MW01519156

Once, We Were Stolen

By Courtney Symons

Dear Michaela,

thanks for taking a chance
on a first-time author. I hope
you enjoy the story~

Symons.

ONCE, WE WERE STOLEN

By Courtney Symons

Amazon CreateSpace Edition

Copyright 2012 Courtney Symons Publishing Co.

This is a work of fiction. Names, characters, places and incidents either are products of the author's imagination or are used fictitiously. Any resemblance to actual events or locales or persons, living or dead, is entirely coincidental.

The ache for home lives in all of us, the safe place where we can go as we are and not be questioned.

- Maya Angelou

We were with him for almost a year as a strange, forced family. Can you hate someone you've spent so much time with? Can you love them? Sometimes it's hard to tell the difference.

I still think I hear him coming down the hall sometimes. I feel the creak of the floorboard and subconsciously count the five seconds until I see his face. The feeling wasn't terror. It was something entirely different, something I couldn't ever put a finger on. It felt ancient and ailing; something deep in your bones that keeps you weak.

The symptoms weren't physical. They didn't remain on our bodies as scars we could point to. They lay somewhere we'd swallowed them down into long ago.

But he wasn't a monster. No more than any of us are.

Once, we were stolen. And this is how it happened.

1

"So what would you like to talk about?"

The question caused Jeremy Ridgeroy to sink down low in his seat. Already he wanted to hide. Instead, he cleared his throat.

"I guess the past, mostly," he said.

The shit we went through, no one should face that alone. It's what his foster brother Derek had said to convince him to show up in the office of Linda Sanford.

Linda had posted an ad in the paper saying she had two ears and wanted to use them. No one should be convinced by such an ad, but it caught Jeremy on one particularly lonely day. Looking through the classifieds, it popped out at him and he found himself longing for those ears.

He'd walked into her Main Street business called Mind Mappers. It was a terrifying name, prompting visions of miniature boats voyaging through his brain, paddling through the grey matter, circulating his skull. But somehow, the name and rates didn't keep him away, and he walked into the office as confidently as he could. He told the receptionist he would like to book an appointment with Dr. Linda Sanford. She smiled generously and gave him some paperwork.

Do you have suicidal thoughts? No, that wasn't it. Jeremy didn't want to end his life, he just didn't particularly want to live it. More accurately, he wanted to survive it.

Linda was still looking at him, expecting him to continue.

"I just don't really have anyone else to talk to. I don't really have many people."

"How about family?" she asked.

"No. Yes. I have foster siblings, but they all have their own families and my foster parents I don't like so much."

"Hmm. Well, we can talk about that too. But how about friends?"

He felt his cheeks grow warm. "No. No one. I don't know why people don't like me, but they don't."

Each time he ended a sentence, Linda quietly waited for him to continue.

"I get scared to talk to people because I think they won't like me, and it makes me worry about what I would say to them, how my face might look, what they expect of me. There's too much to think about, so I avoid it."

"So it's not that people don't want to talk to you," Linda offered. "It's that you're too scared to talk to them."

"Oh, they're scared of me, too. They don't come close."

"Jeremy, if you think that people don't like you, maybe you're sending a negative signal that they pick up on. Maybe they think you don't want anything to do with them."

"Sure," Jeremy said. He knew he never made eye contact with cashiers. He never waited long enough anywhere for someone to start a conversation. He was the last to enter a room and the first to leave it whenever it could be helped. Even his job allowed him to stay away from too many people.

"Well maybe," Linda said jolting him back, "you could focus on trying to make yourself look a little more approachable. What if you smiled?"

"I don't have a nice smile."

"I think you'd be surprised at how many people would beg to differ, if you just let them see it."

This was nice of her and Jeremy smiled in response as a reward.

"I can smile," he said, "but that's too easy. Then I have to deal with them."

"Are you going to be able to deal with me?"

"What do you mean?"

"I mean you're sitting here, having a conversation with me and I'm not going to go away. Are you okay with that?"

"Yeah."

"Why can you talk to me, but not go out and do the same in your everyday life?"

Pause. "It's not the same."

"What makes it different?"

"I'm paying you, to listen. You'll listen to me because you have to."

"That's not entirely true."

"No, it's true, and I don't mind. That's why I came here in the first place. Because I knew you would have to listen, and I'd have to fill in the silence, and I might do that with some stuff that would feel really good to get off my chest. It's like forcing myself to communicate outside of my head."

His arms were erect in front of him and his fingers clamped together like claws as he spoke and sat in her worn patient chair.

She just nodded. He found himself able to continue. She didn't bat an eye when he described hearing little girls being pillaged in the room next to him growing up, girls he was getting to know as his new sisters, by the man in charge of their care. She didn't even flinch.

Once a week he would visit her, bringing with him a box of chocolates. The first session they had together, he saw a box on her desk and assumed it was part of the procedure if a session had gone well; a tip to let her know she had done something good. He figured it couldn't hurt and gave her a box each week after, not realizing she'd brought the first one in from home so she wouldn't end up eating it all herself.

Months later, Linda began doing a bit more talking.

"Jeremy, can I tell you what I think about all of this? My professional opinion?"

He nodded.

"I believe you're suffering from a social paranoia that keeps you distanced from the people around you. You overanalyze every social situation, and you can't allow your body and your mind to relax and enjoy normal, human interactions."

She began to talk about treatment options, but her voice faded away as Jeremy tried to process what she'd said. He didn't know if he should be angry or impressed. He liked it better when she just nodded and listened, but he couldn't help but hear himself in everything she had said. He did walk down the streets faster than everyone else so his stride wouldn't be matched by anyone. He would jot down things to say when he knew he would be faced with a conversation.

But it didn't feel good to think about those things, especially when he felt strongly that there was no way he could change them. Linda suggested putting himself out there slowly; bit by bit, engaging in small conversations with someone like a bus driver or a vendor. Just a quick exchange not meant to last, that he could walk away from almost immediately. Then slowly, bit by bit, he could attempt longer interactions, by chatting with a waitress or saying hello to a neighbour. Then slowly, bit by bit, he could take on larger conversations, maybe by joining a local club or council, by taking walks, maybe trying some online dating.

All of it sounded impossible.

He knew his relationship with Linda had changed. She wasn't willing to just listen to him anymore; she wanted to break him into pieces. He didn't need to be told these things, he'd sensed them his whole life and so had everyone else. There is a reason certain people are picked on in school. They lace their arms across their chests and keep their heads down and try to be invisible. But the problem is that there are other kids who aren't much further ahead of them on the loneliness continuum, and they know how to spot those invisible kids because they're not really invisible, not even close. They instead become overly visible; their deformities, physical and otherwise, inflated and paraded for everyone to see.

Jeremy had always felt like a big, blown-up version of his anomalies. Linda wasn't going to be able to help him change that; she hadn't gotten to him soon enough. He was too far-gone.

That was the last time he ever saw Linda. He left that office and went back to the life that had left him wanting, heading to the only other place he knew to find solace.

He sipped his coffee slowly, took the tentative slurp that affirms if you've added enough milk or cream or sugar. He takes about a milk and a half, give or take, and a sweetener. Sometimes a cream if he's feeling decadent, because you really can taste the difference. It's a richness that rolls over your tongue and clings to your teeth.

Sitting alone in a booth is the only way Jeremy ever eats while he's at a restaurant. Usually, he brings a book providing somewhere to comfortably rest his eyes, but on that particular day, he brought no weapons. Just himself, and the hope that his people-watching skills were discrete enough for others not to notice, or at least not to care.

His hair was disheveled, his head aflame with curly amber locks. Green eyes were his best feature, he felt, but they were always hidden behind his hair and downward gaze. He rarely showed them to anyone.

Someone so long-limbed has a hard time being inconspicuous, but he tried it as best he could. His six-foot-three frame folded in on itself like a spider tucking its legs around its body. Booths are never built to fit his size, so he was used to being condensed.

He sat in the fifties-style diner that exists in every town. One thing it had going for it was that the jukeboxes actually worked, sometimes. Each table had its own, which Jeremy liked. He could put quarters in and choose songs at his leisure, without getting up and gangling in front of the big machine while trying to make his pick. He felt deep satisfaction knowing he controlled what was going into the ears of those around him. As often as he put in a quarter, they had to listen to whatever he selected. And it didn't matter if they liked it or not, because they didn't know it was him who had chosen it.

Last time he was in, he'd picked a song he knew no one would like; a contemporary hit that had somehow found its way into the song selection list, one of those breathy embarrassments with unreasonably sexy lyrics. He'd looked around for reactions, but caught them only from staff members who groaned and rolled their eyes. He'd felt gleeful with power.

That day, he picked a classic. Something he thought the whole diner would enjoy. When feeling particularly grandiose, he considered himself the DJ of the place.

"Did you pick this one?" A female voice broke through the din.

Jeremy's head snapped up out of his reverie to find his waitress smiling and jerking her head towards the jukebox. Her arms were laden with plates, knuckles laced through half-empty mugs, and he imagined her head was her only plausible method of indication.

"Yeah, I did," he muttered sheepishly, a bit unnerved that his secret pleasure had been discovered, but a bit more flabbergasted that she'd taken the time to notice.

"Good choice," she nodded. "I can't stand when people choose the newer songs. It's a fifties diner, you know?"

He did know. His stomach clenched with guilt for inflicting that on her in the past, and he silently vowed never to do so again.

She looked at him expectantly, and he realized he hadn't said anything in return. He wasn't very good at this.

"Um, yeah," he mumbled. "Tell me about it." Stupid.

She didn't appear to mind, asking, "How's your meal?" and reminding him that he still had a landfill of breakfast in front of him that he'd barely touched. "You're not hungry?"

"Oh, I'm hungry. I'll get to it. Thanks." He smiled at her, winningly? Not likely. She smiled back and gave him one more nod. Her arms must have been on fire from all of the weight she held. Other people's leftovers. Ketchup everywhere, egg yolks lining plates like a child's finger painting, edges of bread from people who don't do crust.

"I'll be back with s'more coffee in a bit," she said pleasantly before turning and walking away. Jeremy noticed her long, blonde ponytail swirl around a second behind her, following her lead; that bobbing mane a prerequisite, seemingly, for those who wait.

Tracking her with his eyes, he saw her spastically kick the kitchen door open. The wooden windowed panels swung open just long enough for her to breeze through, then quickly fell back into place.

Breakfast beckoned. Over medium, sausage, brown toast. He never thinks twice before ordering, he just does. Autopilot. With new reverence, Jeremy resolved to eat every last bite before him, cold or crusty. He placed his eggs on top of his toast so that when he cut them, the yolk wouldn't run all over the porcelain plate. There'd be no stains or tidbits left for her to avoid touching as she cleared away his dishes, not from him. He'd even put his cutlery on top, and his empty jam container too, and he might even add his crumpled napkin. He never used napkins but most normal people did, didn't they? It wouldn't hurt to try one.

Jeremy was struck with the sudden panic that she might come back soon. She said she'd bring more coffee. What would he say to her? He could ask what brand of coffee it was, and did she brew it herself? Does she like coffee? What does she take in it? He knew they were meaningless questions that she'd undoubtedly been asked by every other man she'd served that thought she was lovely.

He did think she was lovely, which was strange because he hadn't really noticed it before, even though he found himself there every Sunday morning. It started with a craving for eggs, and perhaps a normal human ritual.

She worked every weekend. She always served him, because he sat alone and she handled the section with the small tables close to the bar, but something had changed. It was the jam, he thought. She'd brought him extra, made sure his coffee cup was full, checked that his eggs were cooked the way he liked them.

"Sometimes it's tricky with over medium," she had said sympathetically. "That's how I eat mine too. They have a hard time getting it right."

Chugging back his coffee, he placed the empty mug along the edge of the table. He would do this with his plate when he was done too, so maybe she'd see it and know he was finished. Maybe it could be their code.

Sure enough, she came back out of the kitchen and looked over at his mug. She made a tiny, almost imperceptible nod of her head; an acknowledgement not meant for him but only for her, and added it to her mental checklist.

She. He wished he didn't have to refer to her in his head that way, and wanted to know her name. He knew he'd never be able to ask without stuttering and stumbling all over his question. Blood rushed to his cheeks and ears just thinking about it. Normal, everyday human transactions were like a foreign language. Interaction with other people was a struggle, a blind search through scripts and codes that he hadn't written and never fully understood.

There she was, a full, steaming pot in hand.

"Ahh, there's your appetite," she said acknowledging his feverish attempt to make his entire plate's contents disappear. Without even waiting for him to ask, she refilled his mug, didn't spill a drop. Didn't splash, and her wrist didn't shake. He'd never seen so much confidence in one small flick.

13

"You're good at that," he said, testing the words.

"At what?"

"At pouring coffee." He was horrified the instant the simple words were past his lips, but she smiled and recovered for him.

"Oh yeah, a real pro!" she joked. "I always save my slopping for when I pour myself a cup."

He didn't know if this was her attempt at being humble, trying to make him feel better by acknowledging her faults. Maybe she was being ironic. Should he laugh? He decided he should; it couldn't hurt.

What came out of his mouth sounded only partially forced. The volume was alright, too. Sometimes he overestimated how loud his outbursts would be, probably because he gave them so infrequently. The result was something close to a friendly chuckle. As close as he could get, at any rate.

"You like coffee too?" He knew this was bad conversation. He could see her eyes wandering and knew that he should accept that he was merely a tick mark on her checklist. Now that she had refilled his mug, he should let her move along to her next task. But he couldn't help it.

"I'm actually more of a tea drinker myself," she said easily. "Coffee is good but sometimes it makes my tummy hurt, you know? If I drink it too early in the morning or I haven't eaten."

Tummy. The sound of that word out of her mouth was incredibly endearing, so informal and childish. She must feel at ease, he tried to interpret.

There wasn't much else to say on the subject, and he couldn't demand any more of her time.

"Well, thank you," he managed. She didn't know it, and he'd be humiliated if she did, but this was the most normal, human interaction he'd had in months. The last time must have been when his television stopped working and a repairman came to fix it. But that guy hadn't had long, bouncing blonde hair or candid grey eyes or been attentive to Jeremy's needs (besides his television). This was something else entirely. He couldn't put his finger on it, but it's what you or I might know as desire.

As she walked away, he returned to his food demolition. There was always way too much food on those plates. Diners could easily serve half the amount and most people would leave happy, but that might have been Jeremy's measly 150 pounds talking. Maybe he didn't know what normal humans wanted and needed. Certainly not this many hash browns. He ate them though, as if it were a quest. After making sure no one was watching, he licked his finger and traced it around the outskirts of his plate to rid it of even the tiniest crumb. He put his cutlery on top of the barren plate, but decided against the crumpling of a napkin. It would be a waste, plus it would hide his clean dish. She might not even see it or realize he had done it for her, to make her life a little easier.

He sat back almost proudly, pushed his plate away and over to the side of the table. Their own special code. Jeremy couldn't think of anything else to say to her besides asking for his bill, but maybe that would be enough.

As she started to head back over to him, he spotted the cheque already in her hand. Really? he thought. She knew I wanted that? Of course it would've been fairly obvious – with not a crumb left on his plate it was evident he was finished his meal, and it wasn't likely he would be looking for dessert at nine in the morning … But she noticed.

She dropped his bill at the table and had written, "Thanks!" with a smiley face next to it. She had also circled something: her name.

Violet.

He ran it over his tongue, noticing the satisfactory vibration as the "V" hummed against his lips, and the way his tongue tapped his teeth on the second syllable. Such a delicate name. A purple, vibrant name. He immediately wanted to know more, her last name, a nickname. All were valid questions but inappropriate for him to ask right now, he guessed. An irresistible urge to use her name in speech filled him. He wanted to go to a garden and find a whole bouquet of her. Put them beside her bed in a vase. A vase for violets. For Violet.

Ridiculous thoughts, he knew. Is this a crush? He didn't feel crushed; he felt light and more alive than in a long while, perhaps ever.

There wasn't much more he could do today, so he left her a tip that consisted of a few more dollars than he'd ever left anyone before, and got up with what he hoped would be perceived as purpose and agility. In reality, he had to untuck his spidery appendages and unfurl his body from around the table. But as he walked away, he passed by her and said, "Goodbye, Violet."

She didn't hear him, busy doing a million other little things. But when she went to his table to collect the tip, she looked up in astonishment and searched out the window for a last glimpse of him. He'd been so generous that she

16

wondered if he'd meant to leave her so much. She was no stranger to men trying to buy her attention, so she pocketed the money, smiled, and made a mental note to pay extra attention to him next time.

2

Violet continued to work. She did so despite having been on shift for almost twelve hours; despite her ankle swelling up and reducing her gait to a penguin-like lilt; despite the plans she had made earlier to see friends, which she had to cancel when work told her she was needed. A clever trick, as she'd spent most of her life wanting to be just that – needed by someone.

She felt a slap on her ass, and wheeled quickly to find Karalee giving a smirk and a wink. Violet had never understood the grabbiness of the serving industry. It was a way to show kinship, she had gathered this much, but why something so unpleasant? Every time she felt an uninvited touch, she would flinch and grit her teeth together, bracing for what she'd find when she turned around. Generally, it was someone she might have granted consent to had they asked, but sometimes it was a cook who snuck a squeeze while her hands were too busy and full with plates to object. Rarely, it was a customer to whom she had been nothing but friendly, polite and respectful. But that is where Violet was blind. She didn't see her friendliness as anything out of the ordinary. She gave out smiles because they were simple, easier than frowning, and because she liked to see them in return. She made a point of ensuring everything tasted as it should, was plated just so, was exactly the way they had ordered it.

It amazed her how often people would ask for her name. Violet, they would often cock their heads and reply. What a pretty name for a pretty girl. They truly seemed to believe that they were relevant to her external life, the shoes she stepped into when she left the restaurant. She couldn't blame them, she supposed, because she'd seen how gloomy other waiters could be and realized she did shine a little brighter. And sometimes those people were relevant to her life, like sweet Mrs. Simcoe who brought her a fresh oatmeal cookie most times she came to eat, or Andrew, the old lonely fellow with the best memory in the world. How's home, he'd ask her, remembering exactly where that was and who was in it. Violet wouldn't be able to make it through shifts like these without people like that.

As her mind trailed off, her body remained active. Autopilot had successfully taken three orders and delivered some food, as well as wrapped up a couple of tables. She shook her head and told herself that being there for so many hours was no excuse to let her head up into the clouds.

When her shift finally came to an end, it was time for side duties; stocking up for the beginning of the next group of workers. In a diner that never closes, there is always a next shift.

The walk-in fridge was a monstrous abyss that swallowed up boxes and spit them out in places of its choosing. Things were never in the same place twice. On hot days, it was a sweet relief to cool your forehead on a big vat of mayo, or sneak a bottle of salad dressing onto the small of your back. But today, Violet hugged herself and shivered as she searched for the salsa.

When in that fridge, she hoped to be left alone. That's why she sighed inwardly as the sticky door swung outwards and Rafa walked in. Rafa was a cook known for his malodour and roaming hands. His were a pair that Violet did not want anywhere near her ass, but they somehow found themselves there quite frequently. She never felt more like an object than when in his presence, as if she were a blow-up doll for him to grab and shove.

She searched harder for the damned salsa, but heard Rafa muttering about how hard she'd been working, how tired she must be.

"You need a kiss," he said. Not a question, because he knew what her answer would be if it were.

"That's sweet, Rafa," she smiled. "But I'm all sweaty, no one wants to kiss me right now." It amazed her how easily she could mask her disgust. She knew she had every right to be short with him, to refuse his advances forcefully, yet she couldn't bring herself to do it. It wasn't only that she wanted to stay in his good favour, although that was part of it. Guiltily, she knew she could return back to the kitchen with a rejected plate, open her eyes really wide, and ask for a quick fix. If her body was a weapon she would use it.

But that day, in that fridge, she wanted her body out of the equation. She squirmed as she felt him, smelt him, get closer.

"Oh, I don't mind," Rafa said. "Just one kiss."

Violet had been through this enough times to know to duck her head. If she was quick enough, he would get only a cheek, sometimes just an earlobe. Her timing was such that he got her right on the cheekbone this time, and she felt enough force for it to have been a goodnight kiss after a date that had gone well. It was something he should have earned, but he stole it instead.

Normally, that was the worst of it. The hardest part was waiting until he was out of sight to wipe the residue from her face, the sticky saliva that felt hot enough to brand. Today, he just stood there.

"Come on," he begged, or something close to it. "One time before I leave here I want a real kiss."

Violet's insides roiled and she dreaded the day she would have to deal with that request. But she made the mistake of thinking that the moment was over and done with because before she knew it, Rafa leaned in again, grabbed her by the cheeks with his meat-stained hands and kissed her. Firmly, long enough for her to say, Oh my god, oh my god, oh my god, oh my god in her head.

He pulled back with a look of such satisfaction; a sly, triumphant smile twisting his forceful lips.

"Mmmm," he said before finally retreating.

She wanted to slap him. She wanted to scream and say her body, her choice, like she'd been programmed to since the start of her sexuality. But instead, she did nothing. She stood there and waited for him to leave the fridge, which he did without looking back. She raised her forearm and wiped it forcefully across her lips, trying to smear off the stain she felt sure he had left on them.

What if I can never kiss anyone again without thinking of him? She couldn't imagine what it would have been like if it were an assault with his whole body, not merely his lips and his hands burning on her cheeks.

The second worst part was that she knew she'd never say a word about it to anyone. The worst was that he knew this, too. He knew her for her smile and her kindness, and that she wouldn't want to make waves. As she walked out of the freezer, she eyed the poster stating the restaurant's zero tolerance policy for sexual harassment.

She finished her stock-up in a haze, counted her cash-out without even bothering to see how much she'd made in tips. She couldn't help feeling like it was a payoff. Yes, you'll be forcefully kissed in dark corners, but at the end of your shift you'll have some money that'll make it worthwhile.

As quickly as she could, Violet left, waving a few forced goodbyes. She scoped out her little red Neon, hideous and functional. She fumbled with her car keys before successfully fitting them into the hole, hoping her poor car didn't feel violated by her force. With her hands positioned at ten and two and her head on the wheel, she took deep breaths.

Some tears came then. Violet didn't cry often and later she was sure she'd look back on that moment and wonder why she couldn't have hardened up. It was, after all, just a kiss. But she felt rubbed raw. She worried for her future and how often she would allow herself to be taken advantage of. She worried also for the present. She would be back here tomorrow to do it all over again.

When Violet graduated from high school last May, she threw her cap into the air in her ridiculous gown; she had gotten tipsy with some friends and camped out in a tent in the town park. Wasn't that what you were supposed to do? There were a lot of pictures taken, a couple of bruises the next day, a hangover that felt like it went for days, and then that was it. High school was over and done with. Most of Violet's friends had gone on to university or college. They all seemed to have clear career plans with ideas of where they were headed to and how they would get there.

No such plans existed in Violet's head. Everyone said she would eventually just know, and she was, after all, only 18. But things didn't seem to be falling into place so easily. A blurry image wasn't slowly constructing itself before her eyes; she didn't feel pulled onto any particular course. For now, the only direction she had was working at the diner, helping her mom out with money wherever she could, and trying not to cry when she heard about all of the great, grown-up dilemmas her friends were getting themselves into all over the country.

A wave of inevitability loaded her shoulders. She felt as if she weighed a ton and wondered how much of her life would feel like this, like she was running around and around on a track that never changed, that never let her change. Those loaded shoulders began to shake, and she felt embarrassed by the display of weakness in the middle of a parking lot. She steeled herself and straightened her back, wiped her tears away almost as forcefully as the kiss. After a few more deep breaths and a headshake, her eyes were almost clear enough to drive. Seat belted, keys in ignition, gear from park to drive, successful autopilot.

Violet thought she might have escaped the whole scene unseen. She didn't see the gangly man sitting quietly in the car across from her, nor feel his heart pounding.

Jeremy hadn't gotten far from the restaurant before he turned around and came back. He wasn't sure why; it's not as if he could go back in and say, Oops, I forgot to have some fries while I was here. Round two? He had no real reason to return, and didn't feel confident enough to stroll in and say what was on his mind, which was, Tell me who you are, Violet. He knew this would be inappropriate. In some fantasy novel it might be romantic, the perfect lover's meeting, a story that would unfold laughingly and lovingly to an attentive audience wondering how two people could be so happy.

But that wasn't quite it. He couldn't define it as simply as that he wanted to love her. He knew next to nothing about her, but when you're starved enough of something, you hold on tightly to anything that will sate the deprivation. He felt an insane desire to protect her, guard against whatever it was that brought salt to her eyes.

For now he let her be, and watched her drive off to whatever home she had.

3

Autumn crept in quickly that year. The leaves, one day green, mellowed seemingly overnight to their reds and oranges and finally brown. Such a quick death.

Jeremy raked meticulously, stopping every few minutes to wipe his nose on his sleeve. The cool air got his insides running. As he paused, he surveyed the seemingly endless carpet of colours scattered at his feet and all around. What a waste, he thought. So many leaves over so many seasons that just fall to the ground to rot.

He found himself thinking of Violet. About how soon he could see her again.

Headlights and crunching caused Jeremy to jerk his head up and see a car crawling up the driveway. Gravel chunks flew up harmlessly, warning the driver to move forward with trepidation. It was Jeremy's boss, Johnny O'Connor, a name that fell just short of rhyming. Jeremy forced a smile in his direction. He didn't appreciate being checked up on, but was thankful to be caught mid-rake.

"Good morning, sir," Jeremy bobbed his head in feigned respect.

"Jeremy," his boss replied flatly, like someone stating an item on a list. "How's the house coming along?"

An old Victorian home like this one was a lucky job to have landed. Working as a general contractor had led to many a tough cleanup. This job was by far the best Jeremy had been assigned since beginning to work for O'Conner & Sons two years earlier.

"Great," Jeremy said. "Feel silly raking all these leaves when tomorrow a whole new batch will be back, but it's peaceful out here so I don't mind." The wind amongst the trees was just the soundtrack he needed.

Johnny smiled. "Yeah, well, I left my raking for too long last year, and the piles were so deep I found two dead squirrels in 'em."

Trying not to wrinkle his nose, and wondering why one person would ever share that with another, Jeremy replied humbly, "Well sir, I guess I'll just have to keep at it then."

He hoped this would be sufficient because he wouldn't do his best work with someone looking over his shoulder. Jeremy could sense his arms slowing, could feel the rake grating against rocks he hadn't felt before. An audience gave him an automatic feeling of clumsiness and inadequacy. The embarrassment from stumbling over a task so simple ruddied his cheeks and salt water filled his eyes, reducing his vision to nil.

Johnny knew this about Jeremy by now. All reports showed he was a good worker, but best left alone. He tried to do that whenever possible.

"Yup, keep at it," Johnny affirmed. "How's the porch coming along?"

"Pretty well sir, I did some sanding yesterday and I'll be priming tomorrow before I start to stain. The boards are all pretty stable, it's a newer addition."

"I'll leave you to it, then," Johnny conceded. "Maybe I'll make a quick round about the place, and then I'm gone." To Jeremy, this sounded like a reward for good behaviour, a timeline for salvation.

The old home was nestled deeply down a long gravel road. The owners were property hounds, real estate junkies who snatch up whatever new listings they could find and afford; who evaluate, pillage, and reconstruct before selling to the highest bidder. The saddest part was that they had moved in for a time, had left behind clothes and abandoned the house's contents, which became like lonely organs left trying to fill an empty body. Heartless, Jeremy thought, to take ownership of something only to tear it apart completely, come up with your own definition of what you think it should be, then discard it for a price.

Jeremy didn't understand the venture, but was still helping along the way. Another contractor had already evaluated the insides, some house doctor trained to see which parts were deteriorating and threatening the structure's wellbeing. Jeremy's job was just the surface stuff. Painting, general maintenance. He was the plastic surgeon of the place, giving a face-lift here, an extraction there. Not a bad gig for someone who had been tossed from job to job so quickly in the past. This place would be his to work on until someone showed an interest in purchasing it. The owners hadn't even come to visit; too many other properties to ravage.

The fingers of his rake snagged ruthlessly on anything in their path; branches, stones, patches of grass if he wasn't careful. He decided to take a break, make sure Johnny had left.

Jeremy walked into the enormous house, past the five bedrooms, sitting rooms, living rooms, dining rooms, rooms he couldn't even think of a name for. He'd been looking after this place for a few months now.

He headed downstairs to the musty cellar underneath, complete with a full wine rack. The house was built in 1893, and the dust-covered bottles could have been ten years old or one hundred.

Jeremy was learning which steps to avoid for their creaking, and which windows let in what amount of light at which hour. There couldn't have been a better job assigned to him. He could retreat there for a full eight hours minding the garden, sanding the porch, coming up with an ever-expanding job list to justify his time spent there.

The house was nearly swallowed by the trees surrounding it. Everywhere you looked, trees. Viewed from the tallest turret of the house, treetops lined the acres like green cotton candy with not another house to be seen. It was such a shame no one lived there, because this sort of home deserved a family. So many rooms with so little sound within them seemed cruel and mocking somehow.

Sometimes, Jeremy imagined he was part of that family. That it wasn't just him, alone, every day. That he wouldn't be nervous by the presence of other people, that he would enjoy their company, and that they would enjoy this home. It was like playing house for grown-ups, except he did it all alone.

When he was five, Jeremy began to recognize loneliness. It had always been there, that hollow feeling in the bottom of his gut, a bit like he'd swallowed something metallic, but he'd never known a word to attach to it. It was his mother herself who had finally given it a name.

He'd come home one day to find her, Gloria, crying on the couch. Wet sobs, where he could hear various liquids pouring out of her nose, her eyes, her mouth. In one hand, a lit cigarette, ashes an inch long with no ashtray in sight, scattered grey bits decorating the carpet below. In the other, an almost empty bottle. She sloshed the dregs around. He knew those bottles meant trouble, as if they were a special sort of pop that had a bit more sugar, or something strange that made his mother equally so.

"Mom?" he called timidly. He never knew whether to speak up or to cower in the corner, sneak to his bedroom and close the door behind him. Usually, that was the best idea. She had seemed so pitiful that day, though, and she actually looked at him. He was emboldened.

"Jeremy," she wailed. "What am I doing? What do I do? I just don't know what to do." This, between hiccupping sobs and slurps of the bottle's last drops. He was terrified, and wondered if she was really asking and waiting for him to answer. To him, it seemed fairly obvious that she was sitting in their makeshift home, on their dirty couch, surrounded by ashes as the smell of that mystery elixir oozed from her every pore.

He took a few steps forward. The little boy of five took the cigarette out of his mother's hand, grabbed the bottle from the other, and began to stroke her hair. He remembered feeling too big for his body; looking down at his hands in her tangled, tatty hair and thinking they looked too small. They should be bigger.

Gloria closed her eyes. She kept mumbling incoherent ideas that Jeremy couldn't understand, but one of the clearest things she said was uttered right as she was about to submit to slumber.

"I am so lonely," she said in a husky, flat voice.

Lonely. Jeremy toyed with the word in his head. If this was lonely, his mother on the couch, not knowing where she was or why, then maybe there was a little bit of that loneliness inside of him, too. He often wondered when he might get a hug from his mother. In school, his teacher said that you should get two hugs a day for maintenance and three for growth. At this rate, Jeremy felt that he would stay stunted forever. There was no one to cuddle him, to stroke his hair when he was the one sobbing. She wasn't capable. Instead, his tiny body huddled next to her, breathing as quietly as his little lungs would let him so that she could finally fall asleep and be at peace, for a couple of hours at least.

When she began to snore, he left. Took himself out the door, and walked down the darkening street.

That was the day he found Buster.

The puppy had been whimpering in the corner of an alley, and it struck Jeremy immediately how similar his mother's cries had sounded just minutes earlier. He saw the outline of the dog's ribs in the streetlamp's glow.

The puppy kept whining and Jeremy began to notice the traces of soft fur, the soft eyes on a body where no softness should have remained.

Lonely dog. Lonely boy. Now that he had possession of the word, he wanted to do something about it. Make it go away.

He inched forward slowly and gently. The puppy retreated as far back into the corner as it could go, digging its dirty paws into the asphalt to push against the wall. But Jeremy crept forward, step by little step, talking quietly to the mutt that he was already beginning to think of as his own.

"It's alright puppy. It's okay. I'm lonely too. I won't hurt you."

Jeremy reached out his hand, and watched the dog lean toward and then away from his palm and fingers, questioning their motives. It didn't take long. By

29

the time Jeremy got close enough to touch him, the puppy was licking his hand. What a sticky tongue, and so much stronger than he expected. That dog kept licking him, on his hand, his arm, even his cheek when he got close enough. Jeremy giggled and fell in love.

"Whoa! Thatta boy, Buster!" The new name popped out of his mouth. Probably fresh in his head from some cowboy movie he'd seen, full of guns and lassoes and things other kids in his class would never have been allowed to see. Buster it was. There was no questioning it.

He had no idea how to bring Buster home with him. Gloria might kick him out immediately. She might scream and yell and terrify the dog all over again. Jeremy was struck with a fierce sense of stewardship. He had rescued Buster, and he would take care of him.

No collar hung around Buster's neck, but Jeremy was afraid he might get startled and run off somewhere. He dug around in a trash bin for something of use; some twine or string. When those failed to emerge, he ripped a strip off a garbage bag, twisted it into something resembling a rope, and made a little noose with a strap long enough for Jeremy to walk comfortably beside him. Buster gently lowered his head as Jeremy applied his new leash.

They walked along the road together and got home to find Gloria snoring, unmoved, on the couch. With an unnecessary "Shhh," Jeremy led Buster to the kitchen and from the fridge took out bits of things he thought a dog might like. A little bit of cheese, a cob of corn, even some crackers from the cupboard. Buster ate it all.

Unexpectedly, Gloria didn't seem to mind Buster. Jeremy promised to walk him every day, to feed him, do odd jobs around the neighbourhood to save money for dog food and, on special occasions, even a bone or two. Gloria remained unaffected.

Once, he caught Gloria on her knees looking right into Buster's eyes. Jeremy froze in the doorway, unsure of what she might do. He thought she might strike him, but when she raised her hand, she did so more gently than Jeremy had ever seen. She stroked that dog's cheeks, grabbed his tail gently.

"Who's a good boy? Who's a good boy? You are Buster, yes you are"

It was just that once he caught her at this, but Jeremy liked to hope it happened all the time when he wasn't looking. Sometimes he would purposely leave them alone in a room. Maybe if she were around Buster more, she would become that gentle with Jeremy, too. Maybe she would pat his head and tell him he was a good boy. That didn't happen, but Buster did end up being a faithful companion.

Buster would have loved the old Victorian house. Jeremy was struck with a fantasy of making the place into a little zoo, an animal farm. He could round up raccoons and try to tame them; lure them with bits of garbage and train them to love him while sitting gently on his shoulder. He imagined them eating ticks out of his hair, although he supposed that was more ape-like than raccoon and hoped he had no ticks to pick.

Jeremy had heard enough silence for a lifetime, and maybe he could deal with a little noise. He wanted to feel like he had rescued something again. As he'd walked that dog home so long ago, he had felt a godlike pride at his garbage bag leash.

Animals would wreak havoc on the property, however, and he knew it. There would be shit all over; too much for him to ever collect alone. On the floors, in the carpets, scratches on the walls. And how would he know what to feed each species? They'd probably all need something different and he didn't like the idea of scrounging up dead bugs and little rodents to shove into their expectant mouths. He would have to think of something else.

Jeremy bent over to pick up a canister of paint. It was mauve. A beautiful purple. Almost like Violet.

4

Violet came crashing out of the kitchen with four plates, two in each hand. She'd only recently learned to do this. Before, she could handle only three, one in each hand and the third balanced on her left forearm. She couldn't help but feel a bit proud when she saw the incredulous looks on her customers' faces as she brought out all four of their family's plates at once. Granted, they always looked a little scared. She was rarely graceful, and sometimes the plates would totter on her capable arms. But she almost always delivered them successfully, with only a few stray slices of toast or fries lost along the way.

People always asked if working in a restaurant took away her desire to eat in them, but the answer was not at all. It felt nice to sit and be served when you're used to doing the serving. On weekend mornings, she would look on longingly at factions of friends who stumbled in together, so hungover they could barely mutter, "Coffee," before their heads retreated into their hands.

Violet saw that the hostess was seating someone new in her section; a redheaded man, alone. He looked tall from behind. She went to get him a coffee, because almost everyone wants one and won't even say hello until they get it. Violet despised some people's willingness to throw away civility so easily. No one needs a coffee that badly. Regardless, she grabbed a mug, filled it, and brought it over.

"Good morning!" she said before seeing his face. She then recognized the long limbs of the friendly tipper from the other day. Her face lit up; she couldn't help it. And not only because she wanted another good tip. It was just nice to know that there were people in the world who appreciated her and chose to let her know she was doing a good job.

"Long time, no see," she added, smiling widely.

Damnit, Jeremy thought to himself. That was the line he'd been rehearsing in his head. He'd thought it would be perfect, acknowledging that he remembered her and poking fun at the fact that he was back so soon. Now he was left wordless, defenseless, and a little embarrassed.

His heart began to pound against his ribs. Blood surged up his neck and blotted his cheeks. He felt transparent; he'd even asked to sit in her section, just in case, which was humiliating enough. "Can I sit by the bar?" was how he had disguised the request. Another of the lines he had rehearsed endlessly in his car before summoning the grit to walk back in.

There were men who came in every day and sat in Violet's section. She wondered what their insides must look like, or their pocketbooks, after eating and paying for the same unhealthy meal every day. She thought of Andrew, who slipped her a dollar after every meal. Very seriously, as if sharing a secret or some prized possession.

The last words spoken had been Violet's and he knew it was his turn. He stuttered for a moment but language finally arrived on his tongue.

"I just couldn't stay away," he said with what he hoped looked like a smile but was really a quivering of his lip. "It's a beautiful day out," he added.

In that moment, Jeremy was glad to live in Canada where the weather changed as often as the time.

Violet didn't mind the small talk. "I know!" she replied heartily. "I feel like it might be one of the last hot days before fall really sinks in." She clasped her hands at her clavicle.

"But the leaves, they're pretty much done for the year," Jeremy found it in himself to add. It amazed him that she smiled and nodded.

"I'm a fall baby," she admitted. "I love the colours of September, how quickly they change. It's over in a heartbeat but so beautiful while it lasts."

Jeremy felt a strong desire to collect handfuls of fallen leaves for her. He wanted to find one of every colour and lay them out so they blended into each other, so that they created a rainbow of greens and oranges and reds and yellows and browns.

"Why were you crying?" he blurted. His hands immediately flew to his lips. She was caught off guard and took one tiny step away from him.

"When?" she asked cautiously.

"The other day. I saw you in the parking lot, I'd been running some errands," he lied. "I saw you get into your car, and you looked so upset. I'm sorry."

"No, it's okay. I'm okay. That was a long day. I'd been here for hours and someone wasn't all that nice to me, and I couldn't help it. It's not a big deal," she quickly added as she saw something more pressing than concern register on his freckled face. She realized she had said a whole lot of words without telling him anything at all, but really, what more could he expect from her?

"Well... I'm really sorry," Jeremy repeated. "I know what it's like to have bad days." His voice wavered. The way he said it made Violet think that every day might be a bad day for him, and it made her heart break. Here he was, this gangly thing, opening up to her. Before she even knew it, her hand was on his shoulder.

"Thank you," she said softly. "That's very sweet. I'm fine. But it's really nice of you to ask. It feels good to have someone concerned about me, and I don't even know you." She had meant this as a compliment but Jeremy felt it as more of a slap. He didn't want a reminder of how incredibly far off he was from knowing her.

"Anyways!" she continued. He liked that she added an "s," it always felt better coming out of his mouth than an anyway alone. "You're probably starving. What can I get for you?"

She'd forgotten the mug in her hand, cooling while she stood and talked, and hurriedly presented it to Jeremy like a gift before he could even answer her question.

"Well, that's a good start!" he said. "I think just the regular breakfast would be good."

"Great! How would you like your eggs?" This was part of her morning script; it didn't vary too much from person to person, but she still made a point of smiling and looking into eyes as much as she could.

"Over medium, please," he asked politely.

"Right! I should've remembered. Next time."

Next time. Jeremy felt a thrill of excitement at the thought.

"What kind of meat would you like? Sausage again?"

She knew! He didn't realize that every person who stepped foot in the place on more than one occasion expected their server to remember their order somehow.

"Yes please, and brown toast."

She said brown toast at the same moment he did. It was a lovely trick when she did remember, Violet had discovered, although sometimes it only served to inflate the very sense of self-importance she loathed.

As Violet walked away from the table, Jeremy followed her with his eyes. He searched his memory for experiences with other waitresses. Were they all this sweet? Did they remember his order if he'd been there more than twice in one week? He wanted to listen to her talking to others to see how much kindness crept into her words. Maybe she was saving all of it for him.

He dressed his coffee and sipped it, not minding that it wasn't nearly as hot as he preferred. He wanted to ask Violet what temperature she liked her coffee. He wanted to call her by name. She did, after all, remember that he liked sausage and brown toast, but was it too invasive for him to use the name that she'd circled for him on a receipt?

Before he knew it, she was back with a plate of food and a steaming pot of coffee. "I figured you'd like a warm-up," she said. "I stood there with it for so long that it must have been awful. It's no good if it's not hot."

He tried not to let his jaw drop, to say not a word except for, "Thanks." For once, he bit his tongue to keep from speaking instead of having to desperately drum up thoughts.

"Cheers," she said. He wondered if that was an acceptable use of the term, but didn't mind either way. Of course she would say cheers; she had cheer pouring out of her. He ate with relish as she tended other tables, and he tried not to stare. When he finished eating, he hesitated to put down his cutlery. He didn't want to push his plate away.

But, inevitably, she came over to ask if he was finished, like the attentive server she was. He nodded. "It was delicious," he said, having no real recollection of how any of it had tasted on his tongue.

"Excellent," she smiled. "I'll be right back with your bill."

Jeremy couldn't help but feel a little discarded. The instant he finished eating, she was done with him as well. He tried to remind himself that it was part of the job description, and he accepted the bill as she handed it over to him.

"Thank you, Violet." He'd done it again, used her name. He breathed in and out before she finally replied.

"You're welcome!" She even smiled. "What's your name?"

"Jeremy," he said quietly. "I'm Jeremy."

"Well Jeremy, it was good to see you again. Hopefully you'll be back soon."

"Oh, I'll be back," he said with what he hoped was confidence.

As he walked out of the restaurant, an idea began tugging at his insides.

What if… he started to think. What if she needed rescuing? What if whatever had made her cry in her car was worse than her cheerful disposition allowed her to show? She might not realize it, but what if she needed him to save her? She had been so kind, so intimate, and maybe she was just what Jeremy needed to feel fully human. They could help each other. She could learn to love him.

5

There wasn't ever a full plan, not really. There were bits and pieces floating around in Jeremy's head. He was on a mission, but his tactics were not clearly mapped. He would have been a poor excuse of a general.

Before the week was over, he found himself back in the diner parking lot. He knew he looked pathetic hovering there alone; he felt naked and bare to his bones. There was a real breeze in the air and he began to shiver. He had taken a cab there. Violet was soon to finish her shift. In a bold move, he'd called the restaurant to ask when she would be done.

Only a few days had gone by since he had found out her name, but already he couldn't imagine what his life would be like if she were to fall out of it.

Jeremy didn't like to take cabs. He never knew if he was expected to speak or be quiet. He preferred when they let him just sit and look out the window. Cab drivers seemed to be ever on the phone anyway, talking in beautiful languages from far away, getting excited and gesturing with their hands. Jeremy would always hold his breath until both were back on the wheel.

The taxi had showed up quickly, but Jeremy was ready and waiting outside with nothing in his hands and his wallet forming a pop-out square in the back left pocket of his jeans. There was a small gun in the back right.

He had bought it at the dollar store. It was jet black, and weighed next to nothing. From a distance, it held weight. Fear could trick the senses into seeing things that weren't really there, or exaggerate those that were. He was banking on that, and yes, it did register in his mind that it was cruel of him to hope for fear.

His cab passed by an after-school camp along the way. It was probably one of the last warm days of the season, and those agile bodies would soon stay shoved behind desks. They would be planted in firm chairs designed to anchor their gaze at the board, at the teacher, at all that was about to be inserted into their brains.

The children were divided into two lines facing one another. Each end had a ferocious hold on a rope that was teeter-tottering between the two. Their movements struck him as infinite, wavering back and forth. Tug of War. Tug o' War. He remembered it from his childhood, how winning hurt more than losing. The rope would go slack and the champion team would fly backwards, landing on stunned backsides in painful victory.

"Now, that's the best kind of war, don't you think?" said the cab driver who hadn't spoken another word, not other than, Where to?

This struck Jeremy as particularly profound. He knew he shouldn't jump to such conclusions, but a vision popped into his head of the driver's family stuck in a war-torn country.

Men don't grow up, his mother used to say to him. They're just bigger boys with bigger toys. He saw world leaders, opposing sides on each end of a rope, pulling for their countries, using their hands alone. Working together as a team. No blood shed, no death. No folded flags, no cannons fired at night to honour the dead.

Before he knew it, Jeremy was outside the diner. He tipped generously. Those few words stayed with him for a long time. Now all he could do was wait.

He peeked in the window to make sure he hadn't missed her, that she wasn't home and out of his reach. The flash of blonde ponytail was visible first, then her smile. He hadn't seen her mouth curved into anything but, and his stomach clenched at the thought that he was about to change that. For a split second, he almost turned away.

Sitting on the curb, he wondered what he would say to her. He had to be likeable, enough for her to listen to his every word and not question it. Did he have to say a lot? Could he simply ask for a ride? He doubted it very much. If there was anything he'd learned, it was that most people weren't willing to go out of their way for him.

He'd have to ask her for a ride; she wouldn't offer. He might have to beg. But it wouldn't be the first thing he said to her. He plotted away with his head in his hands until he heard her laugh.

Oh god.

He began to pace. He wasn't ready. As he looked up, there she was coming through the doorway in her adorable purple shirt with the diner logo on the left breast. How could they put that logo there without willing male eyes to linger?

He tried to meet her gaze. Would she recognize him? What if she didn't? That was something he hadn't thought of. Of course he would remember her face, but how many people did she serve in a day? How many men did she deal with, day in and day out, who expected her to remember?

But she did. He saw the recognition; there was a flicker, then a smile.

"Hi there," she said.

"Hi, Violet," he forced a smile in return. He was beginning to feel a little sad, and wondered if it wasn't too late to call up another cab and turn right back around again.

She waved goodbye to the friend she'd walked out with. "See you tomorrow." She lied unknowingly.

"What are you doing on the curb?" she asked with a laugh. He was amazed that she could say this, could even laugh along with it, and he didn't feel made fun of. He didn't feel pathetic, and he began to breathe a little easier.

"I'm stuck here," he started. "I just, I don't have a ride. I was supposed to meet with a friend, and they never showed up, but I just thought I'd wait and see if they came." He was rambling; he knew it by the way her face fell. There was empathy there. Or was it sympathy?

"How long have you been waiting?"

"A few hours," he lied. He wanted to be the poor little puppy dog on the side of the road that she couldn't help but help. He prayed she hadn't seen him walk out of his cab moments earlier.

"Hmm. Well, do you have a phone number you could reach your friend at?"

She was concerned! She was trying to figure this out for him, trying to find a way to make it right. Not in the way that he wanted her to, not yet, but she might get there.

"No. I don't have a phone." A lie. Who didn't have a phone these days? She'd see through that. "Well, I do, but I left it at home. And I don't remember his phone number. I would've gone to the pay phone otherwise." He gestured to the booth on their right, and was thankful for his peripheral vision.

"I see. Darn, that's too bad. Do you live far from here?"

He could read between her lines. Well, what are you doing just sitting here? Walk home already.

"Yeah, I do," he said, scratching his head. "It's this beautiful old Victorian home out on the 8th Line. I don't think I'd make it there before dark."

This was the begging part. This was where he should have said, Oh, it's alright, I'll find my own way home. I'm a stranger and you don't know me really and you just worked a full shift, so don't worry about me. Just go on and get home safe.

That's what he should have said, but he didn't. He waited now. If she offered, if she ever did, it would be now. If not, he would have to ask. He was alright with that; he'd come this far, and the furrow in her brow was there just for him.

"Do you know what, I can give you a ride." She was nodding, convincing herself of it as she said it out loud. She was probably thinking, Stranger danger! But he didn't look all that strange, just sad, sitting there alone on that curb. It wouldn't hurt anyone for her to help him out.

"Are you serious?" This was genuine. "You don't know how much that would mean to me. I know it's out of your way, and normally I would say no because I shouldn't make you do this, but I just, I really appreciate it."

"You're not making me do anything. My car is just over there," she said, pointing to her little ol' faithful. "I don't mind in the slightest."

And so he got up and started to walk to her car, wondering how the next while would unwind. Maybe he would decide against it at the last minute. Maybe she didn't him at all, and maybe he would do her more harm than good. But as they walked to the car, he saw the bags under her eyes. He took that as a sign that she needed this, that she needed rescuing.

"I have to pick up my brother first though, if you don't mind," she said as she opened her car door.

Immediately, Jeremy felt lightheaded. There was a brother. He had visions of a big, bad man in a leather jacket who would crush him between his thumb and pointer finger. Not even a full fist would be necessary.

"He's just playing over at a friend's," she added.

Playing over. He remembered this term from when he was young. It was what kids said to one another when they wanted to go to each other's houses, eat each other's food.

"Sure, no problem," he said, knowing there was no way around it. "How old is your brother?" He tried to sound conversational and keep his voice unaffected.

"He's six," she said. "His name is Benjamin. Ben. You won't think he looks like my brother." This with a smile. "He was adopted when he was two, he's from Mexico. Everyone always asks." She was so open, sharing the information like offering a mint or a stick of gum. A candid confession wrapped up just for him.

"That's a good age," he said without really knowing what he meant.

"Yeah, he's a doll. He's a really sweet kid. And he's happy to be living here in Canada, I think. He didn't come from the greatest home."

Violet was nervous too. She felt wary and out of her element. She was so good at the small talk of the restaurant, but now that she was alone with an older man she didn't know, her words came out thicker. They took a little longer to process, and she had to grab them from deeper parts of her brain. She took deep breaths and found herself peeking out of the corner of her eye at the man next to her.

She pulled into a driveway. "I'll just be one second," she said as she hopped out of the car. The ignition was still running, so she wouldn't be long.

Jeremy's heart began to hammer. Two people. Violet needed him, he was sure of it. But two people, that was something else entirely. That was a whole other heart and brain, another pair of legs, two more arms, ten more fingers, ten toes. Two extra eyes to evaluate him with. What if this was the most monstrously huge six-year-old ever to exist? Maybe he did wear a leather jacket. Maybe he had to be adopted because he was too huge to fit into the average Mexican home. He glanced at the clock and hoped they would hurry up before he took off running.

When Violet came back around the corner, he saw Ben's hand in hers. A tiny hand, close to the ground. A bare arm, a richly coloured one, and then a full body. A whole little human with a big smile and a pair of chocolate brown eyes.

45

Jeremy's heart did a flip. He couldn't do this. There had to be another way he could get through his everyday life without implicating these people. He didn't know what, but hadn't there?

Ben threw open the car door with little-boy strength and jumped into the back seat.

"Hello!" he said right away, a bit warily but with a real smile, "Who are you?"

"That's – " Violet began, but Jeremy was struck with a panic that she wouldn't remember his name. That she would be left hanging, searching for it in her memory, that she would be embarrassed. He dove in and shouted "Jeremy" at the same time she did. She'd remembered. He smiled.

"Hi Jeremy," said Ben. "Where are we going?" The question was thrown out to either of them, but Jeremy let Violet take it.

"We're going to give Jeremy a ride home, he lives out on the 8th Line. I think it's a little ways up from the ice cream stand you like, remember?"

"Allison's! Can we stop for some?"

She laughed. "It's pretty close to dinner time, so I don't know. But maybe on the way back. If you promise not to tell mom," she added quickly.

"Promise!" He practically squealed it.

So they have a mother, Jeremy thought to himself. Most people did, but he had edited that possibility out to make it easier for himself. Now that he knew there was a mom in the picture, he worried. She would miss them. She would come looking. That's what moms did, or so he heard.

He wondered about a father and guessed, correctly, that there wasn't one. Both of them were adopted, and neither knew the man who had shot out the stuff that allowed them to walk the earth. Jeremy couldn't stand the thought of two parents suffering without their children. But one, just one, it turned out he would be able to deal with. Just one wasn't so hard to bear.

They turned down roads Violet had never been down before, and it took awhile before they began to get close. Jeremy wasn't looking forward to this part. Their smiles weren't going to last much longer, and it would be a long time before they looked at him with any sort of ease or comfort again. He wanted to skip this part.

When they turned into his driveway, it was still a thirty-second trip up to the house. He had precious little time left, but he was not about to turn back now. He was committed, and soon they would be too.

The gravel grumbled beneath the tires, flinging up and around them like battle fire. Violet slowed to a halt when she reached the top of the path.

"Wow!" she marveled. "What a beautiful place to live in! You own it?"

"Yes," he said, the beginning of so many lies. "Thanks so much for driving me. Before you go, I have a surprise for you both."

He instantly realized how disturbing that sounded. Why would he have a surprise for two people that he didn't know would be giving him a ride home? He cringed as we waited for her reply.

"A surprise?" Violet asked cautiously. She knew something wasn't right. Any gracious, normal human being would have thanked her again and gotten out of the car already. She began to press herself against the door, ready to grab the handle. Ben was interested, though, and leaned in to hear more.

"Inside," he added. "There's something really neat I want to show you. This house is over a hundred years old."

Ben's eyes lit up with thoughts of ghosts and ghouls and trap doors. "Cool!" he said enthusiastically, and Jeremy was suddenly glad for his miniature presence.

"No Ben," Violet said firmly. "It'll have to wait." She turned to Jeremy. "We really do have to get back, my mom is expecting us. Thanks though, maybe some other time." She had no intention of returning though, and Jeremy knew it. He would have to use another tactic; the very one he'd been dreading.

He winced and reached into his back pocket. Not the one with his wallet. He pulled out the gun slowly.

"I didn't want to have to do this," he said, and it was the honest truth. Their eyes swelled in size and Jeremy was close enough to see Violet's chest rising and falling faster than before with tiny, stunted breaths.

"I'm sorry. This is awful, I know. But you have to come inside with me. I promise I won't hurt you." He was being too soft. "Well, I won't hurt you if you come with me and don't cause a scene."

"I'm sorry," Violet quivered. "I'm not sure what you want from us, but I just, I thought you were a nice guy, I just wanted to give you a ride home, and maybe I can give you another ride home sometime, but we have to go. We have to go."

48

It sounded like she would repeat the phrase over and over if she could, but stopped herself. She looked at him with big, expectant eyes and hoped for mercy. What did this man want from them? She wanted to ask, but she wouldn't. Not yet. She wanted to see if her plea had struck a chord. Shouldn't it have? He seemed like such a nice man, so innocent and meek, as if he'd been trampled his entire life. But the car began to feel smaller and smaller as the seconds ticked by, and she became acutely aware of just how far away she was from help.

"I can't let you go now," he said. "I can't."

Fear jolted through Violet's body and even her ears began to tingle. What he'd said sounded definite, eternal. I'm about to take you into my basement and chop you up with a machete so you can never tell anyone what I've done.

"I will let you go," Jeremy added, not sure if he was lying. He supposed it was a truth, or at least that it would be someday. Nothing lasted forever, after all.

"What do you want from us? I have some money on me, my tips from today. And if you let me drive to the bank, I can take out as much as I have in there. It's not a lot, but maybe it could get you what you need?"

Soon she was sure he would touch her, he would play explorer on her savage lands while she bucked and revolted against his hands. He would press his fingers into the dimples of her back and try to push her pelvis towards him as she held her breath and willed every opening in her body to close, to lock up and turn out the lights so he would stop knocking and go away.

"Come inside with me," Jeremy said in a low, gruff pitch. He turned back towards Ben, who had been silent for some time.

"Ben," Violet said forcefully. "Ben, don't you go anywhere. We're staying here, okay? We're staying here." The last part was shifted to Jeremy.

"Violet. Ben. You will come inside with me," Jeremy said quietly. "You have to. I'm sorry, but you don't have a choice. I promise I won't hurt you, I won't even touch you. We can just head right inside."

But he looked around, and saw the trees for miles. They could run in any direction and he might not be able to catch them. They could hide. He would have to make a leash. There were no garbage bags to use, so he looked around for something else.

"Stay here," he said with more confidence than he felt, tenfold. "Pop the trunk. Please."

Violet did as he asked and Jeremy got out of the car, grabbing the keys from the ignition as he went. They were too scared to run, he realized. Of course they were terrified. Part of him was tempted to show them the gun up close and say, Look! No bullets in here! It's made of plastic! It can't hurt you!

But he didn't do that.

He looked in the boot of the car and found bungee cords. He wondered if they were part of a care kit included when she was given her first car. Maybe she'd saved up for the vehicle all by herself, and had the wherewithal to think of the need for bungee cords all on her own. He grabbed them, bright red and yellow.

Climbing back into the vehicle, he reached over to Violet and hated the way she flinched.

"I'm sorry," he said, because he had already broken his first promise; that he wouldn't touch her. His hands fumbled awkwardly with the cord. It was so thick, not very long, and proved very difficult to tie around her wrist. He had to pull quite hard to make it stay, and he apologized over and over.

Violet was crying. Drops rolled down her cheeks but she didn't make a sound.

Ben was next. Jeremy grabbed the other end of the cord and wrapped it around his birdlike wrist, so tiny it felt as if Jeremy could snap it if he tied too tightly. Ben flinched, and his cries were audible. They were expelled out into the air so loudly that they echoed back off the trees.

"Why?" Even little Ben had the guts to question. "What's happening?" he asked, presumably to his sister.

"It's okay Ben," Violet sobbed. "It's alright. We're going to be just fine. We're just going to go inside for a quick moment and see this surprise." She paused to close her eyes and clench her mouth in fear. "Then we'll be on our way back home to mom."

The last word evoked even more sobs from Ben, which in turn made Violet cry harder. She had no clue how long this man would keep them.

Jeremy needed to get them inside. His resolve was fading. He needed them secured in place so he could start winning them back in what he knew was going to be a long, trying courtship. But he was sure he would be able to do it if he could only get them inside.

The way to do it was with confidence. No more waffling, no more I'm sorry and I wish I didn't have to do this. He was doing it. He should do it.

"Okay, wait here," he said as he got out of the car one more time. He went to Violet's door, opened it, motioned for her to get up. His impromptu leash still had Ben in the back seat, and he hadn't thought about how to get them both out of the car. Violet stood and Ben had to scramble between the two front seats to follow his sister out.

Jeremy grabbed the cord between their two snared wrists. It was as taut as a tightrope. They were pulling against it, two opposing forces, with every ounce of them. The best kind of war?

He led them toward the front door, up the porch steps and through the entry, the front hallway, to the back staircase, down the stairs.

Violet looked around frantically, her head swiveling to take it all in so she could describe it to someone if need be. It was primal fear, a basic instinct to figure out as much as possible about her surroundings.

Had it been Violet alone, Jeremy could have carried her. But he had two human beings on a leash, being led down the dark, damp stairs into the basement. There were many bedrooms upstairs, but they were full of windows and escape routes. It was too risky right now but when they chose to stay, he could move them up there. There was plenty of room.

"You won't be down here for long," Jeremy said. He meant to be reassuring.

Everything in the house was old and beautiful, full of antiques. There were paintings on the soft, neutral walls. It looked like a home. Violet held onto this observation as tightly as she could as they descended the stairs but was struck with the thought that if Jeremy killed her down there, earthworms would squiggle through the walls to eat her eyeballs before anyone ever found her. When they reached the bottom of the steps, Ben almost tripping down the last one, Jeremy ushered them into the back corner.

The cellar. There was one tiny window facing outside, one tiny source of light casting shadows across the space. Its walls were stacked with beautiful old bricks and below them lay a cement floor, a modern addition on top of the original dirt.

Jeremy knew it was cruel. He had put as many blankets as he could down there, comforters and sheets and pillows. With five bedrooms upstairs, there was a lot of bedding. Jeremy wouldn't have sheets on his own bed tonight, but he wouldn't be able to sleep anyway, he was sure of it.

For a washroom, he'd put a big barrel in the corner with a seat and cover, even a toilet paper holder. He had done the best he could, but it wasn't the sort of thing that led to comfort. It would be hard to convince them that they were somewhere they wanted to be when they had to piss and shit next to each other into a barrel from the garden. It had been dumped of soil and placed down there with a couple of wooden boards.

Jeremy realized he wouldn't be able to do any more convincing right then. He'd be best to remove himself and let them get used to their surroundings. A couple of bags of chips were stashed for them in the corner, some bottles of water too. There was a pot they could use to wash themselves with. He knew they would figure this all out, and decided to leave them. Maybe they would choose to think of it as an adventure. He wondered how long it would take them to realize they could be happy here, with everything they needed provided for them.

"Okay," Jeremy said as he began to untie their wrists. "I'm going to leave you alone now. You should be comfortable down here. I won't leave you for too long, but hopefully you can get some sleep. You two have a big day tomorrow."

Where had that last bit come from? He sounded like a sordid camp counselor advising his terrified campers. He didn't know what about tomorrow would be big, since they wouldn't be able to come out of the cellar just yet. It made him sad to know that he was depriving them of the outdoors, of their own beds. He wished he didn't have to do it this way, but it was the only option.

Violet and Ben continued to cry. They looked at the floor, not at him. Jeremy retreated.

"I'm sorry," he said as he closed the door. He couldn't help it. He was sorry, but not enough so to let them go home.

The door clicked shut. There was a lock on the outside, something he had always noticed and wondered about. In a wine cellar, what would be trying to escape, what would the bolt be locking in? The old bottles wouldn't grow legs and walk themselves out of the room. A burglar would easily be able to unlock the door from the outside and stroll in as he pleased. Maybe the lock was there for this purpose alone.

Jeremy sat down with his back to the door. He leaned against it, and pressed his ear to the solid panel between them. He could hear them whispering. His eyes welled up, and tears just as silent as Violet's began to fall down his face.

He couldn't make out the words on the other side, but it was Ben who was speaking them, Ben who was whispering wetly, "He stole us."

The words hit the walls thickly. The comforters mellowed the sound, cushioning its echo. Just small, sad musings of a little brother to his big sister, wondering what had gone so terribly wrong.

6

It's scary down here.

My sister is scared, which means it's scary. She's brave, most of the time.

I can't stop crying. I know the kids in class would call me a daisy, but I don't know what else to do.

Sometimes, when I fall off my bike, I cry. I try not to when friends are around. I look around real quick, and decide if I can let tears come out or not. If my mom is there, I just cry anyways. She likes it when I cry, I think. Or at least she treats me really nice when I do.

I don't want to think about how much scarier it would be if Vi wasn't here with me. She's shaking. I've never seen my big sister shake. She's not making much noise though, and I wish she would. It might make me feel a little better.

Maybe she's trying to be quiet so the man won't hear us. He could forget that we're down here. I'll bet he's gone to grab some more kids and put them in here with us. I don't know if that would be good or bad.

I want to ask questions. Who is that man and why does Violet know him? But I don't think my words would come out right.

You're supposed to say please and thank you and you're supposed to ask for things before you take them. But he didn't ask if he could take us, and he didn't say please. He just did it.

"He stole us."

I said it out loud by accident, and it feels better. I can't stop.

"He stole us." Because he did. We shouldn't be here. We wouldn't be here if he had asked. We would have said no. Well, he sort of asked but Vi said no.

I know not to get into a car with strangers, but my sister got in there. She's not a stranger, and she's smart. I'm not mad at her, I'm glad she's here. But things keep popping into my head like what will we eat? How will I go to the bathroom? I guess I don't mind missing school but I'll miss my mom, and Jane from my class. I think she might be pretty soon. Just the other day she wore a bow in her hair, a red one, and I know it was her mom who did it, she probably didn't know how to do it herself, but it was still lovely. I think she looked really lovely.

I want some milk. What if he doesn't ever let us outside? What if we're stuck in here forever and we become ghosts? Then at least we could sneak out through the walls.

I should be at home, playing with my toys or riding my bike or having some dinner. Mom probably made me some chicken fingers tonight. Something really yummy. Who is going to eat it?

She'll find us. She will. She'll know somehow, she always knows stuff. Like when I ask her where my favourite Lego set is, and she knows the exact spot where it's hiding. Or when I ask her a question about a place or a person, and she always seems to know what to tell me. Moms know these things. She'll know we're here.

It won't be long.

Maybe I should tell this to Vi. Maybe she needs to hear it, too. I try to do an extra big swallow so I'll stop crying long enough to say something. I whisper really quiet so the man can't hear us and know our plan.

"Vi, Mom will come get us. She'll come soon." I didn't mean for it to, but the last part sounded like a question. I meant to sound sure and to make her feel better, but I don't think it worked.

Vi is looking at me but all I can see on her face are tears. Her cheeks are wet, her shirt is too, and her sleeves from where she's been rubbing them against her face. She still looks so sad. I don't think she believes me.

I try again.

"She's coming for us."

Vi is bigger than me but it looks like she's just as scared, maybe even more. And boys are supposed to be tough. I'll be tough for her.

But she keeps crying, and she keeps being so quiet, and she won't really look at me. And I don't know what to do.

"He stole us." I can't help saying it again. It slips out.

7

There's a place in Japan where lovers go.

You climb a mountain together, stair after stair. You bring a padlock.

When you get to the top, there are locks everywhere. Attached to every tree, every railing, every spot you can see are locks of lovers past.

You lock your padlock to that mountain. It's a prayer mountain. You chain your love to that pinnacle so that it holds tight and strong. And then you take the key, and you toss if off the edge.

What faith, locking your love to a mountain for eternity, with no hope of finding the key, no need. That is the sort of love that should last forever, bound to something bigger.

Jeremy thought about this as he sat outside the cellar door. He'd seen it on a documentary once and for some reason hadn't changed the channel.

He hadn't thrown away the key to this lock. There wasn't one to throw; with the push of a bolt and the twist of a knob, it was done. Easy to reverse.

Maybe this house was his mountain. They weren't his lovers, but he would become important to them. Would it be too aggrandizing to call him their guardian, their keeper? He had already taken care of the padlock part. The rest would come in time.

They had quieted down a bit. Violet wasn't loud, it was mostly little Ben. Jeremy wondered if he should try to find a stuffed animal, something soft for him to cuddle, but didn't know when little boys became too old for that.

He fought the impulse to unlock the door, enter the room and sit with them. He knew it was too soon. He couldn't be the good guy just yet. He had to be the bad one to make sure that they would stay.

Forcing himself to turn away, Jeremy walked upstairs and went to the fridge to get a drink. His eyes stopped on the calendar hanging there, at the red circle surrounding the current day.

Fuck.

The family picnic. It was the one time during the whole year that his family pretended to be one. They weren't a family at Thanksgiving; they weren't a family at Christmas. But for some reason, on a day in the fall, they came together and pretended with games, food, drinks and forged laughter. No one knew one another, not really. When they left, they said, "See you soon!" By that, they meant the family picnic next fall. It amazed him that it still happened, that the Ridgeroy's still attended every year.

After spending a few years with Children's Aid, he had landed in the Ridgeroy household. They had eight adopted children. It sounded like a fairytale but it wasn't.

No one has time for eight children. It's just not possible. No one has that much love, and even if they can muster it up somehow, there isn't enough time in the day to distribute it. The result, at least for the Ridgeroy's, was that no one got enough of anything. Not enough love, that was for sure. Not enough attention or guidance. There was no way for his mother and father to learn all the little things that made Jeremy who he was, with seven other siblings.

The little effort Mr. and Mrs. Ridgeroy put towards the children was rejected as counterfeit. They were in a boarding house, and a toll was collected each time they walked back through the door.

He still heard the sobs of the little girls in the room next door. Mr. Ridgeroy watched them while they tried to sleep. Sometimes, Jeremy would have to get up to pee in the middle of the night and would catch the stooped, miserable man lurking outside their door. Jeremy kept his nose to the ground, but whenever he heard their little girl cries, he would clench his jaw and avert his eyes, disgusted with himself for not doing a thing to stop it.

A stronger man would have barged in there and removed Mr. Ridgeroy from their bodies. Jeremy was not a strong man, though, not now and especially not back then.

Once a year, he goes to the family picnic and sees those little girls' faces all grown up. They come with bad men that change every year, whose wandering eyes are the only constant.

Every time, Mr. and Mrs. Ridgeroy make some punch and a papier-mâché piñata, smiling through the whole spectacle. Jeremy figured it might be their penance, to force themselves to look those wayward boarders in the eye, and know that whatever defeat they saw before them was due to their own failures.

Whatever the reason for the fanfare, the picnic was tomorrow. He would have to iron a shirt, probably shave, grab a bottle of wine to bring. And practise his smile. He didn't know why he felt obligated to go. He shouldn't, really, and he'd fantasized often about cutting all ties. But he would go because they were his family, and you had to love your family no matter what. Didn't you?

Jeremy headed upstairs to his naked bed and curled up in it. He didn't feel much that night. He didn't cry and he definitely didn't smile. But he did sleep.

___

The shirt he chose was forest green, which brought out the emerald of his eyes, and made his hair look extra fiery.

Bottle of wine in hand, he got out of his car and walked up the church steps. None of the children had gone to church a day in their lives, but Mr. and Mrs. Ridgeroy were adamantly Christian. Jeremy wondered if it caused them discomfort to be in God's house with the children they had so badly fucked up. It had to be penance. The ritual was enjoyable to no one.

Eight stairs led him up to the church doors, with a sprinkle of fallen leaves at their threshold. He spotted a brilliant red one and thought about picking it for Violet. With the wine under his left arm, he pushed the door open with his right and was greeted with music, which they had learned was the best way to fill the silence.

There they were. Mr. and Mrs. Ridgeroy, and then from oldest to youngest: Samson, Erica, Derek, Anna, (Jeremy fit right here), Jessie, and Sally. Rose, the youngest of them all, had yet to arrive. She had always been Jeremy's favourite, and the one he felt most guilty for. She had only been five years old when Mr. Ridgeroy had begun to puncture her petite frame. What a bastard. What a poor, sweet little girl.

Not any longer. Rose had covered herself in tattoos and piercings. She had three babies with three different men, and none of them were around. She learned to pay the bills with men's appreciation of her body and for what she would do to them with it. Sad and ironic, or maybe just inevitable.

"Jeremy!" Mrs. Ridgeroy squeaked. He never thought of her as Mother or Mom or anything close. Not even as Amy, which was her first name. Just Mrs. Ridgeroy. It was his way of holding her away from him, keeping her at arm's length. "How ARE you? It's been so long."

She rushed over to give him a hug and a kiss on the cheek. He resisted the urge to wipe the spot where her lips had landed.

"I'm great," he lied. "What sort of piñata do we have this year?"

"It's a giant llama," she laughed. "Can you believe it? Who has ever heard of a llama piñata? But we started to put on the strips of paper, and some bumps started to come up out of nowhere, so we figured we'd go with it!"

By then, she'd walked up to the piñata and was holding it up to show that yes, it really was a llama piñata, albeit a poor one.

"Son," Mr. Ridgeroy nodded at Jeremy, who nodded back in reply. There was never a lot to say between them, or maybe it was that there was too much and where would they start?

Jeremy made the rounds with his siblings. At one time there had been a dutiful bond between them, one of sufferance, and they felt it was their obligation to show up here for each other so that none of them would have to face it alone.

Rose walked through the door as Jeremy finished hugging Anna.

"Howdy!" she said. She was flanked with a child on each side, another on her hip, and definitely one growing in her belly. Jeremy didn't know a thing about his little sister's current love life, but guessed it wouldn't be long before Rose had four babies with four different men.

Jeremy had always loved her spirit. Her hair was short and spiked, this time with a hint of pink. Her colour and style changed with the weather. Her kids all looked happy and smiling, and he wondered how she did it. Rose was the only one who would bring any children along. The rest were too reluctant to put theirs through it.

Being the nearest to her, Jeremy got the first hug from Rose. She had to plop her little chubby one down before leaning in.

"Jeremy," she breathed. "I missed you. It's so good to see you." It was comforting to know she meant it.

She made her rounds also, and soon it was time for the piñata. One of Rose's kids made the final blow, and everyone made a point of scrambling around for a bit of candy. It was humiliating, really; crawling around for cheap, sticky treats in crumpled wrappers.

Lunch was always the same: cold cuts and vegetables with fresh buns and every condiment. They sat together around a large table, which was more than they had done while living under the same roof.

Everyone gave updates on new lovers, old scoundrels, baby due dates, living arrangements. A lot can change in a year for ten people, especially such messy ones.

Jeremy always maintained silence during this part, because he rarely had anything to add. But sure enough, the eyes found him.

"What about you, Jer?" Mrs. Ridgeroy asked. "What are you up to these days?" He twitched at the shortening of his name. She owed him every syllable.

Violet popped into his head, and Jeremy smiled.

"Well... I've found someone," he said shyly and unsure of how much he was about to confess to, and how accurate it would be.

Whoops and outcries around the table begged him to continue. "Who is she?!"

"Her name is Violet," he said, and they all nodded for more.

"Come on, you'll have to give us a little more meat than that!" Rose protested, seemingly in jest but serious.

"Well, she's a server at a diner nearby." He was careful not to name it. "She's very pretty," he continued, "she has this blonde hair that she always wears in a ponytail." (He didn't actually know this, he'd just never seen it down.) "And the brightest grey eyes. I really think she's special. I don't know her too well yet, but I think we're really going somewhere."

Anxiety set in under the gaze of his captive audience but a sense of godliness came back as he bent the truth into words that would make them happy for him.

The lies began to come more easily.

"Wanna know how we met?" He was beginning to sense a story weaving itself in his head and wondered if it would be convincing. Of course, they all nodded their confirmation. Jeremy decided to steal a story his boss Johnny had told him once.

"Well, I'd seen her around an awful lot, and one time she walked by me with a twenty dollar bill hanging out of her pocket, like she tucked it in there quickly but it was about to fall out any second. So next time she came back, I said, 'I'm sorry, but there's a twenty dollar bill about to fall out of your back pocket.' So she reached back, found the bill, smiled at me and said thanks. She said, 'Why are you sorry?' And I said, 'Because I just admitted I was staring at your ass.'"

The whole family giggled with gaping mouths. Where had this confidence come from? How could that line have actually worked?

"After that, she wrote her name and number down on the bill and told me to call her. So I did." He wished so badly that this was the way it had happened and wondered if, over time, he could convince Violet it had.

"She might even come to live with me. I've moved into this home that I've been renovating. I'm there all the time doing work on it and it's completely empty, so it makes sense for me to live there."

Nods of understanding.

"She has a younger brother too," he continued. "His name is Ben, and he might come to live with us also."

"How old is Ben?" Mr. Ridgeroy. Pervert.

"He's six."

"Isn't that a little young for him to be moving away from home?" Anna asked.

"Well, they don't have the greatest home. It might be nice for him to be able to get away." Everyone at the table would understand that. Mrs. Ridgeroy lowered her head the slightest bit. Mr. Ridgeroy looked on steadfastly.

"Good for you, Jer." Rose looked so happy for him. "Maybe soon you'll be the one with new additions to the family and I'll be able to stop!" She said this with one hand on her protruding belly.

Jeremy smiled, amazed at how good it felt to share something. He couldn't let it go just yet.

"I make her tea every morning," he said. It was a lie, but also a pact that he made right then. "I know just the way she likes it. And we eat our eggs the same way. Over medium." He added these bits because they were the only ones about Violet that he knew. But they didn't realize this. They saw him as a punch-drunk new lover.

"Why didn't you bring her along then? We would love to meet her!" Mrs. Ridgeroy said greedily.

"Ah well, maybe next year," he said with a shrug and a smile.

Next year. God, he loved the sound of that. By then, they would be a family. Violet would know all the things about his past he wished he could change, and would understand why he needed to come to the family picnic. She would question it at first, but she'd get it. He wouldn't let her come along though. He would shield her from them.

Jeremy began to worry about her and Ben. He had checked on them in the morning with his ear to the door. He didn't want to rouse them; he feared it would cause their crying all over again. But they'd been in there for some time now. It was only just past noon, but still. No one could be sustained with potato chips forever. He thought about the errands he would need to run on the way home.

"Actually," he said standing up, "If it's alright, I think I might make a couple of sandwiches to go. For Violet and Ben."

He began a deli assembly line. He put everything he could fit inside; every addition an apology. He wrapped them in napkins and prepared to make his goodbyes.

"I should probably go get back to her," he said as lovers often do. As if neither could wait until the other was back in their arms from a day at work, a night out, a trip down the driveway to check the mail.

More hugs were given to say goodbye, alongside flimsy promises to make plans before the next picnic came around again.

He left that church with a new sense of purpose. He would return home (home) with sandwiches in hand like a hero.

He wondered what they would say when he brought them food. Would they think him kind? That was what he wanted, after all, but it might be too soon. Violet was smart, and he was vulnerable to her. She might realize it. What if he was too nice, too soon? What if they weren't scared enough? What if they just appeased him, pretended to oblige, then ran out the door the instant he gave them an inch?

He could easily be duped. Even his gunmanship had been lacklustre. Fear had been in their eyes, but it wouldn't last. They weren't really afraid of him, were they? Violet had seen him before; she'd talked to him. She would figure him out.

He didn't want to, but he would have to find a way to make sure they stayed scared of him just a little longer. They were about to be fed and in a relative amount of comfort, but he couldn't let them feel too at ease. They needed to know they were at his mercy. And he would have mercy, but it was his to give.

At that moment, as if a sign from the heavens or hell, Jeremy saw something on the side of the road. A lifeless body; a furry one.

It was a puppy dog, probably not more than a year or two old. A chocolate lab, it looked like, freshly dead. He could see the crushed ribs, the flattened segment where the tire had run it over, like dough under a rolling pin.

As he got closer, Jeremy saw that its head was still intact with a collar around its neck. This was someone's Buster.

Jeremy thought it would be better to clear the road kill out of the way. That family should never find their flattened friend.

He slowed his car, stopped and got out. Left the car on.

Quickly, before anyone could stop and stare, he scooped the dog up off the ground, cradled its head with one hand and held its haunches firmly in the other. He walked back to his car with the body and opened the door with one hand while balancing the lifeless carcass on his leg with the other. He dropped the dog onto the back seat. It amazed Jeremy how limply the body flopped down.

After getting back into the driver's seat, he headed home.

There was no garbage bag underneath the body. Jeremy didn't even put it in the trunk. He simply drove down those streets with a dead dog that wasn't his own in the backseat.

8

Violet dreamt she was late for work. When she walked into the restaurant sweaty and breathless, a thumping sound made her look to the front window. A zombie was standing there, staring at her and slamming its fist against the pane rhythmically. Maybe it was a code for help. There wasn't time to interpret before Jeremy opened the door and peeked inside.

She woke with a start when the door to their prison opened up. There had been a couple of timid knocks prior, but the weary inmates were tired enough only to register them in dreams.

Violet sat up as fast as she could and breathed in sharply through her nose. She couldn't afford to be groggy.

Ben, somehow, slept on and she debated letting him stay that way, as far removed from this place as he could get. But the chance of him waking up to their conversation, startled by the man who had kidnapped them looming above his head, led her to give his little shoulder a shake. She wanted to be the first thing he saw instead of that man.

Jeremy, she thought to herself. He has a name. A man who knew her name, and had given her his. He should have had the courtesy to be a complete stranger. It was starting to make her feel angry that she knew who he was.

Ben awoke and it broke Violet's heart the way his eyes widened in horror as he remembered where he was. She tried to give him a smile, but it came out haunted and clownish, a miserable parody. The muscles couldn't bring themselves to turn upwards.

"Hi there," Jeremy said in a quiet voice. "I'm sorry I woke you, but there's something I need to show you."

To Violet in that moment, Jeremy looked like a pitiful, wayward boy. It occurred to her that she could probably overtake him. If she and Ben organized a revolt, Ben could bite at his ankles while she swung elbows at his face, and they could tackle him to the ground. She stored this idea away and began to count the seconds until Jeremy was gone from the room. She would tell Ben not to be afraid and that they would be out of there soon.

Violet didn't say anything in reply, and Ben just stared wide-eyed. Jeremy continued. "I want you to know I'm not going to hurt you. I don't want to hurt you. I want us to become very close, actually."

He said this as if it was possible after what he had done, Violet thought bitterly.

"But," he stipulated, "I can only be as nice as you are to me. We're going to be living here for awhile –"

"Whoa." Violet couldn't help but be bold. "What do you mean by 'awhile'?"

Jeremy could see he had gone too quickly, skipped too many steps. It was time to backpedal so he could keep her comfortable.

"Well, a few days," he lied. "Just until I can make sure that everyone will come out of this safely."

"Look, Jeremy," she would try to use his name as much as she could. "Nothing bad will happen to you. If you let us go, our mom will be so happy to see us that if we ask her to, she'll leave you alone. If you let us go, we'll let you go. We don't ever have to see each other again."

Jeremy just stared at her sadly, and she saw she had said the wrong thing.

"Neither of us is hurt," she kept trying. "And you've been very nice to us. And," she didn't know if it was appropriate or not, but decided to try to make him smile, "you are a really great tipper."

He did smile.

"I don't know what we're doing here, but my family doesn't have a lot of money. I mean, I can try to give you a few thousand dollars. That would be no problem. Just take us to the bank, or let me call my mom so she can put aside some money."

Jeremy was shaking his head. "I don't want any of your money."

Then what? Being kidnapped for ransom was terrifying, but being kidnapped for something else was even more so. There was only one other reason she could think of as to why they were there. She again felt the premonition of his hands all over her, covering her mouth so she couldn't scream.

Violet took a deep breath from a reserve hidden within.

"No?" she asked. "Well, even if you didn't want it to begin with, I'm sure we could figure something out. I know we can give you whatever it is you need. Whatever it'll take to get us home, we'll do it. I mean, we have extended family too, they have careers and connections…"

She stopped because she didn't know what else to say. How many times could she tell him she would give him whatever he wanted before he asked her to take her clothes off? She thought of him railing against her body as Ben watched right beside them. Violet tensed. Her arms locked across her body and she refused to let go, like her sense of wellbeing that was slipping away as she clung desperately to it.

"No, that's not it," Jeremy explained uselessly, "It's not anything tangible that I want."

Violet clamped her eyes shut.

"We don't need to talk about that part right now," Jeremy said. "Let's just not worry about it, that'll figure itself out, okay?"

Nods from Violet and Ben. The rest of their bodies were frozen in place.

"For now, I need you to look at something." Jeremy leaned over and grunted with exertion as something furry appeared in his arms.

Violet realized it was a dog. A large and dark one. A pet? How long are we going to have to stay here that we need a pet?

The dog's head rested on Jeremy's shoulder and kept very still. With its head facing the other way, there was no way to know if a friendly tongue was wagging about, but Violet sensed instinctively that something was wrong.

Jeremy opened his mouth to begin what looked like it might be a speech, with a deep breath and a sudden, sharp upturn of his skinny shoulders.

"I don't like to be violent," he started. "I don't want to hurt you. But sometimes, if things don't go the way they should, I might have to. This dog here, Buster, he was my pet. I brought him home after finding him in an alley one day. But he started to misbehave. He was killing animals and knocking over things and barking at everything that went by. I told him to stop, but he wouldn't. He wouldn't listen." Jeremy shrugged, a somewhat muted gesture with the weight of the dog still in his arms.

"He would even run out into the street, and it was only for his own sake that I wanted him to stop, but he wouldn't. So I had to do this. I had to kill Buster," Jeremy lied. "I didn't like doing it, but I did."

His voice shook, and his eyes misted over. Violet could see he was feeling something genuine and mistook his words for truth.

"It had to happen," he justified. "And I don't mean to scare you too badly, and I'm sorry if a dead dog is a strange thing to bring down here to show you, but I wanted you to know that you have to listen to me."

He paused to clear his throat.

"Now, I'll be as nice to you as I can. I want you to be comfortable here. But the thing is, you won't be able to leave until I say that you can. So you should try to accept your new surroundings and listen to everything I tell you. Don't try to escape.

"I'm going to put security cameras in here so that I'll know if you're trying to get out. There are electric fences all along the property, and there's no way for you to get out of here without hurting yourself and setting off an alarm. I don't want to cause you any harm, but I need you to cooperate. Does all this make sense?"

No, thought Violet, none of it did. She still had no idea what he wanted from them, or for how long. But the dead dog that Jeremy held onto crept into her bones. She sensed that there was something incredibly off-balance about the man before her. For the first time, she began to fear for her life and not just their safety.

Violet merely nodded. Her stomach was plagued with the unsettled feeling of her faulty evaluation of Jeremy, but the image of him sitting passively in a diner booth still pervaded her thoughts. He wasn't a sinister, coal-hearted man. She could see him trying not to quiver. He kept swallowing in an exertive attempt to hold back the waver that snuck in and around his words.

But she realized she had no idea what he was capable of, and her fear forced her to comply.

"Okay," Violet said. "We'll stay here and wait for you to figure things out." Her voice shook. She tightly held Ben, who had been sitting in stone silence, staring at the stranger.

That seemed to please Jeremy, and with a nod, he retreated from the room.

"I'll get you guys something good to eat," he said from the doorway. "I know you can't live off of chips. I have some sandwiches, but what else? Any requests?" What an inappropriate question. Well, I'd really like it if you would let us go. No? A ham sandwich then, please.

Violet and Ben shook their heads in tandem. They just wanted him out of the room, out of their space and their vision, just gone. Jeremy answered their silent will, closing the door behind him. They heard the lock latch into place behind the wooden barrier.

Violet looked at her brother.

"I love you," she said. "I'm so sorry we're in here. I never should have given him a ride. You should never give rides to strangers. But I did know him, I served him at work, and he just seemed so..."

"Why does he want us here?" Ben asked.

"I honestly don't know. There's something wrong with this man. He doesn't see the world the way we do. He might not even realize it's wrong to be holding us here like this."

"But it's stealing," Ben said earnestly. "Everyone knows you're not supposed to take things that aren't yours."

"You're right. But we're not things. Maybe he thinks he's borrowing us. He could just be really, really lonely. We need to keep him happy and do everything that he tells us to, as long as it doesn't involve us getting hurt or leaving each other. We should stay together no matter what, okay?"

Ben gave a small nod.

"I won't leave you," Ben said. "If you won't leave me. Promise you won't?"

Violet looked into his big brown eyes. He'd said goodbye to a lot of people in his short life. "I promise, Ben."

She was reminded of what a tiny, quivering mess of a thing he'd been when he arrived at the age of two.

Holly, their mother, took a trip to Mexico and found him. Fell in love instantly, is how she tells it. After all the paperwork and red tape, she brought him home where fourteen-year-old Violet had been waiting patiently. Bits of that feverish little boy, now almost completely transformed, remained in Violet's memory.

Ben would dart through the house, pausing to poke his head around corners and say proudly, "Hola!" before giggling impishly and running off.

And dinnertime. When putting a plate of food in front of him, you had to be careful to draw your hand away quickly. He would bite with the skill of a scavenger fighting for his share. He would grab fistfuls and shove them into his mouth like a caveman. Chewing voraciously, he swallowed as fast as he could. Holly learned never to ask him if he wanted more, because he would say yes, yes, yes every time. It took him months to learn that he didn't need to fight for it anymore.

Bits of this instinct still leaked through when he was startled or uncomfortable. He still shied away from the touch of people with new faces, and sudden noises caused him to whimper. Four years had passed, though, and six-year-old Ben was endlessly more confident than his two-year-old counterpart.

He was a quiet boy, a bit secretive. He was curious like his sister, but where she wanted to know everything she could get her hands and ears on, he would often wait patiently and trustingly for the information to come to him.

Violet had an image of Ben as a kitten that might run off on its own if startled. Just tear out into the forest and hide underneath some small shelter. She feared the survival instinct he had perfected as an orphan might come back to haunt them. She wondered if he would bite at her hand if she tried to share a plate of food. Hopefully she would soon find out – somehow in all of the terror and strangeness, her tummy began to rumble.

Until Jeremy came back, they would just have to sit and wait. Maybe eat some more of those damn potato chips lurking on the edge of their cotton-sheeted lagoon. Who provides chips as sustenance? How could he have thought they would be enough? For a moment, her disgust overpowered her fear.

She continued holding onto Ben, thinking about how sad it was that she shouldn't have given a seemingly friendly stranger a ride home. Her Girl Scout good deed gone all wrong. What sort of karma was that?

9

Jeremy was miserable after leaving the cellar. He felt like the Boogeyman, the Abominable Snow Monster, Boo Radley. A misunderstood freak who would take forever to learn to love.

Violet and Ben had looked genuinely scared when he brought in that dog, which had been the point. But he didn't calculate how awful it would feel to cradle a dead dog in his arms for so long. The shattered bones crunched as he shifted the dog's weight against his body. He could feel squishy bits where he knew none should be. He'd wanted to cry for the poor dog, especially after calling him Buster. Instead, he remained stone cold, barely allowing his voice to falter.

Jeremy went outside to the barn and got out a shovel. Buster II deserved something of a proper burial.

His mind wandered as he lowered the spade, stomped on it, heaved the loosened soil over his shoulder and started again.

How did I get here? He wondered. What started all of this? The dirt was heavy and he found himself wanting a helping hand. But, just as he had been since childhood, he was alone.

He remembered something then, about why children are the cruelest humans of all.

One day, a few boys ventured over to Jeremy, who was about to visit the corner store for a cold drink. He was thirteen years old. He remembered, because he was riding the bike that he'd saved up for and bought for his birthday. It was green, and the cheapest one he could find. There weren't any fancy gears, no kickstand or bell or basket, and the seat was as uncomfortable as someone shoving their fist up his ass. But it was his bike; he had earned it and now he owned it. His next priority was to buy a lock because he didn't trust anyone in that town.

That's why he was skeptical, even more so than usual, when three of his schoolmates sauntered over to tell him what a nice bike he had. Jeremy gripped his handlebars and thought of ways to escape.

"Thanks," he said softly. He hoped they would leave it at that. He didn't even entertain the idea they might want to stay and play with him; he'd given up hoping for that.

"How fast does it go?" the tallest boy, Roger, asked him.

"I don't know, about as fast as yours, probably." He really had no idea, and hoped this wasn't the beginning of a proposition to race. Another thing he hadn't bought yet was a helmet.

"Mine's pretty fast," Roger said.

Here we go, Jeremy thought miserably.

"Say, wanna do a dare?" Roger asked. His two sidekicks, Johnny and Mo stood by, silently smirking.

Jeremy felt like prey. He didn't know what to say to them.

"I don't know," he said finally. "Depends on what it is."

"That's not the way a dare works, mate." The term sounded unnatural coming out of Roger's small, tight-lipped mouth, like he was trying out a new word he hoped would catch on.

"Yeah," Mo chimed in, "You'll either do it or you won't."

Jeremy squirmed. "Well, what do I get if I do it?"

"We'll leave you alone," Roger said, "Simple as that."

He wasn't sure what Roger meant. Did he mean they'd walk away from him right now and leave him to his cold drink? Or did they mean forever, as in, they wouldn't chase him with taunts down the hallways every day? That he might not hear Bewaremy and Here comes the Ginger Giant whispered behind his back as he passed them in the hall. And if they stopped, would everyone stop? Would three people really make that much of a difference out of a whole school's torture?

He was getting ahead of himself. "And if I don't do it?" he asked.

"We get your bike." Roger jerked his head in the direction of the brand new two-wheeler. Jeremy didn't want to take that bet.

"No thanks, guys." He had no idea what they might dare him to do. They'd probably have him eating worms or sneaking a peek up the woman's skirt behind the counter. The thought made him feel sick.

"Come on now, Jeremy," Roger said in a singsong voice. "You might want to rethink that one. I mean, we were just gonna steal your bike anyway, dare or no dare. But we figured it would be only fair to give you the chance to win it back."

Win it back?

"It's my bike," he replied lamely. "I worked hard for it. Save up for your own bike."

The trio looked at each other with wide eyes and laughter.

"Oh, we have our own bikes," Johnny piped up. "We just want yours, too. Add it to the collection."

"Why?" Jeremy asked. He meant it in so many ways. Why do you want another bike? Why are you doing this? Why me? Why am I always your target? Why do you act like you're so much better than me? Why can't I defend myself? Why does everyone think you're so much better than me? Why does it make you feel good to make me feel worthless?

Roger's answer addressed all his silent questions. "Because we can."

Jeremy sighed and knew he didn't have a choice. They might smack him upside the head regardless of the dare, grab his handlebars and make a getaway down the street until all he could see was the retreating green glimmer from the setting sun. But it was worth a try.

"Alright. I'll take the dare. What do you want me to do?" He held his breath.

They hadn't thought this part through. Looking at each other dumbly, they waited for someone to come up with a solution. Jeremy took secret pleasure in their tongue-tied silence.

At that moment, a woman walked by the store with a purse dangling from her left hand.

"Steal that." Roger said. "Grab that purse."

The boys snickered.

Jeremy considered his options. It's them who would be stealing the purse, he rationalized, not me.

Should he cover his face? It was a small enough northern Ontario town that she might know him. He knew better than to ask for a mask. The boys would laugh at his yellow belly.

"Better hurry up," Johnny said. "She might live in one of those houses up there, and you don't want to have to follow her inside."

Jeremy slowly mounted his bike and contemplated pedalling off into the distance. He knew they wouldn't give up so easily. If it weren't that day, it would be another.

The woman with the purse was a petite Asian lady who looked to be in her mid-fifties. She wasn't swinging her bag in a childlike, carefree way; she had it secured in her fist and held it alongside her body. Jeremy's quickly hatched plan was to ride up beside her and swipe it at the last second. He would hopefully be way down the street before she even knew what hit her. She'd have a hard time identifying him from behind, although his bright green bike might be a dead giveaway. He gulped at the thought of having to paint it another colour so he wouldn't get caught. There had to be plenty of other green bikes around. He couldn't be nailed by bike colour alone. Probably.

It didn't take long to catch up, and as he pulled next to her he reached out and grabbed for her purse as quickly and violently as he could. Her grasp hadn't been as tight as it looked. Jeremy secured the bag on his arm, put his hand back on the handlebar, and pedalled as hard as he could.

"No!" she screamed after him. "That's my purse! He took my purse! Help, someone, help! He took my purse!" She yelled so loudly that Jeremy thought people would surely come streaming out of their houses to see what all the commotion was about. She sounded insane, like if she caught him she wouldn't know whether to cry or rip him to pieces.

He was the reason she screamed that way. He had done that to her. Looking back (he couldn't help it), he saw her chasing after him on legs made futile by his wheels.

"Yosonoabeech!" she bellowed. Her accent caused her words to run together, but he knew what she meant.

"Bastard!" she howled after him. That one was clear as day.

"I'm sorry!" he yelled back, uselessly. "This isn't who I am!" She probably couldn't even hear him, but he couldn't help it. His actions were so off-kilter from what he thought he knew about himself that it made him feel ill.

It wasn't my fault, he told himself. I would never have done it if those boys didn't make my life miserable all the time.

Her angry voice ran through his head. He never thought he'd be on the receiving end of words loaded with that much hurt and disgust.

His hand and his alone had been the one to reach out and grab that purse. That was the day Jeremy realized he was capable of doing awful things when put under the right kind of pressure.

Jeremy snapped back to the present and eyed the deep hole he had dug. He always seemed to lose himself when digging, as if he was shoveling down into his own depths. He set the spade aside and picked up the dog's dead weight one last time. Gently, he lowered the defeated body into the bottom of the grave and stared at it. It seemed so sad to pour dirt over the dog, and he regretted not finding a burlap sack or a makeshift coffin. Jeremy took the shirt off his back and wrapped the dog in it.

"I'm sorry you were hit by a car," Jeremy said out loud. "You're a beautiful dog, and I'm sorry I brought you here but I'm glad this is where you ended up. It's nice here. You're under the shade of a beautiful willow tree."

He lifted the shovel and began to suffocate the grave with dirt, trying to hold onto the present so he wouldn't get lost in any more reveries. That was enough remembering for one day.

It felt bizarre to insert such a large body into the ground. From above, no one would ever know. They'd walk right over top without realizing, as he hadn't brought any cross or stone to mark it with. He looked for a rock. He didn't want Buster to be walked over unnoticed.

What he found was a big grey boulder. It wasn't pretty, and he wouldn't be able to write on it, but it would do. He would always know that it marked the spot of the dog that marked the beginning of his journey with Violet and Ben. Maybe someday the three of them would stand side-by-side at the gravesite and think about how that dog had helped bring them together.

Jeremy smiled.

He started to think about what else had to fall into place before he finished the first part of his plan. He wondered where his cunning had come from. No one thinks they will be good at holding someone captive. He knew he had no right to feel proud of himself, but something inside started to feel good. Increasingly good, in a way he hadn't known before.

The power of the puppet master. Violet and Ben were stuck where he had placed them. They were under his care and he wouldn't let anyone harm them. Besides himself, of course.

<u>10</u>

My sister keeps making weird noises. One second I think I hear her sniffling, and the next she clears her throat really loud like she's coming down with a cold. I don't know what to think, but I hope she's not getting sick because who will take care of her?

These chips aren't even the good kind. Mom would never let us eat them.

I miss her. I miss home. I don't want this to be where I live. I didn't have a choice where I lived when I became a Ben Wrigley, like the gum, but I got lucky. That was a really nice place to be. But it would be really unlucky to live here. I'd be scared all the time, and all I would get to eat would be chips. I mean, I like chips. But my mom would kill me if she knew I'd just been sitting here eating them for every meal.

The thing is, she doesn't even know I'm eating chips, because she doesn't know I'm here. She must be looking for us. She probably got so mad when we didn't come home for dinner.

I kinda want to ask Vi if she is alright, but I don't know if she wants to talk about it. She hasn't said anything in a long time. I'm glad she isn't going to leave me here by myself, but scary ideas keep popping into my brain. Like what if she left and meant to come back for me but couldn't find her way, or what if the Jeremy man wouldn't let her back in? I try not to think about it.

"Vi? Are you okay?" I know it's a silly question, because I know she's not really okay, and I'm not really okay either, but adults always tell us there's no such thing as a silly question, so you're always supposed to ask.

Vi raises her head up and looks at me and nods. She's okay, the same kind of okay I am right now. "Are you thirsty?" she asks me.

I open and close my mouth for a second to see if I am. It's a little sticky in there. I nod my head back at her and she reaches over to grab a bottle of water. I wish it was pop. I know I need to remember to stay hydrated, because that's what my mom tells me whenever I'm not feeling well. Stay hydrated. I think it's because hydrate sounds like hydrant and there's water in those.

I drink a few gulps of water and wipe my fist over my lips to get the drips.

"Vi," I say even though I know I shouldn't say it, "Do you think we get to go home soon? I think Mom is getting worried."

When I say this, she starts to cry and I feel bad. I know she misses Mom too so I just hug her, and she hugs me, and we sit that way for a while. Then I hear footsteps.

We both suck in our breath a little bit, and make sounds kinda like when you shake a pop bottle and untwist the cap. I don't know if I want him to come down here or not. I'm scared, but I would like to eat some food.

The lock on the door comes undone and the door opens. I see a big bag in his hands.

"Hi again," he says and he's smiling. "I brought you guys something to eat, are you hungry? You must be. Sorry I was gone so long." He places a bag down on the floor in front of us.

"I made you sandwiches, nice fresh ones from this picnic lunch I was at. I'm sorry you couldn't go with me."

He mentioned those sandwiches when he came in with the dog, and I wonder why he didn't just give them to us then.

87

He opens his mouth like he's about to say something else, but then closes it. Like a fish. He hands me the bag of food. I take out a sandwich and give it to Vi, and then I take one for me. I think maybe I should wait until the Jeremy man leaves the room, but I guess it can't hurt to eat and listen and watch him all at the same time. Vi just holds on to her sandwich though. Girls are weird sometimes about eating.

"I have something else for you guys, too." Jeremy was still standing there. He's so tall and skinny, like a lamppost. His pants are too short. They don't cover his ankles and I can see his black socks. All of his bendy bits sort of look like doorknobs. I wonder if I could count his freckles.

I have no idea what he has in his bag, but I hope it's something good and not something scary, like handcuffs or blindfolds or something else dead.

He pulls out some comics and chapter books and pencils and paper and a thing you play music on, but not the new kind, an older one for CDs, I think they call it a Wokman. But we don't have CDs, and so then he pulls some out. I haven't heard of any of the people he pulls out, but they all have hair that's dark and oily, both the men and the women. And then he pulls out some batteries and some headphones, so he really thought of it all.

It feels a bit like Christmas. We're getting all these presents, and we didn't even ask for them. Maybe he feels bad for keeping us down here because, really, he should.

I remember when I was littler than now, I saw the news one night. I don't know why people like to watch it. It's just boring-looking people sitting and reading stuff, using big words for names and places. But one time, I saw a news about a dad who killed his two kids, and then killed the mom too. That's three different people. It was the person he had kids with, and his own two kids, and he killed them. That really scared me because it seemed like he did it the same way I squash bugs that buzz in my ear or spiders that spin webs in my room.

I didn't understand it so I said to my mom, "Why did he do it?"

And my mom looked at me with a sad face, like she was in pain or I had a huge lump on me that I couldn't see yet. She said, "It's because he doesn't know what's up and what's down."

I didn't know what that meant, and I didn't want to give up so easily.

"What do you mean?"

"I mean, he doesn't know the difference between right and wrong."

"But didn't his mom teach him?" I turned a little red then, because maybe he didn't have a mom to teach him that it was bad to kill people he loved.

My mom didn't notice though, and she said, "Someone taught him, and he probably used to know it was wrong. But sometimes, things happen to people that are too much for them to take, and it changes them. It muddles things around in their head, and they don't know wrong from right. They don't know up from down."

I remember the word muddle because it sounded like mud puddle mixed in to one word, which is pretty much what it means, I think.

I still didn't get it. I couldn't think of anything that would make me forget that something so wrong was wrong, except maybe if I whacked my head really hard.

That's probably not going to happen though because I always wear a helmet when I ride my bike.

I wonder what happened to Jeremy so that he doesn't know up from down. I feel like pointing to the floor and the ceiling for him so maybe he'll be less confused and remember.

What I really want to do is ask him what happened to make him want to keep us here. I think sometimes people think I like to be quiet. But really, there's all kinds of things going on in my head that I want to ask about and just don't know how to. I should ask Jeremy because there's no such thing as a silly question. But maybe that's another of the things he forgot.

"I know it's not the nicest place to be down here," he says. I think the reason he started talking again was because me and Vi weren't saying anything. I was still eating, but she was just sitting there, looking at him but not really looking. She could have been staring at a big rock or something, because she wasn't moving anything on her face or blinking very much.

"But I'm going to do everything I can to make sure you guys are okay. And we'll work day by day to see what happens next. If you're good, then I have a bunch of rooms upstairs, and you could come live there instead. There's a lot of land here, and the trees are beautiful. There's so many fun things to do, like gardening and picnics and a porch swing. The sunsets here are so pretty, and you can really see the stars when they come out at night."

My mom told me once that the stars are shy, and they don't like to come out when it's too noisy or bright. They figure the streetlights and big buildings are enough to light the night, so they focus on the dark places that need them more. It makes me glad to live in a town with not a lot of lights.

"It might take awhile before I can let you move upstairs," he keeps going and I wonder when he will leave. "But I'm willing to learn to trust you, if you earn it."

I see Vi's lip twitch. When she smiles, her lip curls in this weird way that my Mom says looks like Elvis, but I don't know who that is. Vi does it for little smiles, but also when she's baring her teeth at someone. She doesn't even know she does it. I asked her once about it and she turned all red and carried around a mirror with her all day to see if she could catch herself doing it.

Anyways, I know that this kind of lip twitch means she's not happy.

Jeremy keeps talking to us about how we can earn little things, like gifts and food if we're good and listen to him. Next he reaches outside the door and grabs a whole new bag. At first I'm scared there might be another dead animal in it, but it's some sort of black box, and it has a red light on it, and it's got this little top part that screws into the ceiling. I know this, because he takes it into the corner by the door, and starts to screw it up there. He keeps talking while he does it.

"This is just so I can make sure you guys are okay. If you run out of water and get thirsty, I'll be able to see that and come give you some. Or just in case a light bulb burns out or something, or if you have a nightmare and you get scared." He looked at me when he said this, and I gave him a dirty look. I've had bad dreams forever, but I don't wet my pants or call out to my Mom to come help me. And I definitely wouldn't call out for him.

"Just in case you guys misbehave, I'll be able to see that too. I'm going to be very reasonable, and I'm not going to hurt you, you know, like punch you or anything. But it's in your best interest to be on your best behaviour."

He sounds like Mrs. Smiley on my first day of Grade One.

"There's one more thing," he says, and I'm hopeful again. But he pulls out more black stuff, this time two long black straps that he hands over to Vi.

"These are security bracelets," he says. "Do you mind putting them on?" I'm really glad he's not putting them on for us. I don't want him to touch me, and plus, I know how to put on bracelets.

"It's got a GPS that shows me where you are. And even when I'm sleeping, it'll start to beep at me when you're moving around a lot, so I'll wake up and come check on you. Because if it's anything you need, I don't mind getting it for you." I couldn't tell if he was being really nice or really mean, but I think it was a bit of both.

I put on my bracelet right away, but Vi is still holding hers in her hand and staring at him with her blank, rock eyes.

"Why do we need to wear these? We're locked in here anyways, and we're not going to run away, we already told you that." She sounds like she's mad, and I don't think she means to. I think she means to sound strong, and she is because I wouldn't be brave enough to say all that to him. But she should probably stop talking, and I kick out my foot at her, just gently to try to say, Stop talking so he'll leave and we can eat. She moves the leg I kicked a little, so I know she felt it, but she just keeps going.

"If we're going to be living here with you, and we're going to be gaining your trust, then you have to gain ours too. Trust goes both ways."

I don't understand what she's trying to say. Trust is one of those things that my mom and my sister talk about a lot. It gets taken away when I do things like eat an extra cookie when no one's looking, or when I sneak downstairs in the middle of the night to watch TV. But then I get some of it back when I play outside and don't jump out in front of a car or something. I think trust is a sort of money. You get some, and you give it away, and you get some back sometimes but only if you do something right. Someone can't just hand it to you for no reason, or else it's fake. And you can't steal it. I know that much.

Jeremy gets what she's saying I think, because his eyes sag a little and he looks sad.

"I know I have to earn your trust," he says. "And I'm going to do that. Let me know anything you need and I'll get it for you. I'm going to buy you guys a TV so you can watch some movies and shows. I'll bring you, I don't know, some weights so that you can exercise if you want."

He looked at Vi when he said this and I think that was a mistake because you're not supposed to say things to girls about exercise or what their belly looks like. I said something like that once and Vi threw a hairbrush at my head. I would warn him about this but I don't think he's earned it.

"No, I know you'll give us everything we need." Vi is being too nice and I know it's not real nice, but I don't think Jeremy can tell. "It's just not ideal to have to wear this bracelet all the time so that you know every time I go to the bathroom."

His cheeks turn red and he starts mumbling stuff about how he isn't going to do anything while she's in the bathroom.

"I'm sorry," he says. "But there's no way around it. That's just the way it's going to go. So I hope you'll wear it, and if you do, then I'll keep doing nice things for you, and maybe soon we can work on an outdoor day for us all."

I think Vi realizes he means it, and that we're just going to have to wear these things.

"I'll leave you alone for a bit," he says. "So you can get something to eat and get used to the camera and the bracelets. I'm sorry to have to do all this." He sounds like he really is. What if he did know what way was up, and he was doing this anyways? I didn't know what to think about that.

11

That's how time passed for awhile, Violet and Ben in the basement and Jeremy living above them.

He didn't have the heart to continue forcing them to use that old barrel as a bathroom, soiled by the earth and their bodies. He knew he wasn't about to win them over if he kept them in a state of discomfort, so he began escorting them back and forth to the bathroom four times a day. As humiliating as he knew it must be, he used two dog leashes the owners of the house had left in the front hall closet. Soon, he started to leave the leash slack so they could walk more easily, and eventually he stopped with the ritual all together. He locked the upstairs door so that if they ran away they couldn't get out, but he let them walk at their own speed and would simply follow behind them. He felt a bit inappropriate lurking outside the door while they went to the washroom, brushed their teeth or tried to shit, quiet and embarrassed. But it had to be done.

He felt a strange, grotesque pride at being able to provide them with a bathroom, like he had when taking Buster for walks when he was young.

Jeremy wanted them to move upstairs, to spend time during the day with him. They could have family dinners, just the three of them. They would be roommates and there would always be someone to watch a movie with, or go for a walk with, or talk to if needed. He'd have attention and affection, things he hadn't had enough of for years, and maybe not ever. Things he hadn't even known he wanted.

Violet and Ben had been living with him for a few weeks, and he liked to think they were getting used to it. You can get used to anything.

Jeremy scoured the news. It wasn't that he was vain. He didn't want to pin up stories about himself. He wanted to burn them instead. He wanted one less newspaper in circulation so that one less person would read about what he had done and maybe try to find him. It wasn't anyone's business but theirs, and no one else would understand. The media were getting it all wrong, Jeremy thought, painting him as a fire-breathing dragon and questioning whether Violet and Ben were still alive.

It took a day or two before the news outlets began to swarm on the story like maggots. At first there was a hunt to find out if Violet and Ben's birth parents had gone on a jealous, regretful rampage, claiming back the children they had long since given up.

"Two children have been reported missing in Blind River. Ben and Violet Wrigley, ages six and eighteen, were last seen on Monday afternoon. Ben was wearing a green t-shirt with a pair of khaki-coloured shorts and Violet was wearing a purple t-shirt bearing the logo of the local diner where she worked. No suspects are currently in custody. If you have any clues as to the whereabouts of these two individuals, call..."

"MISSING SIBLINGS" was the bolded headline on the front page of the Blind River Eyes the following morning. "Little brother and big sister gone for three days."

But wars went on. People got shot. Stocks went up and down, animals still looked cute. And the three names Jeremy had been hunting for appeared less and less.

He considered the odds of being found. He knew there was no sign of a struggle because Violet had allowed him into her car willingly, and wasn't alarmed or visibly distressed when she went to pick up Ben. Ben wouldn't have looked suspicious either, because he had no idea Jeremy was even in the car. Violet had a cell phone, but he had taken that away from her and removed the battery.

He never noticed any signs of attempted escape. There were no claw marks on the door, no smashed windows or little tunnels dug into the cement. It made Jeremy feel good. The house didn't have a working landline, so there was no fear of them sneaking upstairs and making an emergency phone call. The same was true of an Internet connection, and it was so far out in the middle of nowhere that there was no hope of picking up any wireless signals.

Other technicalities worked in his favour as well. Jeremy tried to evaluate them realistically. Their mother must be putting up a fierce search party for them. With two of them gone, it might be double the search effort.

What would he do if someone rang the doorbell and asked if he had seen Violet and Ben Wrigley? Of course he would have to lie, but would a simple No do? Would he have to feign concern, ask about when they were last seen and if there were any distinguishing marks on them, or if he could have a picture? Was there such a thing as being too concerned, or not enough? Perhaps he would look cold and suspicious if he merely said No and waited for them to tip their caps and leave.

If that happened, he decided he would say: No, I'm sorry I haven't. Not too many people make it out here. Do you have a flyer with contact information in case I see anything? He acknowledged that if an officer showed up at his door asking if he had seen the two people currently hidden in his basement, he might not be able to access his pre-planned script. In all likelihood, his mouth would go dry and his lips would stick together so he'd have to lick them before he could even open them at all. Then he would bluster and bumble out words that would hopefully convince them there was no reason he looked so nervous.

What if they called him in for questioning? If they hooked him up to one of those lie detectors, he'd send bright lights flashing and loud noises honking out LIAR! LIAR! But maybe they only used those in the movies. Could he learn to beat the system? He didn't think so. He'd heard that if you press your heels really hard into the ground and breathe really slowly, you could sometimes get the lines to stay straight.

The thought of facing that situation kept him up at night and made him wonder in the dark if it was worth it. But he decided, every time, that it was.

He could hide them in the barn, where he'd also hidden Violet's car. But no, they would search there. What if he tied them up and took them out to the forest while he waited for the police to search inside? They probably had search dogs though, which would patrol the fields and forests searching for their scents. Perhaps Mrs. Wrigley would have given them some laundry so they'd know what to smell for. Jeremy had known that scent for the first two or three days before it was replaced with dirt and sweat. That was when he knew he had to offer to do their laundry. He enjoyed having purposeful things to do for them, things they would appreciate. They both said thank you after he returned their clothes washed and ready for them to put back on. They drowned in the clothes he had given them to wear while they waited.

The next day, he walked into their bedroom to ask what sized clothing they wore. Their eyes widened like he had just said he wanted to fillet their bodies and was wondering how many they would feed.

"I just thought it might be nice for you guys to have something to wear besides your one outfit and the big clothes I gave you," he explained quickly. "You can even tell me what stores you like!" He spewed his justification as fast as he could so they were scared and confused for as little time as possible. "I need to know your size so that I can buy you stuff that will fit."

Violet hesitated, then launched in. "Why do we need clothes other than these? We have lots at home. We could just go there and grab some."

Jeremy hated when she said things like that. She would be so well behaved, so docile; he would think she was finally coming around to him, and then she would say something like that. Just when he thought he was gaining control, she would try to steal it back.

"I know, I'm sure you do," he replied patiently. "But that's not going to happen, so I'll just buy you some new stuff. When you go home, you can take them with you."

He thought it might be a good selling point, maybe not so much for a little boy, but for a teenaged girl at any rate.

"It depends," Violet said.

"What do you mean?"

"It depends on the store, what size I am. My waist is 28 inches, but sometimes they'll use smaller numbers, and in that case I'm a 6. Sometimes a 4 if it looks big. And with length, my legs are about 32 inches."

Jeremy regretted not bringing a pen and paper. He asked to use some of theirs and Violet nodded and handed it over.

"Why are there so many sizes? Why can't they all be the same?" he thought out loud.

"I don't know, but it's really hard to get other people to buy clothes for you. Maybe we could come to the store with you. That's really the only way we can know for sure."

She didn't usually try it again so soon. It made Jeremy angry, but also sad.

"No," he said softly. "That would be nice, and maybe sometime soon we can do that, but I don't think any of us are ready for that yet."

She admitted defeat for the moment. "Well, for shirts, I'm a medium. Unless it looks really big, and then you could buy a small instead."

He nodded. He had no idea what really big looked like, but figured he could buy both sizes and return the one that didn't fit.

"What sort of colours do you like? Any preferences?"

She didn't answer right away, just looked at the floor and shook her head.

She looked down at her dirty shirt. It didn't matter if it were her least or most favourite shade. She wouldn't feign joy out of being dressed in clothing that she liked.

"It doesn't matter," she finally said in a small voice. "The colour doesn't matter."

She would only see the shirt about four times a day when she went to the washroom, and even then she barely glanced up at herself. She looked too tired. The bags under her eyes were too blue, her cheeks too puffy. Her hair was knotted and tangled. Jeremy probably hadn't noticed what a rat's nest it had become in captivity. She thought of something then.

"Do you think you could buy me a hair brush?" she asked.

Jeremy's face lit up. "Of course! I'm sorry I didn't think of it earlier!" He sounded like he meant it. "Do you want some elastics too, maybe some clips? Just let me know the sort of things you need."

"Well... we need showers. Real showers," Violet began to negotiate. "We can't just sit in here and not bathe. There's only so much washing up you can do in a sink. I'm starting to feel filthy and it's really uncomfortable."

Those were magic words. Jeremy slapped himself on the head. "I didn't even think of that. Of course you need showers. That's no problem at all."

He decided that from then on, he would escort them up to the main level once every other day, one at a time, so they could shower before returning to their cage. It wouldn't be luxury, but at least they'd be clean.

"Ben, what about you?" Jeremy asked. "What sort of clothing would you like?"

"Well," he pouted his lips and made a thinking face. "I think maybe something with a wolf on it. Or a turtle."

Violet smiled at her little brother, in a sad, proud kind of way.

"Okay, that sounds good, I'm sure I can find something like that. And what size are you?"

Ben looked to Violet, who leaned over to check the tag on her brother's pants and shirt.

"A size 10 for his pants, in the kid's section," she told him. "And a medium for the shirt. But a kid's medium, not a regular medium." She said this with conviction. Maybe it did matter to her a little bit.

Ben was still confused. "I don't have any money, and my mom isn't here to give you any. We could get some money." He said this with an expectant look at his sister, trying to ask her, Did I do that right? Does he know that means we should go home?

Jeremy answered as fast as he could. "I'll pay for it. I don't mind at all."

He said it so excitedly that Violet realized he expected them to be happy about it. She tried to see how that could be possible, made a list of the things that so far had made life bearable.

Jeremy doted on them. He was there when they needed him, willing to do whatever they asked, as long as they stayed in the basement. He gave them attention and asked how they were doing. They didn't have to worry about going to school or to work.

Work. Until that point, Violet had put aside any thoughts of it. Her boss would be wondering why she hadn't shown up for her shifts.

"What about my job?" asked Violet.

102

"You don't have to do it anymore!" he said cheerfully, thinking she was finally catching on.

"No," she said with frustration. "I mean, I'm still on the schedule. They're counting on me to show up and they're probably really mad at me. Maybe I've already been fired. I know I'm not going to be working while I'm here, but when I get out, I'll need a way to make money. I like it there, and I don't want them to fire me."

"Oh," Jeremy said as he looked at the floor. "I thought maybe you'd be excited not to have to go back there. But I don't think it's possible for you to go in for your shifts. I'm really sorry."

"I know that," she said sharply, "but is there some way I can tell them I can't make it?"

Jeremy tried to interject, but she kept going. "You could be right there when I called. You could call for me, it doesn't matter. I just want to let them know that I'm not just fucking off – sorry, Ben – for fun, and deciding I don't feel like going in to work. Would that be okay?"

He didn't think it would be okay. Maybe she had a secret code word that she'd prearranged with her co-workers in case anything happened to her. Maybe if she said she was feeling a little "under the weather," they would know she really meant she was under the ground, in someone's basement. He couldn't take the risk.

"I'll call for you. I'll let them know you're okay. I'll tell them you're in the hospital but you're okay."

"And that I'm really sorry I haven't been able to call before now, can you say that too?" She sounded so concerned. He thought young people hated to work. He thought this would be a holiday for her.

"I will, I'll say that too," he said. He wasn't sure if it was a lie or not. How could he call them for her, who would he say he was? An estranged uncle no one had ever heard of? Their mother had probably already called into work, asking if they had heard from her. Maybe the police had the diner's phone lines tapped so they could trace the call. It wasn't worth the risk. She could get her job back when she returned home, whenever that was.

The future was a foggy place for Jeremy, a shape-shifting mist lingering ahead and slightly out of sight. He would deal with the future when it came.

But that's the thing about the future. It always stretches out before you, and never arrives.

12

Violet lost count of the days.

She knew she should be angry. She should be pounding on the walls, screaming for him to let them go. She should check every time he left to see if the lock hadn't clasped; tap the walls in search of hollow spots she could chip away at slowly. She and Ben should be working on a secret code to pulsate out into the world somehow. But for some reason, the fight just wasn't in her.

She knew she wasn't where she was supposed to be, and that fact distressed her in the beginning. But she was fed whenever she got hungry. She took showers when she felt she needed to. She spent endless amounts of quiet time reading and writing and drawing, and was spending more time with Ben than she ever had before.

Violet couldn't figure Jeremy out. It would take a cruel, malicious person to do to them what he had done, but she couldn't find any of those things in him when she heard him speak, or when he looked at her. His eyes weren't hard. They were green. Bright green, actually, and they usually seemed like they were giving everything away as she looked at them. He would smile at the unlikeliest of things, and was always so pleased to do whatever it was they asked of him – as long as it wasn't to let them go.

One morning, she woke to the sun seeping in through the tiny window above their heads. She'd tried to look out so many times, but all she could see was grass.

Something had begun to weigh heavily on her mind. Where was their mother? Why hadn't she found them? Was she even looking at all? Violet knew they were ridiculous thoughts, that of course their mother was looking. But it wasn't enough. She wasn't here. She hadn't found them.

Hadn't anyone seen her give Jeremy a ride that day? Wasn't someone looking for her car, her licence plate? It was scary to think that the world could just go on without them, the same as always, without skipping a beat. It made Violet want to scream. Instead, she remained silent.

"Ben," she nudged her brother, who had fallen asleep in her lap. "Wake up, sleepyhead."

He opened his eyes and looked around. The fear was gone from his gaze. It had faded into cautious acceptance.

"What time is it?" he asked. Violet thought it was a silly question. What did it matter? Nothing about their situation would change if it were 8 a.m. instead of 10. Her watch, however, still worked, so she went to check it for him.

Violet had taken it off her wrist about a week ago – was it a week? Maybe two? – after realizing that all it did was make her feel helpless. It didn't do her any good to remind herself that time was passing while they stood still.

"It's just past nine," she told him. "Sorry I woke you, but I want to talk to you about something."

Ben propped himself up, nodded, and sat still. She had to give him credit. He was coping well, and his crying had stopped after the first few days. Violet's had lasted longer. It was a good thing they had stopped crying, right? From her point of view, it was a lot easier to get through the days, the hours, the minutes, without sobbing beside Ben and knowing there was nothing either of them could do.

"Jeremy has done an awful thing to us," Violet started.

They had both taken to calling him Jeremy out loud. It was less scary than that man or the kidnapper.

"But," Violet continued, "He doesn't seem to be a mean man. Do you know what I mean, have you noticed?"

106

"Well, yeah," Ben said. "He brings us stuff. He talks to us pretty nice, and he doesn't hurt us. I guess he's okay, but still mean at the same time."

"Right," Violet said. "I think he likes us. And I don't think he wants us to suffer, I think he really means it when he says that. Every time we need something, he says yes. But it's too little down here. You're a young boy, you should be running around, out exploring things, not cramped down here like this. It's not fair. Right?"

Ben nodded. "But Vi, all of it isn't fair."

"I know that. It's not. But I think that maybe, if we keep asking him for things, just little things, we might be able to move around a little more freely."

"He won't let us," Ben said. "We're like his animals and we're in a cage. He won't let us out because he's afraid we'll run away."

"Yes, but we won't run away." Violet saw Ben's expression shift to angry confusion.

"I mean, eventually we will," she continued placing her hand on his arm. "We will get out of here. Both of us, together, I know we will. But we need to gain his trust. You know how he keeps talking about that, the trust thing?"

"Yeah. But how are we going to get his trust and be asking him for stuff all the time too?"

Violet nodded. "I think we'll have to do it slowly. Just start by asking for something small, like being able to go for a walk to stretch our legs. It wouldn't hurt to ask, right?"

"I guess not," Ben said warily.

"I'll try it," Violet pressed. "Just follow my lead and if I ask you something, just say yes. Jeremy isn't a normal man but I don't think he's a mean man. And I think he might listen to us."

Violet was excited. She began to feel a bit of the fight rise up in her again. She had learned more about Jeremy and what a lonely creature he was, and she knew she could use that to help them escape.

Jeremy came in with breakfast not long after their discussion. Eggs, bacon, and fresh grapes.

"Thank you so much," Violet said with what she hoped sounded like sincerity. "This looks delicious. Jeremy, do you think I could ask you something?"

"Of course," he said eagerly. "What is it?"

She took a deep breath.

"I've been thinking and… It's been a long time that we've been cooped up in here. I mean, I know we're still learning how to get along with each other, but this is a tiny space. Have you ever been stuck in one tiny room for this long before? It's not easy."

She read the shame on his face instantly.

"Oh," he said sheepishly. "I didn't think of it, I was thinking it would be nice and relaxing here and you wouldn't have to do anything you didn't want to."

He paused and his eyes wandered around the room. "I guess a walk to the bathroom every now and then doesn't count."

"No," Violet said. "And we've started to get these leg cramps, deep in the muscle. They sort of seize up and I think we're really losing muscle mass. Ben couldn't sleep last night because his legs hurt so much."

Violet looked over at Ben with expectant eyes.

"Yeah," he said. "It really hurt."

Jeremy was easily convinced. "I'm so sorry," he said. "That's awful. I just didn't think of it."

All the things he hadn't thought of reminded Violet of Jeremy's poorly laid plan. He was so disorganized, she thought. There was no way he had spent months plotting, stalking her and learning her habits. He had grabbed them and was trying to figure it out as he went along.

Violet found hope in this. He would mess up. There would be something he never considered that Violet would think of and use to get them out.

Jeremy's face lit up. "I've got it! Wait here," he said before quickly leaving the room and shutting the door behind him.

What a cruel comment, Violet thought. Wait here. As if they had a choice.

Nearly an hour later, Jeremy returned.

He grunted as he lugged a large box into their room that he wedged through the doorframe and squished the pillows against. Violet squinted at the description on the cardboard.

"A treadmill?" she observed incredulously.

"Yes!" Jeremy said, his voice full of excitement. "I'll help you put it together, and you can go for runs or walks on it whenever you want! It's electrical, but we can put the cord under the door and plug it in from the hallway!" He saw something flicker across her face. "I have extension cords," he added.

Violet's hands balled into fists and her body shook. Her rage swelled over her like a tidal wave.

"YOU IDIOT!" she screamed. It spouted out of her before she even knew it was coming. "We don't need a treadmill! We want OUT of this cage! We don't want a fucking hamster wheel that we just run and run and run on and never get anywhere!"

Jeremy's eyes went wide and his lips glued together in a rigid, pink line. He didn't move. She couldn't stop now. Her plan to gain his trust had taken a backseat.

"Do you have any idea what it's like to be trapped in here all day long? Have you ever had anyone do this to you? Is this some sort of crazy revenge because you were tortured and you want someone else to feel your pain?" she screamed.

She sounded so angry that Jeremy was scared to respond. His heart contracted when he heard the word torture. That wasn't what he had done. That's not what he had meant to do.

"No. I haven't. That's not it."

"Then what is it? Do you even know? Do you even have a reason for keeping us here? It's not for money, then what is it?" She threw her hands into the air. "Are you going to rape us, is that it? Is that what you want?" Her voice was hoarse.

She was disgusted, at both herself for saying these things in front of Ben, and at Jeremy for forcing her to do so.

"No!" Jeremy said, so quickly and genuinely that she almost felt a twinge of guilt.

"How the fuck do we know that?" she stampeded onwards. "You took us away from our family, from everything and everyone we love. Do you know how cruel that is?"

Every word was shouted. It felt good to yell.

"I didn't mean for... I gave you food and shelter and I wanted you to be safe in here," Jeremy stuttered.

"Safe? Safe in here? Are you listening to yourself? YOU are the reason that we are not safe! We're trapped here! We're kidnapped!"

"You stole us!" Ben's little voice jumped in. Violet and Jeremy both looked at him for a moment, alarmed, but then Violet started up again.

"You did steal us," she said. "Like we were something dispensable that you could just pick up and drop whenever you felt like it. We're humans, Jeremy! We need sunlight! We're trapped down here and we can't even stretch our legs or look out at the trees or sit in the sunshine. Don't you know how important those things are?"

"I'm so sorry," Jeremy whispered, his eyes leaking fat, salty drops that he kept having to wipe away. His hands lingered on his cheeks as he did it, grasping his face as if to say, What have I done?

"Then let us go!" she screamed. "Let us go if you feel so damn sorry! Because you saying sorry, and that you didn't think of it, means nothing. Absolutely nothing! Do you realize that?" She pointed at him. "I don't want your apologies. I want my mom. I want my friends. We want our lives back! You can't just 'sorry' all of that away, that's not how it works. Why can't you see that, Jeremy?"

The strained way she said his name cut right into the deepest part of him. All he wanted to do was keep saying he was sorry, but she'd taken those words away from him. Now he had no idea what to do. He didn't want to walk away from her while she still had things to say, but he didn't know how much more he could take.

"I can't let you go," he said. "I can't do it right now."

He didn't explain why. It wasn't because he was afraid of the consequences. He couldn't because in his heart, they were becoming his family. They were what he woke up in the morning thinking about.

Some feisty part of him wanted to scream back at her, to say, I'm giving you everything I can, why isn't it enough? Don't I mean anything to you? But he already knew what the answer would be it and It broke his heart.

"You can't let us go, like hell you can't," she spit. "All you have to do is open the door. We'll walk. Just don't follow us. It's as simple as that. We'll never have to see each other again."

She was so far from understanding all that Jeremy wanted her to.

"Just let us go, please? Please!" she pleaded with her hands on her collarbone. "Look at this, you have two human beings trapped in your basement, begging you to be let go. Does it feel good to see us beg? Are you happy? Fine, I give up. I'm not going to dance around it anymore. I'm begging you to let us out of here. Please."

Her eyes full of tears stung her pale, puffy cheeks. She shouldn't be crying. She'd lost almost all of her dignity, and she didn't need to lose tears as well. But she couldn't help it.

"I can't," Jeremy said. "I'm sorry."

He didn't know what else to say. He couldn't form more words without his throat closing up. It felt as if someone was choking him, like Violet held her palms around his neck and squeezed tighter and tighter with every angry word.

He couldn't take any more. He turned and retreated for the door, arms out in front of him to make up for his blurred vision.

"I'm not done!" Violet screamed. "Don't you dare leave while I'm talking to you! You at least owe us that! Hey! I'm not done!"

He shut the door behind him, locking it quickly, afraid she would storm it, kick it until it crumbled to bits. Jeremy pressed his back against the door. His breaths came out in frantic gasps. He gulped and sputtered and wiped his cheeks.

"YOU COWARD!" she screamed right behind him, pummelling her fists into the door. He could feel every blow. They reverberated throughout his whole body, jangling his organs, shaking his insides around.

"HOW CAN YOU DO THIS TO SOMEONE? HOW DO YOU SLEEP AT NIGHT? YOU'RE A COWARD, JEREMY! WE SHOULDN'T BE DOWN HERE, WE DON'T BELONG IN YOUR FUCKING BASEMENT!"

He put his hands over his ears. I don't have to listen to this, he thought. I don't have to take this.

But still he stood against that door, the pounding of her fists piercing his body like gunshots, listening to every miserable word she screamed.

13

Violet cursed herself over and over. She had gone too far. Everything she had been working for, put up with, all the smiles she had given him, trying to gain his stupid trust. Every step forward she had taken back.

Ben started to cry the instant Jeremy left. Violet couldn't tell if it was fear or pride that kept his tears locked up until the door followed suit.

"I'm sorry, Ben," she whispered to him. She rubbed his back. "I lost it. I didn't mean to go that far. I'm so sorry."

He curled up into a ball beside her and she wrapped her arms around him. What would happen next? Jeremy could take away all the little comforts he had given. She had to admit, it would be much less bearable with nothing to do or watch or read or write with. These objects were no freedom, but they were something to pass the time. Something to allow Violet to imagine her freedom was still out there somewhere, suspended only temporarily.

Time passed slowly that day. Violet and Ben didn't say anything more to each other. Violet's throat was raw. She felt as though if she coughed, it would bring up blood and the sting every time she swallowed was a constant reminder that she had lost control.

Jeremy brought in their lunch at noon. They didn't say a word to him, just stared. Violet toyed momentarily with the idea of a hunger strike. Maybe she wouldn't eat anything until he promised something would change.

The grilled cheese sandwich with a side of sliced cucumbers sat untouched for four minutes before she gave that idea up.

Ben ate his sandwich ravenously. He was starving, and able to pretend for a moment that life was normal. Violet felt ashamed at how much better Ben was coping than her. Until today, she had been calm. Maybe he had locked up his frustration as well. Maybe he needed a way to get it out.

"Ben… What do you think about all the things I said earlier to Jeremy?" she asked.

"Well, you said a lot of swears."

"I know, I'm sorry about that, I lost control. But what do you think about what I was trying to tell him? Do you think I did the right thing?"

He put down his sandwich, a simple gesture that made him seem decades beyond his years.

"I don't know, I think you just got mad."

"Is there anything you wanted to say, too?"

"Not really," he said. "I think he already knows it all. But thanks for the part about the leg cramps. I haven't had one yet, but I bet I will."

Violet smiled. "Maybe, baby," she said, as their mother had so many times before. Ben cried again, but Violet wasn't sorry. He should miss their mother. She fought through her feelings of frustration and found that she, too, missed Holly. She needed to try to forgive their mother for not finding them yet.

Violet's head snapped up when she heard the door unlock again. So soon? Maybe it was time for their bathroom break, or perhaps he was checking to see if they'd been so enraged they were attempting escape. They wouldn't though, not today. Today, Violet would walk submissively, head down, into the bathroom, squeeze out her urine as fast as she could so he wouldn't have to wait for her. Should she be embarrassed at this complicity? There was only so much fight that could be held within one body, and she had drained hers dry for the day.

Jeremy entered the room with his head down, looking as submissive as the part Violet had meant to play. He shut the door and sat on the floor. He'd never sat with them before.

"I just wanted you to know," he began, "I've been thinking about all the things you said. You're right, I was a coward to leave when you were talking to me, and I'm sorry for that."

He looked Violet right in the eyes, which she could tell was very difficult for him to do. He looked pained. She nodded her head slightly and waited for him to go on. She had already told him his apologies were no good without action.

"I know that things have to change around here. I know you were really upset this morning, but like I said, sometimes I don't always know the things you need. I don't... I don't respond to things the same way most people do." His hands were outstretched and clenched like claws.

Violet wondered if he meant it or was merely repeating it.

"I want you to come and live upstairs with me," he said slowly, with trepidation.

Violet and Ben looked at each other, not knowing whether to feel excited or scared, or both.

"I have a lot of rooms up there, it's a really beautiful home. I'm doing some renovations right now, so there's lots you guys could help with." He scanned their faces. Violet tried to keep her eyes blank, free of rage or fear, but had no idea how successful she was.

"I don't understand," Violet finally said. "We would be able to live upstairs, with you, and have our own rooms? And move around whenever we want?"

"For the most part, yes. You'll still have those bracelets on," he gestured to her wrist. "So I'll always know where you are. And the electrical fences are still around the property so you wouldn't be able to go any further than that. But otherwise, yes, you could move around as you wish."

Ben chimed in next. "You mean I would be able to play outside?"

"Yes," Jeremy said seriously.

"Are we going to have to be on a leash?" Ben asked.

"No," Jeremy responded.

Not a physical one, Violet thought. But there was still something wrapped around her throat. She was bound by her hands. She wanted to go so much further than the boundaries, but her fear doubled as a restraint.

If nothing else, Violet thought, it was a start. Living upstairs with Jeremy would provide chances every day to convince him they would never run away. Until they could run away.

Violet wondered how Jeremy remained so deluded. Simply moving them upstairs wasn't going to change the way they felt about him. Different walls, same prison. But, she admitted, it would feel damn good to be able to go for walks and into the kitchen whenever she wanted. To be able to open the fridge, look around inside of it, decide against it, and close it again. To be able to use a whole tray of ice cubes in her water if she chose. The everyday luxuries she hadn't even known she missed.

"How do we know we can trust you?" Violet asked. She could see that this stung Jeremy.

"You don't," he said candidly. "You don't trust me yet, and I guess there's no way to prove that you can right now. But I do think it'll make you more comfortable, because everyone deserves a little space of their own."

"Okay," she said, "We'll do it." She looked over at her brother. "Ben?" she asked.

"Yeah," he said. "Upstairs sounds good. Jeremy?"

Jeremy just nodded.

"Do you think I could get a Frisbee? Or a basketball?"

118

Jeremy smiled for the first time all day.

"Yes," he said. "I can get those for you."

"Awesome," Ben said. Violet supposed this was as close to awesome as they had gotten since arriving.

"When is this going to happen?" she asked.

"Today, right now. If you guys want."

Brother and sister looked to each other with wide eyes. Violet surveyed the room; it wouldn't take long to gather their new belongings.

"Do you mind helping us carry some of this stuff up?" she asked.

"Not at all. And also, grab a sheet and a comforter each. I took them off the beds upstairs, so you'll need them."

Violet chose a lavender one she had spent most of her time sleeping on. She couldn't help but have a predisposition towards the shades of her name. Ben grabbed something blue.

"What about pillows?" Ben asked.

"Yeah, you'll need one of those too." Jeremy said, another thing he hadn't thought of.

They scooped and gathered and stacked their things until all three had heaping armfuls.

"Are we ready?" Jeremy asked, as if they were about to embark on a road trip or a roller coaster ride. Violet was glad to hear the enthusiasm dripping back into his voice slowly; it gave her hope that her emotional flood hadn't ruined everything.

"Yes," Violet and Ben said in harmony.

Jeremy opened the door. Violet shrunk as it creaked. She was so glad to be freed of the awful sound.

They ascended the stairs together; Jeremy first, Ben next, then Violet. Jeremy walked slowly and Violet wondered if he was catering to the disintegrating legs they had complained about.

The main floor was spacious with so many windows. Sunlight streamed in and trees surrounded the whole house. A large sitting room sprawled to their left, and on the right a staircase led upwards. Further ahead was the kitchen. From what they could see, it was buttercup yellow with light blue borders all around.

How can someone like Jeremy have a kitchen the colour of sunshine? Violet thought.

Jeremy led them up the next flight of stairs. At the top was a narrow hallway with three bedrooms to the left, two bedrooms and a bathroom on the right. Violet revelled in anticipation of going to the bathroom whenever she pleased, even if she didn't have to go.

"There are four empty bedrooms," Jeremy explained. "Mine is just over there," he pointed to one next to the bathroom, "So you can pick whatever other one you would like."

Violet noticed all the beds were stripped of their sheets, including Jeremy's. "Do you sleep up here?" she asked.

"Yes," he said, without explanation. She wondered why he hadn't brought up a set of sheets for himself, and if he had slept on a naked bed the whole time they'd been there, close to a month. Three weeks and two days had gone by while they'd been underground.

Violet pointed to the bedrooms furthest from Jeremy's. "We'll take two down there. Does that sound okay, Ben?"

Ben was already lumbering towards a door.

Violet hurried along behind him and claimed the room right next to his. She threw the sheets down on the bed, dropped her books and things on the floor, and collapsed onto the mattress. It felt so good to have something soft beneath her. Not just sheets, but something made for sleeping on.

The room itself was simple. There was a window above the double bed and on the right side, a bedside table with a lamp. A dresser lined the other wall next to a closet. No desk, nothing fancy.

She found Jeremy leaning tentatively on her newly chosen doorframe. "Do you think this will be okay?" he asked her.

"Yes," she replied. "It's going to be so nice to sleep in an actual bed."

She meant to sound gracious, but the blush that rose to Jeremy's cheeks told her he was ashamed.

It's great," she added for his benefit. "I think I'll like it a lot."

Jeremy smiled.

"It'll be like staying in a hotel," she added then, to emphasize that it should be temporary. He just nodded, then walked to the room next door. She heard him ask the same of Ben, followed by a muffled reply, and then Jeremy spoke to both of them, saying he would give them some time to get used to their rooms. He would be downstairs.

Violet lay back on her new bed. She hadn't thought of how difficult it might be to live so close to Jeremy. It was one thing to be locked into a tiny room with someone you loved. It was another to be locked in a larger space with someone you didn't. She sensed he would probably be nervous by their presence and hoped he would keep his distance.

Violet's hands crawled over her body. She wanted to search for all her parts to make sure they were still there. It had been so long since she'd been able to check. She ran her hands down her hips, rubbed her finger between herself and held her breath at the pleasure she had been denied. At least she could have the little things back, instead of monitoring her brother's breathing in and out as he slept against her.

At least she could look at herself in the mirror and not forget who she was or what she looked like. She could talk to herself again, sing little songs, do the things people do in the privacy of their own rooms. She was thankful for these small pleasures.

Violet eased herself off the bed and went to visit Ben next door.

"Knock knock," she said as she arrived in the doorway. She smiled down at her little brother who was lying on a real bed and not on the floor. That looks better, she thought to herself.

"Hey," Ben said smiling. "I have a desk."

She followed his eyes to two stacks of cinder blocks topped with a big slab of wood. Eloquently primitive. She wished she'd found this room.

"That's nice," she said. "You can do some writing and drawing there. Maybe you'll even let me use it sometime."

"Yeah, anytime," he said casually, which was funny to her. If she'd said the same thing a month ago, he would have told her fat chance.

Violet wondered if tonight she'd have a hard time sleeping without the rhythms of his breathing to ease her into slumber. He always fell asleep before her. She could count on the next breath, and the next. The silence tonight in her new room would be deafening, but she hoped it would be enough that he was nearby and that she was lying between him and Jeremy.

She surveyed her brother's room; evaluated the windows for their size and distance from the ground. The house was tall and skinny, and the earth looked so much further than a storey below. Her eyes skimmed the ceiling and found a little black box with a little red light. She instantly felt sick to her stomach. She should have known.

"Ben," she said. "I'm not going to point at it, but there's a camera in that corner over there by the window."

"Oh," he said, unconcerned.

"I just want you to know it's there. There could be microphones too, we'll have to look around. I'm just going to look in my room, okay?"

"Okay," he said, but she was already gone.

There hers was, facing her bed. She was so angry. How dare he? Hot tears burned her eyes. She was furious. Bastard.

She fought the urge to jump up and snatch it, rip at the cords, throw it on the floor and stomp. She had never trampled an electronic device before, and had thought it to be a purely male desire. Now she knew better. She wanted to pretend that box was Jeremy and squish it like a cockroach.

Violet was alarmed. In everything she had felt towards Jeremy, the fear and anxiety and anger, she had never felt something so violent. A word only one letter way from her name.

Take hold of yourself, she counselled the devil within. Those thoughts won't do any good. She would be sleeping in a bed, on a mattress tonight. She would get to eat dinner at a kitchen table and take a walk outside tomorrow. The bedroom was a blessing and she would be crazy to call him out. He needs to know we won't run away, she told herself, fighting the sinking feeling of disbelief that she was excusing him for planting a camera to film her sleeping body. She consoled herself with the thought that it was a small price to pay for the step towards freedom they'd been given that day.

Her only relief was that she found it when she did. Jeremy had probably crept downstairs to the receiving end of the camera, was probably looking at it now, watching her watch him behind the black box.

Violet ran her hands over her comforter. She had never seen it in so much sunlight before. It looked clean enough; she had wondered about that. Leaning closer, she could see the tiny threads weaving in and out, the warp and the weft.

124

A long time ago, she had been a student at an arts and crafts camp with an eccentric old woman named Jezebel who had tried to teach little girls how to weave. They set up their own looms, chose their own colours. It was November, and the theme was remembrance. Violet's colours had been red and orange. Red for blood. Orange for firefight. Or the torch, thrown with failing hands. She had woven a fairly simple piece, but Jezebel had breathed over and over about how amazing it was, marvelling that something so violent and simple could bring so much peace.

"It's like infinity," Jezebel had said wispily. "The thread, if you look closely, it weaves over and under, back and forth. It's like waves." She explained how life was like a wave. Soundwaves, heatwaves, energy waves, ocean waves; we are surrounded by systems of ebbs and flows.

Violet wondered if she'd ever be able to look at that blanket and feel peace.

Jeremy hadn't specified any boundaries for living upstairs. Could she just go and make herself some toast right now if she wished? Could she give herself a tour of the rest of the place if she felt like it? What about sitting on the front porch? Her survival instinct reared its primitive head, and she wondered if there was a way to collect sticks and bramble slowly and inconspicuously. She could say she wanted to have a fire; collect some kindling and stash some for herself. After a week or two, she could write a message on the ground with them. She'd need only enough to write out the most basic of letters, a simple SOS. That's only three.

As for now, she wanted the pleasure and comfort of the kitchen. Just to stand in it, or sit on its floor. Most of her crises before then had been endured on the kitchen floor.

She used to like the bathtub. Something about being squished into that cold, ceramic cask made her feel the tub understood her misery. It was the best place to be during heartache.

When Violet's first boyfriend broke up with her, she spent hours in that tub. She'd just had her wisdom teeth removed and her face was inflated. The painkillers made her vomit because they were too hard on her empty young tummy. She'd wanted her boyfriend to just sit next to her so she could lean on him and be still. Instead, he came over one day, looked her right in the tired, drugged eyes, and told her that he thought it was best if they took a break. That was code for, I've met someone else, but Violet didn't know that. No one had deciphered it for her yet, so she nodded dumbly, gargled an agreement through her swollen, bloody mouth, and hugged him goodbye.

After leaving her house that day, he went over to his new girlfriend's place. She lived just down the road, a new girl in town. By default that made her sexy.

These were some of the things she thought of in the tub. Not a bath, no water involved. Just her and the ceramic, a cold kiss on the shoulder blades.

The kitchen was comforting in the same, cold way with the addition of space to move around. She wondered if that space would be ruined because of Jeremy's presence.

126

Violet decided to head downstairs to the kitchen anyway. She popped her head back into Ben's room to invite him along, and promised to bring him a snack when he declined.

Sunshine streamed in through the kitchen windows. Violet was stunned by the way its light softened everything like butter. The walls radiated the same shade as the sun and the effect was comforting. It was then she noticed Jeremy sitting at the table in the corner.

"Oh," she said. "Hi. I can't believe you have a kitchen like this."

At least he wasn't hiding away somewhere, peeking at his video surveillance. She tried to clear her head of the thought.

"Do you like it here?" Jeremy asked.

Violet tried not to cringe at the inappropriate question, but fully believed he had no idea how offensive it was.

"Do I like it here," she repeated with her head down, and something of a sadistic smirk on her face. "I'd rather be at home, if I'm honest."

"Oh," he said in such a sadder way than her Oh had been seconds earlier. "Yeah. Well, I guess I should've figured."

"But, it's a beautiful home," she added. "It's really nice to see the sunshine. I can feel its warmth on my skin, even from in here."

Rays of it beamed down on her arm, lighting up little blonde hairs. She had hairier arms than average, she thought.

Jeremy appeared to be appeased. "Well, I'm glad. Are you hungry?"

Violet shook her head. "No. I just wanted to be in the kitchen."

She glanced around the room and hesitated. Slowly, she slid downwards while leaning against the cupboard doors, ending on the floor with her legs bent like triangles enveloped by her arms. It felt really nice. There was no reason she should feel comfortable enough to do so in his presence, but she couldn't resist. She craved the ceramic tiles underneath her, and the feeling of safety that came with it.

"Jeremy," she said, in a conscious effort to speak his name as many times as she could, "What are the ground rules here?"

"What do you mean?"

She pursed her lips. "You know what I mean. We can't just go from being locked up in a dungeon – sorry – to being able to run around wild. Right?"

"Well, I mean, I do want you to be able to run around in here, as much as possible."

"But that's my point," she explained, "I don't know how much is possible. If this were real life, I could walk down the hall right now, open the front door, grab my car keys and drive off to get myself some ice cream. I could go to a friend's. I could go for a drive with some music on and the windows down and see where the road took me. These are all things I could do, and I would do, if I were able to run around 'as much as possible.'" She paused. "But I'm guessing that you're not going to be okay with all of that, are you."

Not a question.

"You're right. I'm sorry," he said. "But you can move around the house whenever you like. You can go in and out of your room whenever you want to, go to bed whenever you please and wake up when your body wants to."

She itched as she heard her body on his lips.

"What about outside?"

"Outside," he said seriously, with a nod of his head. "Well, this is a big property. Basically, you can roam around it as much as you like. I don't know if you noticed on the way in, but there are a lot of trees out there and a lot of acres."

She could tell this was meant to be comforting, but instead it made her feel anxious. She hated the thought of her staying long enough to conquer the acres of land surrounding the place.

"Do you think I'd be able to take a walk right now?" she asked.

"Right now? Wow. Um, yeah I guess that would be fine. And if you get lost, you have your tracking device so I know where to come find you."

"Thanks," she said. "I just really want to stretch my legs, you know?"

"Yeah, I know. Can I come with you?" he asked timidly, the way you ask a question you know you won't like the answer to.

"I don't think so. No. I sort of want some time to just think about things. But I promise I won't run away. You don't have to worry about that."

Ben was still upstairs and there's no way she'd leave without him. But it didn't mean she couldn't start to evaluate their options.

She grabbed an apple, ran one up to Ben, and asked if he wanted to come along. He said no. Violet paused in the doorway. Could she really leave Ben alone in the house with Jeremy? What would she do if she came back and Ben was missing? Or crying because of some invisible and irreversible injury Jeremy had inflicted on him? Her heart began to pound as her brain conjured countless images of what could go wrong.

After a deep breath, she decided she would go. She had to trust Jeremy, at least pretend to, for now. He wouldn't hurt Ben, not while she was out for a walk. That would be cheap. He wouldn't do that. She knew little about Jeremy, but she knew he wouldn't do that.

Violet descended the stairs again and waved goodbye to Jeremy who hadn't moved from his perch in the kitchen.

When she stepped outside, she paused on the porch for a moment to take it all in. First, there was a porch; a beautiful one that wrapped around the entire house. Second, the house was surrounded by the greenest, most vibrant looking grass. Trees of all kinds and sizes and shapes, bushes, shrubs, flowers. There were gardens. Fresh, dark dirt that had been watered recently. Dew soaked leaves on stalks and herbs. It was the land of someone who loved it.

She walked along the side of the house towards the back. Her breath stalled in her throat when she saw just how far the trees went. She couldn't see the fence, but she could see the miles of land before it. She fought the urge to call it lovely. In any other circumstance, it would be.

Violet tried to clear her head again. She wanted to make an emergency sign that people could read from above. It had been some time, but there might still be people looking for them. She hoped their mother was, at least. It wouldn't be preposterous to think that a helicopter might fly overhead and see a sign for help.

It was a disadvantage to know nothing about the property. She had no idea which areas Jeremy wasn't likely to visit. She didn't want him to stumble on her SOS sign, but she'd need a large clearing where the three letters could be seen from a great height.

I need him to come with me, she realized.

She returned to the front door. There was a back door but she didn't know if it would be unlocked or where it would lead. All decisions made in this house should be ones that erred on the side of caution, she figured.

"Hey Jeremy?" she asked loudly from the front foyer.

"Yes?" He still hadn't moved.

"I know I said I wanted some time alone. But do you think you might be willing to give me a tour, show me around a little bit? I just want to make sure I don't get lost or anything."

He nodded enthusiastically and was out of his seat before she'd even finished asking. "Sure I can," he said. "Do you want some sunscreen? Bug spray?"

"Just some sunscreen, yeah, that would be great."

Appearing with sunscreen in his left hand and a hat in his right, he passed Violet the bottle.

"I think I'll grab an apple for the road, too," Jeremy said with a smile, excited at the chance to be a tour guide around his garden.

"Do you know what kind of flower that one is?" he said as they stepped outside, pointing to a batch of bright blue blooms with five petals and a yellow centre. She did.

"Forget-me-nots," she said.

"You're right. Do you know how they got their name?"

Violet shook her head, trying to hide her irritation. This wasn't the kind of tour she'd asked him along for.

"There's a legend that a long time ago, a knight was gathering a batch of blue flowers to show his lady how much he loved her. They were walking along the riverbank but all of a sudden there was a flash flood, and the knight was swept away by the current in his heavy armour. They say he tossed the bouquet back to her, and shouted, 'Forget me not.'"

"That's a very sad story," Violet observed.

Jeremy looked at her then as if to say, Is it? She supposed it was beautiful in a way as well.

"The Queen of England ordered them all to be exterminated in the U.K., did you know that?" he asked.

"No. Why would anyone do that?"

"I'm not sure. I think it's because they're too beautiful. Flowers were supposed to be modest. These ones were too boastful."

"What kind of person banishes something because it's too beautiful?" she asked. "That's crazy."

Jeremy delighted in her involvement. They walked deeper into the garden, down a hill. He wished he had an interesting fact for everything they passed by. He wanted to keep talking to her, teaching her, making her stop to wonder about things she never would had before.

He doubted he had enough tricks up his sleeve. He had rehearsed telling her about the forget-me-nots hoping that he would get the chance to show her around. He was out of material.

Violet walked along quietly beside him, looking way up, straight down, and all around her.

"Can you show me your favourite places?" The instant she said it out loud, she cringed. It sounded too obvious to her, but Jeremy didn't notice. He veered them to the right and stopped in front of an old structure too small to be a barn.

"This is the gardening shed. There's a tractor mower, all sorts of gardening tools, and a whole lot of mice."

"Mice?"

"Yeah, all kinds of them. Every time I open that barn door, they scurry out all over the place. I'm always afraid I'm going to run them over."

It wasn't usually so easy for Jeremy to talk to people. He rarely said out loud the things running through his head.

Violet smiled quietly. "The Mouse House."

"That's a great name for it. The Mouse House, I like that."

"That's what my grandparents call their shed."

Jeremy smiled in a quiet sort of way.

"Where is my car?" she asked. Now that she was outside and her car was nowhere in sight, she felt the right to know.

"It's in the barn over there," he pointed. "I parked it in there. I hope you don't mind."

His politeness drove her insane. If he was going to keep them there against their will, he should at least have the decency to stop apologizing uselessly. If he's so sorry, she thought, shouldn't he just let them go?

"Why would I mind?" she said sarcastically. It was only her car, her licence plates, her method of transportation. Why should it matter if he locked it away? He was doing the same with her body.

They kept walking towards a beautiful vine-covered gazebo at the end of a stone walkway.

"You really take good care of this place," she commented.

Jeremy paused, remembering that Violet still thought it was his property, his home. Another set of lies he would have to keep. He was, however, the one who maintained the garden, and he did put a lot of time and effort into it.

"Yeah," he said. "I do. It makes me feel productive, like I'm doing something good with my hands."

"Tell me..." she trailed off then continued. "Tell me something about yourself. Something I don't know."

It was the sort of pick up line she saw straight through when it was used on her, but she needed to figure out more about the way Jeremy worked.

"Something you don't know?" He didn't make any great effort to conceal his pleasure. "Well, that should be easy. I don't really talk about myself that much. I mean, I'm doing more of that with you than I have with anyone in a really long time."

So he was a loner. There might be no one who ever came to visit. This made Violet sad, for her and Ben, but also for Jeremy. Someone should be there for him, it just shouldn't have to be her.

"Okay. Here's something. One year I got a Power Rangers backpack. I was young, grade three I think. I'm pretty sure it was second-hand. I can't even remember who gave it to me. Probably a woman named Mrs. Cassidy, she always seemed to look after me for some reason. Anyways, I had this backpack and I loved it. I went to school with it one day, and I should've known better."

Violet looked at him with new eyes. She knew where this was going.

"The kids liked to tease me. I wasn't always the cleanest and I didn't have the best clothes. Sometimes I wouldn't have a lunch. I know I was weak, and I guess I made myself an easy target, but I was never mean to any of them.

"So I brought this backpack to school, and we're lined up outside before the day started, and I'm at the end of the line. I usually was. But all of a sudden I felt a shove from behind, and I smashed into the boy in front of me. I hit my nose on the back of his head and it started to bleed right away. I got some blood on his shirt. I turned around to see who had pushed me, but they were gone. Everyone was laughing.

"The boy I crashed into, his name was William Bellamy. He was a normal kid, he teased me along with the rest of them but he'd never been that bad. I said sorry and was really hoping that would be the end of it. But he turned around to look at me, touched the back of his head and felt the blood. I said I was sorry again, but he just got so angry." He shook his head. "I think he was worried he'd be made fun of for having my blood on him." Jeremy began to fidget with the memory.

"He started to yell, calling me an idiot. He spotted my new backpack. I hadn't had one before, I just used grocery bags to bring my things with me.

"He spun me around. He grabbed at my bag and just started to pull. It made no sense to me. I tried to tell him to hit me instead, to leave the bag alone, but I'm not even sure I said it out loud. He kept pulling and I kept trying to lean my body in so that the straps wouldn't break, but he pushed me away. The left strap snapped. He just laughed. Not even one person tried to help."

His eyes were unfocused. Violet kept thinking he'd end his story, but he kept going.

"After the strap broke, he just grabbed the other one off my arm and threw it on the ground. He jumped on it, over and over. I had an orange in there for lunch, and he squished it so that the whole inside of the bag was sticky and full of pulp.

"I cried. It was the worst thing I could have done. I should've pushed him back. I mean, I'm not a violent person, but I think that kid deserved a shove. I just stood there and cried instead, I couldn't help it. I'd only had that backpack a day, and I was so embarrassed to see Mrs. Cassidy and tell her why it was already broken.

"When I started to cry, he pushed me again. Everyone was still laughing and watching, and I think he could sense that. I think he got caught up in it. He pushed me to the ground and kicked me once, in the gut. That was it, just one kick, like I was a sack of dirt."

"That's awful," Violet said softly.

"Yeah. And the worst part was I still had to wear that backpack. Only one of the straps was broken and it was still better than using a plastic bag. But every kid remembered what had happened to me every time they saw it. Whenever I would unzip it, I would catch a whiff of orange. I tried to clean it out but the smell stayed forever, this rotten, sour citrus smell.

"Maybe I should've just thrown it out, I don't know. After all was said and done, I got pissed off. Really mad. It drove me crazy that he thought he had the right to do that, and it drove me even crazier that I had let him."

They had covered a lot of ground, but Violet was surprised to feel more interest in Jeremy's story than in her new, expanded, surroundings.

"I've been bullied my whole life," he continued. "After school it got a lot better, there weren't kids talking about me right in front of my face. But the older people get, the more secretive they get. I still turn around sometimes and see people whispering about me. I don't know what it is that makes me so fun to whisper about, but there's something."

"Do you have anyone to talk to?" Violet asked.

"No. Not really. There's no one around very often. I'm out here by myself most of the time. Before today, even you didn't really talk to me much."

This shouldn't have made Violet feel guilty, but it did.

"But it's nice... It's nice saying things like this out loud. There was one other person who would listen to me, but I had to pay her, and it didn't work out," he said with a weary smile.

Violet had no idea if he meant a prostitute or a therapist, and didn't care to find out.

"Well, I don't mind," she said. "I like it. It's nice having someone to talk to. All I've had is Ben, and I don't really want to say anything that'll scare him, and he wouldn't understand a lot of the things going on in my head, so... I appreciate having someone to talk to as well."

She didn't fully mean it. She did like having someone to talk to, but she was learning that it was uncomfortable finding out so much about her kidnapper. He should probably remain a stranger, kept at arm's length. But she could use this to her advantage, she was sure of it. This was a very lonely man who might be driven to aggression, but only if provoked. That was her guess. Her plan was to keep him pacified and feeling as if she didn't resent him for keeping them there. Somehow, Violet thought, she'd find the strength to do it. If not for herself then for Ben.

"Thank you," he said. "Thanks."

The rest of their walk was in silence, both having said more than they planned. He continued to lead her around the property on the grassy areas easiest to walk over.

"So I can just come out here, whenever I want to?" she asked, to clarify.

"Yes, you can. It's really nice out here. There's no reason you shouldn't enjoy it. Maybe later, Ben will feel like taking a walk and you can show him around."

"Definitely," she said. Today wouldn't be the day she started her sign for help. It would be suspicious heading out on her own again. It could wait.

<u>14</u>

Vi says we've been here for more than two months. I don't know how she knows that, I just wake up in the morning and go to bed at night and don't really think about the days going by.

I spend my days doing normal stuff. I watch TV and play with toys, I draw sometimes. I don't have to go to school, which is neat, but there aren't any other kids my age here, which isn't so great. It'd be nice to have someone to play with.

I wanna play hide-and-seek and go to make-believe worlds and have sword fights, but Vi never seems to want to. I don't think she has the best imagination.

So I had to come up with some friends of my own. Their names are Deedee and Dodo. I don't know why they came to me. I think I might've asked for them one time when I was trying to fall sleep and feeling sad I didn't have anyone to play with. I haven't told Vi about Deedee and Dodo yet, she wouldn't get it. I guess I'm a little old for them, but they spend time with me and they're really nice. They look like big blobs with arms and legs and faces. I'm pretty sure they live in the forest. They don't stay with me at night, and they don't like to come around when I'm with Vi or Jeremy. I think they're a little shy.

Today I was outside playing hide-and-seek with them. There are so many trees here, and all sorts of things to hide behind. Every time, I like to hide a little farther away so that I can keep exploring. I always watch out for the fence though, and make sure I don't go too far. Jeremy will know if I do, and I don't want to make him mad.

So I was it, and I was talking to them, you know, telling them I was looking for them and that they can run but they can't hide. They were hiding though, so that doesn't really make sense, but you always hear people say that so I wanted to try.

All of a sudden I felt like there was someone there, I mean someone besides Deedee and Dodo and me. I turned around, and it was Jeremy.

"Hey," he said. I didn't really want him around. Deedee and Dodo went off and hid somewhere I'd never find them, they probably even went home.

So I said "Hi" in a grumpy voice and started walking back to the house because I didn't really feel like playing anymore.

"Who were you talking to?" he asked.

"No one," I said because that was sort of the truth but not really.

"It's okay, I don't think it's silly. I used to have imaginary friends too."

I wanted to tell him they weren't imaginary. They were real to me and I liked to play with them, and they liked to play with me. But I wanted to know about his friends, so I said, "You did?"

"Yeah, I did." I hoped he would say more, but he didn't, so I asked him to tell me about them.

"Well, there were three of them." (Three!) "They were named Joey, Jesse and Sam. They'd come and play with me when I didn't have anyone else to play with."

"Why didn't you have anyone to play with?" Maybe he had been taken away from everyone too, just like us.

"There were people around to play with, it's just that none of them wanted to play with me."

"Why not?" I knew Vi would tell me I was asking too many questions, but he kept not saying enough, and besides, she always asks too many questions.

"I don't know, I guess they thought I wasn't cool enough, or that they would get in trouble from their friends if they played with me. I did have one friend, his name was Billy, but he wasn't around too much. And there was a girl too, named Sarah, and she would play with me sometimes but only when no one was looking. Whenever anyone else was around, she would pretend she didn't know me."

I knew the type of kid that Jeremy was. There was a boy named Harvey in my class like that. He was small and he cried a lot, and no one really ever talked to him. He always sat by himself. I never played with him.

Jeremy kept going, without me asking this time. "So when there was no one else to play with, that's when Joey, Jesse and Sam would come around. They were good friends to me."

I liked the way that sounded. I think he might have understood. I decided I could tell him about my friends.

"Well, I have two of them." I liked that he'd had one more than me. "Their names are Deedee and Dodo, and they live in your forest. They're pretty shy. I don't think they're going to come out to meet you."

I wondered if maybe he'd be able to see them. Some people might have something special in them that lets them see all the imaginary people. But not today.

"That's okay," he said. "Another time. Just so you know though, if they're ever not free to play, you can ask me. I know it's not the same, but it might be better than nothing."

He'd already offered before, and he doesn't know how to have fun the way I do. But it was a nice thing to say, so I said thank you because I know Vi would have elbowed me if she was here and I didn't say it.

"Do you want to come inside for some lunch? I can make you a grilled cheese."

He makes really good ones. He has this press thing that makes them into two triangles and seals in all the cheese. And he uses real cheese too, not the slices. Plus, he always has ketchup. Vi thinks it's gross to use ketchup but I think it's the best.

I told him okay and started to walk back up to the house with him. Jeremy's hand was kind of dangling towards me and I think he might have wanted me to hold it. I definitely wasn't going to do that. I turned around and waved goodbye to Deedee and Dodo because it turned out they hadn't run away from Jeremy after all. They were still in their hiding places, peeking out from behind them, and they waved back to me.

15

Violet put off making her sign. Jeremy would be suspicious about her wandering off alone. She found herself sticking close to the house's walls. It comforted her in a way she didn't understand.

When she needed time to herself, she plopped down on the front porch with a book. This house had a library, the kind she had always dreamed of. Books lined every wall from top to bottom, so high up there was a ladder on a track to wheel it wherever you needed to go. It was beautiful. She could read for the rest of her life and still not be able to get through all the words that were in those walls. But she was certainly putting in a dent.

She would sit out on the porch in the rocking chair with a cup of tea. It used to creak, but Jeremy fixed it. She hadn't even asked him to. One day it creaked and the next it didn't.

Sometimes, Jeremy would bring her a snack. Crackers and cheese or little bits of chocolate. She'd never had anyone bring her snacks before, and she tried very hard not to find it endearing.

She had to get out of there. Her eyes were open, and if an opportunity to escape presented itself she would jump on it. She would. There just hadn't been one yet.

With each passing day, she knew it was less likely a helicopter would be searching for them and see the sign she had yet to make.

Tomorrow, she thought to herself every day.

Halloween was approaching. It had always been a huge holiday for her and Ben, and for years they had dressed up in elaborate costumes together. A tiny bit of hope inside her wondered if some trick-or-treaters might come to Jeremy's door. She was going to have a note ready and written.

HELP! We have been kidnapped by a man named Jeremy who lives in this house. Our names are Violet and Ben Wrigley. Please contact our mother, Holly Wrigley at... She would slip the letter into their bags along with the candy.

"Hey Jeremy," she said to him later when he walked up the porch and past her, about to head inside.

He stopped and swiveled. "Yes?"

"What's the date today?"

She could see him hesitate.

"The reason I'm asking," she decided to make it easier for him, "is because I think it's getting close to Halloween, and Ben and I love that day."

"You do? I do too!" He sounded convincing. "And you're right," he added, "it is coming up. Today is October 23rd."

They had arrived on August 18th. Violet couldn't believe how much time that was, how many days had been lost. She kept notches on the side of her bed, inscribing a new one each night. There was probably a night or two she had forgotten, and she'd had to guess how many days had gone by in the basement.

"Do you think we might be able to celebrate?" she asked.

Jeremy paused. "I don't see why not."

"Could we go somewhere to pick out costumes?" she ventured.

"No, but there's a whole closet full of clothes upstairs that you can look through."

"Are they all yours?" she asked, surprised. He didn't seem the type to have clothes for all occasions. As far as she could tell, he had about three pairs of faded jeans and an assortment of one-coloured t-shirts. Mainly grey.

"No," he said. "They're—" He wondered how he could answer smoothly so she wouldn't know he was lying. "They were in here when I moved. I just never cleaned them out. You'll find some good stuff up there. Boas and hats and jewellery, all kinds of things."

Violet was excited to tell Ben.

"Do you usually get trick-or-treaters?" she asked, trying to sound casual.

"Mmm, sometimes." He had no idea, because he'd never spent a Halloween there before. Without another house for miles he doubted it, but decided it couldn't hurt to embellish.

"One year, I got five kids. That was a big one." He lied for fun. Because he could.

All sorts of ideas popped into his head. There were pumpkins to carve, seeds to roast, pies to bake, candy to buy, the house to decorate, costumes to assemble... He didn't know why he hadn't thought of it. What a way to spend Halloween! They could sit around a fire and tell each other ghost stories while eating candy in their costumes. He knew he was a little old for it, but if Violet was excited then he had every right to be.

There was no way Violet and Ben should miss out just because they were away from home, he reasoned. Jeremy made a resolution that from then on, they would celebrate every passing holiday. They had missed Thanksgiving, but could observe the American holiday instead if they chose, or pick an arbitrary day to celebrate just because.

Violet got up then. "I'm going take a look in that closet, if that's alright."

"Sure, go ahead," he said. "It's in my room."

The bedroom of her captor wasn't a place she should volunteer to enter, but she did. She walked in, saw that his bed was made and no longer bare, and that no real traces of him had leaked out into the room. There weren't any pictures, no obvious accents of his own. Violet wasn't sure if it was comforting or eerie.

The bedroom walls were wood panelled. One faced the property and had a little window seat with pillows. It surprised her that Jeremy had thought to put soft things there. Another wall held his tidy bed, the opposite had a door on each side of it, one of which had to be the closet. She swung open the big wooden entrance and marvelled. The closet extended from one end of the room to the other, the opposite wooden door marking the end of it. Violet was greeted with a rainbow of colours and patterns and shapes; tops and bottoms and dresses. Even shoes! A tie-rack! The sloped ceiling was just high enough to hunch beneath and there was a light on each end. It was a hidden treasure trove.

She couldn't wait to show Ben. A closet like that was the perfect spot for hide-and-seek, which he had been playing a lot of. Usually all by himself.

A soft, thick fabric tickled Violet's arm. Velvet. When she was a little girl, Violet's favourite dress had been made of velvet. It had been purple with a black belt around the middle that came to the front in a little bow. She had never been crazy about the two puffed sleeves.

She fought the memory that came along with that dress. She'd been fighting it since they'd been taken, and had been successful until now. The fabric allowed the details to flow back, to creep into her conscience. She hadn't realized she could remember so clearly.

It had happened when Violet was five. There was a park across the street from her house. The rule was that she had to tell her mother when she was about to go play, so that Holly could see her through the front door if she left it open.

But one time, Violet didn't ask. Dusk was setting and Holly was in the backyard with a man. Violet didn't remember his name, was too young to realize it didn't matter. There had been a string of nameless men already, and there would be many more to come. They would stay late into the night, long after Violet had gone to bed. Sometimes, they would even come back early in the morning and have breakfast. Violet didn't like it when that happened. They always tried to talk to her but never knew how.

While Holly entertained in the backyard, Violet decided to go to the park. It wasn't very far, and no one would notice. She had been set up with a couple of puzzles and toys in the living room and left to rot while they giggled out back.

Slipping her shoes onto her toes, she stomped her heels down. No coat; it was summertime. She reached up, grabbed the doorknob and turned it deliberately. Thankfully, it was unlocked. She couldn't have reached that high.

Cars drove by all the time so she knew to stop at the end of the driveway and look both ways.

Shuffled steps took her across the road after squinting into the fading light. Hopping onto the curb, she kicked her way through the gravel and onto the slide, down the slide, over to the swings. After learning to propel herself, she couldn't get enough of them. Instead of waiting for her mom to push her for only minutes at a time, she could now sit for hours, pumping her own legs in and out.

Violet was high in the air when she heard deep voices. That wasn't so strange; lots of dads and boys lived in the neighbourhood. She was used to seeing them around, but paused to think if she would get in trouble. It could be Mr. Saunders out walking his dog. He might not even see her if his thick glasses weren't trained right on her.

But it wasn't Mr. Saunders. It was two younger men, ones she'd never seen before. Violet's eyes had grown used to the dying light; she hadn't noticed it had gotten so dark.

She stopped pumping her legs. It was time to go home. She wanted to hop off the swing while it was still in motion but never summoned the courage to do it. She was a slave to the slowing movements bringing her back and forth.

The two men weren't just walking by as she'd thought. They stopped, standing in the gravel like children. Maybe they were, but big ones, much older than she. Violet's heart began to beat faster; she could feel the heat in her ears.

One of them spotted her and spoke, said something like, "Hey little girl, what are you doing out alone so late?"

Violet knew not to talk to strangers, and by this time her swing had come to a stop. She hopped off and began to walk quickly. All she had to do was leave the playground, cross the street, walk up the driveway and back into her house until she was safe.

The two men didn't let that happen. They rushed towards her. One gripped her arm; the other grabbed her legs and swung them upwards. She was suspended between them before she could even yelp. Violet didn't utter a sound. Somehow, she convinced herself it would be worse to scream and have her mother find her breaking the rules.

They carried her underneath the play structure, the part with the little benches and fake kitchen, and laid her down on the ground. Violet caught sight of her purple velvet dress shining in the light.

"You shouldn't be here all alone," the one at her feet said. Violet still didn't make a peep.

"Keep holding her arms," the man said to the other. She might as well have been chained.

The one at her feet reached under her dress. Violet closed her eyes and sucked in her lips, willing them to stay shut, shut, shut. Everything shut. Her small body tensed so much that one man whispered in her ear, "Relax little girl."

The nerve.

Violet remembered his foul breath, like her mom's after a long night with one of those nameless men. Stale, dank, rotten.

He left her dress on. The purple velvet with the pretty bow and the puffed sleeves. But her underwear came off. Little white ones, nothing fancy, and Violet wondered why he wanted them, why he smelled them before tossing the cotton aside.

He touched her down there, laughed about something, then spit on his hands and rubbed them on her. She wanted to scream then. She didn't understand any of it and had no idea what he wanted down there.

Only a moment later she felt a sharp jab into her body. She wondered if she'd been stabbed but realized it was his fingers. This time she cried out, in pain and not by choice. The man at her head clamped his hand over her mouth. No one could hear her, no one could see her, and there was no way she could get away from them on her own. She was trapped. She wouldn't be able to get up and walk home until they let her. She wondered if they ever would, and started to cry.

Violet heard the man at her feet fumbling with his belt buckle. He made strange, grunting noises and she thought he might be in pain. Well, she was too. He had taken his hands off her, but she could still feel his phantom fingers conquering forbidden land. And then it got worse.

With each stroke, Violet shrank further away, deeper and deeper into herself. She wasn't sure how long it lasted before she heard the shout. Without knowing whether it was another one of them or someone who would help, Violet tried to stay silent, her scream ricocheting in her head.

"Hey!" she heard the voice shout.

"Shit," the belt-fumbler whispered. "Shit, shit." He stopped playing with his pants and let go of her. The second one followed suit, and in an instant they were off and running. Violet lay there, wide-eyed, fully clothed except for her underwear, and waited for the voice to approach her.

"Are you alright? Violet? Is that you?"

It was old Mr. Saunders. How he of all people had managed to spot them was beyond her, even to this day.

"Hi, Mr. Saunders," she said quietly. "I'm fine. I was just playing." She instinctively lied. Hopping up quickly, she ran away.

"Are you sure?" he called after her. "I think I should take you home and speak with your mother."

"No," she said, already almost across the asphalt. "No, it's okay. My mom has a friend over. I was just playing. I'm okay. Thank you."

Violet opened the door to her house slowly and quietly, waiting for her mother's concerned voice to greet her on the other side. But there was nothing. She walked in further and heard her mother giggle from the backyard. A strange, horrible thought popped into Violet's head. If she was still out there with those men, maybe her mom would have noticed she was gone and come to find her, screamed at the men to go away, rocked Violet in her lap.

Tears rolled down her cheeks and they alarmed her. Normally when she cried, she made a lot of noise and only a few drops went along with it. But she wasn't sobbing. She didn't want these tears to come out, no one was there to see them. What were they for?

She grabbed the banister of the stairs and slowly made her way to her bedroom. Each step stung and made her wonder if that man had torn her.

Gently, she laid herself down on her bed and touched her dress. She'd forgotten her underwear in the park. Her hands reached under her hemline, the way the man's had but much slower and gently. Arriving at the top of her legs, she felt how wet it was down there from his spit. The worst was the grit. Grains of sand, all over and inside of her.

It burned when she went pee for the next few days, causing her face to scrunch up as bits of sand came out of her bit by bit. Violet was embarrassed. What if her mother saw? What would she say?

She thought about it every night when she was alone, but she never told her mother. Mr. Saunders never mentioned it either, to her or to Holly. From then on, Violet went to Mr. Saunders' house periodically to leave a couple of flowers on his porch. Dandelions and daisies mostly.

She'd never talked about it with anyone. She'd filled in the blanks on her own now, and was glad Mr. Saunders had come before that man could do anything else with his belt. Constantly, she wished she could go back and sit on the bedside of that little girl that night. If only she could console her, tell her that wasn't the way it was supposed to be. Explain why that man had wanted to shove his fingers inside her like she was a piece of meat he was testing for doneness.

Was it crazy that she knew Jeremy would never do that to her? It just wasn't in his bones, she could tell. He would apologize the entire time, he would be so gentle that she could push him off. It wasn't possible. He was insane in some ways, but not this one. She was almost sure of it.

Violet took note of her surroundings and let go of the velvet jacket that had started it all. It would not be a part of her costume; at least she had ruled that one out. Shuffling towards the door on her knees, Violet got out, stood up, and walked briskly back to her own room. She sat down on her bed. Smoothed the sheets. Put her hands between her thighs and left them there a moment to warm them.

16

Halloween came and went. Their costumes were ridiculous collaborations of prints and accessories found buried within the closet.

Jeremy had come home the day before armed with a pumpkin, carving knives, decorations and loads of candy. He left bowls of it around the house, each with a different treat inside.

At first, Violet wasn't sure how she felt about sitting down and carving a pumpkin. It was something you did when you were comfortable and happy and warm. It was something you did at home. They shouldn't do it here; they shouldn't celebrate being kept. But by the time she told Ben about the costume closet, it was too late. His eyes lit up too brightly, and she wanted him to have this; a normal holiday, something to remind him of home.

So, they carved. A goofy pumpkin, nothing scary. Big long eyes with pupils of pumpkin, a crooked nose, a gaping smile with teeth akimbo. The classic sort of pumpkin you'd find on any given street, ten to a neighbourhood.

Ben had drawn the design and scooped out the guts, then set up the seeds to be roasted. While he did that, Violet looked inside. So many strings were left to ravage. She grated the scoop against the sides and tried to hollow it as best she could. When she finished, it was completely empty She wondered how close she herself was getting to that sort of emptiness.

No one came knocking on their door on Halloween night. They sat, the three of them in their costumes – Ben in a suit and tie ten sizes too large; Violet in a long, white dress with an enormous hat, feathers galore, and a cigarette holder; Jeremy in a purple velour jumpsuit. Violet had actually giggled at the sight of it, prompting Jeremy to give a spin.

Jeremy couldn't remember ever liking Halloween so much.

As the clock crept closer to midnight, they knew no one would arrive. The only place any of their candy had gone was into their own mouths. Violet tried not to show her disappointment; Jeremy his relief.

For the next batch of mornings, the three of them woke as usual, stretched, ate some cereal and headed outside. Ben and Violet would sometimes go for walks, but more often they would help Jeremy with the yard work. Ben's favourite jobs were to ride with Violet on the tractor mower or shuttle around the wheelbarrow.

On one particular day, Violet pruned the front garden. It didn't feel like labour because Jeremy didn't demand it of her. She enjoyed it more than sitting in front of the television all day, and it meant she got to be outside while staying in Jeremy's good favour. She could see Ben playing out of the corner of her eye.

Jeremy was still working on the porch; sanding and levelling, hammering and sawing. It was almost as good as new.

What made that day different than all the rest began with a noise that perked up all three sets of ears, like prairie dogs in the desert. Tires on gravel, that's what it was. It wasn't something Violet or Ben heard very often, and when they did, it was Jeremy who was coming or going.

Jeremy recognized the truck as it came into view, winding its way up the driveway toward the house. It was his boss coming to check on the property.

Fast, sporadic bursts of blood shot through Jeremy's veins. There was too much for Jeremy to process all at once. He would have to please his boss, update him about the renovations, while explaining why he had two helpers on the job who weren't getting paid. He also had to ensure that Violet and Ben didn't run straight into the car and be gone forever. And, if he could swing it, it might also be nice to extend the illusion that this was indeed his own property.

Jeremy had no idea what to say. He looked over at Violet, who was looking wild-eyed at Ben.

Fuck.

They were going to make a run for it. Of course they were, why wouldn't they? Johnny was the first person to show up in weeks. Jeremy had still given them no indication of when they would be allowed to leave, and he didn't plan on it any time soon. They would be crazy not to run.

Jeremy swallowed deep and squeezed out a smile. He knew he probably looked insane, but tried to keep his breathing steady. Time would pass; the situation would end; he could get through this.

He waved hello at the truck that had slowed to a stop. There was no time to say anything out loud to Violet or Ben before Johnny opened his car door, so Jeremy shot a desperate look that he hoped communicated everything he couldn't say: Please don't leave, I promise I'll give you everything you need, just pretend you're supposed to be here. Please don't leave. It was a lot to convey in one look.

"Hi there Jeremy," Johnny said as he walked towards the house. "Sorry to pop in like this, but it's been awhile since I've heard from you. Just wanted to make sure everything was alright." Johnny looked over at Violet and Ben. His eyes lingered on them.

Jeremy figured he'd better do as much talking as fast as he could, to leave minimal airspace for Violet or Ben to cry out an SOS.

"Oh yeah, sorry about that," Jeremy bumbled, "I've just been working away. I'm almost done the porch! There were some rotting beams but I took them all out. It won't be long before I'm staining it."

He searched his brain for a lie to explain the two extra bodies beside him.

"Sorry, I didn't introduce you. This is Violet and Ben. They're my cousins, they're visiting from out of town. They didn't have plans today, so I asked if they'd come give me a hand."

It was then Jeremy realized that Violet and Ben were standing stock still and silent. There was no running, no screaming or yanking open car doors to slam shut behind them. No movement of any kind. He wondered if they were frozen in fear or if they were just waiting for the right moment to make their move.

"Pleased to meet you," Johnny smiled first at Ben and then Violet. And then at Violet's chest. She crossed her arms in front of her, but still she said nothing. She nodded at him instead.

When he began to see stars, Jeremy reminded himself to keep breathing.

"Yup, it's been great to have them around. I'm getting three times as much done." He was talking just to talk, to fill up the time before his boss would leave.

"Excellent," Johnny said. "Well, I suppose I shouldn't keep you. The porch looks great. I hope you all have a wonderful afternoon. Don't work too hard," he said, and then laughed because he was the boss and of course he wanted them to.

Violet was baffled as to why no words had come to her lips, why her legs hadn't fled to the car. Was he safe? What could happen if they went with him? Something in her gut told her not to trust Johnny; the way his eyes grazed over her breasts made her uneasy. But then again, her gut had also told her she could trust Jeremy.

"Bye, thanks for the visit!" Jeremy said quickly. He found himself slowly able to exhale as Johnny turned and retreated to his car. His footsteps on the gravel were about ten times slower than Jeremy's racing heart.

"Sure thing. Take care," Johnny said before sealing himself into the vessel that could have taken both Ben and Violet to safety.

Making a three-point turn, he headed back down the driveway and drove off. The sound of the gravel under his tires returned. When it had completely faded away, Violet fell to her knees and began to sob.

17

What is wrong with you?

Violet asked herself the question over and over. Why hadn't she said anything? Why hadn't she screamed or started to cry a few moments earlier so that the man would have said, What's wrong little lady? Please name the many ways that I can help you.

Ben was right there beside her; she wouldn't have had to leave him behind, but she still couldn't do it. If Jeremy had just turned his back, or gone inside to fetch something, the spell might have been broken and she could have found the right moment.

Violet had no idea who the man even was; Jeremy later told her he was a contractor who was working with him on renovating the house. She had no reason not to believe him. It shouldn't have mattered who he was; anyone could have taken them home.

But that was the thing, maybe not just anyone could. No one ever came to visit that house. The man, Johnny, obviously knew Jeremy. What if he was in on it? What if he had been stopping by to check out the goods, to see if he might have any use for them, too? Maybe Violet in her garden gear getting her hands dirty turned him on.

Jeremy was many things, but physically cruel was not one of them. She had no idea if the same could be said for that other man. Besides, the last time she had gotten into a car with a stranger, look what had happened.

Ben hadn't known what to think. He just stood there with his eyes stretched open as far as they would go. Violet wanted to cradle him in her arms after that, rock him back and forth, telling him how sorry she was for letting their potential rescuer drive away without them.

After the sound of the grinding gravel had faded away, no one said a word. Violet stayed on her knees with her hands over her face. Jeremy walked away.

He went to the backyard and picked a bouquet of flowers. Chrysanthemums, the only ones still blooming. He chopped their jagged ends into a sharp, diagonal line and put them in a vase filled with warm water. He carried it up the stairs and into Violet's bedroom. He set them on her chest of drawers gently.

Jeremy wasn't sure why she hadn't said anything. A new feeling was racing from his heart and jolting through his body. Flowers wouldn't be enough, but they were a start, the beginning of a very long thank you.

He turned away from the flowers and saw Violet standing in the doorway, blocking him.

"What are you doing in my room?" she asked. Hot flames flew out with her words, aimed directly at him. He had seen her like this only once before.

"I was just – I picked these flowers for you." A measly hand gesture towards his offering.

"Why?" she asked icily.

"I wanted to say thank you."

"Thank you?" He hadn't known these words could invoke such fury. "Thank you? That's what you wanted to say to me. Thanks because I kept my mouth shut? Because I didn't run to that man and tell him we aren't your cousins? That we're two people you don't even know, who you just grabbed off the street and stole out of our lives and into yours? Is that what you're thanking me for?"

Jeremy didn't know what to say besides the truth, which was, "Yes."

"No way. No way Jeremy. You don't get to thank me for that. I didn't do it as a favour to you. I have no idea who that guy was, and I wasn't about to hop in a car with him and risk him hurting Ben or me. I'm that fearful of people. Does that make you feel good about yourself? You made me scared of a man I don't even know. Are you happy? Does it make you happy that I was too scared to say anything and get away from you?"

"No," was the simple answer he gave with his head down.

"Good. Do you know what I think of your flowers?" She walked over to the dresser, grabbed the vase, held it up in front of her for a moment, and let it go. Glass shattered all over the hardwood floor and onto the little circular rug beneath her feet. The flowers looked defeated and dangerous amongst the liquid that raced to the corners of the room around the shards of glass.

Jeremy felt the water splash his leg. He was tempted to run and grab the broom and dustpan so that she wouldn't cut her feet. But he needed to say something first.

"I didn't mean for you to have to go through that," he said. "I had no idea Johnny was coming today. He shouldn't have shown up like that, and you shouldn't have had to face that situation. But you dealt with it really well, so that's why I wanted to say thank you."

"Stop it!" So loudly. "Just stop with your thank yous! I don't want your thanks. I didn't do it for you! But if it meant so much, then tell me one thing. Tell me you'll answer this one question."

161

"I don't know Violet, I can try, but I can't promise –"

She didn't care; she cut him off. "How long are you going to keep us here? It's been months. What are you gaining? Why are we here? I asked you these questions forever ago, and I still haven't gotten an answer. Don't you think you owe us that? Instead of your stupid flowers, can't you give me a thank you like that instead?"

"I'm not sure."

"What do you mean you're not sure? You mean you haven't planned that far ahead? You're not sure if you can tell us that you're never going to let us go?" She paused and her face fell. "Jeremy, you have to let us go at some point. You know that, right?"

He looked her right in the eyes. "I know that. I know I can't keep you here forever. It's just... You won't be going home today and you won't be going home tomorrow."

"So the day after that?"

"No."

"The day after?"

"No."

"Then when, Jeremy? When?! We were here to be your little freaks for Halloween, we've been peaceful and helpful and obedient for months, what more do you expect from us before we leave?"

162

He couldn't put his answer into words. It wasn't an action or an end that he wanted out of them. It was the time itself, the time they spent in the house, even if they were doing nothing at all. That was what he wanted from them.

"A month from now," he said. "That's when I'll let you go. One month."

She jumped on this. "What day is it today?"

"November 19th."

"So a month from now, on December 19th, you'll let us go home?"

"Yes," he said.

"We'll be home for Christmas?" she asked hopefully.

"Yes," again.

Her fury had faded. The rage had seeped out from her eyes, and the colour in her cheeks headed back down into a healthier rose.

"Can I tell Ben?" she asked. By this she meant, Can I actually count on this to happen, and tell Ben without getting his hopes up?

"Sure," he said.

She decided right then that she wouldn't. It would be too risky. Ben might start to ask questions, like why they had to wait a month, or how she knew that Jeremy would really let them go, or what would happen after he did. She didn't know the answers.

Violet had been amazed at Ben's willingness to submit to his captivity. Perhaps he thought of it as just another home. He might just assume that this was his new family, and that no one had bothered to let him know.

"Jeremy?" she asked before he could walk away from her.

"Yes?" He turned and looked her in the eyes again. She was impressed, having assumed he would look at the ground in shame instead.

"One month," she said firmly.

He nodded. "One month."

After walking out of the room, Jeremy made a pit stop for the broom.

One month was four more guaranteed weeks he could spend with them. American Thanksgiving was approaching, and they could have a big feast together. They could even decorate the house for Christmas; people normally did that around the beginning of December, didn't they? Maybe one month would be enough. When it passed, maybe he would be ready to say goodbye.

<u>18</u>

The rest of the leaves grew tired of turning beautiful colours and fell to the ground in exhaustion. Bare tree limbs extended to the sky. Snow fell, cold enough to cling and turn them into vanilla gloves. A million gnarled fingers, stretching to the stars.

Violet looked out her bedroom window. It was December 19th, which meant it was time to go home. Each day, the three of them had eaten together, worked alongside each other and said goodnight before going to sleep. But each night, Violet added another notch on her bed. She marked each day bringing her closer to freedom.

Dusk weighed on the landscape, and the darkness allowed her to see Jeremy in the reflection of her window. With a start, she whirled around.

"What?" she asked, startled.

"I'm sorry," Jeremy said. "I didn't mean to scare you, I was just about to knock. I was wondering if you'd like to help me start a bonfire out there."

"Like a campfire?" she considered.

"Yeah," he pointed out the window. "There won't be too many more nights like this where we can sit outside and not freeze. I've got some chopped wood ready to go."

"Okay," she found herself agreeing. As the days got shorter and colder, they ended early with Violet alone in her room, Ben alone in his, and Jeremy off doing things she couldn't see and didn't care to. "What's Ben doing?"

"He's lying down in bed, and it didn't seem like he was interested but you can ask him to come," Jeremy said.

"I will," Violet nodded. She removed herself from the window, passed Jeremy in the doorway and knocked on her little brother's door.

"Hey Ben?" she said gently. "You awake?"

"Yeah, just resting."

"Feel like coming outside for a fire?"

"Nah, I'm okay in here. Thanks."

So polite. He rarely lost his temper and never forgot his manners. It was almost eerie. Violet walked over to his bed and sat down next to him. In a gesture that was more maternal than she'd intended, Violet brushed the hair off Ben's forehead. It needed to be cut, badly.

"You sure you don't want to come? I'll bet we can even swing some s'mores." She paused for effect, but didn't seem to have any. "Not even tempted?"

"I'm just tired. I just sort of feel like being alone."

Alone, as if he didn't spend all his time by himself or in the company of only two other people. More alone time wasn't a reasonable excuse, but she knew better than to push him. She shouldn't force Jeremy-time upon her little brother. He'd be safe and sound and resting while she sat right outside.

She walked back into her room to grab her favourite mustard-coloured sweater; favourite in comparison with the two others she now owned. They included a black one Jeremy had picked for her and a long grey frilly cardigan she'd found in the dress-up closet alongside the mustard one. She almost welcomed the cold weather for the excuse to wear the yellow sweater. Its v-neck extended into a big triangular hood that fit around her head perfectly. Two u-shaped pockets with bunched openings sat right where her hands would first reach. Just the right fit, with a ribbed band along the bottom.

Sometimes it felt strange to think she was wearing clothes meant for someone else. How could anyone leave behind a whole wardrobe?

Violet had a nightmare once that the woman whose sweaters she had stolen had shown up at the foot of her bed, rotting and putrid, eyes eaten away, her bony hand extended and waiting for the return of her garments.

166

She shook the memory and walked downstairs. Jeremy waited patiently by the back door with a flashlight, some newspaper and a lighter.

"Ready?" he asked.

"You go ahead. I'm going to grab some snacks."

He nodded and headed outside.

Violet walked into the kitchen and found some chocolate chips, whipped cream, and soda crackers. It was the best she could do. She was almost outside before she turned back for some foil. Marshmallows were meant to be roasted, but she couldn't very well roast whipped cream. She could prepare the sandwich, wrap it in foil, then let it sit in the embers to toast.

As she walked outside, she saw the flashlight trained on the fire pit; a ring of rocks lay in the shape of a lopsided circle. Jeremy's hands were the first part of him that Violet saw, assembling bits of kindling with newspaper in anticipation of the first spark.

"Can I help?" she asked. Jeremy jumped and she smiled smugly. It was nice for him be the one in fear once and awhile, she thought.

"No, it won't take me long, you just sit and relax," he said in his best attempt at chivalry.

Violet settled into a fold-up chair, happy she had worn full pants. The wintry breeze snaked around her ankles and snuck up her leg.

"I haven't had a campfire in ages," Violet admitted. "I used to go on camping trips when I was a Girl Guide, and every night we'd end up around a campfire, singing." She mentally ran through all the songs she'd learned, ridiculous ones that only other Guides would ever know.

"We had these things called sit-upons, they were just little pillows that unfolded so you could put them on the ground and sit on them."

She was rambling. Normally, she felt no need to fill the silence with Jeremy. Tonight, however, she wanted to nudge the issue of their homecoming, and was on her best behaviour.

When Jeremy finally created a spark, he threw in some extra newspaper, gave the fire a little nod of approval and sat.

"Shouldn't take long for this to really spark up," he said and Violet detected a hint of pride. She resisted the urge to tell him she could have had a fire going in a minute flat, and allowed him to keep his fiery glory.

Turning her head to the sky, Violet held her breath for a moment as she caught sight of the thousands of stars above her head. That was one thing she did love about this place; no other lights to interfere with the nighttime show. She wondered if she'd be able to count the glowing dots, and if anyone had ever tried.

"Hey Violet?" Jeremy asked in a voice more gentle than normal.

"Mmhm?"

"Would you like a glass of wine? I don't normally drink much, but it's such a nice night and I was thinking why not?"

She was underage, but didn't pause for a moment.

"Yes," she replied. "I'd love one."

Most of her wine drinking experience had come from family Christmas parties. Her grandparents bottled their own wine. She would be permitted one glass, which she would top up when no one was looking.

"Good girl," they would comment. "It's better to enjoy it slowly."

A few times, Violet had even snuck down to the cellar to steal a bottle. The next time she went to a friend's house, she'd bring it out and revel in the shrieks she was greeted with. They would pass it around from hand to hand and glug from the bottle. It hadn't exactly made Violet feel grown up; in fact, the gesture looked a bit like a baby slurping from a sippy cup, but every time she pulled out a bottle, she was a hero. As much as she enjoyed it, she resented the way the other girls began to slur their words and start touching each other as the bottle's contents depleted.

"You're the best."

"No, YOU'RE the best."

"No, YUUUUUUUR the bessst."

Violet was sure that one bottle of wine wasn't nearly enough to get five girls drunk, but she participated anyway, passing along her love to whoever requested it.

Jeremy walked back outside, a glass of red wine in each hand, the bottle tucked under his arm.

"Do you drink red?" he asked.

"Yes," she said. No hesitation. She'd only ever tasted white wine before, but she'd give it a try.

Her first sip was dry and tart. It filled her whole mouth with a warm flavour she felt course its way down her throat when she swallowed.

"Thank you," she remembered her manners.

"Sure," he said. "Help yourself to more whenever you want it."

"Jeremy," she started, as she always did when she tried to extract information from him. "Can you tell me more about you? I don't really know that much and we've been living here for so long."

"Oh!" He seemed surprised at her continued curiosity. "Well, sure. Okay. What sort of things do you want to know?"

"Well, do you have a job? And if you do, when do you do it?"

Jeremy squirmed. He toyed with the idea of telling her. One more glass in and it would've been simpler, but the choice was still tricky in his sobriety.

"I'm a general contractor," he said honestly. "I do odd jobs, mostly construction."

"Are you working on anything right now?"

"Nope," he lied. "Dry spell."

"What sort of work have you done other than that?"

"Well, one time I did data entry for a computer company. I sat at a desk and inputted pages of data. It sounds boring, I know, but I didn't mind it. I didn't really have to talk to anyone."

Violet wondered if this was a slight at her, a polite way to tell her to stop asking questions, but he kept talking all on his own.

"I also worked for a call centre. That was the worst by far. People hate you. They think it's you that wants to ruin their meal, or interrupt them right when they're trying to put their kids to bed." He shook his head. "It's like they believed I sat by the phone knowing exactly what they were doing, and waited for the most inconvenient time to call."

"Well seriously, those survey people always call right in the middle of dinner! It really is like they have some sort of radar," she argued.

"I know," Jeremy defended, "but that's only because the company knows people will be home then. Now when I get those calls, I tolerate it because I know what it's like to be on the other end of the phone."

"How long did that last for?"

"Only two weeks. I've never had so many people yell at me. You'd think it wouldn't affect you as much because it's only over the phone, but it really cuts into you," he shrugged. "I started calling the same numbers over and over, the ones I knew were out of service or would just ring forever, so I wouldn't have to deal with anyone."

Violet stopped to think. "Yeah, I've never had a job at a call centre, but serving is a bit like that."

"How do you mean?"

"Well, think about what a server actually does. They say hi to you, they talk to you, they take your order, check to see how you like the food, and then they clear your plates and give you the bill. They don't always even bring the food out to you, and they certainly don't cook it. Right?"

171

"Right."

"But somehow, whenever something is wrong with the food, it ends up being the server's fault. I've been screamed at before, just because some woman's eggs weren't cooked the way she liked them."

"Do you like working as a waitress?" Jeremy asked.

It had been so long since Violet had worked a shift that she probably wasn't even a waitress anymore. The mention of the job reminded her how behind she now was on her savings for school. She pushed the thought aside.

"Sometimes," she said. "It depends on the day. Restaurants bring out the worst in some people, but the best in others. I mean, you say hello and give them a smile and it's like you've handed over your heart."

Jeremy blushed. He was thankful for the red glow of the fire that would prevent Violet from seeing. He knew the feeling, and could very easily see why people would want Violet's heart after seeing her smile.

"At least they like you," Jeremy said. "I mean, for the most part. At least you can smile at them and they'll automatically like you."

"Yeah, I guess," Violet said noncommittally.

"I mean you," Jeremy added. "I don't mean waitresses specifically, I meant you have a really nice smile."

It was a roundabout way to give a compliment, but the wine and the fire were warming him and he'd never really, truly given her a compliment before. He figured it was about time.

Violet smiled with her lips closed, a smirk but less sinister. "Thank you," she said.

"Did you ever go to school?" Violet asked him.

"Well, I went to high school, which was awful. But then I graduated, and that was it. I didn't have a lot of money, I come from a family" (could he really use that term?) "of a lot of kids, and I didn't get a job early enough. The time just kept passing and I never got up the gumption to go."

Violet smiled again, this time at his use of the word gumption. "Did you ever regret not going?"

"No. Well, sort of. I don't know. It might've been easier for me to meet people if I'd gone on to school, but the thought of it ... I'm not very good at making friends."

"What would you have gone for?" She reached for the wine bottle.

"I don't know for sure. Probably something with my hands. Maybe I could have been an electrician or a carpenter. I could've started my own business."

Violet could tell they weren't well-formed dreams. They came out of his mouth slowly and she sensed they weren't ambitions he'd ever spoken aloud before.

"Well, with all the stuff you do around the house, it seems like you're already pretty good with your hands." She prayed, prayed that he didn't interpret her words in a sexual way and held her breath for a second. Jeremy didn't notice at all. She exhaled.

"Yeah, I guess I'm not useless." Violet cringed at the wording.

"No, not at all," she tried to make him feel better. "I didn't go to school this year either. I graduated from high school last spring, and I'm waiting a year before I go anywhere."

"Why did you wait?"

"Oh, you know. A bunch of reasons. Money. Indecision. Ben."

"Ben?"

"Yeah. He's still so young. And our mother..." She drummed her fingers on the chair's armrest. "She's amazing and we love her, but she's not always the most present. She tends to get preoccupied with things. Like men. I sort of thought it might be nice to stick around for another year and make sure Ben was okay."

Jeremy nodded. "But Ben seems like he'd be okay."

"I know. I know. I wonder if it isn't just an excuse because I'm too scared to leave. But I don't think so. I figured I might as well take the year to save as much money as I could, maybe even apply for a couple of scholarships, and then wait until next September."

"What would you take?" It was unbelievable that they had lived under the same roof for so long and not had this conversation yet.

"Journalism," she replied with confidence. "I love to write."

"Isn't that the wrong reason to go into journalism?" he questioned.

"What do you mean?" She was caught off guard.

"Well, isn't it more about the reporting than it is about the writing?"

"Oh. Well, yeah, I guess you're right."

"And it's not exactly creative writing that you get to do."

She hadn't thought about that. "I don't know." She felt a lump in her throat. "But I know I want to go to journalism school. I would write human-interest pieces, I wouldn't be a hard-hitting, everyday reporter, that's not what I would want to do." She wasn't sure why she felt the need to so fiercely defend her decision.

"Well, that's perfect then." He paused. "I'm sorry, I didn't mean to attack you. I don't always know how my words will sound until I say them."

She knew all about his social awkwardness, but it was nice to hear him admit it. The lump in her throat diminished a bit.

Jeremy continued. "I just realized that it might sound like I was discouraging you from going away to school but that's not what I meant. I think you'd really regret it if you didn't." He spoke the words like he could tell what was best for her, and Violet wasn't sure why she didn't mind.

"You know what one of my biggest regrets is?" she asked.

"You're fairly young to have big regrets," Jeremy replied. "But yes."

She ignored his comment. "I was in grade school when the Rwandan genocide happened. I'd never even heard of the country before, but I started bringing in my toonies to school from family and friends, raising money to send over there. We had a big jug to collect it all in, you know the water jugs they use in offices? And we would just pour our toonies in there and congratulate ourselves as the jug filled up. It took a long time, too. It took us a few weeks, and all we filled was this measly container with two-dollar coins."

Jeremy nodded solemnly. "I remember hearing about how awful it was." He didn't understand her passion, but was glad to be experiencing it. "We're so far away from it though. I have no idea what it would have been like."

"Yeah, and I was a little girl collecting little bits of metal to send over so that the two sides could shake hands and call it a truce," Violet said. "Go out and buy each other a beer with the toonies we'd collected. That's deluded. Isn't it? I mean, I understand I was young enough at the time so that I couldn't even really understand what war was and wasn't. But what about everyone else who was older and wiser and should have known better?"

He looked at her then and wondered what she thought she knew about war. Jeremy had fought his battles in other ways, but he always wondered if he could talk about war validly, giving it the credit and introspection it deserved.

"What's their excuse?" she was still talking. "How did grown, educated, rational people believe that slopping money over the situation from afar, throwing it out of helicopter windows, could actually work? It's ridiculous."

Jeremy was interested. He found words clouding his head with all the things he wanted to say. He started to organize them, put them into the order they should come out of his mouth. It was unusual. He normally grasped in the dark.

"I understand your point. And I think for the most part I agree. But the thing is... Is it really our business what's happening over there?"

Violet leaned back to put distance between them. "Well, they're humans too, right?"

"No, I know it's horrible. I don't know how I would deal with that if it happened here," he replied. "But think of all the people in the world. Think of how much our population is growing all the time. A baby probably just popped out right now. And right now, somewhere."

Violet smiled, then stopped herself.

Jeremy kept going. "Basically, we're just animals that are overpopulating. But when that happens in nature and there's too much of something, some of them die off. It always happens, it has a way of regulating itself. Some of them have to go. It's natural selection, the way things evolve, the way the world works. But whenever it's a human, it's an outrageous thing to suggest. Like we're the most supreme beings of all, and that we have more right to live than any other creatures living on the planet."

"Whoa," Violet said, surprised at how much he was communicating. He wasn't apologizing, he wasn't promising her anything or appeasing her, he was just talking. Having a discussion, an incredibly human interaction. She had never thought it possible.

"I don't actually think that genocides should happen," he continued. "That's not the way I would want the population to stay under control, not even close. A one-sided war isn't fair."

"No. So how would you want it to happen, for the population to stay under control?" she asked.

He thought for a moment. "I wouldn't want it to be something we planned. If we just buggered off a little bit," he immediately regretted the expression. He wasn't British, and it was really hard to pull off otherwise, "and let things happen as they happen, we wouldn't have to worry about it. It would worry about itself."

"Well basically, you're just excusing things like genocide then, if we just stand by and let it happen!"

"No," he said, in the closest tone to exasperation that Violet had ever heard him use. "I meant I want all people to fuck off in terms of population control. I mean, assuming we could find a way to live without war, go back to being nomads or something, I don't know. But if people would just let the plague take them when it came, and starve when the crops dried up, then things would even themselves out... Does that make sense?"

She had never heard him swear before. She liked it. He seemed more human.

"Yeah," she said. "It makes sense."

They stopped talking for awhile and looked into the crackling fire instead. Sparks flew up and landed on Violet's feet, but she knew they wouldn't hurt her so she didn't move. She kept them in the line of fire willingly.

Finally, she spoke. "So, yeah," she said far from eloquently. "I think that's part of the reason why I want to go into journalism. I want to talk to people about this sort of thing. I want to make it obvious how stupid we can be sometimes."

"We, as in humans?"

"Yeah, we as in humans."

Violet looked into her empty glass. She'd noticed Jeremy refilling his earlier too, and wondered if there was any left in the bottle. She reached; there was a splash.

"Wanna split this?" she asked.

He shook his head. "No, you go ahead. I still have a bit."

"Thanks." She sloshed the last of it into her glass, ran her tongue over her teeth and felt a red film. Violet remembered looking at adults with red stained mouths and wondering if they knew they looked like idiots. Here she was, one of them.

She couldn't wait any longer.

"When do we get to go home, Jeremy?"

He looked at her then, really looked at her. Violet found herself actually looking back at him too. His eyes were green; so green she could see them by the fire's dim and tricking light. His hair looked like it was on fire; wild and chaotic. Freckles framed his face, concentrating around his nose, which was smaller than average. He looked immensely sad, and Violet wasn't sure if that was the way he always looked or if that look was just for her, right then.

"I don't know," he said.

"What do you mean, you don't know? We talked about this. Our month is up, Jeremy. It's time for you to let us go."

"Violet, I know I said that. I know I told you one month, but the truth is, you caught me off guard that day. I didn't know what to say to you, and you were so upset, and I just said a month on a whim and you seemed to be okay with it. I just didn't want to upset you more."

She took in a deep breath. "Didn't want to upset me more. So you didn't think I'd be angry when I waited a whole month and then found out you'd only said it to appease me?" She spoke the words more calmly than she thought she was capable of. The wine had turned her voice to honey. She couldn't raise it, couldn't summon the right amount of anger.

"Of course I knew you'd be upset." He looked down at his hands. "I just didn't know what to say and I was trying to buy myself some time."

"Fine." She said. "Fine. We'll miss Christmas. I hope it makes you happy, knowing that we won't be able to have Christmas with our family because of you."

"No," he said in an almost whisper. "That won't make me happy."

"Well then tell me. You've bought your time, you should've been able to figure it out by now," she began to find her anger. "When do we get to go home?" Each syllable was stretched through her clenched, red teeth.

"If I told you another month, would you believe me?" he said with the trace of a smile.

"Are you trying to be funny? Because it isn't working. Not now."

"I know." Crestfallen, again.

"Why can't we go now? You keep saying we can't, as if there is some upcoming day that we need to be with you here for, so when is that day? When do you need us to stay with you until?"

She didn't understand, she still didn't. He was disappointed. "It's not a specific day. I don't know when that day will be. It's not that. I just... you need to be here for a while longer. Violet, you and I work differently. I'm not going to be able to explain it in a way that makes sense to you. You just have to trust that eventually, I will let you leave."

"How can I trust you? I trusted you to let us go in a month."

He wanted to say, I can't let you go because I'm beginning to love you, and Ben too. I'm slowly starting to feel like this is a family and that we should be together. I might never feel like you and Ben should leave.

It would sound absurd coming out of his mouth, and so he held his tongue. He wouldn't say it, not now, not even with half a bottle of wine in him. But he knew he had to say something, so he took a deep breath.

"Two more months." He looked at her to gauge her response. Her eyes were surprisingly flat. "I know that sounds like a long time, but I promise there will be lots of fun things for us to do. What do you think?"

"Jeremy," she began slowly. "I don't know how you can ask me what I think. What I think is that we should be at home right now, with our family, for Christmas. I don't think it's a good idea for us to be here for two more months. I'll never think that."

Violet realized she hadn't brought Ben into the argument at all. Would it have gone differently if she pleaded with him to let a little boy have a holiday at home?

"I'm sorry," Jeremy said. "And I'm sorry that I'm apologizing because I know you hate when I do that." He paused and looked up at her with big eyes. She wanted to slap him.

"Are you going to be mad at me from now on?" he asked pathetically.

What a little boy thing to say, she thought.

"No," she summoned up this bit of truth from inside her. "I mean, I'm mad right now. Really, really mad, Jeremy. It was so unfair for you to let me hope and wait for a day that wouldn't change a thing." She closed her eyes. "But I won't always be mad at you. We have two more months to live here, and it wouldn't make it any easier on anyone if I was mad and miserable all the time."

Jeremy wondered if it meant she might be happy. He didn't ask. He just smiled, cautiously. He knew he shouldn't say too much more tonight.

"But you have to let us go in two months," Violet pressed. "That's it, Jeremy. That's all the time you get."

They stopped talking then, and their heads turned to the stars. The big and little dippers shone proudly, right through a gap in the trees. A shooting star leapt across the sky just then. Flicker and flame. Violet gasped.

"Did you see that?" Jeremy pointed and looked over at Violet.

"Yeah, I did."

He kept his eyes on hers and tried to draft what he wanted to say so that it came out right.

"That star was just for us." He'd never caught a shooting star with anyone before.

Violet looked at him with an immense sadness in her eyes. She simply nodded at him, then looked back up at the stars.

She would never again catch a shooting star, and neither would he. No more flicker and flame.

<u>19</u>

I didn't realize it right away, but I was screaming. Really loud too, and kinda squeaky. I thought it was someone else at first, but it was me.

I opened my eyes. I was in my bed. My body felt okay. I wiggled my toes. I lifted my hands in front of my face; all ten fingers waved back at me.

Jeremy was in my doorway all of a sudden. The door flew open and he ran in, but not really ran, just took really quick steps and was beside my bed faster than I'd ever seen him move.

"Are you okay?" he asked, and I think he really wanted to know. His eyes were all red and bulgy and his mouth was hanging open.

"Yeah," I said, because I was, but my voice came out all soft and wimpy and I didn't know if he would believe me.

"Did you have a bad dream?"

I guess I did. I don't normally get that scared anymore at night because I'm getting bigger, and even when I do have bad dreams, I can usually remember them.

I used to have this nightmare all the time where Frankenstein was pounding on the front door of my house, and I was scared in my bed hoping he wouldn't be able to get in. But he always found a way to open the door, and then I would hear his footsteps on the stairs, one by one, and then he pounded on my bedroom door, and he'd open it, and he'd walk towards my bed and fall right on top of me. I'd always wake up then, and there was no Frankenstein. But my tummy would feel like there was all kinds of air in it and I wouldn't be able to breathe right. I haven't had that one in a long time, and I don't think I had it just now.

I don't think I've ever screamed like that.

"I guess so," I answered Jeremy, "but I don't remember what I was dreaming about."

"I know that kind," Jeremy said, and he sat down on the bed beside me. I moved away from him a little and I hope he saw. I don't think he's supposed to sit down on the bed with me.

"I used to shout things in my sleep, and I would wake myself up with my voice, but I'd have no idea what I was saying or why," he told me.

"Was I saying anything?" I was curious.

"No, just making noises."

"Oh." I wish I'd been shouting some secret message or something, maybe a password.

"How are your friends doing?" he asked me. I knew he was talking about Deedee and Dodo, but I didn't want to make it easy for him.

"What friends?"

184

"You know, your friends you play with when you're outside."

I didn't know what to say. Maybe he was making fun of me, because I know I'm kinda old to have friends that most people can't see. But I guess I was sleepy and didn't really think about it too much because I said, "They're good."

"Why don't they ever come inside? You could invite them to dinner if you wanted."

I gave him a good long look. That sounded like being made fun of. I'd been thinking lately about how it might be nice to have them around more often, not just when I'm outside and in the mood to play. Sometimes I just like to stay in my room, and it might be nice if they came in too. But I'd never really invited them, I guess. They always just went home to the forest.

"Well… I don't know if they eat the same stuff as we do." They might not even eat.

"I could make whatever they want. Or, I could just put out plates for them and they could bring some food from home."

Thankfully, Jeremy wasn't moving any closer to me. He was still on the edge of the bed, and I didn't mind it too much as long as he stayed there. So far, he was okay.

"Yeah, I think that would be alright. I'll have to ask them, though."

Jeremy nodded. "Sure. Well if you see them tomorrow, let them know they're invited for dinner."

I nodded, too. "Okay. I will."

He got up but stood near the bottom of my bed for longer than he needed to. "Goodnight, Ben. I hope you have a bit of an easier sleep now. You can come get me if you get scared again."

I wanted to tell him that I hadn't been scared, not really. I'd been as surprised as he was by my yelling. But nodding was easier, so I did that instead. He left my room.

Vi didn't come in to see if I was okay. She was probably just in a deep sleep. When I was little, I would walk into her room and jump around, and she would just lie there, her face all squashed up against the pillow and her mouth open. Sometimes she would drool.

We used to have penny sales, me and Vi. That's where you take some of your stuff that you don't want anymore, and you arrange it on your bed, and someone comes in to look at it and finds the things they want, and they ask you, "How much?" and you have to answer them, but it can only be in pennies. Most of the things we put in penny sales were only three or four cents. And if you sold something that you thought Darn, I still wanted that after it was gone, sometimes it would show up again in another sale and you could get it back.

Sometimes, I'd sneak into Vi's room when she was sleeping and set up a sale on her floor so she'd see it in the morning. She never woke up while I did it.

I guess she was just in one of her deep sleeps and didn't hear me. It's a good thing Jeremy doesn't sleep like that.

I can't wait to invite Deedee and Dodo to dinner. It was nice of Jeremy to ask me that. They don't pay a lot of attention to me anymore, Vi and Jeremy. Vi is always screaming at him about something, and I don't say a word.

When I'm quiet, they don't bother me. Jeremy doesn't talk to me much, and Vi doesn't try to be like Mom and touch me on the head anymore, mostly. Being outside a lot of the time helps, too. Sometimes I get back and Vi will lift her head up from her book and say something like, Oh! Where did you come from?, like she forgot she even had a brother at all.

We've been here a long time. I don't know how long, but it's starting to get cold, and the ads on TV are for Christmas. I think it's getting close, and I think it might be a big surprise that we get to go home for the holidays, but I'm not sure. By now, I've usually sent off a letter to Santa Claus asking him for a present, but I think it's too late. Plus, I don't really want him to bring me anything here. I think my present would be for him to get me home, but he has an awful lot of kids to worry about so I don't think he would have time to pick me up, Vi too, and fly us back.

Anyways, I'm still here and Vi is still here and I think we're stuck. But it's weird. I can still move around all I want, I just can't pass the fences. So it's like we're not really stuck, but we're stuck.

I really miss my mom sometimes. Like the other day, I fell and scraped my knee and started to cry, just quietly though, but I was yelling, "Ow, OW!" out loud. My mom used to hear things like that, and she'd come find me and grab me and clean me up and put on a bandage. Sometimes even ones in really neat colours.

And she'd kiss it, which was the part that really made it feel better. No one does that for me here, though. I just sat, holding my knee and yelling "Ow, OW!" but no one heard me.

Maybe it means I'm supposed to be grown up. I mean, I'm six, so I guess that's kinda old. I'm not a little kid anymore, but I thought I was still a big kid. Maybe being a kid is done now. Does that make me an adult? I don't think that's right. Maybe a young person? My mom used to say that when she watched the news at night; she always talked about young people and how they did things and talked in ways they shouldn't and wore fewer clothes and had less respect than they should.

I didn't really ever understand, but maybe I'm now what she meant then. Young people. Maybe yelling ow was talking in ways I shouldn't anymore. Next time, I'll bite my tongue and suck in my cheeks and pinch my arm so that whatever I've hurt doesn't hurt so much, and I won't have to make a sound.

20

Violet was helping Jeremy in the kitchen. They had made a habit of cooking together. Everything went faster that way, and there was no remembering or reminding who had cooked the night before and whose turn it was next. It wasn't as if they could go out to dinner, so someone had to cook.

Ever since they'd shared that bottle of wine, Jeremy made sure there was always some in the house, red and white.

She had tested a theory the other day when hit with an irresistible urge for ice cream. Chocolate chip cookie dough, the most clichéd flavour for a reason. Violet found a way to casually mention her craving to Jeremy, casting it like bait.

Sure enough, not two days went by before there was a tub in the freezer.

Violet felt a silent satisfaction. She knew it wasn't much power, but it was something she had and would wield.

There they were in the kitchen, Violet and Jeremy, preparing dinner as usual. Except this time, Jeremy set the table for five.

Violet's heart began to pump in double time.

"Who else is coming to dinner?" she asked in her fake casual voice.

"Oh," Jeremy smiled. "Their names are Deedee and Dodo."

"What? Who are they?" She thought he was making fun of her.

Jeremy looked around the room to see if Ben was nearby. "They're Ben's friends." Violet's look of confusion led him to continue. "You know, the ones he plays with, outside?"

"Oh my goodness," Violet said when she realized what he meant. "His imaginary friends? They have names? They're coming to dinner? What does that even mean?"

"I know it's a little strange, but I asked Ben if he wanted to invite them and I think he really liked the idea. I think he feels lonely."

Violet turned so he wouldn't see her face. Lightning-quick rage boiled through her body. How dare he play the hero, inviting imaginary friends to dinner because he felt bad about Ben being lonely. Do you know why he's so lonely?

she wanted to scream. Because you keep us in this fucking house. She felt as if her body temperature had risen 20 degrees.

How did he know so much about Ben's imaginary friends? How did he know their names, or that Ben would want to invite them to dinner? Couldn't Jeremy see that they weren't real people, and that no one would sit in the chairs he'd put out for them, no one would eat the food on their plates? What an idiot. It would be embarrassing for everyone.

Violet couldn't resist. She wouldn't say nearly all she wanted to, but she had to say something.

"How do you know about Deedee and Dodo?" she asked, trying to waive the anger from her voice.

"I just asked him about them and he told me."

Fuck you. And you're the hero because I didn't ask and I'm his sister and I should have.

"Do you talk to Ben alone a lot?" She let the accusation drip from her words.

"What? No! God no," Jeremy said, guessing at what she had implied. "I just found him outside talking to himself one time and asked him who he was playing with, and then last night he had a nightmare and I was talking to – "

"What do you mean he had a nightmare?" she interrupted. "You went into his bedroom when he was sleeping?" She was getting angrier by the second.

Jeremy looked at her with a mixture of pity and pleading. "Violet, he was screaming in his sleep. You didn't wake up, and I did, so I went to him. I didn't want him to be alone when he was scared, so I just went in to see if he was okay."

Violet took a deep breath. So Ben had been having nightmares again. He'd been doing so well, they barely happened anymore. How could she not have woken up? Worse, how could Jeremy have woken up and been the one to comfort him? Her bedroom was right beside his, they shared a wall, and Jeremy was all the way down the hall. She hated Jeremy in that moment.

"So now we're just going to sit around the table with two empty seats and pretend everything is normal."

Jeremy frowned. Good. She wanted him to hurt.

"I just thought you might think it was a good idea, since it's something that would make Ben happy," Jeremy said.

Fuck you, she thought again. Kidnappers can't take any moral highroads. She wanted to scream it, yell and kick at him. Still, she kept the peace. For Ben's sake. She kept breathing and moving and cooking until everything was ready.

"Ben," she called out, "it's time for dinner. You can tell your friends too." She didn't think she had the capacity to yell out Deedee and Dodo's names to ask them personally to come eat, and figured it was fair to pass that job along to Ben.

"Coming!" he shouted from upstairs, his outburst followed by staccato foot thumps, gradually drawing nearer and nearer until there he was in front of her, a big nervous smile.

"What's for dinner?" he asked.

"Stuffed chicken," Violet said proudly. She hadn't known what she was doing, but she'd sautéed some sweet peppers, mushroom, onion, garlic, fresh basil, feta and some dried herbs, then slit open a chicken breast and filled its insides. It smelled delicious. That was the thing about living at home, her mom had cooked most of the time. Or, rather, heated things up.

Ben scrunched up his nose at her description of dinner. He liked his food separated, little piles of this and that to be eaten one by one. The idea of a chicken stuffed with all kinds of different things sounded scary. He was gracious enough to wait until Violet's back was turned before the scrunch.

"Okay Ben, want to pour the milk?" That was his job for every meal as well as helping clear the table at the end of it.

"Yup," he said, heading towards the fridge. Violet loved watching him do it, especially when the milk bag ran out and he had to slice open a new one with the little magnetized cutter stuck to the fridge. His hands moved so assuredly. He had the mannerisms of an old man performing an age-old duty.

The three sat together, plates steaming with chicken and rice, fresh salad on the side. Violet looked at the two empty plates next to Ben and somehow felt rude.

"Are they hungry?" she asked, almost saying their names before second-guessing her memory of them and stopping herself.

"Oh," Ben said shyly. "They brought their own food from home. But they say thank you very much for having them." He said it so quickly, like he didn't want Violet to be offended that they didn't like her cooking.

192

She smiled at her little brother who was trying hard not to notice how many types of food he was eating in one bite. She could see him hold his breath a little bit, chew quickly, swallow, and wash it down with a pull of milk.

"What did Deedee and Dodo do today?" The names had come back to her.

"They were just playing with me mostly," Ben said apprehensively. He glanced at Violet with an evaluative look; gauging her mood. The anger had seeped out of her.

"That sounds nice," she said with a smile. She looked at Jeremy then, who was more silent than usual. Violet fought the urge to ask him how his day was. It would sound too familiar, too close to camaraderie. Thankfully, he saw her look and decided to speak on his own.

"So... Christmas is coming in a few days." He hadn't wanted to say the words, and it was obvious in the strained way they came out. The truth was that he hated to announce it because he knew they would have to spend it with him, and he was worried it would make them hate him.

Ben's eyes grew wide and he looked to Violet expectantly. She just shook her head. She knew what he asking, and the answer was no. As if he didn't believe her, he turned his gaze to Jeremy instead.

"You're not going to be able to go home for Christmas, Ben. I'm really sorry about that."

The table went silent for a minute, except for the scratch of forks and knives. Ben broke the silence, and he whispered, "You're the Grinch."

"The Grinch?" Jeremy asked sadly.

"You stole us. And now you stole Christmas. Like the Grinch." His words were deliberate and designed to wound. They sounded so melodramatic coming out of his tiny mouth that Violet put her hand over hers to stifle a laugh.

"I know," Jeremy said, "I know it's awful. If it makes you feel any better, I never have anyone to spend Christmas with. This will be the first time in a long time that I'll get to be with people I care about."

This was met with a glare from Ben, and a blank look from Violet.

"Look," he continued, "I know this isn't where you want to be. But I'm going to do my best to make this a great Christmas for us. Do you know how much fun we could have here? Look at all the trees out there," he gestured, palm up, to the snow-filled backyard. "We can pick one out, cut it down, and decorate it in here. And Violet," he turned to her, "I can buy any sort of baking supplies you'd like, maybe we could all make some sugar cookies or something."

He was going a mile a minute, making another hard sell. "And... well, I know you guys won't be able to go shopping... But if you put together a list of things you'd like to give each other, I'd be more than willing to pick them up for you."

"How will Santa know we're here?" Ben asked skeptically.

Violet raised her eyebrows. Ben still believed in Santa Claus? Wasn't he a little old for that? She searched back through her memory, hoping she hadn't made any grown-up faux pas' denouncing the existence of Old Saint Nick. If Ben was still able to believe, she wanted to let him.

"Oh, he'll know," Jeremy recovered quickly. "We can even leave him out some cookies and milk."

"And carrots for the reindeer?"

"And carrots for the reindeer."

Ben appeared to be evaluating the offer, as if it was something he could accept or reject.

"Okay," he finally said. "What day is it today?"

Jeremy glanced at the fridge where the calendar used to hang. He had taken it down when Violet and Ben moved upstairs. "The 22nd," he finally gathered.

"That's not a lot of time. Why didn't we talk about this earlier?" Ben scowled at Jeremy. "How am I supposed to decide what I would like from Santa, and what I want to get for Vi so quick?"

"Well," Violet stepped in, "I've been thinking lately that I might like a new notebook that I could write in. And maybe a warm sweater or some wool socks."

Ben scrunched up his nose again. He couldn't understand why anyone would ask for socks when they could choose whatever they wanted.

"And Ben," Jeremy added, "If you let me know by the morning of the 24th, then I'll make sure I have everything ready in time. I'll even buy some wrapping paper and bows and things so you can wrap them however you want."

Christmas wrapping was a whole new experience for Ben. His mother had always slapped his name on gifts from herself to Violet, or sometimes he wasn't included at all. Something about being able to give gifts made him feel warm inside, and very grown up.

"Okay," he said. "That sounds good. Can I get something for Deedee and Dodo too?" he asked, looking over at the emptily filled seats.

"Sure," Jeremy said, "Whatever they would like. Just add them to your list."

Ben ate with a new zeal after that. He finished everything on his plate and quickly asked if he could be excused to go work on his wish list. Violet told him he'd have to do extra cleaning up tomorrow to make up for it, but secretly, she was clenched up with happiness. It was nice to see him excited.

"Oh – and can Deedee and Dodo please be excused as well?"

"Of course," Violet and Jeremy said in unison. She looked at Jeremy in surprise.

When Ben and invisible company had cleared the area, Violet sucked up her pride. "That was really nice, what you suggested," she said.

Jeremy shook his head to shrug it off. "I love Christmas. I mean, I don't normally get gifts, and I don't usually have anyone to buy gifts for, but I like the idea of it. Families coming together and staying warm inside while it's cold out..." He trailed off.

"Tell me more about your family," Violet said.

"Right. Sure. Well, I never knew my father, and my mother decided she didn't want me." He didn't know how else to phrase that part.

"I lived in an orphanage for awhile. Eventually I was adopted by this family, the Ridgeroy's, and there were tons of us kids. Eight in total. They didn't have time for us at all. It was like they were collecting as many as they could. I think it was for the money.

"Anyway, pretty much all of us got out of that house as soon as we could. Most of them have their own families now to spend the holidays with. I just never really found anyone else." He sounded embarrassed, as if it was shameful to be so alone.

To Violet, it was just sad. She felt her heart warm a shade. "Well, you know that Ben is adopted, but did you know that I'm adopted too?"

"Really?" He looked at her with an intensity that she hadn't yet seen from him.

"Really. I was only a few days old. My birth mother was just really young and couldn't afford a kid. And my mom, the one who adopted me, she didn't have a husband or a boyfriend or anything, but she just decided it was time for her to have kids. So, she found me, and then a few years later, she found Ben too."

"Does she have a man around now?"

"No. Well, no one special. A whole lot of ones who aren't so special, though. They're around by the dozen." She laughed a little. She hadn't realized she was bitter.

"But," she continued, "My mom's parents are both still living and pretty healthy, so we have grandparents. No aunts or uncles or cousins or anything, but we do alright."

"I know this is a rude question," Jeremy said, "So I'm sorry in advance. But do you love her like she's your real mother?"

She wasn't offended. "Yes. I do. I mean, I don't remember my actual mother at all, so it's not as if I'm pining after her, or comparing. Sometimes though... Well, yeah. I love her like she's my real mom."

"Sometimes though...?" Jeremy prompted.

"I don't like talking about it. But sometimes, I wonder if my mom knew what she was getting herself into when she adopted us," she pointed up the stairs towards Ben's room. "I mean, she didn't carry us for nine months, she didn't eat right and touch her belly and feel us kicking around, and she didn't have to go through labour... I just think that maybe my mom didn't fully think it through."

"How so?" Jeremy sat very still, looking right at Violet.

"Well, the ins and outs of being a mother. The having to be there, every second, for every tear and every first. Sometimes, she didn't notice things. She told me that I learned to walk all on my own, and seemed proud of me for it. One day she just turned around, and there I was, walking towards her. She hadn't helped me up or anything. Doesn't that seem strange to you?" she looked to Jeremy. "I mean, I feel like if I had a kid and she was getting close to walking around, I would watch her every move and have the camera on at all times and have my hand ready to dart out, and have all the sharp edges covered in case she walked into them. But my mom just turned around, and there I was, walking."

Jeremy paused to make sure she didn't have anything else to add. "Yeah," he said finally. "I know the feeling. There were so many of us that whenever we all went somewhere, they did a head count. Didn't call our names or anything, just numbered us off."

198

"Did you ever wish you had a smaller family? Or just a different family?" Violet asked, and knew that this time she was the one asking the rude question. She didn't apologize.

"Yes. I guess now I've sort of resigned myself to it, and I do love some of my siblings. Like my sister, Rose, is really something. She's so spunky and finds a way to be positive about all the bad things she's been through. But I only see her once a year. One day out of the whole year, and it's not even Christmas. It's a random day at the end of summer so we can gloat about the things we've accomplished and ignore any of the bad stuff that might be going on." Jeremy held his hands out in verbal claws that punctuated his words. They were birdlike talons; his long skinny fingers rigid and slightly angled. "It's not family time, it's not therapeutic, it's just show and tell. And I usually don't have much to do of either."

"Hmm," Violet said. "That's sort of sad. I don't mean about the show and tell part, I just mean that you have such a big family and you guys don't even take advantage of it."

"I know," Jeremy said. "I guess I could try a little harder. It's not like I make the phone calls, or send the cards. I don't even know when any of their birthdays are. It's to the point where if I did get a hold of any of them, it would be strange. I wouldn't know what to say and I would feel like I was intruding. We're all off doing our own things, on our own little islands."

"Yeah well, you know what they say."

"I know, 'No man is an island,'" Jeremy anticipated.

"Oh," Violet said. "I was thinking more along the lines of, 'You can't choose your family.'"

"Well, I don't know about that." Jeremy contested, a rare moment that he disagreed with anything Violet said. "I feel like us in particular, people like you and I, we're not tied down by biological bonds. I feel like we can choose our families. And the one I was in wasn't one I would have chosen for myself."

She thought about it. "I'd still choose my family. I love Ben and I love my mom, even if she's distant sometimes. I don't think she means to be. And if I didn't have them, I wouldn't have anyone. I'd rather have a dysfunctional family than none at all."

Jeremy watched her recoil like a flower shrinking back into itself, as if in need of watering. He knew he wouldn't be able to reach her again that night. The only thing to do was to clean up after the mess they'd made. He stood up, gathered the dishes and washed them one by one.

Violet sat at the table with her head in her hands. She didn't say another word.

21

Sure enough, Ben and Violet were able to come up with their Christmas lists by the next morning. Violet's choices for Ben were simple: A peppermint patty. A pair of blue pajamas. A bug catching kit. A deck of cards.

She didn't know what Jeremy's budget was, and she wanted Ben to have a few things to open. The peppermint patty was a tradition of theirs; each Christmas they found one in their stocking. It was the only time of the year they would eat them. Violet dropped her list off first thing in the morning without a word.

"Hey Ben?" Jeremy called up the stairs. "You awake?"

He felt the thuds of Ben's heavy feet before he heard a response. Thumping down the stairs, the youngest held one hand in front of him with a piece of paper in it.

"Here!" Ben said. "This is my list. Don't show it to Violet."

"Okay, I won't," he replied.

"Thanks, Jeremy," he said before racing back up the stairs.

Jeremy paused to smile. Rarely did Ben use his name, or thank him. Determined more than ever to give them a good Christmas, he went out the door. He had a lot to prepare. Looking down at Ben's list, Jeremy saw that there were two columns. One for Violet: Peppermint patty. Warm sweater (purple?). Notepad. Lip stuff.

And one for Jeremy: Peppermint patty. Candy cane.

Jeremy felt a weight within him. Not so much a burden, just the heaviness of his thoughts taking up space inside of him. Sort of a happy space. His hands resisted the urge to flutter at his side. Even though Ben's gift to him would be purchased with his own money, Jeremy so looked forward to having something to unwrap on Christmas morning, something someone had chosen for him.

Jeremy shopped for hours, finding the items from Violet and Ben's lists, as well of some gifts he planned to wrap himself. He bought lights, ornaments, tinsel, garlands, a wreath, a mini Santa Claus. He bought all the things that most people have stored underneath their stairs, in a big plastic bin labelled, CHRISTMAS, the knickknacks that normally take years to accumulate bit by bit. It would take another trip, on another day, but Jeremy would now also need to buy the plastic bin he could store everything in for the rest of the year. He would keep it in his own closet upstairs though, as a reminder that it was there, waiting for the next jolly holiday season.

Christmas songs played on every radio station he flipped through. He settled for O Little Star of Bethlehem. Its eerie resonance always struck a chord, and he found it comforting somehow; that there was depth and sorrow to the holidays, too. Next was a new-fangled carol sung by a modern artist. Enough time has passed by now, Jeremy thought, that all the good possibilities for Christmas songs have been used up. There is no need to keep writing new ones. He shook off his judgments and tried to hum along to the new song with the same old sentiment. Tiny snowflakes fell on the windshield of his car but he didn't use his wipers to clear them, choosing instead to let them build up one by one as they formed an ever-melting quilt along the glass.

He quickly rerouted to a grocery store. After all, Christmas is only partially about the decorations, and more about the food. Jeremy roamed the aisles, eyeing shortbread and candy canes and eggnog. The rich yolky liquid had made him sick as a boy, but he knew it would taste differently now. On a whim, he also bought a jar of nutmeg to sprinkle on top.

When he arrived back home, he rode the gravel curves up to the glowing house and fought the sense of dread he always felt when returning up the drive. Please still be there.

He saw Violet in the kitchen and found that he could breathe again. No sign of Ben, who was probably off playing somewhere. Maybe Violet was baking Christmas goodies. He felt the urge to stay there for hours, to sit in the driveway and observe the home he had created for himself and for them.

Weren't they as much of a family as anyone else? They might hate him sometimes, but didn't hate go hand in hand with love? He took a mental picture. The house, the light snowflakes softening the scene. His car full of goodies like a real life Santa Claus. A warm home waiting for him.

Everyone deserves this, he thought to himself. A family to come home to. A little weight dropped off of his shoulders. Ben was right; he had felt a little like the Grinch earlier. But he felt like he was on his way to making things right.

Turning the key and pulling it out of the ignition, Jeremy got out of his car and grabbed the first load. He found all the gifts and snuck them inside before Violet or Ben even heard a thing.

"Hey!" he called out when he had safely hidden the parcels. "Who wants to help me bring in some Christmas supplies?"

Ben's approaching thumps resounded immediately. Violet came around the corner a little more slowly, peeking past Jeremy out the window, to the car. Ben and Violet threw on their boots and jackets, another of Jeremy's former gifts.

All three loaded their bodies with boxes and bags. Dumping the goods in the front hall, Ben began to pluck through them.

"Cool!" he called out when he got to the small Santa, promptly pulling it from the bag and setting it out on the front porch. It was about half the height of Ben, and much too small to represent the entirety of the porch with its presence, but neither Violet nor Jeremy wanted to move it from Ben's desired site. Besides, who else would ever see it?

Violet pictured the house covered top to bottom in lights, flashing red and green strobes across the sky. Would a car see it from the road? Perhaps some nosy holiday hunters would turn up the drive to get a better look at the lights. She was hit with an urge to decorate furiously and excessively.

"Can I put the lights up outside?" she asked.

"Yeah!" Jeremy said, misinterpreting her enthusiasm. "But maybe you should wait until tomorrow. It's starting to get a little dark and I wouldn't want you to fall on the ladder."

Violet resisted the urge to tell him that she was just as likely to lose her balance in the daytime, but held her tongue because he was probably right. "Well, what about a tree? Think we could go pick one?"

"Cool!" Ben shouted again, and Jeremy couldn't resist.

"Definitely," he said. "Just let me get a flashlight so we can make sure we're not getting a Charlie Brown Christmas tree." Although those had always been his favourite.

With a flashlight, an axe and mittens, they crunched their way into the woods in search of a tree.

"This one!" Ben said to every evergreen they came across.

Violet laughed. "Ben, think a little more critically about this. We want one that we'll be able to hang lots of ornaments and lights on. That last one? Come on."

Ben wasn't concerned by her constructive criticism, and he scampered on ahead until he was out of their sight. He didn't leave their ears for long, though – excited exclamations soon rang through the trees and back to them.

"Guys! I found it!" Jeremy noted the plurality. It was a small victory. He beamed behind the glow of his flashlight.

When they caught up, there was indeed a fine tree before them. Arms reaching in every direction, pine needles coating them like fur.

"Violet, what do you think?" Jeremy asked.

"I think we found our Christmas tree," she said, more quietly than she had planned.

"Alright then. Ben, wanna hold the flashlight?"

Ben quickly accepted his new responsibility and took the big light into his little hands.

"Stand back, guys." Jeremy swung his axe at the trunk, as low to the ground as he could. He took small steps in circles around the tree, slowly chipping away from all angles. Violet began to shiver, and the light of the flashlight wavered in Ben's frigid hands.

"Okay, here goes!" Jeremy finally announced when he saw the tree start to lean in one direction more than any other.

"TIMBERRRRRRRRR!" Ben roared suddenly, surprising Violet and Jeremy. They looked over at him, alarmed at first, then started to laugh. It was probably the only time Ben had, or ever would have again, the perfect opportunity to yell such a thing.

They dragged the newly fallen tree back through the woods. Violet soaked in the whispering sound of the needles sweeping the thin layer of snow coating the ground.

That night, to any onlooker, would have seemed a delight. The house quickly filled with the sound of Christmas music; the smell of cinnamon, ginger and nutmeg; the bright, colourful lights of Christmas strings. A transformation took place. The tree stood proudly in a corner where a rocking chair had been. Balls and bells dangled from its branches; lights twinkled and traced lines around its figure.

Jeremy even went back outside to get some wood to spark up a flame in the fireplace. Soon, the crackle and smell of scorching wood added to the stimulation of their senses.

The next day, Christmas Eve, Ben sliced up some carrots and put out cookies and milk.

Sorting through the parcels, Jeremy made a drop off in each of the three bedrooms – Violet's gifts for Ben; Ben's gifts for Violet and Jeremy; Jeremy's gifts for Ben and Violet. Later, they retreated to their rooms. Each could hear the crinkling of the others' wrapping as they cut and taped and tied. Each came up with a different way to label their gifts. Ben wrote right on the package in big, bold letters with a permanent marker. Violet folded bits of wrapping paper in half to create a tag. Jeremy used full-sized Christmas cards, envelopes and all, for each parcel. He didn't have anyone else to send them to, and had bought a whole package.

When Jeremy finished wrapping, he snuck his boxes downstairs to the tree. Ben had already done the same. He stood looking down at the gifts, glowing green and red in the tree's light. There were four crumpled items for Violet, two for him. It didn't matter that he knew exactly what lay beneath the paper. Didn't matter at all.

He heard feet on the stairs and turned to look. Violet, balancing her gifts in her clumsy but able arms, walked carefully down each step.

"Hi," she said. "You're not supposed to see me put these under there."

"Oh, oops," Jeremy said, unaware of the protocol. "I'll get out of your way." He turned to walk up the stairs. "Goodnight, Violet. See you in the morning."

"Goodnight," she said. A few seconds later she added, "Jeremy? Thanks."

He was halfway up the stairs by then. He paused and felt that happy, heavy feeling again and willed his arms to stay still. Turning slowly, he didn't know what else to say except, "You're welcome."

There weren't many times when Jeremy felt like he was doing the right thing lately. But something inside told him that this, the holiday season he had created for them, was something he had done right.

He went to bed with a smile on his face. So did Ben. Violet did not. Instead, she looked out her window at the moon. The man within it looked right back, and she wondered what he was trying to say to her.

You're doing a good thing, staying strong for your brother while you're in this place.

How dare you still be there.

She remembered when she was little and her grandfather would hold her in his arms underneath the sky. He would look to the moon and say, I look at the moon, I look at you. I look at the moon, I look at you. I'd rather look at the moon.

She hadn't understood that it was a joke made at her expense, she just threw her little chin up in the air and giggled, because he had inevitably begun tickling her.

Her mind strayed to a place she didn't often let it. She thought about what everyone else in the world was doing at that moment. Her grandparents had gone to church that night, she was sure of it. What about her mother, had she gone too? Had she prayed to someone, anyone who might be listening, to find her daughter and son and bring them home? Did she have a Christmas tree up, did she buy them gifts just in case? Violet wasn't sure whether she would prefer the house to be undecorated and miserable like a place of mourning, or for her mother to find it within her to celebrate. There was probably a man there, perhaps some champagne, some chocolate.

Violet visualized their home. She mapped the walls and made a mental note of how many photos of herself and Ben were hung. One of Ben, one of her, one of the two of them together. She wondered if her mother walked by them every day and cried. Did she put them next to her bed like a shrine, vowing not to truly sleep until she found them? Or were they turned around, taken off the walls, hidden away in the closet? Maybe the men she brought over had no idea that a Violet or a Ben existed at all.

She hated herself for even thinking it. Holly must be missing them, remembering every little bit of them constantly so that the details wouldn't fade. But Violet couldn't ignore the termite that had been chewing away at the back of her brain for months.

Why hadn't she found them? She should have fought long enough, hard enough to find them. They weren't needles and the house a haystack. They were alone for miles. Any search of the region would lead to a visit of this very house, wouldn't it? Violet didn't know how search parties worked, but she would've given theirs a failing grade.

She puffed her cheeks and held her breath. Those sorts of thoughts wouldn't get her anywhere. She tried to remember the good in her mother, to forget that she was adopted and the awful notion that Holly's hurt could be lessened by this fact.

Years ago, when Violet was old enough to start wondering about it all, she'd asked Holly how the two of their lives had collided.

"Why me?" she'd asked, eyes wide, when she was about six years old.

"Why you," Holly repeated with a smile. "Well, because you were the baby I was given. I didn't really get to choose you, you weren't like a robot that I got to pick how many fingers and toes you came out with."

Violet giggled as Holly tickled her fingers and toes in demonstration of how she'd come with just the right amount.

Holly paused before continuing. "But I think that even if I did get to choose, I would've ended up with the same Violet. You would have those ocean grey eyes that you don't know how to use just yet, but someday you will. You'd have your golden blonde hair that shines in the sun. You'd be kind and friendly and know how to make people smile. Those are all things I would've picked, but you came out just right without me picking any of them."

Looking down at her hands, Violet felt a little better. Her next question was harder though.

"If I came out so good, why didn't my real mommy want me?"

"Oh, Violet," Holly said with furrowed brows and long eyes, the saddest face she had ever allowed in front of her daughter. She didn't say anything more, her eyes just welled up as she hugged the curious little thing in her lap.

Violet remembered confusion, not knowing if she'd said something wrong or why her all-knowing mother didn't have an answer. She was old enough to know that Holly was her real mother, and that maternity had nothing to do with biology. She wasn't quite old enough to realize, however, that her questions might burrow themselves painfully into Holly's heart. Both of them had been unwanted enough to have ended up together.

They made great companions; they were good at reading each other and gauging their needs. Violet quickly learned it was simpler to leave out the fact that she was adopted. People had too many questions paired with too many pitying looks, and Violet was tired of the explanations to everyone who thought it was their business.

It didn't stop Violet from asking questions herself, however, and she was thankful for Holly's openheartedness. Schoolyard friends were jealous of the questions she got away with, as well as the answers she received and shared the next day at school. Children huddled around as if her words were currency.

"What is sex?" she'd asked one day after seeing a movie where it was all the actors could talk about. Violet had an inkling. One of her friends from school named Stacy had an older brother, and she heard stories about him and the strange noises that came out of his room. Stacy had tried to explain something about a sock that boys put on their bodies to protect the girls.

"Sex!" her mom had replied with her eyebrows up as high as they would go. "Sex, already." This was said quietly, more as a note to herself. Violet was, after all, only eight. Wasn't Holly supposed to have a little more time before this conversation? She had no book handy, no useless pamphlet with diagrams that weren't quite raunchy or accurate enough. Remembering back to her own endlessly inadequate sexual education, Holly realized she was glad to use her words instead.

"Well, sex is what happens when two people put their bodies together for a certain purpose." It was the best she could come up with on the spot.

"What purpose?" Violet responded, ever the inquisitor.

"That depends," Holly said slowly, sloshing through uncharted waters and not knowing how deep she was willing to go. "Sometimes so that they can make a baby together. Sometimes just for fun."

"So what happens?" Violet said, a little confused but excited that she hadn't been shut down with a non-answer like Stacy who had tried with her mother.

"Well, men and women both have different parts that fit together if you put them just right. And there's a way to do it so that it can feel really nice, like a massage or a hot bath." Pause. "But it's not something that's fun to do with just anyone. It won't feel good if it's not with the right person." The last thing she wanted was a call home tomorrow from a teacher telling her that Violet had been trying to fit her body together with a little boy in class.

Violet sat quietly with this for a minute. "And how do you know if it's the right person?" she asked.

"You don't," she said more honestly that she ever imagined she would be in a conversation like this. "You don't always know. But you can try really hard to find out in advance. You can make sure that the person likes you, even with all the silly stuff you do." Holly poked Violet on the nose. "And you can see if you feel comfy being around them, and if it doesn't scare you to be alone with them. Oh my god," she added hastily, "and you don't even have to start thinking about this for a long, long time. You won't be ready for awhile yet."

"How will I know I'm ready?"

Holly got up from the couch where they were stationed. Violet was worried she'd scared her off just as they were getting to the good stuff. To her relief, Holly only went to grab a wine glass.

"I need some help to answer that one," she said as she poured herself a glass from the open bottle in the fridge.

Violet smiled as she remembered the conversation and how long ago it had been. It had paved the way for Violet to ask her mom anything.

Contrary to some whispering parents' opinions, those talks didn't lead Violet on an endless quest to dominate men and make her body fit with theirs. The words did not magically transform her into a fiendish slut. Slut, a word so much like sludge; bottom of the barrel residue. A word sometimes used to describe her mother, and it made Violet squirm when she heard it whispered. Her mom wasn't like that. Violet and Holly carried this justification with them like a weapon, slung on their hips and ready to be drawn for battle.

Remembering what a team they'd been made Violet ache.

Enough, she thought. Tomorrow was Christmas morning. She didn't need to worry about it right then. In that moment, she felt deplorable. She forced her eyes to close. The light of the moon still burned on her retinas. With deep breaths as slow as she was able to bring them in and out, her heart rate began to slow and she tried to concentrate on nothing but her own breathing. She would fall asleep. She wouldn't be kept up tonight. She wouldn't...

She was out like a light.

Violet was awoken by the pounding of Ben's fists on her door.

"Vi!" he shouted excitedly. "It's Christmas!"

Violet wiped the sleep from her eyes and looked over at her clock. Seven in the morning.

"Ben," she whined. "Really? Right now? The gifts aren't going to run away or anything. Give me an hour."

"No, Vi, it's Christmas!" he said, this time swinging the door open. He stood there with his hands on his hips as if to say, C'mon sis.

"Fine," she gave in, like all older sisters do when their little brothers wake them on Christmas morning. "Just do me a favour and go turn on the kettle so I can make some tea."

"No, Vi," he said again, "I can't go down until we all go down."

It was true, it was a Christmas tradition. Ben, Violet and their mother would huddle at the top of the stairs before all heading down together.

"I don't know," Holly would say. "What if Santa didn't come this year?"

"He did, he did!" they would argue without budging from their faith. And sure enough, every year, Santa had come.

Ben left Violet's doorway, no doubt to rouse Jeremy so that they could all meet at the top of the stairs. Violet didn't have the heart to tell him that the only gifts under the tree would be from her, and probably Jeremy. Maybe it was time the kid stopped believing in Santa Claus, anyway. She didn't realize that the gifts from Santa weren't the point.

Violet dragged herself out of bed, put on some pants, a sweater, some slippers, and headed to the top of the staircase where Ben was already waiting. Jeremy stumbled out of his room, fists in his eyes, at about the same time Violet did.

"Okay, ready?" Ben asked, anxiously.

"Yes," Violet and Jeremy said at the same time, in similarly scratchy voices but different keys. Violet was impressed he'd made it out of his bedroom so quickly.

They descended the stairway together, all three pausing a moment to admire their tree. A light snow fell softly on the morning. The gifts were sparse and wrapped with varying levels of ability, but they looked just the way presents under a tree should, Violet thought. She bit her cheek for a moment, willing herself not to cry. It looked too much like Christmas at home.

Ben launched himself off the staircase and down to the tree in an instant.

"Can I deliver them?" Another job of Ben's back home, to be the giver of the gifts. Neither Violet nor Jeremy fought him for the job, and Ben quickly delegated them to a seat so that he could begin.

Five presents sat in front of Violet, five for Ben and, Violet noted curiously, two in front of Jeremy.

Ben? she thought. She wasn't sure how she felt about Ben giving Jeremy gifts. But it would have been awfully sad if only the two of them were opening while Jeremy looked on, she admitted.

Ben asked if each gift should be opened one at a time, from oldest to youngest. Violet squirmed at the thought. She hadn't handpicked her gifts; they weren't things she'd been hiding for months and couldn't wait for Ben to see. They were last minute afterthoughts that Jeremy had picked for her and she'd thrown some wrapping paper over. She told Ben that for the first time in his life, he was allowed to tear into his gifts at whatever pace he chose.

"Cool!" he said, which was increasingly becoming his catchphrase.

"Thanks, Vi!" he shouted when he got to his bug kit, mid-peppermint patty bite. Violet smiled when she opened her chocolate as well – he hadn't forgotten. Her new purple sweater was lovely, and she had to give Jeremy credit for eyeballing just the right size. It was something she would actually wear, at least while she was still stuck in here.

Jeremy sat looking down at the two gifts in his lap. He smiled, and lifted the first one gently. He undid the wrapping paper bit by bit, taking off one piece of tape at a time. When he revealed his treat, Violet saw him raise his head, looking for eyes, wanting to show it off. Look, I got one too!

A strange lurch hit Violet's stomach. It reminded her of when she'd been in the first grade and the teacher had asked the students to pair up, leaving one poor boy standing all by himself looking down at his hands. Lucas, that's what his name had been. Violet remembered a strong urge to run up and hug him, but she had no idea why. It was the same feeling she had now.

"Excuse me for a sec, I'll be right back," she said as she removed her gifts from her lap and headed upstairs to her bedroom.

She reached under her bed and grabbed for the card she had made the night before. It was for Jeremy. Even as she had written it, she wasn't sure if it would end up in his hands or the garbage. But she'd gone to the effort of making it, so shouldn't he get to see it? It was Christmas, after all.

Vaulting back down the stairs, she slipped the card onto Jeremy's lap and sat back in her chair in one long, fluid movement. He was surprised; she could see it right away. He hadn't expected anything from her, and to be honest, it was a surprise to Violet as well.

The card didn't contain a lot of fanfare. It was a big piece of wrapping paper, folded in two, with a rough sketch of a Christmas tree on the left half (she'd been trying to fill up space without having to write too many words), and the other side very simply said,

Jeremy, I hope you have a very Merry Christmas. Thank you for letting us have one, even though we're away from home. It means a lot. Violet.

Nothing fancy. Jeremy looked down at it for much longer than it would have taken him to read. Violet wondered if she'd done something wrong. When he finally raised his head, his eyes were shiny with tears he was trying not to spill.

"Thank you, Violet." That's it. A card so unsubstantial didn't really warrant more than that, she supposed. But she could tell there were other things he wanted to say to her and wouldn't or couldn't. She merely nodded and turned her eyes back to her lap. All that was left to open was their gift from Jeremy. Violet felt uneasy. What if it was something she hated, would she have to pretend to like it? Shouldn't she, for once in her life, be allowed to just say, This is not even close to something I would choose. What were you thinking?

She unwrapped deliberately, like Jeremy had. She dreaded what was within. The first thing she saw was colour – bright, fiery red and deep, burnt orange on a large piece of cloth. She grabbed a corner and began to unfold, revealing a wall-hanging depicting a beautiful woman sitting cross-legged, fingers together in meditation. Violet's mouth opened as she took it in.

"That's Irene," Jeremy explained. "The Greek goddess of peace."

He shouldn't have known that she would love it. She hadn't disclosed enough. But here was this beautiful wall hanging that if she had passed in a market, she would have felt compelled to have. And here it was in front of her, chosen by Jeremy.

"I love her," she surprised herself by admitting out loud. "It's absolutely beautiful."

"Good," Jeremy said simply, smiling.

She resisted the urge to say Namaste to him in thanks, steeple her fingers and rest her chin on them as she lowered her head. I bow to you. But bowing signified submissiveness, or supreme respect. Neither felt appropriate, and so her hands remained on the cloth instead.

Just then, her eyes caught a glistening in the wrapping paper, and she looked down to discover a silver necklace that must have been swaddled in the cloth. She untangled the chain to discover three stars hanging from it at various lengths. One short, one medium, one long. She knew immediately it was because of their shooting star. It twisted her insides to know that now she could never forget she'd seen one, and that it had been with him.

Violet preferred gold to silver. But somehow, the little necklace immediately found its way onto her body. She wrapped it around her neck.

"How does it look?" she asked the boys in front of her.

"It's alright," Ben said, disinterested and about to tear into his last gift.

"It's beautiful," Jeremy said. Violet looked at him them, one of the few moments when she truly did. She heard his voice catch. He really did think it looked beautiful on her, and Violet was surprised at the way that made her feel. Did he think she was beautiful? Or just that the necklace looked beautiful on her neck? She internally slapped herself for even wondering.

Getting up to look in the mirror, she fingered the chain. It really did look beautiful, she soon discovered. The three stars ran right along her collarbone. Violet felt a little naked then, more vulnerable. She thought she'd remained removed, but there must have been moments when she'd let him in enough for him to siphon these details from her.

"What's this?" she heard Ben ask. He held up a set of keys.

Dear god, Violet thought.

"Go take a look in the backyard," Jeremy said with a contented shrug.

Ben flew to the window and looked out. "No way! Is that for me?" Violet joined her brother and saw what he was looking at. A mini Jeep. Violet had always wanted one as a kid. Not the sissy Barbie kind that told you to go to the mall, but one of those Jeeps that let you drive.

"WOW!" Ben shouted and ran for the door. "Can I ride it right now? Even in the snow?"

"All season tires!" Jeremy said. Violet was concerned with the lack of instruction manual, the fact that Ben had never driven a car before, and also that Ben was still in his pajamas. She decided she could let it all slide, except for one small thing.

"Don't forget your boots!" she shouted. He'd be fine without the rest, she was sure. Violet had no idea how much one of those things cost, but she could guess.

"Jeremy," she said when Ben had slammed the door behind him, "This was too much. You shouldn't have spent so much money."

He misinterpreted and instantly started to explain. "I know, his did cost a bit more than yours, but I just figured... Well, I could go and pick you out another gift if you like?"

"What? Jeremy, no! That's not what I meant at all! I love my gifts. I think you were too generous with the both of us. Seriously. You didn't need to do all of this."

Violet heard her mother's words in the back of her mind. Never refuse a gift from a man.

Jeremy did owe them an awful lot for what he had done, she supposed. It's not as if she wanted to give the gifts back, either. So instead, she just held her new wall hanging against her newly decorated neck and said, "Well, thank you. Merry Christmas to us."

Ben had already figured out his first vehicle and was driving around the lawn in crazy figure eights, his hair flying wildly in the snowy wind, wearing the ugly pajamas that would soon be replaced by the new blue ones.

The rest of that day was enjoyable for all. Violet and Jeremy took to the kitchen, cleaned the turkey, prepared the stuffing, got the vegetables ready, mashed the potatoes, and began to breathe in the slow release of the smell that meant Christmas was almost over, and a great feast was about to begin. The house would be redolent of turkey for days.

They each went for seconds of everything, finding themselves laughing and talking freely. Jeremy had poured wine for himself and Violet, and had given Ben some sparkling juice that he was very happy with, especially since he got to drink it out of a wine glass – something he had never done before. Their mother had always been too worried he would break one.

Wine kept finding its way into Violet's glass as the night wore on. Bottles kept reappearing when the previous drained dry. Violet noticed her cheeks getting hotter, her steps becoming less assured, her words stumbling out of her mouth in ways that she was sure her brain hadn't meant them to. Ben just looked at her funny and continued playing, but Jeremy laughed every time she bungled a sentence.

"I'll just clean up in the morning," she had said, which had come out as something close to, "I'll jus' clin up n' the morn."

Or, "I sh'd prolly stop wining s'much drink," greeted with a burst of laughter from Jeremy and her own throat.

"Oh god," she said, "What an idiot!" Instead of putting down her glass, she clinked it against Jeremy's. "Well, cheers, to us all being here together," she found herself saying.

Jeremy paused for a second. "Really?" he said.

"Oh, shut up. Don't ruin it. Just... cheers."

And he did. It was the best Christmas Jeremy ever had.

22

New Years passed without a countdown. Guilt had sunk in for Violet, and she decided it would be inappropriate to observe New Year's passing. How could they ring in the new year without feeling as though they were celebrating being stolen? The private resolution she made was that she would get herself and Ben out of there. She hadn't forgotten they were caged birds, and she worried they were learning to sing on the inside.

Beautiful Irene hung on her bedroom wall, shining with colour and presence. It didn't feel like home, but like a familiar friend's.

Storms arrived with the colder weather, which often found the three of them snowed in together, constantly boiling water for some hot drink. Violet was up to about four cups of tea a day. No sugar, just a drop of milk.

Ben's newest favourite thing to do was drive his Jeep around in the snow while holding a shovel out beside him as he tried to clear the way. Violet cringed at the sight of him driving with only one hand on the wheel while the other reached out wildly, wielding a heavy, metal weapon. No casualties had yet occurred, and she supposed this was when someone would feel justified in commenting, Boys will be boys.

All of January passed this way. Slowly, leisurely, life trickled by for the three of them.

Violet still put a tally on her bed every night, but had a feeling there were an increasing few she had missed. Nights she'd fallen asleep on the sofa watching old reruns of I Love Lucy, or when she stumbled into bed and the number of glasses of wine she had drank diminished the notches' importance. Every week or two, Jeremy and Violet would find themselves sitting up late at night, much past Ben, drinking together.

One night in early February, Jeremy decided to try something.

"Do you know what day it is?" he asked.

"I don't know, early February? I need a calendar," she added.

"Oh, sure. Yeah, I guess. So you know we're getting closer to the day I said I'd let you go?"

Violet nodded, took a tiny sip of her wine. She kept her head down as she said, "But you're not really going to let us go, are you?"

"No," he said simply, matter-of-factly, like it wasn't as if he'd lied to her, like it should be no big deal that he wouldn't be letting them go. Again. He prepared himself for her fire.

"I know," was her response in a voice much calmer than he expected.

"You know?"

"I know. I knew it was just a day you gave to hush me up again. I knew that when the day came, and I asked you if it was time for us to go, you'd just tell me that you were wrong, you hadn't realized it but you'd need to keep us for who knows how much longer."

Jeremy's mouth was open but he didn't know what to say.

"Jeremy..." she continued. "I'm not going to put up a fight this time. I'm not going to yell. But I think you need to explain yourself. We've been with you for half a year and I deserve some answers. Don't you think?"

"Yes." He knew she was right. Gripping his glass tighter, he was glad to have wine in his hand.

"Why?" It was the simplest question, one she had asked many times before.

"Okay," he said slowly. "I've told you bits and pieces about my life, but I haven't told you the whole story."

Violet settled back in her chair. She was determined to hear him out. He was the type of person who said bin instead of been. She loved hearing him say new words and trying to catch the tiny twang inside of them.

"My mom left me on a doorstep," he said quietly.

"What?"

"Yeah. She did. It's funny, I can barely picture her face anymore but I just remember her long, red hair. It was so curly and I'd always get my hands caught it in. She hated that."

He readied himself to tell her a story that he'd only ever spoken aloud once, to Linda Sanford.

"We went to go get ice cream one time, it was a really hot day," he began.

Little Jeremy chose Rocky Road, oblivious to its recipe. He'd pointed with his grubby finger and said, "Please!" So polite, wasn't I?, he thought to himself now. He did everything he could to please her.

She'd ordered strawberry, like her hair. He said this out loud, and she didn't even smile. When he tried to grab onto her curly locks as evidence, she shoved, yes, he's sure he remembers it correctly, shoved him out of the way. Hard enough for his startled little hands to let go of his Rocky Road. Tears welled up before he even knew he was upset.

There's something irresistible about a little boy who has just lost his ice cream, and the bejewelled teen behind the counter offered to scoop him a new one. But his mother, Gloria was her name, said no. "It'll teach him to take better care of his things," she justified. Even Jeremy was old enough to know she was wrong, but he didn't know how to put it into verbs and nouns and was too afraid to try.

Gloria grabbed his hand and took him outside. She sat him down on a bench as she enjoyed her strawberry ice cream and Jeremy looked on longingly.

"Mommy... Some?" He asked in the childish way he had learned to ask for more.

"No," she said sharply. "You would still have your own if you weren't so clumsy." Where other mothers radiated compassion, adoration and patience for their children, Gloria flat lined.

Jeremy remembered that her eyes were green, and that they were beautiful. Especially with her hair that looked like a campfire when caught in the wind. But looking into them, he never saw himself reflected back. There was no sparkle, nothing he could find that indicated he truly belonged to her.

One day, they were driving and Jeremy felt curious. As far as he can remember, he was asking the questions every child asks, and should.

Why is the sky blue, Mommy?

Do you think that the trees can feel things like when you pull off a leaf?

Where does the sun go at night, and how does it always know to come back? Simple questions with complex answers. Most parents, Jeremy imagined, would smile and feign knowledge, or simply announce that they didn't know either but offer congratulations on having such an inquisitive mind.

Gloria looked at him with furrowed eyebrows. Jeremy didn't realize it was the last time he would ever see her, but that expression is still branded into his memory somehow. He couldn't tell if it was hatred or confusion, impatience or concern.

"I don't know, Jeremy. Why don't you go find someone who does?" she gave a rare reply.

"Who?" he asked innocently, as it was only the two of them in the car.

She turned off the main road onto a smaller residential one. "I don't know," she said again, almost mockingly. "Why don't you go knock on one of those doors and see if you can find someone who knows?"

Confused and a little scared, Jeremy undid his seatbelt and got out of the car. He waddled to the nearest door, looking back gingerly at his mother to make sure he was doing it right. She nodded and smiled, looking happier than he'd ever really seen her. He rang the doorbell after standing on the tops of his tippy toes and pushing all of his weight against the tiny button. The loud chime that his efforts evoked was very rewarding, he remembered. Looking back proudly, he saw her watching expectantly. No one answered.

"Try the next one," she shouted. "I'll bet they know the answer."

He scurried to the next house, excited by her involvement in something to do with him.

Again, a tippy toe thrust to ring the chime. Right away he heard the bark of a dog and the clip clip clip of its little claws scampering towards the door. Heavier, denser human footsteps followed shortly behind. The door opened, and Jeremy beamed up at the tall and smiling man who stood before him.

Little Jeremy turned to make sure his mom could see his progress, but her car was no longer there.

He was five years old.

The man in the doorway thought him a boy scout, out to sell cookies or collect non-perishable goods, but quickly registered the panicked look on Jeremy's face.

"You aren't here all by yourself, are you?" the man asked. Jeremy burst into tears. He didn't know what else to do. The man put his hand on Jeremy's shoulder and tried to coax him into explaining what was wrong, but his tongue felt thick and heavy. His vocabulary wasn't nearly developed enough to explain abandonment.

"She's gone," he finally sobbed. "Mom... Gone..." He hiccupped it out clearly enough that the man at the door ran down the driveway in search of a frantic figure looking around for her precious baby boy. But there was no such person.

The man, whom Jeremy later found out was named Earl, ushered him inside with a reassuring hand on his small, shaking shoulder. "Don't worry, little man," he said soothingly, "We'll find her."

She didn't want to be found though, and she never was.

Jeremy took a deep breath. He didn't want to say anything more.

Violet squirmed, and couldn't help but think back to her own childhood; the countless photos of her on her mother's lap, holding hands in the park, getting a piggyback ride. When Ben had come along, the photos had just expanded to include the three of them. For all that Holly lacked, there was still much she'd done undoubtedly right.

"Oh Jeremy," she finally said. "I had no idea. I'm so sorry. I just... I'm so sorry."

"Yeah, it's okay. Anyways, I guess I have a father out there somewhere but I never knew who he was, so I ended up in an orphanage with a bunch of other kids. And that's when I was adopted by the Ridgeroy's. And that's it."

"How old were you?" Violet asked.

"I was five. I was old enough to remember it all."

He was shaking his head now. His words had gotten more heated and slurred. Frenzied. He couldn't stop.

"You probably don't even realize how many people you have behind you," he said to Violet. "I'll bet there are so many of your friends and family back home who think about you everyday and wish you were back. And I'm sorry, I know that's a shitty point to make and I know you want to say, 'Let us go back, then.' I know." He inhaled sharply. "But the thing is, when I took you and Ben, even though I didn't know he was coming, I was finally creating a family for myself. Living in this house with you two has given me a reason to wake up in the morning."

His mouth opened again as if about to continue, but he stopped there instead. He looked up expectantly at Violet, waiting for her response.

What am I supposed to say to that? she thought to herself. You're a crazy person? Thanks for messing up our lives just because yours was? But she didn't say that. She pushed those thoughts back, and chose instead to act on the twinge, the one that made her want to hug Little Jeremy abandoned on a porch.

"I don't know what I can say to that," she began. "Because it sounds like you've gone through a lot of suffering in your life. As much as I hate you sometimes – and I do, Jeremy, sometimes I really, really do," she clenched her jaw. "But there are times when I like you a little. You're not awful. You don't yell at us, you don't hurt us or lay your hands on us, which were all fears I had about you at first. I was positive that you couldn't continue to be so docile towards us and that your top was just going to blow sometime. But Jeremy, besides the fact that it was completely insane for you to kidnap us – you do realize it was insane, don't you?" Jeremy nodded eagerly.

"Besides the fact that it was crazy," she rephrased and continued, "You have been wonderful to us. You have been gentle and kind and a good listener and... I'm starting to feel weird about giving you so many compliments. But you're not awful." Violet found her hand reaching out to touch his arm.

"There is nothing intrinsic about you that should repel people. Your life shouldn't have turned out this way. Your mom was a piece of shit. I'm sorry if that offends you, but honestly? She was a worthless piece of trash for doing what she did to you, and it's a good thing you got away from her. I know it might not seem like it, but the rest of your life with her would have been even more awful."

Jeremy hadn't thought of it that way before. He supposed he was a little hesitant to think of his mother in any way other than through a softened, nostalgic lens where he could pretend she used to love him.

"I know things haven't been easy for you, Jeremy. But life isn't easy for anyone. And I'm sorry you've been through so much, and that you don't have people around to support you the way you should be, but you can't force someone to be that person for you. It's a choice they have to make for themselves. I am never going to feel that way about you, because it wasn't up to me to come here. I never got to choose."

"I know," Jeremy said sadly, "I know you're right. But you were just so nice to me in the diner, and I convinced myself you might be that person for me. You were so friendly, and you smiled, and you asked how I was doing..."

Violet fought the urge to tell him, Of course I was nice to you, I was trying to get a good tip! She realized that would be cruel. She didn't want him to think his whole vision had been a lie. She would grant him that one, small decency.

"Violet," he said then, "I will let you go. Both of you. I know that my words hold no weight now because I've said it so many times before. But I know that you and Ben can't stay here forever, and the longer I keep you, the more you'll hate me. I realize that. But I'm not ready yet. This Christmas was the best in my life. Getting to spend it with an excited little boy, and you, was incredible."

He said you with such reverence that Violet was taken aback. Her? She wondered what made him feel it was such an honour to spend the holiday with her. She felt something close to butterflies but forced herself to swallow and breathe until they were gone.

"Just as long as you know that then," said Violet. "I'll try to be respectful of your deciding when you can let us go. But please just remember that Ben and I do have a family and we do have friends, and they're missing us. They're probably very worried about us. So to let us go back home to them would be a gift you could give us that we would never forget."

She knew her words would hit him right in the gut. She saw it register in his eyes. He would let them go, she knew it. But there had to be a way she could speed up the process.

Violet's legs were half exposed in a skirt. She crossed them, and noticed that Jeremy's eyes tracked her movement. She searched for his gaze's intention but found none. She lifted her hand to scratch her collarbone, right below her new necklace, and saw his eyes slip to her breasts.

When did this start? she wondered. Certainly not right from the beginning, she would have noticed long ago. His eyes hadn't always wandered like that; they hadn't shown any interest in her curves or the parts that made her different from him. She would know. She had watched for it.

It wasn't a skill she was proud of but she had learned, not inherited, from her mother the gift of manipulating the opposite sex. She had never thought to try it on Jeremy. He had seemed so asexual, so distant and untouchable and ultimately disinterested. But Valentine's Day was quickly approaching and Violet decided she would take her New Year's resolution into effect as fast as she could.

Her mother would be so proud.

23

Violet was right. Something had changed in Jeremy. It hadn't happened in small steps, slowly inching deeper into his brain. It had hit him like a brick, right in the stomach, only a couple of days earlier.

He had gone upstairs to ask her if she'd like a cup of tea. She drank so many these days that any time he put on water, he asked just in case. She usually said yes.

On that day, he caught her unaware. Her bedroom door lay open, and he peeked in to see her sleeping body sprawled across the bed. Clothes fully on, blankets fully off, her eyes and mouth closed delicately and she didn't make a sound. It was the silence that intrigued Jeremy, and the complete lack of motion. She could have been dead lying there. He walked into her room where he knew he didn't belong and lowered himself so that his own cheek hovered inches from hers. There was her breathing, so calm and regular, no hesitation or fear. Just tiny, sweet breaths.

Her eyelids fluttered against each other and he wondered what she was dreaming of. Her hands were clasped around the comforter crumpled beside her, evoking an image of Violet as a little girl gripping a baby blanket. She looked so innocent. He wanted to take a picture so that he could look at her like this every night, without fear of her noticing his eyes lingering on her for far too long.

How smooth her legs looked, hooked around her blanket; how lithe her arms. A strand of hair had fallen over her left eye and he fought, physically fought, the urge to reach down and smooth it away.

Suddenly she moved, and Jeremy took a step backwards. Her sleepy eyes opened slowly and unseeingly. The pupils within her ocean grey eyes were enormous, and they focused on Jeremy before he found a way to escape.

She didn't scream. He thought she might. She didn't snarl, either. She simply said, "Jeremy?"

"Hi," he whispered. "I'm sorry I woke you, I just boiled some water and was wondering if you'd like a cup of tea."

"Yes, please," she whispered back, then closed her eyes. That was it. Instantly, her breathing returned to its quiet, regular stride. The ease with which she had fallen back asleep made Jeremy's heart feel warm. Wasn't that trust? Allowing herself to close her eyes while he still stood over her bed?

He rushed back downstairs, made her a cup of Earl Gray with a tiny bit of milk (he wondered why she bothered putting any in at all), and ascended the stairs back to her room.

She was still curled up; she hadn't moved. He gently placed the mug on her bedside table and left it there. He was tempted to wake her before it got cold, but she looked so peaceful that he didn't have the heart to. He turned to walk away, denying himself the pleasure of looking at her any longer, and heard her say in a tiny, babyish wisp, "Thank you."

"You're welcome," he said in the doorway before forcing himself to turn away.

That was it for him, the moment he noticed there was no one in the world he cared more for. It terrified him.

The timing could not have been better. Or was it worse? Four days after Jeremy found the sleeping Violet, she began her new plan.

234

She would seduce Jeremy. She knew she could do it. She would wield her new power to set herself and Ben free. The video camera above Violet's bed was something she had avoided as much as possible. Always careful never to take off her clothes in its path, Violet had for months huddled in the corners to change or get ready for bed. When she touched herself at night, she did so lying on her side, away from the camera, underneath the covers. She hid her mouth in her pillow and bit down on it. The thought of him watching her always crept into her mind. As hard as she tried to keep it at bay, there was no preventing it. Sometimes she would stop, shake her head, force him out of it and restart. Others, she would just let it be. In those times, she moved angrily, hungrily. Is this what you want to see? she'd think to herself. Is this why you've kept us here? Well feast your eyes on this then, you bastard. As much Violet was getting used to being around Jeremy, she still hated his presence in her room; she wanted to cry every time she looked up and saw that black box.

Lately, she'd been looking up and wanting to do more than cry. She wanted to strike back and use that black box against him. That night, four nights after Jeremy's revelation, Violet walked into her room and over to her bed. Her back was to the camera, but by Violet's best guess, she was dead centre in the middle of its lens. She took her shirt off slowly and threw it aside. Lifting her hands over her head, Violet smoothed her hair back and pulled it into a loose bun. It was getting long enough to tickle the small of her back, the longest it had ever been.

Bending over, she shimmied her legs together until she had worked her pants off each limb. She stood slowly and started to get nervous about what would come next. Should she really be doing this? What if Jeremy came barging into her room and expected her to continue under his watch? Didn't men get off on that sort of thing? Pretend I'm not even here, he might whisper.

Her hands reached behind her and unclasped her bra, the very decisive movement that men always seem to have an easier time doing than women. The motion was almost like snapping your fingers, except softer and sometimes double-handed. Her bra was mustard yellow, like her sweater, and had lace on both straps and cups. It was the bra she had worn to work that day so long ago, and had worn every day since. It was a fate better than the alternative – sending Jeremy on a bra hunt for her. Hmm, she thought, maybe now is the time for that.

She hugged her body so that the straps fell down, then lowered her arms to let the fabric fall to the floor. The last part would be the hardest. She felt acutely aware of how naked she already was, and clenched her teeth in discomfort. She couldn't imagine taking off anything more; it would feel like shedding a necessary layer, skinning herself for his pleasure.

Violet took care not to look directly into the camera, not yet. She kept her back to it, put her fingers inside the elastic of her underwear, and bent down while holding on tightly to the soft nylon material. She stepped out of it one leg at a time, and slowly ran her hands up her legs until she stood once more, skinned alive. Her nipples were hard with excitement and fear. She wasn't sure which was more overpowering, but prayed it was the latter.

Next, she turned around. Took down her hair, shook her head so that it fell gently around her shoulders. She wasn't sure she was sexy enough to be standing in front of a camera like that, but it was only Jeremy on the other end.

As her naked body faced the camera, her eyes trying desperately not to look into it, she wondered what would come next. In a successful seduction, Jeremy would walk through the door, take her into his arms and admit to watching. He might guide her hand onto himself to prove it. It wasn't what Violet wanted, and knowing all she did about Jeremy, she realized she shouldn't worry.

With newfound reverence, she stared at the camera violently, barely blinking. Her hand reached down her body to the tuft of course hair, her weapon in hibernation beneath it. The shield made her feel safer somehow.

Stepping backwards, Violet sat on the edge of the bed. She propped herself back on both elbows and raised her legs off the floor. As if imaginary stirrups cupped her feet, Violet's knees did their best to touch the comforter. She spread herself wide open to form a diamond; her left knee, her toes, her right knee, her sheath.

She knew he could see all of her. Pink lips he'd want to kiss. He had to. What if he didn't? She shook the thought away. Her left hand mapped a route to her clitoris. She used three fingers, ran them in circles over herself, and focused on keeping her legs still. She never succeeded.

Violet felt like a beast on the bed, bucking and groaning. She lowered herself off of her elbows, her back flat against the cool, smooth cotton of the duvet. The small of her back curved up a tiny bit. One hand stayed on herself, the other found its way to her face. Her wrist touched her lips and she settled her fingers down over her eyes.

She caught herself holding her breath and forced it out in a large burst of exertion. Dizziness gripped her, as if she had a new centre of gravity she had yet to figure out. Her eyes started to leak too, tears of a different kind, coursing down her cheeks, her neck, settling into her collarbone. No sobs accompanied them. She fought every instinct she had to make a sound. Lives were meant to have highs and lows, but that moment was the lowest. Out of eyes squeezed as tight as her clenched jaw, under fingers that caged her eyeballs, she still saw slivers of light. She couldn't keep it all out.

There it was. Her body tightened, her muscles taut and ready. Breathing came a bit louder; it couldn't be helped. Violet was shocked at the viciousness, by the power of her hand in that moment. She came forcefully; it almost hurt. When her body released, she let her feet drop to the floor. Now, her hand lay flat across herself, covering her pulsating loins like a fig leaf. No more. That was all. Her other hand stayed on her face, and the tears stayed too.

Gasps escaped her lips. Her left forearm throbbed with exhaustion. She wasn't sure how she would ever muster the courage to uncover her face or leave that room.

Part of her hoped and imagined that would be enough. Jeremy would see her, fall desperately in lust and decide it was too dangerous to have her around. Her irresistibility would be too much for him to take, and he would have to let her go.

But nothing happened as she lay there, body clenching and unclenching, waiting for her door to open. He would knock, of course he would, and she'd say, Come in. She wouldn't cover her breasts or fumble for the blanket. Instead, she would lie there, presenting her skinned body for his viewing.

He wouldn't touch her. Not today. Not yet. She shivered at the thought. Blood still pumped furiously between her thighs, bursts of warmth ebbing and flowing. Her whole body hummed in anticipation.

Why wasn't he there yet? Didn't he know he should go to her? Perhaps to watch was enough for now.

Violet wiped her tears. She tossed her underwear so they caught on the black box, blocking the camera. She did it quickly, so that he couldn't enjoy one more second of her.

With the camera covered, she was left with the remainder: A young, naked woman alone in a room that was her own but not her own. The full-length mirror caught her eye, presented her as others saw her, in reverse of the way she saw herself.

Turning her head slowly to the left, then to the right, she looked at her ears. She touched the left one gingerly. She hated them. It baffled most people. If they hadn't seen them, her description made them wonder if her ears were deformed in some way. They were, but only to her.

It started at a birthday party over a decade ago. The birthday girl's older brother hung around, and all the little girls giggled. He wasn't even handsome.

He was just older and a boy, which had always been a deterrent, but had somehow transformed into something desired.

Looking back, Violet remembered the exaggerated gestures and winks he had given them all. She now thought him pathetic, but in the moment, each girl had pushed the others out of his line of vision. Each girl wanted to be the only one he saw.

He had seen Violet. She had noticed his eyes on her, and her cheeks deepened in colour instantly. The heat rose before she even had a chance to stop it.

"Hey monkey ears," she heard him say.

Violet looked over at him, eager to see which unfortunate girl he was making fun of. She probably would have even laughed, little bitch.

But the older brother, David was his name, was looking right at her. He tried again.

"You with the monkey ears," he said right to her face, chin jutting out in her direction, "You're in the way."

Violet looked left, right, then finally behind her where David's mother was standing with the cake and trying to get through.

"Oh," Violet said embarrassedly. "I'm sorry." She shuffled to the side and retreated. Little backwards steps until she was far enough to turn and rush into the bathroom. She slammed the door behind her and peeked into the mirror. She didn't want to look. Surely he was joking, her ears were normal.

Tucking her hair behind them, she suddenly realized how monstrous they were. They stuck out like rounded mountains. From then and every day after, she would see only monkey ears.

Soon, she'd almost forgotten where the idea had come from. Violet started to assume she'd realized on her own that her ears looked like elephant flaps, enormous protrusions she would hide behind her hair. Even ponytails would be loosely pulled back with hair covering both ears.

Standing in front of that mirror, in the present, she wondered if someone had deflated them. They didn't look so big. They jutted out more than average, but there was nothing apelike about them. Violet turned her head back and forth again, amazed at the transformation. Her ears were normal. It occurred to her that she hadn't been playing attention; she didn't evaluate herself in the mirror on a daily basis the way she used to. No makeup was in the house; it was another thing she couldn't bring herself to ask Jeremy for. She'd gotten some lip gloss for Christmas, that had been nice, but she didn't blacken her eyelashes the way she used to, or rouge her cheeks that turned pink all on their own.

Her eyes drifted to her hips. Birthing hips, some would say, although she'd never been able to ask her real mother if it were true. Holly had tiny hips, bones that stuck out of unstretched skin.

But Violet had curves to spare. She ran her hands down the sides of her body and wondered if she could call her figure an hourglass. Was it sexy, or just fleshy? She supposed it depended on the person.

The curved figure in front of her was not one of a little girl. She had only just graduated from high school. She knew little about love and being desired. But those curves, her breasts, her eyes were distinctly those of a woman. Did it happen that quickly, the transition from a girl to beyond it? Would other people notice? Maybe it had happened just now, only after having done something with her body she hated herself for. Was that the reason some people grew up so fast?

With one hand across her breasts and another across her belly, she looked for a long time and wondered if she was beautiful. She'd been told she was.

Violet smiled at the mirror. Was that really what she looked like? A strange, forced smirk was all she could muster. Jeremy wouldn't be visiting her tonight. She had waited long enough to know, and to be slightly relieved. Too much too soon would be risking it. She needed to seduce him slowly, revealing a bit more of herself each time until he was the one vulnerable to her. In that moment, she felt loaded with power. It coursed from her pores and gushed from her limbs.

Violet hugged herself and turned away from her reflection. She peeled her sheets back and settled down beneath them. Without even the strength to brush her teeth or wash her face, she collapsed into bed, light on, her black underwear still hanging from the box in the corner. The show was over, both the one for Jeremy and the one she had put on, just now, for herself.

24

On February 14, Ben woke up first, Jeremy second, and Violet last. Always last, even though her feet hit the floor before 10 a.m. most mornings.

She smelled something drifting from downstairs. The saturated air had been the culprit, the one who woke her. Something sweet and buttery. Pancakes, maybe French toast. Tousling her hair to discourage the cowlicks, she threw on her purple sweater and headed downstairs. Not a sound escaped from beneath her toes and heel; she walked lightly, like a dancer without poise.

The morning after she made love to the camera, life had continued as normal. Violet kept her head down while talking to Jeremy, but upon peeking up, she found no indication that anything had changed between them. No embarrassment, no awkward bumbling, no drifting of his gaze down to her (hopefully) desirable hips or breasts.

Since then, she had made no other move; hadn't summoned the courage yet. And, if he hadn't seen the first time, she didn't want to waste another unveiling.

Turning into the kitchen, she saw that it was indeed pancakes that were being flipped on the stove.

"What's this?" she asked with a smile.

"This was supposed to be breakfast in bed," he said shyly, "but I guess now it's going to be breakfast in the kitchen."

Breakfast in bed for her? For Ben too? Part of her wished she could go back in time, stay in bed and wait for him to come knocking, carrying a tray with fresh pancakes. A pot of tea with a tiny jug of milk. A mug, a fork, a knife. Would he have included a fresh flower?

He would have. From the corner of her eye, Violet saw Jeremy sweep a blossom into the garbage. It was a swift movement she wasn't supposed to see. She wondered if he was embarrassed to have been caught in the sweet act.

Sitting on the barstool, Violet asked if she could help.

"Well," Jeremy said, "You could track down your brother. I have a feeling by the time you find him, breakfast will be ready."

"Where is he?" she asked, pushing herself up from the stool.

"Outside, with Deedee and Dodo," Jeremy smiled. Violet was coming around to the imaginary friends, although she hadn't seen or heard much of them since the family dinner.

Violet rolled her eyes warmly. "I'll be back, but you might have to set out two empty plates in case I bring home more than just Ben."

She went out the back door after slipping on her boots and jacket. The frost nipped at her nose and ankles, but it wasn't a cold winter. Not by northern Ontario standards. It was pleasant and bearable and she could barely see her breath. Her dripping nose didn't freeze and her throat didn't burn as she smuggled cold air down it.

"Ben!" she called, seeing no clear sign of him anywhere. Footprints, yes, but no flash of blue. "Breakfast is ready!"

Only a moment's pause passed before she heard his booming reply, "COMING!" and another before she saw him bounding towards her. He was, by her count, alone.

"Hey!" she said. "Good morning! Are Deedee and Dodo coming for breakfast?" She didn't want to be rude.

"Nah, they're back at home."

"Oh, okay," she said as they turned and headed towards the house. "Do you know what Jeremy made for us to eat?" she asked.

"No, what?" But they were already inside, and he saw for himself.

The table was set with a red tablecloth, a rose in a vase at its centre. Perhaps he'd retrieved it from the garbage after all. Wine goblets filled with orange juice sat beside plates heaping with pancakes. Butter and a boat of syrup sat waiting to be dripped over their warm counterparts.

"Whoa!" Ben said, and Violet resisted the urge to say the same. "What's all this for?"

"Happy Valentine's Day!" Jeremy said happily with a little shrug that said This is special and This is no big deal all at once. Violet had known the day was coming because she had planned her seduction in tandem, but it hadn't occurred to her that it would be on anyone else's radar but her own.

The three of them sat down in the seat that had become their own; Violet at the head of the table, Jeremy to her left, Ben to her right. The empty chair across from Violet didn't make her feel as sad as one might think an empty chair would.

"Dig in," Jeremy said needlessly as Ben dove to be the first one holding the butter.

"This is really nice," Violet stopped to make sure she said it. "Thank you."

"It was nothing," Jeremy said, not meeting her gaze and instead fiddling with his cutlery. "They're nice and thick, the way you like them."

She had told him that once, she didn't know how long ago.

"Good memory," she said.

Most of the meal was eaten in silence. When they finished, Ben the only one capable of having seconds, Violet announced that she and Ben would clean up since Jeremy did the cooking.

Ben groaned at the same time Jeremy protested. "No, not today. It's Valentine's Day," he said. "I want to do this for you." He looked right at her as he said it. Not for them, for Ben, just her. Valentine's Day was a day of romance, after all, and love of all kinds.

"You're sure?" she asked, knowing he would answer yes, which he did.

After thanking him, she headed upstairs to dress for the day. When she walked into her room, she immediately saw that Jeremy had been in there.

A box of chocolates sat on her bedside table, as well as a card with her name on it. How...? She supposed he had rushed upstairs while she went outside looking for Ben.

Violet was written on the card lightly and so carefully that some of the letters were shaky. She opened the envelope and slid out the card. Classically cheesy, a bouquet of red roses and a heart adorned its front. Be Mine it read, and Violet wondered how literally she was supposed to take that message.

Aren't we already yours? she thought to herself, and the copper taste of bitterness crept back onto her tongue.

The inside was blank, save for Jeremy's own words.

Dear Violet, he had written, Roses are red, Violets are blue, But none is as beautiful a Violet as you. Happy Valentine's Day. Jeremy.

Before his name, he had drawn a little heart. Did that mean love, or was he just using the logo of the holiday? She wasn't sure, and didn't know why she cared. His little rhyme was, surprisingly, something she hadn't heard before. No blushing schoolboy had left her a poem like it on her desk at school or in her mailbox.

Violet didn't know how she should respond. Jeremy was fond of giving them gifts for any or no occasion, she knew that by now. But something about the card felt different. She quickly snuck into Ben's room to see if there was anything there for him, and there was. A smaller box of chocolates. No card.

She smiled as she thought about the way Jeremy bumbled and fumbled around his compliments, the modest habit he had of looking away from the television when a particularly racy bit came on, while Violet found her own eyes glued to the scene.

The unrest in her stomach reminded her of something she'd felt before, and somehow, Damien's face appeared in her mind. The one who had eventually broken her heart as her mouth swelled too large for her to protest

Before all that though, things had been good. As good as a young girl thinks it can get when she doesn't know better. They had been in love, the kind where you feel woozy when your foreheads and noses touch. Violet's lips had automatically reached out to him in those moments, starved for something they were only just beginning to know.

The first time she received an I love you from someone she loved too had come from Damien. They had sat by the lake together, their legs dangling off a rock overlooking the water.

Without a word, Damien had gotten up and walked to the water's edge, leaned over, and picked up a handful of wet sand.

"Oh, no way!" she had said, sure there was about to be a mud fight while she wore one of her favourite dresses. But instead, he walked back slowly towards her. He stopped and plopped the sand onto her foot without warning. As soon as he did, he turned away, bent down, and did it again. Violet had no idea what he was doing, but tried desperately to keep her foot still so that the wet mound wouldn't slip off.

After his last handful, Damien began to rub her foot, smoothing out the sullied sand until flat and even. He shaved off the excess until the mud was perfectly moulded to the top of her foot.

"What are you doing?" she asked quietly with a smile, not really caring if he answered or not. He didn't, only grinned back as he carved a heart in the middle of the canvas he had created. He dug his finger in with such patience and care, held her foot as if it was the most important thing. When the heart was complete, Violet thought hers might burst. She resisted the urge to blurt out her love.

Next he carved an "I," right above the heart. It could've been a line, she wasn't sure. Then he wrote a "U" right underneath the heart. And then she knew. It was a real heart, and it was the real thing.

"I love you, Violet Wrigley."

For once, he looked nervous. "I love you too," she said happily. "I really do."

They sat on that rock for awhile, and when they finally rose to leave, Violet hesitated. In just the shake of a limb, her first "I love you" would be erased like an Etch-a-Sketch. She had no camera to take a picture. It was so fragile, this love business.

"Come on, let's go. I don't mind," he assured her.

Not wanting to seem too sentimental, she shook her foot. Cleared it off except for the stray couple hundred grains that stayed glued to her skin. The I love you was gone. In real life, the I love you would last another four months.

She had lost her virginity at his house, after school one afternoon when no one else was home. They huddled in his room, his door recklessly open, daring anyone to come home and interrupt. They lay in his single bed with bright green sheets. A little boy's bed. They had fumbled for each other and Violet noticed that their breathing was a lot louder than normal; that their kisses became a desperate mashing of lips, a constant clash of teeth and tongues. Clothing came off bit by bit, her taking off her own, him taking off his.

Damien's hands shook as he ripped open the plastic wrapping he'd pulled from his wallet, and Violet was relieved to see this was new to him as well. He put it on carefully as she lay there, nervous and dehydrated.

Their attempt was almost comical, slamming into each other like bumper cars. Violet kept her ears open, tried to tune out Damien's grunts. Twice, she could have sworn she heard a key in the lock, or maybe that was what she said to get him to ease up, to relieve her body of being smashed against like a ship beaching on the sand. It ended unsuccessfully when Violet muttered a defeated, "Okay," which wasn't obvious enough for a boy having sex for the first time. She repeated it, louder. When that still didn't work, a firm "Stop!" was what it took. But he listened, collapsed beside her in a fit of deep breaths and repeated exclamations of "Wow" that somehow left Violet feeling smug and successful. She tried to keep her mind off her throbbing body. It felt like she had rug burn, or like someone had rubbed sand all over her insides, again. She felt raw and heavy, trying desperately to erase the feeling of the sand. Tears filled her eyes. Damien looked at her and said (quite romantically), "Shit, what'd I do?"

Sex with Jeremy would be something similar to that experience, Violet feared. He wouldn't know his way around her body; she would have to try desperately to match his stride. But she was getting ahead of herself. Jeremy had given no real indication he was interested. She feared that if she brought up the idea, he would run away screaming. It had to happen organically.

Every night, sometimes every other night, she would put on her show for him. She took off her clothes, bit by bit, bending over in front of the camera and touching herself. Increasingly, she found herself staring right into the red dot that told her the camera was on. Look at me, Jeremy, she told it. This is for you.

She stopped hating it about two weeks in. It became natural and even enjoyable, most likely because when it was over, she turned off the light and went to sleep, safe and alone in her bed. She wondered how many times Jeremy had caught her in the act, and how many times she was performing for the camera only. Could he rewind and play the tape back? If Violet were ever to come across tapes of herself this way, she would immediately rip them open and tear them apart. Light them ablaze so no one could see what she was convincing herself she was capable of. She cringed at the thought of her mother seeing her like this. Would she be proud? How could she?

Still, Jeremy kept his distance. The days passed, the nights too. Violet woke in the mornings to the smell of breakfast. It amazed her that he never tired of treating her, or of thinking of her when he brewed a pot of tea. She couldn't help but feel that her and Jeremy were doing some sort of dance, skirting around each other, shyly sneaking looks.

She caught him glancing at her at the most unlikely of times. When she was stumped on something and sitting with her brow furrowed and her chin in her hand; when she would laugh quietly to herself after thinking of something that struck her. She would look up in those private moments and see him staring at her. But not quite staring; it wasn't so obvious or rude as that. More as if he was noticing her completely, taking her in.

This coyness added an element of excitement to her days. It was something she woke up and looked forward to. A game of cat and mouse, except she wasn't sure who played which role. Sometimes it switched. Sometimes she would look at him intensely, for as long as she could get away with before embarrassment set in, thinking, C'mon Jeremy. I'm right here. What are you waiting for? But if he could see the messages her eyes were sending, he didn't give any indication he understood or accepted.

March drifted on leisurely; the snow began to melt and the days became a little brighter, a little warmer. Violet never woke up wondering where she was anymore. In the beginning, she had bolted upright with a start on many nights, wondering whose room this was, whose bed. Now, the scenery of her room had become so commonplace that she knew instantly where she was the second she woke up. It was both settling and deeply unsettling.

So much time passed, in fact, that soon it was April. Violet decided it would be best if she let Jeremy know that Ben's birthday was on the 10th.

On the morning of April 1st, she came down the stairs to the smell of dinnertime. Garlic and vegetables and meat. Probably chicken, she guessed as she approached the kitchen.

"Hey," she addressed Jeremy who was leaning over to look into the oven, "What's for breakfast?"

"Dinner is for breakfast," Jeremy said with a goofy smile.

"What do you mean?"

"We're having a roast chicken with garlic potatoes and grilled vegetables for breakfast."

She was surprised by how good it sounded, albeit bizarre. "I've had pancakes for dinner before, but never dinner for breakfast," she admitted. Her tummy rumbled in anticipation.

"April Fool's!" Jeremy shouted like a little boy.

She paused. "April Fool's as in, we're not actually having dinner for breakfast?"

"No. April Fool's is the dinner for breakfast!"

"So we are having roast chicken for breakfast," she clarified, "and the fact that we're doing so is the joke?"

"Yeah," he said, as though it should be obvious.

"Jeremy, I think you have the wrong idea about what April Fool's Day is about, but I'll take it." She shook her head in mock exasperation.

"Oh." Jeremy wasn't sure if he should feel flattered or embarrassed that his prank didn't fit the bill.

As they heard Ben's clomping feet heading downstairs, Jeremy looked questioningly at Violet. She nodded yes.

"What's for breakfast?" Ben asked.

"Dinner is for breakfast!" Jeremy said as energetically as the first time.

"What?"

"April Fool's Day!"

Ben just rubbed his eyes and went to pour himself a glass of orange juice from the fridge. "April Fool's Day," he repeated, "That means my birthday is coming soon." He said it neutrally, like a birthday wasn't something a young boy should get overly excited about.

"Really?" Jeremy asked. "What day is it on?"

"Umm... Violet?"

"The 10th," she filled in for Ben. He wasn't so good with dates. When he'd been adopted, they hadn't known his actual date of birth, so they had chosen the first day that he'd come to Canada as his birthday.

"Well, we're going to have to celebrate then!" Jeremy said. "What do you think you might like?"

Ben sat on the barstool with his orange juice, and appeared to give it some serious thought. "I think I want to go home," he said. Just innocently, without any malice. His words weren't meant to sting, but of course they did. Jeremy recoiled from the impact.

"Oh," Jeremy said softly. "Yeah, I know. That'll happen. But that's not a birthday gift. I want to give you something you can play with or keep forever."

The reasoning appeared to make sense to Ben, who nodded. "A suit," he said simply, as if it was the most logical thing a seven-year-old boy could ask for on his birthday.

"A suit!" Jeremy commented with surprise. "Maybe a tie as well?"

"No, not that kind of suit," he shook his head fast like a wet dog. "I never want to wear one of those. I want a suit for when I ride my Jeep and get splashed with mud."

It was true; he had been returning from his rides on his Jeep increasingly soiled with melting earth. As the snow thawed, the dirt began to surface beneath it. Ben seemed to be an expert at stirring the soil. Most of it landed on his clothing.

"You mean, like a wet suit that scuba divers wear, but one that you can wear in your Jeep?" Jeremy asked.

"Yup," Ben said simply. "Yes, please," he added after looking at Violet. She hadn't even noticed, but smiled after hearing him self-correct.

"But really," Ben asked. "What is for breakfast?"

"Roast chicken, garlic potatoes and grilled vegetables!" Jeremy repeated as he pulled the pan from the oven. The aroma of seared skin reached their nostrils, each of them amazed by how ready they were to eat such a meal in the morning.

"And this is for April Fool's?" Ben asked.

"Yeah," Jeremy replied sheepishly.

"Jeremy," Ben said gently, "I don't think you get what April Fool's is."

Violet giggled. Jeremy started to as well. Ben didn't see what was so funny, but threw his head back and laughed the loudest of all.

Later, to teach Jeremy the meaning of a true prank, Ben searched the kitchen. Finding a large bag of flour, he dumped it into a bowl and climbed up onto the counter to hide it above one of the cupboards. He tied a rope around the bowl, tied the other end to a hook inside a cupboard door. When Jeremy opened it later that evening to prepare dinner for dinner, the bowl of flour fell upside down onto Jeremy's head with perfect aim. The flour dusted his shoulders and covered most of his body.

Standing with a bright red mixing bowl on his head, Jeremy turned to face the giggler he could hear behind him.

"April Fool's!" Ben shouted.

Violet walked into the kitchen when she heard the commotion, and saw the flour-covered body with a mixing bowl for a head. She let out the laugh that Jeremy found increasingly infectious. He smiled from beneath the mixing bowl, and realizing they couldn't see it, let out a hearty laugh. He never wanted to take that bowl off and wondered how long he could keep it on before moving from silly to idiotic.

When he finally took it off, he puffed out his cheeks and blew, resulting in an explosion of white in all directions.

"That's how you do a real April Fool's," Ben said proudly.

No one minded cleaning up the flour that day.

25

Today is my birthday.

I'm not sure if I should celebrate. We're still here. We didn't get to go home yet, and Jeremy says that's not a birthday gift but it would have been the best one ever. Instead, I think I'm getting a suit I can wear in the mud. That'll be good too.

I'm seven now. Seven is a lot older than six. Six is still little kid age, but seven is definitely a big kid. My mom has a chart back home where she measures how tall I am on my birthday every year. The mark is always a little higher than the last. I wonder if Jeremy would measure me and I could bring it home with me when I go. The mark would be a lot higher this time, I'm pretty sure. I feel bigger.

I guess since I'm seven now, I can't play with Deedee and Dodo anymore. They don't know yet though. I haven't told them. I don't want to hurt their feelings. I don't know. Maybe seven isn't such a big age after all. Maybe eight is the age when I'm not allowed to have friends like them.

This morning I was sleeping when Vi opened my door and said, "Knock, knock." I don't know why people say it instead of doing it. Usually, I'm up first and Vi is still in bed for a long time. I asked her once why she was so lazy, and she rubbed the hair on my head and told me I wouldn't get it until I was older. I guess she does stay up later than me. Sometimes when I go to bed she tells me she's going to bed soon, too, like it matters to me. I don't care when she goes to sleep. I go to sleep because I'm sleepy. Maybe that's one thing that's nice about not being at home, is that I get to pick when I get up and go to bed, and no one tells me it's too early or too late.

I'm sorry, Mom. It's not nicer than being home. It's just a little bit nice.

Vi brought me breakfast in bed, which I don't really like because it's hard to eat in a bed. I usually slop and get crumbs in there that I feel at night on my toes. I always wish I hadn't eaten in bed. Plus, I don't have a TV in there, so I just eat and stare at the wall. But I know it's nice, so I smile and say thank you.

Every Mother's Day, Vi and I bring Mom breakfast in bed. We make toast with peanut butter and a pot of tea. Mom has her tea with a lot of milk, but no sugar. She likes about three times as much milk as Vi does, so we pour her a jug. Usually, I have a card made from school or daycare, so I put that on the tray when we bring it to her. One year, I learned a poem and stood beside her bed to say it to her. There were only a few rhyming words and I didn't even write them, but her eyes got all watery and she said it was the best Mother's Day gift ever.

Maybe that's why Vi thinks I like breakfast in bed, because we do it for Mom. Vi brought me grilled cheese.

"For breakfast?" I asked, because she always told me it wasn't a breakfast food.

"Lunch for breakfast," she said while bobbing her head back and forth, and I smiled. Cool.

Vi didn't leave me alone to eat like we do with Mom. She sat there looking at me and it was weird.

"Thanks," I said, in case I'd forgotten and that's what she was waiting for, but she didn't move when I said it.

"What?" I asked. I know it came out rude, but it was the quickest way to ask.

"Nothing," she said, and leaned back a bit. "Sorry. It's just, it's your birthday. I didn't want you to have to eat alone."

I guess that makes sense.

"Now, what do you want to do today? It's up to you," Vi said. I know that's not really true because it's up to Jeremy. I didn't answer.

"I think there might be a surprise downstairs waiting for you," Vi said with a smirk.

I smiled big at that. I like surprises. I ran out my door and down the stairs and all I could see was string, everywhere.

"What's this?" I asked. It looked like a giant spider web. The whole main floor was tangled in it from bottom to top.

"I don't know," Vi said, but I think she knew. I looked down and saw a ball of yarn attached to all the string.

"Do I –" I started to ask Vi but realized I knew what to do. I picked up the ball of yarn and started to roll it back up. It was wrapped around all kinds of things; chairs and lamps and tables and railings. Probably about a million feet of string. I just kept rolling it up, walking all over the house.

When I got near the end, I slowed down a bit. I didn't want it to end. I'd never had a puzzle like this before.

"Vi, this is so cool!" I shouted, because I wanted her to know I appreciated it. But she just shook her head.

"I know," she said, "But this was all Jeremy."

I didn't know what to think about that, but I think I really liked it. I kept collecting the yarn, and I finally got to the last bit. It took me to the big closet by the front door. I opened it up, and Jeremy popped out and shouted, "HAPPY BIRTHDAY!"

I sort of made a sissy noise, because I didn't expect him to be there. Jeremy laughed, and Vi did too. I like how I can make them laugh.

Jeremy held out my suit for me.

"Just like you asked for," he said as he handed it over.

Badass Ben was painted on it in bright green paint. My mouth fell open, because I wasn't supposed to say that word, and I looked back at Vi to see if I was in trouble. But she was smiling.

"How does it feel to be badass, Ben?" she said. I couldn't believe it.

I decided to try something. "It feels... badass," I said. I almost chickened out, and it didn't sound cool coming out of my mouth, but I said it anyways.

I put on my new suit and went to use it on my Jeep. I felt like a real racer. The backyard was a desert I was exploring at my own risk. I saw cactuses and camels. I splashed through the muddiest puddles I could find. When they weren't muddy enough, I grabbed the hose and turned it on and sprayed it. I got mud everywhere. From the desert, I found my way to the swamp and I watched out for alligators and elephants. Loud shouts started ringing in my ears, and I didn't even realize it was me. I was having so much fun.

No one even came out to tell me to slow down, or stop, or that I was going to make a huge mess of the house, or to keep it down. My Mom would be so mad. Sorry, Mom. But it was way too much fun.

I finally got tired, plus I had a chunk of mud in my mouth I wanted to rinse out. My new suit was a bit tricky to get off, but I slipped out of it while I was still outside.

"Shower time!" Vi said when she saw me. It wasn't in a mad or mean way. I looked down at myself and she was right – I was covered top to bottom in mud. Some had even soaked through my new suit. A shower was a good idea.

After that, I got to watch movies with dinosaurs and robots and aliens. Jeremy turned the lights down and made popcorn. I even got to drink Cream Soda in the middle of the afternoon.

For dinner, Jeremy went out and brought us back hamburgers. I had three of them. Three! Vi only had one, Jeremy had two, but I got three. My tummy hurt real bad after that, but I wasn't going to say a word about it because it was too cool.

After that, Vi and Jeremy snuck into the kitchen. Whenever someone does that on your birthday, you always know it's a cake. It's not a real surprise, even though they won't let you peek and pretend to be all sneaky while they're doing it. I sort of like it though. I pretended like I didn't know what they were doing, just to be a good sport. I think you're supposed to.

They sang me Happy Birthday. I wasn't even embarrassed. I really liked it, and I wanted to sing along, but I don't think you're supposed to sing to yourself on your birthday.

I got to cut the cake. Mom never lets me use a knife. When I looked at Vi, she said I was a big kid now and I should be able to cut my own cake. To be honest, I didn't really want to do it. I was nervous I wouldn't get the pieces right and that it would fall apart when I put it on a plate. It was something really grown up and I didn't want to blow it. Turns out, it wasn't so bad. The trick is to do it nice and slow. Don't try to rush it.

Vi rushed out of the room again in that not-so-secret way. She came back with a gift in her hand. I sort of thought the mud suit was from both of them, but this one was just from her. I said thank you before I opened it.

When I ripped the tissue paper out of the bag, I wasn't sure what was in there right away. A book of some kind. I looked at her, but she just stuck her chin forward, and I knew she meant, Open it.

Inside was all sorts of writing. It was Vi's writing, I could tell by the way she draws the letter a like a backwards s with a stick attached, and the way she writes e like the Golden Arches, only sideways.

I flipped through the book. There were pages and pages of bits all starting with Do you remember when…

"Vi, you did all this?" I think it was the same question my Mom would have asked if she got a present like this. I was proud of that.

"Well, I didn't have any of our old photos, and since we're away from home, I thought you might like this to help you remember."

It was a really good idea. Sometimes I missed being able to look at my Mom anytime I wanted to. You don't realize it's something you like to do until you can't. I didn't realize I loved the way my Mom kissed the top of my head when she said goodnight to me. I wouldn't want Jeremy to do it, and I think it might make Vi sad. I didn't realize I loved the way my Mom made different versions of a meal for me without ingredients I don't like.

Reading all the things Vi had written would be weird right in front of her, plus I can't read as fast as she can. I closed it and said thank you, but I hoped she could tell it was the nicest gift I'd ever got.

I could've stayed up as late as I wanted that night, but I started to get sleepy and there was no one to impress. Vi and Jeremy were both heading upstairs, and I didn't want to sit alone.

When I got into bed, Violet came in to say goodnight. She kissed me on top of the head. I never told her about how Mom used to do that, and I was pretty sure I hadn't said anything out loud when I was thinking about it earlier. I have no idea how she knew, but it felt really good and I hoped she would come in and do it every night.

When she left, I opened the book she gave me. This memory was my favourite:

Do you remember when you were really little and you were taking a bath in Mom's big Jacuzzi? You must have been sick, because that was the only time we were allowed in there. I'm not sure what you'd done to annoy me, but it was something bad because I was really pissed at you. I unplugged my CD player and I brought it into the bathroom where you were. I held the thing over my head, and I told you that if I dropped it in the water, it would electrocute you. I think I must have seen it on TV or something, because I have no idea how I would have known something like that. And, for the record, it wouldn't have electrocuted you because it wasn't plugged in, but I didn't realize this at the time so I guess it's no excuse. You looked up at me with real terror in your eyes. I was scared that you were scared that I would actually do it. Because Ben, you know I never would. I don't know what I was thinking that day. But when I saw the fear in your eyes, I immediately left and put it back down in my room and started to cry. I'm not sure if I ever apologized for that. I'm sorry, Ben. It was an awful thing to do and I wish I'd never done it. I just wanted you to know, and I never knew a way to tell you before now.

It was a weird memory to choose as my favourite, but I remembered it so well. I always knew she wouldn't throw it in. But she looked so powerful with it in her hands that I had been scared just because I knew how much smaller I was than her. I know exactly what I did to make her so mad. I looked through her diary. I snuck into her room and dug it out, because I'd seen her put it away after writing in it. I was sitting in her room reading it, but she came upstairs and caught me. She started to scream, so I just ran. And I wasn't sick that day, I was just brave and asked Mom if I could have a bath in the big tub, and she said yes.

I never told my Mom about Vi's threat. And she never apologized for it either. I'm not good with times and years but I think I was five when it happened. We never said a word about it, and it felt nice to have it down on paper. It was like we'd talked about it when we never really had to. It felt like we cleared the air. That's something my Mom used to say when I would sit and pout and she told me to just let it out because it would feel better that way. It didn't always feel better that way. But this time, it did.

Jeremy came by to say goodnight to me too. He just stood in the doorway. I didn't feel sad or anything that he didn't come in and give me a kiss on the head. I don't even think I would like that.

I told him thank you for my birthday.

He stood there for awhile and didn't say anything. A bit like Vi earlier when she was sitting on my bed. Finally, what he said was, "You can call me Jer."

He left then, and didn't wait for to me to tell him if I was going to call him Jer or not. He just pulled the door shut behind him and that was it.

<u>26</u>

Violet was frustrated. Her evening burlesque shows were having no effect on Jeremy, or at least none she could see. There were moments when she wondered if she just wasn't his type. Maybe he was gay, or wasn't into blondes. But she had seen the way he looked at her.

The next stage would have to begin, and it was going to happen that evening. May had arrived. Buds were sprouting. Most of Violet's time was spent outside, gardening and shovelling and wiping grime and sweat off her forehead. She had taken to going for runs around the property in the early mornings or evenings when the air was crisp and cool. The ground squished beneath her toes, and the only sounds in her ears were the birds chirping, her own breathing and the blood pumping through her veins. Her lungs felt as if they could expand for hours. She frequently took huge gulps of air in, just to see how much she could fit. Back home, she had wheezed. Runs were cut short by the ache in her chest, the metallic pressure of her lungs turned to lead pipes about to burst. Here, she felt she could run for days. Just not away.

The deadline for applying to school for the fall had come and gone. She wouldn't be accepted anywhere that year. She refused to let herself really think about it. It was inevitable, she supposed, since she hadn't been able to save the money she needed anyhow. What was one more year? She was only eighteen. There was no rush, no voice in her ear telling her that life was passing her by. There was only time, and so much of it.

If she were still at home, Violet knew she would have returned from work each night to a computer screen with university websites pulled up. University of Guelph. Carleton University. Brock University. Her mom had mentioned them all, had done more research than Violet ever had or would. Have you made up your mind yet? She never had.

But at Jeremy's house, she slept late, spent time outside, got her shoes covered in dew from early morning runs that took her breath away more from beauty than exhaustion. Ben, too, seemed increasingly happy. Violet had grown so used to her everyday life that sometimes she would go for days at a time without questioning it.

Not today, though. Writing down memories for Ben had pulled at something she'd kept hidden. What if the police tracked Jeremy down? And what if, when they arrived, they discovered Violet had done nothing to get them out of there?

It was time to make a move, for her own sanity and so she could tell everyone she fought as hard as she could to get out. Nine months, that was how long it had been. Violet could have conceived and given birth by now. A whole human life could have been created in that amount of time.

Four loops around the property took her an hour to run. She had her own route carved out. Sometimes she could even spot her footprints from the day before in the mud or carved into the grass. Other times, she'd see bunny tracks, bird feet that had crossed her path on their own journey.

Once, Violet tripped over a stump and fell, hard. The wind had been knocked clear out of her and she lay on the ground wriggling in pain before hoisting herself up and wobbling back to the house. She hadn't even sprained her ankle, only scuffed up her knees a bit. When she hobbled back into the house, Jeremy's eyes had widened to saucers and he immediately fussed and fawned over her bloody knees.

Her cuts had healed, but on that dewy morning Violet remembered how good it felt to have Jeremy's undivided attention.

Violet let her legs give out underneath her. She collapsed to the ground, hitting one knee on the soft earth as the other bashed into a rock.

"Motherfucker," she muttered. She hadn't meant to really injure herself, but she supposed authenticity wouldn't hurt. Her pants had ripped and she could see the mashed up skin beneath it, already beginning to secrete thick, red fluid. Before convincing herself it was a bad idea, Violet lowered her head to the rock.

I can do this, she thought. With a strange, sick dedication, she raised her skull a couple of inches above the boulder, scouting out its sharpest edge. Quickly, with more force than she thought she would be able to summon, she smashed her head against the rock. Bright lights flashed and her head began to thump in pain. Wooziness filled her. She felt something trickle down the side of her face. She hoped... yes, it was blood. Sufficiently bedraggled, Violet lay on the ground motionless. The pain in her knee came and went. It felt as if someone had wrapped a tourniquet around the cap and was pulling tightly on it then letting it loose again and again. Her head felt as if it was in the process of exploding. She lay still for five minutes until she finally got the strength to pull herself up. Thinking of her body as a puppet, she visualized pulling herself up by the strings. She had no choice but to straighten, rise up and begin to walk back, her own marionette.

Jeremy was in the garden. He looked over at her and waved. Violet wasn't sure if it was theatrics or light-headedness; it happened too quickly and she can't remember it right, but she collapsed to the ground. Her puppet strings came loose and her joints unlocked, sending her tumbling back down to the earth. Her eyes were closed, her head throbbing, and sound filtered into her ears sporadically. She knew Jeremy was calling her name, but she couldn't bring herself to respond. Stars flashed across her vision.

She felt strong hands underneath her legs and around her waist. Light, she felt light, floating upwards. She tried to open her eyes but shut them again quickly from the pain and hot blood hovering around her eyelids.

Jeremy carried her into the house. Fluffy comfort greeted Violet's body as he lowered her into the royal blue easy chair in the living room. She was alone then. Violet realized she had smashed her head harder than she should have. There shouldn't be so much blood and so many stars.

"Hey," she heard Jeremy and felt a cool cloth on her forehead. "Are you alright?"

She nodded. She opened her eyes tentatively, waiting for the blood to seep in but it didn't. "I fell," she said simply.

"No shit you did," Jeremy said, and Violet's mouth curved upwards into a tiny smirk. She loved when he swore. "Were you out for a run?" A small nod again.

Part of him always worried that she would just keep going, that she would run for miles and miles. But she'd never leave Ben alone like that, and Ben didn't like to stray far from the house.

"Maybe you should take a break from running for awhile," he said gently. Violet grunted agreement.

"Say something," Jeremy asked her, "What's your name? Where are you?" He didn't know much about First Aid, but knew enough to know she should be able to answer those questions, even after some deliberation, or she was in trouble.

"Don't be stupid," she said. "I'm Violet Wrigley and I'm here and I'm okay." She tried to push herself up into a more comfortable position. "God, my head," she said, raising a hand to her warm, wet forehead.

"You really did a number on yourself this time," he said, wiping her forehead with the cloth. The blood just kept coming. Head wounds scared him. A little chunk of skin had flapped upwards on her forehead. He pulled it back down and tried not to grimace.

"Is there anything I can do to make you feel better?" he asked. Violet had known the question was coming.

"Yeah," Violet said decisively. "I want a campfire and a big bottle of wine. Tonight," she added to make sure he didn't go spark up the fire right there and then.

"Oh," Jeremy said, taken aback and clearly delighted. "Sure, we can do that." He ran his fingers though her hair, and kept doing it. At first it had been functional, to smooth the locks away from the sticky, clumpy blood. There was no reason he should keep going, but he couldn't find a reason to stop. Violet leaned into his hand. He ran his fingers along her scalp and she was amazed by the nerves that tingled all over her body.

Ben walked in soon after, oblivious to her injuries. "What's wrong with you?" he'd asked, looking at the bag of ice she held to her forehead.

"I'm concussed," she said. Ben just gave her a strange look and walked out of the room. Violet couldn't help but feel a little hurt. But, true to adorable form, Ben poked his head back around the corner, just as he'd done when he was little to shout, Hola! This time, he said, "Are you really okay?" She just nodded and let him go off to play.

Violet stayed in the big blue chair and watched soap operas. She humbly accepted the soup and crackers that Jeremy presented her with; she drank the tea he brought. She didn't prepare dinner or clean up after it. It was easy to revert to having someone tend to her every need. Sometimes, you just need looking after.

The days were stretching longer. The sun was still hinting on the horizon past dinner; a big improvement from the winter nights when Violet had looked out the window and seen only her reflection in the darkness by late afternoon. The sun still belonged in the sky at that time. It wasn't fair that it should shy away from the cold, taking the only part of the season that could warm them from the ice.

Violet eased herself off the chair to put on her spring jacket. Jeremy peeked in from the next room. "Is it time yet?" he asked.

"Yes," she said quietly. The sky was darkening.

They shouldn't be there. Sometimes she repeated the sentiment in her head like a mantra. They shouldn't and they wouldn't be, not for much longer.

Jeremy gathered newspapers, a lighter, a bottle of wine with two glasses.

By sundown, they were stationed around a blazing fire. Ben peeked outside to ask what they were doing.

"What does it look like?" she shouted jokingly. "Wanna join?"

"Nah," he said. "I'm fine in here."

Violet was relieved, and felt guilty for it. "We can make s'mores," she shouted back in negotiation.

"Nah," he said again, and pulled himself back in the house.

"I wonder what Ben's life would have been like if you hadn't found him," Jeremy said when the door closed. Violet hadn't found him. She'd simply been waiting at home when he arrived. But she didn't argue the point.

"I don't know," she said honestly. "When we first got him" (instantly, she regretted her word choice. He sounded like a goldfish they'd won at the county fair), "he would wake up almost every night screaming from some nightmare."

"Like he did that night awhile ago?" Jeremy asked.

"Yeah, except he normally remembered what the dream was about and he'd be so scared. I thought it was over with."

"What sort of things did he dream about?"

"Mostly that he was back at the orphanage. Another one of the boys would have a knife to his throat or a gun to his head, telling him he couldn't leave to live with us. He also had one where he was in a car with me and our mom, and it

272

crashed into the river, and my mom and Ben were alright but I didn't make it. Ben said he could see my body all blue and floating down the river. He would wake up sobbing."

"A little boy had dreams like that," Jeremy said with a shake of his head. "That's scary. I wonder if it was because he didn't think he deserved to go from an orphanage to a home like yours. It must have felt like heaven."

"Hey," Violet said quickly. "Life wasn't always so amazing in our house."

"That's not what I meant. Just comparatively, from a little boy's perspective. I know no home is perfect. There's always the good and the bad.

Violet wondered how different his home had been from her own.

"I guess we had it pretty good," Violet admitted. "I didn't have a father, but I did have a mother who loved me." She caught herself using the past tense. Her hand shot to her mouth. The sentence scared her.

"Would your mother have loved you no matter what?" he asked.

"What do you mean?"

"I mean, do you think she would love you no matter what you did or how you turned out? Unconditionally?"

"Well," Violet thought, "I think that's part of being a mother. I don't think you really have a choice. I don't even mean a moral choice, I mean a physical one."

Jeremy didn't like her answer. He was shaking his head before she'd even finished. "No, it's a choice," he said definitively. "And I'm asking if your mother chose it."

"Well then yeah, I guess she did. She puts pressure on me to succeed, but I'd like to think she'd love me no matter what." She paused. "Although you've bought me a little time before I really find out."

"Why is that?" Jeremy asked. Violet didn't normally talk so openly about his kidnapping them, especially not in a positive way.

"I was supposed to go to school this fall. I took a year off to work and figure things out. And here we are, past application deadlines, and I'm still no closer to knowing what the fuck I should do."

Jeremy was quiet for almost a minute. "Violet," he finally said, "I didn't even think about the fact that you being here would get in the way of applying to university. I'm so sorry. I should've offered you the internet to research programs..." His voice faded.

It baffled Violet how out of sorts Jeremy got about the strangest things. He had no qualms about stealing two people for months on end, but the fact that his doing so got in the way of university applications really distressed him.

"It's fine," she said. "I would have been in the same boat even if I were still at home. I wouldn't know what to do either way." She almost stopped, but continued.

"Hey Jeremy? Do you ever feel like even though our generation has had the easiest lives out of anyone, that some parts might be harder than anyone else's ever before?"

"Sure," he said. "People can live wherever they want because it's easy to get around. There are thousands of occupations to choose from. How is anyone supposed to decide?"

Violet could tell he'd thought about it before. She couldn't help but wonder if he'd anticipated her comment somehow, stayed up late the night before with cue cards practising.

"Right," she said, glad he seemed to understand. "We're expected to do it all. To travel the world, to get the best education possible, the best job, the most money, the biggest house. But what if life would be better without all this stuff? Without all the choices?"

She paused for a breath.

"Sorry," she said. "Tangent. I'm just getting worried about making those decisions. I wish I had a crystal ball so I could see what job I should pursue, what education I should get."

"That would defeat the purpose," Jeremy said.

"Of what?"

"Of living."

"Yeah, well," her voice trailed off with a shrug. "But I can't help but feel scared that I'm too young or naïve to be making the right choices."

"Don't be so hard on yourself," Jeremy said kindly. "There's no training for those big decisions, and they don't get easier as you go. Just take it day by day, Violet, and you'll be okay."

Violet poured herself a second glass of wine, and topped up Jeremy as well.

"What about the most basic decisions though? Like sexuality?" She decided to make a conversational leap that she hoped wouldn't be too obvious.

"I don't know," Jeremy said, confused. "I guess it's just one of those instinct things."

"But is it?" she asked. "What if it's just so engrained in us at birth that we're supposed to fall in love with the opposite sex so that we can make babies, that some of us don't really have a choice?"

Jeremy was uncomfortable. "I don't know," he said again.

Violet let out the memory that had led her there. "One night after I finished a shift at work, a friend offered me a ride home on her motorcycle. She was new to the job and I didn't know her well. She was pretty, but she'd be mad if you told her so, I think. She wore a leather jacket. We both got off the evening shift at the same time, and I started to call a cab. My car was in the shop and my mom was busy that night. Her name was Farrah. Like she should have the big feathery bangs, but she didn't. She had bleached blonde, jagged hair that made you want to just muss it up even more than it was.

"Anyways, she saw I was calling a cab and offered me a ride home. I'd never been on a motorcycle before. I said yes, even though I was a bit nervous, and she reached into a bucket under her seat to get out an extra helmet. I fumbled with the buckle, but I didn't get it quite right. She was already on the bike at this point, so I just hopped on behind her. I had to hold on really tight, she told

276

me to, because she took her corners hard." She smiled at the recklessness of youth. "So I sat behind her with my hands squeezed around her waist.

"All of a sudden, I felt the helmet clasp come loose, and then it just flew off. I didn't even say anything right away. I had no idea what to say, I felt so uncool and like I might have just ruined her helmet forever. Eventually, I had to tap her on the shoulder and shout in her ear what had happened. We turned around, and there was a man on the sidewalk just holding the helmet up, so confused. I guess it had skidded onto the sidewalk. So much could have gone wrong, but there were no cars on the road, and the helmet didn't even have a dent in it. Farrah just laughed. She did my helmet up for me that time.

"I got back onto the bike and I held on even more tightly. A minute later I was home and I was thanking her and took off the helmet. I barely knew this girl, but I reached in and gave her a big hug. She hugged me back, and we held on for much longer than I thought we would." She thought about it. "Maybe five seconds. That doesn't sound like a lot, but it is when it's someone you just met.

"I always wondered if she wanted to kiss me, or if I should've kissed her. Maybe I misread her, but there was something there. She quit working at the restaurant soon after, so I didn't see her much. But I feel like, if I hadn't have held back, I would've wanted to kiss her."

She looked over at Jeremy. The story had been meant to turn him on. It was true, it had happened just the way she had told it, but she'd never told anyone else before.

"Well," Jeremy added, "In ancient Roman times, it was considered more respectable to have a homosexual relationship than a heterosexual one. Women were the baby-makers, but they weren't who the men turned to when they wanted real physical pleasure."

Not the reaction she'd been hoping for.

"Good point," she said wryly. "If no one ever told us it was wrong to love someone of the same sex, I wonder what would happen."

"I guess we'll never know," Jeremy said. "But I've always felt that you shouldn't be judged for who you fall in love with."

She looked at him sharply then. She would be judged if she loved him. But how could she? Why would she? Her wine glass was empty and she remedied that using what little was left in the bottle.

"There's another one inside," Jeremy said. "How's your head feeling?"

"A bit better, she said, holding her cool glass to her forehead. "The wine is helping."

"It is or it isn't?" he asked. He hadn't heard her.

"It is," she clarified. "Hey Jeremy?"

"Yes?" He was tending the fire but looked at her when she said his name.

"When you think about me, what do you see?"

He paused. He didn't understand the question, but didn't want her to know. "I see a young, beautiful girl who has a lot ahead of her." Maybe she was still seeking affirmation from her decision-making phobia.

"That's nice," she said, "But I mean, do you see me as a sister? A daughter? A friend? Or something else?"

"Oh. Well. I've never tried to put it in words before. Sort of like a daughter."

Violet tried not to grimace.

"I'm sorry, I know that's weird to admit." He would never have done so if he hadn't drank so much wine. "But also like a friend. I like talking to you and just being around you."

Violet leaned in towards him gradually. She didn't want him to know she was moving closer. "But do you ever think about me the way I thought about Farrah?"

Seduction was coming more easily to her than she had imagined. The wine smoothed her words and she didn't feel dirty or cheap. She wanted to whisper in his ear.

Jeremy swallowed. He didn't say anything for awhile, and then he did. "I – It's crossed my mind," he admitted.

"Really? So you've thought about what it might feel like if I were to lean in, like this, and kiss you?" A pause that felt like a lifetime. "Like this?" And she did.

She had thought it might take longer. She'd been planning to wait until she knew Ben was sleeping soundly in bed, until even the crickets had quieted, until the dead of night. But she hadn't needed to. She didn't want to.

His lips were soft, and they held on. It wasn't over in an instant. Neither of them recoiled in horror. They held on.

When Violet finally pulled back, she felt a little dizzy. Her eyes didn't open as quickly as she wanted them to. They were leaden. Glancing at Jeremy then, she would have guessed he'd look transformed. More handsome, more repulsive, different in some way. But he was the exact same. The expectant eyes were the same ones he had always given her, with just a bit more urgency.

"What was that?" he asked. She wasn't sure. Before she could decode it, stamp meaning on it and be too embarrassed to continue, she leaned in again. Kissed him harder. Her hands stuck to her sides, pasted like glue, but she felt his move onto her; there was one on the small of her back, and the other crawled to the nape of her neck. They were just where she wanted his hands to be.

Her leaden arms grew light. They reached around his neck. His sweater felt thick and fleecy beneath her fingers, and she was filled with an urge to feel his bare skin against her own. His shoulders would be freckled. She could picture it in her mind.

Their lips formed a rhythm quickly, in a way that some people never can and that others take time to get just right. It was like their lips knew what the other wanted.

He kissed softly, gently, with more passion than urgency. He held her tightly, and she tried to ignore the fact that it made her feel safe.

Jeremy's mind raced. He was convinced he must be in an alternate reality. Maybe he'd fallen asleep, or was lost deeply in a reverie while Violet sat beside him saying, Jeremy? Hello?, wondering where he had gone.

But it didn't end. She kept kissing him, each deeper than the one before. He was so confused. She wouldn't want to do this with him, why would she? How could she?

His body felt liquid, warm and unstable. He monitored her level of passion. He would match it, but not exceed it. There was not a bone in his body that would have allowed him to kiss her. She was untouchable. But here she was, touching him.

His conscience forced his vocal chords to act up. "Violet," he said amidst kisses, "What are we doing?"

"Just shut up," she said. It wasn't playful, it was a plea. He pulled away.

"I'm sorry," he said, "It's just that Ben is right inside and I don't want him to see this. I don't know what he would think."

Violet cursed under her breath because she knew he was right. She felt embarrassed.

"Okay," she said looking at him intensely. "I'm going to go up to my bedroom and stay in there with the door closed. Ben will probably go to sleep soon after. When he's asleep, come knock on my door and I'll tell you to come in. Will you do that?" she asked.

He didn't know if he could, but nodded his head in apparent agreement. She nodded back, and bent to pick up her wine glass and the empty bottle. "See you soon," she said with a lopsided smirk.

He heard her breathe a huge sigh as she walked away. He hadn't been meant to hear it, of that he was sure. He had no idea what it meant. Was it relief or disgust or excitement? If he knocked on her door, he might find out the answer. But he wouldn't.

Violet's silhouette stood out in the glow of the doorway as she opened it to go inside. She paused, but shut the door behind her.

This time, Jeremy was the one exhaling. He hadn't realized he'd been holding his breath. He sat still for a long time watching the logs burn down, the embers holding on to the heat of flames that had faded long ago.

The hose had never been fully put away since Ben had destroyed the back yard with his Jeep. He drenched the last of the burning coals and listened to their sizzle. It was such a satisfying, long-lasting sound. Slowly, he headed back inside, unsure what he would do next.

Ben was in bed, Jeremy could tell from the lack of noise. He climbed the stairs, slowly, skipping the third board for the squeak. Violet's door was closed, Ben's also. He pressed his head against the youngest one's door, convincing himself that he heard steady breathing coming from within.

Jeremy stood frozen in the hallway. He knew what he wanted to do, but knew also that he shouldn't. He didn't want to ruin her trust, make her feel violated. Such a shame that her name was so close to that word, violate. His feet refused to move, even to turn him away from the door. His mouth opened and shut with indecision.

No good could come of him knocking on her door. Short-term good, yes, but surely not long-term. He was about to turn away but the doorknob turned instead. Violet opened the door slowly wearing all of her clothes; no sexy nightgown or anything scary. Her bright purple sweater still sat atop her shoulders and covered her belly. She was beautiful.

He couldn't resist. "You're beautiful."

Jeremy wasn't sure what she was thinking. She looked at him strangely. It was an expression that could as easily have been hatred as affection. Taking a step back, away, he felt a hand on his arm.

"I'm coming with you," she said. Where Jeremy had planned to go was downstairs, to the kitchen, back to the bottle of wine. But that's not where she meant. Grabbing him by the hand, Violet led him towards his bedroom. She looked back at him. The message she tried to convey with her eyes was, It's alright, come with me.

The message he got was, Don't say another word.

<u>27</u>

Jeremy's hand was in hers. Violet wasn't sure how it had gotten there. She must have grabbed it. Their fingers were locked together and they fit more nicely than either of them imagined.

Violet sat down on the bed. She had no wine glass to hold now. There was nothing to look down at, to fiddle with, to take a sip of when she didn't know what to say. It was only her and him, in his bedroom, at night. The inevitability of what was to happen made her cringe, but they were trapped in the moment before it began; the moment where they just sat looking at one another.

Are you serious? Violet thought. I have to make another move? She'd never had to do this before. Any other boy she'd shown interest in had taken it from there, had leaned in and touched her chin and kissed her like he meant it. But Jeremy did nothing. He sat rigidly beside her, his hands clamped to his body.

"You can kiss me now," she said softly.

All he needed was permission. He leaned in slowly. He grabbed her chin, just as she'd mentally ordered, and kissed her firmly. His weight gently eased her backwards until they were lying down together. Jeremy's fingers twirled strands of her hair. The opposite hand ran up and down her back.

Jeremy was trying to hide his shaking. His solution was to keep kissing her, over and over, so that she wouldn't notice him tremor.

They lay on his bed together, on top of the blankets, fully clothed. Violet waited patiently for his hands to stray downwards, to linger on her breasts then tickle her belly button then reach for the elastic of her underwear. It was the natural path for them to take. But his hands stayed on the small of her back and tangled in her hair. They would not move. They caressed and slightly relocated, but they would not move down or under.

Violet grabbed Jeremy's hand and pressed it to her breast but he pulled it back quickly. "No," he said firmly.

"What do you mean, no?" Violet said, trying to decide if she was about to feel offended, hurt, embarrassed or a mix of them all.

"We can't do this," Jeremy said. She had never met anyone who shook his head so much. "We can't do this."

"Yes, we can Jeremy. It's okay. I want to. I'm here because I chose to be." She was surprised at how calm she sounded. Not a trace of a quiver. If she didn't know any better, she would have convinced herself.

She pressed his hand to her left breast again, harder this time. Forcefully, as if she would not take no for an answer. She reached for his lips, but he pulled away.

"Violet, I can't," he said quietly. "We can't. Not right now. Not like this. I would never forgive myself."

"Jeremy, there's nothing to forgive!" She was exasperated now. "You won't need forgiveness. I am old enough to make these decisions, and I'm fully aware of what I'm doing. It's okay."

Violet wondered then if it was worth it, begging to bed her captor. Embarrassment began to seep in.

Maybe he doesn't want me. Relentlessly, she pressed her body against his and fought to meet his lips with hers. He held on to her tightly, his hands still stationed on her, but he would not kiss her again.

"Violet, no. I won't." She knew he meant it; there was no changing his mind. She felt like she'd been slapped. Here she was, tipsy and young and vibrant, in the bed of a man who would likely never again get next to the likes of her, and he shunned her.

She tried to turn her body away from him. The strength wasn't in her to get out of that bed, but she wanted him to know she'd been stung. He held on tightly and ran his fingers through her hair, reaching around to stroke her cheek. The tears on them met his finger and dissipated.

"Trust me, it has nothing to do with not wanting to," he assured her. "But you've had some wine and you hit your head earlier, and I've never done this before." The three-tiered excuse spewed out of his lips so quickly that Violet only caught a few words. But she heard the last part.

"You've never been with a woman?" she asked quietly and curiously.

"I've never been with anyone," he admitted to her. "That's probably not much of a surprise. And I just... Violet, you're Violet. You deserve someone who knows what they're doing, someone who is confident and self-assured. I'll just stumble around and it'll be uncomfortable for both of us."

Violet was struck with the urge to tell him that she'd teach him, guide his hands in the right direction and tell his fingers when to stop. The thought didn't disgust her. But she didn't do any of it, not then.

Instead, she settled her hips into a neutral position and stopped thrusting them in his direction. She put her hands on his shoulders and turned her body to face him. Never had she been so close.

"Is that a chicken pox scar on your temple?" she asked.

"Oh, that," he fingered the small crater. "Yeah, it is. I have tons of them. We didn't have any calamine lotion. Come to think of it," he cocked his head, "I'm not even sure if my parents knew I had them. I sort of just suffered through it, but I scratched too much."

Violet had started smiling a few words in. "Me too," she said. "I had calamine and everything, but I still scratched. My legs were covered in them, and I clawed at them in the night. Sometimes I didn't even know I was doing it, and I'd wake up with blood under my nails."

She felt the urge to share the little stories she had about her body, to map out her physical history. "You see this?" she asked, pointing to the top of her left arm, above her armpit. He nodded.

"It's my butterfly birthmark. Can you see the butterfly? When I was young, it was really dark. It's faded now, but you can see it if you try."

It was a stretch. He saw two bars of colour on her arm but couldn't make out the butterfly. He nodded again. He could pretend to see it for her sake.

"And this one too," she said, pointing to the big toe on her right foot. "See that scar? Ben and I were playing hide-and-seek or tag or something and I was chasing him. He hid in the bathroom but I was right behind him and he slammed the door on my toe. Sliced it right open. I had to get five stitches."

"Ouch," Jeremy said, reaching to touch the scar. Violet flinched but recovered quickly.

"The funny part is, I don't remember it hurting. I know my brother started to cry when he saw the blood because he felt bad. My mom sat with me while they stitched it up and she went white, but I remember thinking it was more exciting than anything else."

When Jeremy allowed himself to close his eyes, he felt dizzy and intoxicated. He felt like he could breathe in the scent of her hair for hours and wondered how long it was acceptable for him to just lie there, stroking her back. She leaned in to him and he felt her body fully relax against his. Her breathing slowed. He didn't have long before she would be asleep and oblivious to his attempts to make her feel good in his arms.

"Hey Violet?" he asked quietly.

"Mmm?" she mumbled.

"Can I kiss you goodnight?"

She didn't answer him out loud, simply turned and kissed him, full on the mouth. It was wonderful. Her lips were like cushions and tasted of mint. He would let her fall asleep now and would lie there holding her tired body until he fell asleep himself. It wasn't long before he submitted to a deep, easy slumber.

The hours passed quickly. Both Violet and Jeremy woke up a couple of times. They each looked at the clock, at one another, then closed their eyes and let sleep take them again. Every time Jeremy awoke, he was shocked to find the beautiful young woman still in his arms. He fell back asleep with a smile on his face and his arms still around her. He had no feeling in one of them, but the other felt good enough to assure himself he could pump enough blood back in there in the morning, on any other day he didn't have Violet in his bed.

When Violet awoke in the night, she did so with a start. Panic kicked in. Where am I? What's going on? She looked over at Jeremy and remembered right away. His arms had stayed around her all night and she settled back down into them gently.

Things hadn't gone as she'd planned, but perhaps she had overestimated the amount she would need to give Jeremy to win his heart. Maybe he just needed someone to hold.

Both wondered what would happen in the morning. Who would speak first, who would put their feet on the ground before the other. Would there be breakfast in bed, should she sneak back into her room before Ben awoke, would Ben even notice? Neither had any idea what the morning would look like, but both kept re-shutting their eyes and falling back asleep, willing to wait and see.

Finally, the sun began to stream in too brightly for them to ignore. Violet's eyes were open and her body was alert. She considered how she could get up without disturbing Jeremy's sleep. When she looked over, she saw his open eyes looking right back at her.

"Oh!" she said startled. "You're awake!"

He just nodded and kissed her hair.

"Violet," he said, his voice hoarse with sleep, "I know that once you get out of this bed, this will never happen again. But it was so nice to have you here. Thank you for spending the night with me. You have no idea how much it meant."

289

His breath slunk into her ear, hot and humid, triggering a nerve deep in her lower back and making her spasm with intensity.

Jeremy was convinced their night had only happened because of the wine and the concussion. Violet wondered if he would let it happen again. For now, she decided to let it rest.

"So I'll just sneak out of here, back into my room, before Ben notices?" she asked quietly.

"Yeah," he agreed. "I think that's the best idea. And if you stay in there for awhile, I'll bring you breakfast in bed."

She smiled. Perhaps he's in love with me already, she thought.

"And things will go back to normal?" Violet asked innocently. She wasn't sure how she wanted him to answer. Mostly she hoped he would say no, that things had changed and would never go back to the way they were. He didn't say that.

"Yes, back to normal," he said with a stiff jerk of his head that she took to be an exaggerated nod.

She crawled out of bed, still fully clothed. She couldn't recall ever having had such a good night's sleep dressed in jeans and a sweater. She had forgotten the clothing was there at all, hadn't felt any need to remove it all night. Maybe there was comfort in covering something. She had tried to lay herself bare before him but that wasn't what he needed. Maybe he was too worried he would need to strip down too.

"Okay," she said as she got to the door. "Well, see you in a bit then." It sounded phony coming out of her mouth. There was no way things could be the same. It was bound to become strange. It had to, didn't it?

When Violet turned the doorknob and pulled it inwards, she gasped when she saw two brown eyes waiting right outside the door.

"Jesus, Ben!" she breathed. "You scared me. What are you doing?"

"I heard you guys talking," he shrugged, "I wanted to see what was going on."

Violet's heart jumped in her chest. She had no idea how long he had been hovering outside that door, and she certainly wasn't able to ask. Thank god she was fully dressed.

"Oh, right," she said in her best attempt at an everyday, normal tone of voice. "We had a bet last night that whoever went to bed first would have to make breakfast in the morning. He fell asleep first, so I was just reminding him that he owed me breakfast in bed." The lie came easily.

Ben seemed satisfied. He wasn't even jealous; he didn't like breakfast in bed anyhow. He went one way and she went the other, back to her bed not slept-in. She wondered how much Ben noticed, what he took in. Would he notice the change in them? As if the pressure had dropped in the room or there was a silent stranger sitting in the corner that they guarded their words around. It had to be evident. It would definitely be noticeable. She decided to get to work at coming up with an excuse. Easiest would be to tell Ben she hated Jeremy, and that she was just angry because she wanted to go home. The effort of carrying out the lie was unappealing.

Violet closed her door behind her and pushed her weight against it. She slumped to the floor and wrapped her arms around her buckled legs. She was forced to remind herself the purpose of her plan. Perhaps she could ask Jeremy later that day if they could go home, and he'd be too vulnerable to say no, too desperate to please her. She wasn't confident enough to try yet. It would take a little more time, which was all she had. Grain upon grain of it; time she could hold in her hands and spend as she pleased, but not really. It slipped through her fingers bit by gritty bit. It made her sick, that her time was so dispensable.

If I went home tomorrow, she told herself, I would be in the same spot I was a year ago. I would have to get a job, work myself crazy, save money, apply for programs I haven't chosen yet.

If she went home tomorrow, there would be no more late night campfires. No unexpected gifts. No lazy Sundays, or weeks, lazy months. No gardening, no fresh air. More stress. Less time for herself. More responsibility, more guilt, more questions. The guilt might be the hardest part. How was she going to explain to the world that she had stayed with this man for so long? Why she hadn't found a way out sooner? How she could let her little brother spend so much of his childhood in a place like this? Why hadn't she fought harder? She could imagine the skepticism, the judgment, the heavily lidded eyes staring at her in accusation. She would be made the villain, just as much as Jeremy.

292

Could she go home? It wasn't a question she had ever thought to ask before, because of course she could. As soon as they escaped, they could head right back home and life would continue as normal. But so much time had passed that she knew it wouldn't be that easy, could not be. A part of her might never be able to forgive her mother for not finding them. A part of her mother might never forgive her for being away for so long. What would become of Jeremy? She would turn him in. She would have to turn him in. It was the only logical solution.

A knock behind her jolted Violet's head and attention. She shimmied away from the door, pulled herself up and opened it. Jeremy stood there, tray in hand, steam rising from everything fresh and hot he had prepared for her. Eggs, toast, tea, and a bowl of yogurt.

"This is all for me?" she asked, although she knew it was. She walked over to her bed, propped her pillow and leaned against it.

"All for you," he repeated as he set the tray in her lap. "Take your time, I'm making some for Ben too, don't worry."

"He was in the hall," she reminded him.

"I know," he said. "It sounded like he wasn't too concerned though. Do you think?"

"Oh, definitely not," Violet agreed. "He's fine." She made a mental note to sit down and talk with Ben just in case.

Jeremy was already retreating toward the door. She could tell he wasn't comfortable in her space; the space that had become hers. He would never have laid his head on her bed. As he left, she puzzled over his reluctance to get into bed with her. How could a man morally depraved enough to kidnap someone be incapable of intimacy with them? She knew it was gruesome, but shouldn't that have been part of the plan? Why would he have chosen her; young, relatively fair, a waitress – a role that, by definition, involves submissiveness. Why her if he hadn't meant to touch her? It made no sense. Perhaps Ben being along for the ride had changed things. She couldn't decipher his moral code. She would just have to keep trying.

That night, Violet sat up in bed waiting. When all the lights had gone out and Ben was snug in his bed, Violet crept out of her room, gently eased open her old wooden door to avoid the creak, and tiptoed down the hall to Jeremy's room.

Knock, knock. There was no sound from within. She tried again. Knock, knock, knock. A little louder this time. Still nothing. Violet rested her hand on the doorknob and wondered if she could just walk in. She held her breath and told herself that on the count of five, she would open it.

One, two, three, four, five. She didn't open it. She tried again. And then she did.

"Jeremy?" she whispered into the darkness. "Are you awake?" It was fairly obvious he was not. Taking small steps forward, she relied on memory to lead her to his bed. Her eyes hadn't adjusted to the dark after sitting in her light-flooded room. She stubbed her toe on the leg of the bed, and stifled a whimper. A rustling of sheets before her said that at least he was there.

"Jeremy." She said it louder this time. She didn't want to startle him; he might shout and wake Ben. A figure hovering over his sleeping body – does that sort of thing scare men the way it does women? She wasn't sure.

Peeling the covers back from the lonely side of the bed, Violet slid her body underneath and next to Jeremy's. He radiated heat. He'd been asleep for some time; Ben had lasted longer than them with something on television.

His back was to her, curled up in a ball facing the empty air. She reached out and rubbed his back. He groaned in an innocent way and leaned his body toward her, still sleeping. It amazed her the way human bodies respond to touch even in the deepest of slumbers. Violet burrowed herself against him and nudged her knees into the back of his. The movement of her shorter body left her head midway down his back, but she pressed her lips to his spine and instantly felt the warmth of his body transferred onto her mouth.

A sharp intake of breath followed by a jerk and a hand reaching back toward her indicated Jeremy was awake.

"It's okay," she soothed, "It's just me."

He breathed out. "Violet? What are you doing here?"

He hadn't invited her, after all. She had snuck into his room and his bed without asking permission. What if he had done the same?

"I couldn't sleep," she said, which was partly true. She hadn't allowed herself to, waiting to sleep next to him instead.

Jeremy turned to face her, suddenly alert. "Violet?"

"Yes?" She feared he was about to ask her to leave but it was the opposite.

"Do you like living here?" he asked.

She paused, not sure what he was asking. "Yes, I do." What else was she to say while lying next to him?

"What do you like about it?" he pressed.

"Oh, okay," she said, not sure how she felt about listing reasons why she didn't mind being held captive. What alarmed her was the quick list that sprung forth in her mind. "Well," she continued, "I like waking up when my body tells me to. It's been months since I've set an alarm for anything, and that's really nice."

She hoped that would satisfy him but he asked for more.

"What else?"

"Hmm. I never minded my job because I liked the people and bringing in money … But it's not the worst thing in the world to not go to work every day."

He didn't ask her to continue, but his silence did the job. She should've stopped there, but she didn't.

"I like getting to spend so much time with Ben. I like being able to put off real life for a while and not think about the decisions waiting for me at home. I like not having to live up to my mother's expectations." She didn't need to be so honest. He was probably only looking for one thing, true or false, and it was the thing she said next.

"And I like getting to know you," she said. After the words were over, she sucked in her cheeks and lay there, dead silent, waiting.

"I really like that as well." He bought it. It had been a pretty good sell. "Do you ever wish you were back home?" he asked.

"Yes," she said firmly. "I do miss sleeping in my own bed. I miss my mom. I miss my friends, and the regulars at the diner. I miss being able to go wherever I want whenever I want to. I miss going out for dinner. The movies. The gas station, even."

Experiences she never knew she'd enjoyed were now absently ached for. The mundane adventures; the everyday safaris.

"Yeah," Jeremy said after a moment. "I guess you would."

She hated him again, then. She wanted to get out of his bed and run to her room, slamming the door behind her. She didn't, though. Didn't move at all.

Facing her, Jeremy said what he'd been dying to for weeks. "Violet, what if I asked you to stay here with me?"

"What do you mean? I am here with you. Ben and I both."

"No, I know," he said sheepishly. "But I've been forcing you to stay. Do you think there's a way you could ever choose to stay with me? To live with me?"

"Jeremy, no," she said quickly. "I couldn't. I can't just be cut off from the rest of the world for the rest of my life. That's cruel."

"I know," he said again, "but you wouldn't have to be. If you chose to live here with me, then I wouldn't have to force you to stay. You could leave whenever you wanted, just as long as you always came back."

Violet couldn't believe her ears. It was perfect. Her fingers gripped her wrist, where that dreadful bracelet had been dangling for months. Mostly, she could ignore it. Pretend it was part of her outfit. But sometimes she was struck with such an urge to rip it off her arm. How dare he strap something to her body like a brand, a searing hot shackle to mark her as his. If that bracelet was removed from her wrist, Jeremy wouldn't be able to track her any longer. She could drop off the grid, get as far away as she could, and never come back.

"Yes," she said quickly, before he could rephrase his offer, take bits of it away. "Yes, I would do that."

Jeremy mistook her firmness as fact. It sounded to him as if she had thought about it already, on her own, long and hard, and had come to the conclusion that she wanted to stay with him forever. How could he be so lucky?

"You would?" he asked excitedly. "You would stay here, of your own free will?"

"I would," she lied. "I would stay here with you."

Neither of them mentioned Ben, whether they should ask him as well, whether he would get to go home or be forced to stay. Violet didn't want to get Jeremy thinking about the details, and Jeremy didn't want to say anything that might make Violet change her mind.

"This is amazing," he whispered.

"When would this happen?" Violet asked.

Jeremy wanted it to start right then, that very moment, but knew he should do it bit by bit. "In a week," he said. "One week, and it'll all be over."

Violet felt freedom rise to her throat like bile.

28

She went to his bed every night after. Crept in when the lights were off and stayed until the sun started to crawl up the walls. The same routine; she would curl up against him and kiss the middle of his back, slither down to get the small of it on her lips. It became easy, but she had no idea what would happen if Jeremy decided he wanted more than just warmth.

On those nights, Violet closed her eyes and pretended she was next to someone who kept her safe every night and held her hand every day. Jeremy was the only man besides Ben she had ever lived with, and she found herself playing the childhood game of House, except in a real one, with a real man. With eyes closed against the moonlight, he could be anyone. He was warm, he held her tightly and he smelled like comfort. The rest, she could block out. The gangly limbs, the freckles and wild hair, the nervous tic that crept into his speech sometimes, not allowing him to say what he wanted on his first attempt. Those things could be erased in the night.

At the end of that week, though, on the last night that she knew conclusively she would be under the same roof, under the same sheets, as Jeremy, she allowed it to be Jeremy. She allowed all of the things she had discovered about him to stay in bed with them. Running her fingers through his hair, she remembered how the sun made it look aflame. As she traced her fingers over his lips, she saw them moving slowly, trying to get the words out.

Against her will, or maybe with it, her hips began to press themselves against Jeremy's stock-still body. It felt natural and intimate. Her hips had remained still next to him for far too long. Would he really not respond to her touch?

He stiffened. He didn't relax or wrap his arms more tightly around her, but she knew he had noticed and was trying not to. Her hands traced a line from his jaw to his chest.

"Jeremy?" she whispered.

"Violet?" he responded.

"We can. I want to," she said.

"You do?" Incredulously, as if she couldn't know what she wanted, and if she did, it couldn't be him. By all rights, it shouldn't have been him. But he was the one who had been next to her for months on end.

"I do," she said firmly. She didn't want to argue or convince. No more words needed to be spoken, and she hoped he realized it.

He didn't. "I just don't want to make you do anything you don't want to do," he protested.

"I know," was all she said in reply. Then she kissed him, and kept kissing him more deeply whenever he tried to mutter anything else.

He started moving with her, his hips arching in time with hers. She rested her thumbs on the elastic of his underwear and pulled them down. She wanted no time to second-guess herself.

Jeremy's body moved perfectly with hers. Violet's mouth clamped shut in attempts to stop from moaning from pleasure and shame. He touched her gently, he went slowly, he didn't race her through the process. There was sweat, there was fire, there were moments when Violet thought her body might burst.

Violet didn't close her eyes. She looked right at him. He looked right back. Eyes that big couldn't be bad, could they? All she saw was desire and adoration. There was no evil in them. In that moment, she could think of no good reason why she should not be in that bed.

When it was over, Jeremy took deep breaths and looked at Violet nervously, worry etched all over his face. She only nodded. She didn't want to say anything more, too busy focusing on her body humming. She hadn't come but was close; she could have gotten there but he was out of her too quickly. Jeremy read her mind, or seemed to.

"Can I touch you?" he asked.

"Yes." There was no reason for her to say no, not after they'd come so far. She guided his fingers and rose above him, on the precipice she had been dangling near. It didn't take long before she fell off the edge. Her body convulsed and released.

"Oh, god," Violet said out loud, unable to help it.

"Was that okay?" he asked with genuine curiosity. Violet could hear its depths.

She nodded and found herself searching for reasons to go back to her room. There were a few, but not enough to deter her from the warm body next to her, sticky with her sweat and his.

"Jeremy?"

Nothing.

"Tomorrow is the day," she pressed.

"I know," he said after an uncomfortable moment. "I know it is."

He had been thinking about it constantly. Hadn't been able to get it off his mind. Two things could happen if he released her. She could disappear, leave with Ben and be out of his life forever.

But. There was another option, a hope that clung to life in the back of his mind, silently pulsing in the background. The other option was that she would stay. He couldn't convince her; there were too many months of her life he had already decided for her. Now, it was back in her hands. He thought about what it would feel like, to see her come back up the driveway after he let her go. His own beautiful boomerang.

He would love her. Everyday, he would tell her so. Fresh flowers would be always on their table, and he would have picked them for her. He would remember all of the important days. They could create their own family. Ben could grow up there. Soon enough, his little Jeep would be replaced with a big one. Images flashed before him like a premonition.

Stop, he told himself. Sleep. There was nothing else he could say to convince her to stay. Her mind had to be made up by now. It was out of his hands.

That's when he fell asleep next to Violet, pressed against her side in a way that was increasingly familiar. She was already sleeping, the steady rise and fall of her chest giving it all away.

When he opened his eyes in the morning, Violet was already staring at him.

"So what's going to happen?" she said, propped up on the arm behind her pillow.

"I'm going to let you go," he said, too simply.

"I know that." She sounded impatient. "But what will that mean?" She held up her wrist with a questioning look.

He nodded. "I'll take the bracelet off. I'll deactivate the fence so you can come and go whenever you please. The cameras, all of it, it'll be gone. This will be a normal house. And we can go grocery shopping and to the movies and out for ice cream." He knew he sounded like he was pleading. It didn't bother him, because he was.

"And Ben?"

"His bracelet will be gone too," he reassured her. "You're both free to do whatever you please."

Jeremy wanted to keep talking, as if his words would wear down some resistance inside of her. He had one last weapon, a morsel he could feed her that might change her mind about him forever.

"Violet?" he began. "If we've decided that you're now a free agent, then there are some things I should tell you."

Her face looked puzzled. Not worried, but curious.

Jeremy took a deep breath. "I don't actually have to cut off your bracelet. Or remove the cameras."

Violet started shaking her head before he could continue. "No," she interrupted. "No. They're going. We agreed." Her voice began to rise and he held his hand out to calm her.

"I know, I know that was the deal," he said. "But the thing is that you can still leave the property with those bracelets on. They're made of magnets and rubber."

"I don't understand," Violet said slowly.

"Violet, they were never tracking devices. I was never keeping tabs on where you were. I just needed you to think I was so you wouldn't leave."

His words were met with silence. Her eyes shifted from him to her wrist. She started to rub at it, slowly, massaging it. Quickly, her hands became vicious. They grabbed and tried to rip it off her wrist.

"No," she said again. "That can't be right. I wore this fucking thing every day, every night." A battle between confusion and anger began inside her.

"I'm sorry," he said, "I know it was wrong, but I didn't know how else to keep you here. I needed us to be together."

"So you gave me a fake bracelet and forced me to wear it like a dog, so I would know I was yours? No," she said. She couldn't stop. Jumping off the bed, she stormed to her bedroom. Her stomach was turning and she thought she might be sick. First, she needed to check something.

Pushing her door open, she looked up at the camera watching over her bed. The camera she had posed for, time after time. The camera she had dreaded and desired and feared and fucked. For months. She climbed on top of her shelf to reach it. She grabbed. Pulled, ripped with all her might. When that didn't work, she wriggled it until it came loose.

The stucco crumbled and the device came off in her hands. She hopped down and stared at it closely. There were no wires. No cords at all. The red dot that had been perpetually on, the one that told her Jeremy was watching, that red dot was not part of the camera. Using her nails, she chipped off the black paint and saw the tape underneath. Just a red light. A battery-operated red light that signified nothing. The camera wasn't recording her and never had been.

Violet started to shake. With rage, with embarrassment, with rejection. How dare he, she thought. Jeremy had no idea what it felt like to be a prisoner in a house and a bedroom you were trying desperately to make your own, just to survive. Every night she had spent in there, that fucking red light had stared her down, making her feel like the victim sometimes and the villain others. Judging the movements she made and the ones she couldn't.

And it was all a lie.

"No," she moaned. Tears streamed down her cheeks. The fence was what she thought of next. The electric fence that would buzz them if they crossed the line, like cattle in the field waiting to be slaughtered. She had to find out if that, too, was a lie.

Slamming her door as hard as she could, she walked down the hall and saw Jeremy standing next to his bedroom door. She wouldn't look at him. He didn't dare try to stop her; he couldn't even move.

When she got outside, Violet gasped in the early morning air. It felt cool and crisp in her lungs. She realized she'd been forgetting to breathe. Depriving herself of something basic that she needed to survive, as Jeremy had been doing to her for months. Left leg, right leg, she felt the need to look down at her limbs and engineer their stride. She couldn't get them to move at the right speed, to step forward at the right angle. The world was about to knock her over, or her knees were about to give out. Either way, she felt she would soon be on the ground. She followed the gravel driveway that wound its way down the property. The last time she'd been on that road was the day she'd driven them there. She hadn't tried to escape, not even once. Too much could have harmed her if she did.

Running seemed out of the question, but she pushed for it. Left leg and right leg began to move faster, almost in rhythm. Her breathing matched her pace. She needed to be on the edge of it all, to see the boundaries that Jeremy had carved for them so long ago. It took time to get to the end of the drive. Her frenzied mind began to convince herself there was no way out; that they had been locked away so long that the rest of the world didn't exist anymore. She imagined rounding a bend and seeing the very house she was running away from.

Because she was running away from that house. It was something she had never done before. It felt strange and scary and her lungs were burning, but she couldn't stop. She sobbed but it caught in her throat, sounding stunted and shallow like a child gasping between cries.

And there it was. She saw the end. How had she not wanted to come back down there? Why hadn't she sat, cross-legged, every day waiting for someone to drive by? Why hadn't she?

Her run down the driveway felt like a punishment, a kick to her body for every time she hadn't tried to escape. Her SOS sign that she so long ago had begun still lay unfinished and stagnant in the yard. Her fear that Jeremy would find it had been too great; he would realize she'd been spending too much time in one spot. He would have found it. Except that he wouldn't have. He'd never known where she was, there had never been a red dot mapping her strides over the property.

The road. Looking back and forth, she searched for the fence, and it was there. She did see it; there was a fence. It was wooden and traced the outside of the property. From her walks and explorations, she'd seen it; she knew it existed. But she had stayed far away, just in case.

Now, she stood before it, panting and crying. A minute passed. She was frozen in fear. It had been so long since she'd crossed that line. What would happen to her if she did? What would happen if she didn't?

Her legs found a way to move forward. Her toes lingered just behind the fence line, but she took a deep breath and hopped over it. Bracing herself for a jolt through her body, Violet's eyes hid underneath her eyelids. She waited.

There was nothing. Opening her eyes, she found herself faced with a road going in two directions, both of them away from here. No scrapes or bruises or aches were on her body. Turning around slowly, she looked back from where she had come. That's how simple it had been. She had put one foot in front of the other, and she had crossed that deadly boundary. That arbitrary boundary. Counterfeit. Make-believe.

Her knees gave out then. They couldn't hold her any longer. She sunk to the ground and landed in the gravel. It should have stung, but it didn't. Still, no feeling sunk into her body, only a void. On her knees wasn't low enough. Falling forward, both elbows struck the ground. Her head went down with them. Over and over, she slammed her forehead into the gravel. Little bits of rock lodged themselves into her forehead and then fell out, leaving small dents behind. Some were sharp and stuck.

Animal cries escaped her. Her throat opened and sounds from the deepest parts of her emerged. Sobs she hadn't let out for fear of Ben hearing, or Jeremy.

She had been shackled to this place, but not by anything from this earth. It hadn't been chains that kept her there. There were no locks, but without locks, there were no keys. How was she ever to escape if she couldn't find the key that would set her free? Where was her release?

Violet lay on the ground, face down. She couldn't think of moving, of what would happen next. What she was to do, what she would tell Ben. When she returned to the real world, would she tell everyone? Jeremy hadn't kept them there. She had kept them there, in fear of things that didn't exist.

What would everyone say? The newspapers, the police reports? When she was questioned, what could she tell them?

"Did he tie you up?"

"No."

"Ever?"

"Just when we first arrived."

"Did he lock you up?"

"Yes. At first."

"For how long?"

"A couple of weeks."

"And then, he unlocked you?"

"Yes."

"So what was stopping you from leaving?"

"Fake cameras, rubber bracelets and phony fences."

They would judge her. That poor little brother who didn't know any better while she refused to find a way to get him home. People would pass her in the street and furrow their brows, shake their heads with distain.

Maybe they would have her committed. They might try to test her sanity. It would be easier for everyone to believe if they thought she was crazy. It would excuse the many months she had stayed, passive and weak. It would be her fault, all hers, because Ben was too young to know better and Jeremy stopped restraining them long ago. He'd never even hurt them, never raised a hand to strike.

I could say he raped me, she thought miserably. I could say he forced me to sleep with him and that if I didn't he would hurt me. And Ben. And my family. Poor little Violet, the sex slave.

But how could she stand up in front of someone, in front of the whole world, and tell them Jeremy had violated Violet? He had been gentle and loving and kind. He hadn't hurt her in any physical way. In fact, he had hurt her less than many people in her life had. To think about telling the world otherwise made her nauseous. She realized that for the world not to hate her, she would have to hate him. She would have to summon up that old hatred and feast on it, force it on anyone who would listen. It was still in there somewhere; it festered and bubbled up from time to time. There had been no way to put out that fire completely, but it was a weak flame that flickered smaller and smaller each day. She'd have to feed it, the whole world would need to feed that flame.

Summoning an inner strength she wasn't sure she had, Violet pulled herself up from the dirt. She straightened her knees, tentatively put some pressure on them, and sighed with relief when they held. There were a million directions she could have taken but the one she took as she turned and walked up that long, winding driveway was the only one that led her back to Jeremy.

<u>29</u>

Vi stormed into my room without knocking, or without even saying, "Knock, knock." I knew that meant that something was wrong.

I'll never forget the words she said to me next, how red her cheeks were when she said them, her hands holding both sides of her head and her hair.

"Ben, what do you say we go home?"

At first I wasn't sure what she meant. We were home. Homes change, they come and go, I know this. I wasn't sure which home she meant, especially since home wasn't something we talked about a lot. Or at all.

I didn't know what to say back to her. I needed more information. I asked her what she meant.

"Home, Ben. Home, to mom. Back to life, back to school, away from this place. Back to where we came from."

A weird little part of me wanted to argue. Where I came from was a different place than where Vi had come from, and both of those places were different than where our mom lived. So we wouldn't be going back to where we came from, not really.

"How?" She'd never mentioned anything like this before. We were always waiting, being silent and good so that Jeremy would learn to like us and let us go, that's what Vi always said to me. I'd stopped even thinking about it. There were a couple of nights when I stayed up late in my bed and put my thumb in my mouth and thought about what it would feel like for my mom to walk into the room and rub my back as I fell asleep. That would've felt really good. But Jeremy wasn't so awful. Really, I can think of tons of worse people who could have taken us. There are a million things he could've done to make this a worse prison. But I have a Jeep that I get to drive around like a grownup and I get dessert every night after dinner. This isn't the worst home I've been in.

Vi started speaking really quick. The words were sloppy and slurred.

"Jeremy can't keep us here anymore. You know our bracelets, the ones he told us would let him watch us wherever we went? They're fake. They're fake Ben, they're nothing. Made of rubber."

She looked so angry, and she kept pulling at her wrist. Next, she went to the corner of my room where the camera was. Really, I don't mind it that much. I don't do anything too weird in here, and Jeremy can see me when I'm outside of my room so I guess it's okay that he wants to see me when I'm in my room, too. But Vi hopped up on a chair and grabbed at the camera. My mouth fell open really wide. We'd never done this. Jeremy would be mad, wouldn't he? Those cameras cost a lot of money, I bet.

"They're not real, Ben! All of it, all of it was a lie! This isn't a camera that records us. It's not hooked up to anything. And the fence, there's no electric fence Ben. It's just a regular, everyday, ordinary fence."

How could they not be real? Jeremy had to keep us here, and he had to have all of those things so we would stay in one spot. I knew the fence was real, I'd seen it. And I'd never gone past it so I was still okay.

"How do you know, Vi?" Maybe she had it wrong.

"He told me. It's time for us to go home, Ben. Jeremy promised me that he would let us go and now he's going to do it. Only, here's the thing." She squatted down on her knee. "Jeremy thinks we want to stay here. I told him, well, I let him believe that if he let us go and stopped keeping us here by force, then we would always come back. But when we leave here, we're not coming back. We have to

312

make him think that we are, but we're not. Otherwise, he won't let us out. He'll put us back in the basement."

Too much stuff ran around in my head. How could all of this be happening so fast when it had been months since this had even come up? I hadn't asked questions in so long. I'm not even sure I wanted the answers. Part of me wished Vi would stop talking, walk out my door and leave me alone to play. But I couldn't say that to her.

"How do we do that?" I asked. It sounded like maybe she had a plan and that I wasn't really going to have any choice but to go along with it.

"The first time he lets me leave here, he probably won't let you come with me. He'll probably keep you here, just to make sure I come back. Because I would never leave you." She grabbed my arm and I knew she meant it.

"But when he lets me go," she said, "I'm going to come back, and I'm going to get you, and then we're both going to leave. Forever. We won't ever come back. Do you understand?"

I nodded, but I wasn't sure I did. I couldn't help but ask.

"Why now?"

"Because Ben, we can't keep letting him do this to us. We have to leave here, and he's not going to be the one to drop us off on our driveway."

I searched through my memory for everything I knew about Jeremy and how he had kept us here. Except for the beginning, which was really, really bad, he hadn't done anything mean at all. He'd given me most things I'd asked for, more than my mom ever did, and I sort of liked living here. Deedee and Dodo don't come around much anymore, but I don't want to just abandon them. What happens if I have to leave before I get to say goodbye?

I thought of one more thing then, and it made my tummy hurt a little bit. "What about Jeremy?" I asked her. I knew right away that it was the wrong thing to say.

"What about him?" she said, in a mean way. "He's done enough to us."

Still, I didn't know what she meant. He hadn't done all that much to us, really. Sometimes he would even read me stories at night. When Vi wasn't around, I would call him Jer. He had asked me to, after all. I didn't think Vi would like it though so I kept it hidden, like a secret.

There wasn't anything I could do to change Vi's mind. If this was the plan she had decided on, then it was what we were going to do. I definitely wasn't going to stay here without her.

"Well, when are you going to leave?" I asked. I figured I had a right to know all the details, plus I needed to make sure I had time to pack and say my goodbyes.

"Tonight. I'm going to run to the corner store, wherever the nearest one is, to rent a movie or buy some chips, I don't know. It doesn't matter. Just something small, so that I won't be gone for too long and I can come right back so that Jeremy will think that's what I'll always do. If I can get that over and done with tonight, then tomorrow morning, you and I can leave here for good. We have to trick him. Okay?"

314

Her eyes were so big when she said this. I didn't think I had a choice but to nod my head to tell her this was not okay, but close enough.

She nodded back at me, stood up and started to walk out the door.

"Ben? You can't say a word about this. You need to pretend you don't know a thing about it, like you don't even know I'm leaving here tonight."

"I won't," I said, but it was a lie. I was going to tell Deedee and Dodo, because I had to explain to them why I wouldn't be coming back. But I didn't know if Vi would get that, and besides, I knew she was really talking about Jeremy.

Vi left my room then, and I heard her walk down the hall to Jer's bedroom. She shut the door behind her. Mom never let her have boys in her room.

I went downstairs. I tried to start looking closely at everything, because who knew how many more times I was going to see it.

Outside, it was a sunny day. It would be sort of nice to spend the summer here, with all the flowers and the space to run around. I tried not to cry.

I looked for Deedee and Dodo. I really needed them. I tried whispering for them at first, but that didn't work. They lived deep enough in the forest that they definitely wouldn't hear whispering. I tried shouting, over and over. I kept yelling. I stopped caring if Jer or Vi heard me.

Deedee and Dodo never came out. They ignored me, or they'd gone off someplace else, to some other little boy who needed them.

I never saw them again.

30

Violet clenched and unclenched her fists as she left Ben's room to head back to Jeremy. He knew she was upset. The key would be to convince him somehow that she wasn't anymore, that she understood why he had lied. She wanted to make sure their agreement still stood, and that she would be allowed to leave as planned. As long as she came back.

Knocking on his bedroom door, Violet peeked in and saw Jeremy standing in the corner, facing the door in wait for her return.

"Hi," she said softly. Her breaths were short and shallow, and she had to focus on inhaling and exhaling so that her heart would slow, so that her words might come out less shakily.

He replied with an equally quiet, "Hi, Violet."

"I went to the fence," she admitted, because it was obvious that she had. "I went past it. I wasn't even sure if I believed that it wasn't real. I kept bracing for the shock." She harnessed herself; the details weren't necessary.

"I'm sorry," Jeremy said again, as he always seemed to.

"It's okay," Violet said, trying her hardest to sound convincing. "I mean, there were a lot of lies, for a long time. But I understand why you did it." The words were thick on her tongue.

"You do?" he asked. He didn't sound at all sure that she did.

"I do," Violet reassured him. "I get why you needed safeguards to keep us here. We needed to think we were being forced to stay so we wouldn't leave. I didn't think I was going to admit this," and she didn't, "but I used to look into that camera and do things I thought you would see. I tried to send you messages so you'd know how I was feeling." Her hands unconsciously rose to the necklace around her throat.

"It used to make me sad and frustrated that you didn't seem to notice, so at least now I know why."

Jeremy wanted to ask what she had done in front of the camera, what she had wanted him to know. But he didn't. He knew he had no right.

"I put those in there because I needed you to think I had control over you. I needed you to stay."

Violet's heart felt heavy, and her stomach as if it had been gutted. Before that day, awareness had been slowly slinking through the deepest folds of her brain, but she had always pushed the feeling away. The knowledge would have sunk in on its own, eventually. She hadn't needed him to tell her. But hearing him say the words out loud, knowing that there had been no chains around herself or Ben at any point made her feel useless, stupid, tricked. She felt robbed. He had stolen her ability to realize she could leave. She wanted to scream at herself for not seeing that she'd always had the option to.

Looking back, Violet realized she should have known all along. She should have realized it was an illusion. But that's the thing about hindsight.

Summoning up every last bit of gumption she had hidden inside, scraping up the last residual layer of revolution, she threw her shoulders back. She would not let him know what was going on in her head. Never again.

"I know that now. But Jeremy, you don't need restraints to keep us here. You don't need to use force or threats. This is home to us now. This is it. We could leave now, but where would we go?"

It had to be obvious she was lying, didn't it? She was sure he wouldn't buy it. She regretted her words instantly, but he didn't question them. He bought them, invested in them. The muscles in his face seemed to relax; his eyes became softer. Violet could see it.

"So this is where we want to stay," she continued to lie. "But now that I know there aren't any chains holding me here, I really want to leave for a moment. I just want to get in my car and go for a drive and remember what it feels like to be able to choose to stay or go."

He looked so sad, then. "How do I know you'll come back?"

"Because," she said confidently, as she was about to tell the truth. "I promise that I will come back. You have my word. And I know there's no way to prove that to you until you let me leave. But I can't come back if you don't let me go."

"Where?" he asked. Jeremy had visions of her travelling the country, driving further north to find herself in the cold territories above, returning months later to tell him about a world he had never seen.

"To the corner store," she said simply. "Just out and about, so I can buy something, see people, say hello to someone."

"Oh," he said, relief registering on his face clear as a billboard. "The thing is... You have to be careful about where you go and who you see. I don't know if

318

it's the best idea if people know you're living here with me. There would be a lot of questions. I wouldn't want anyone to take you away."

She wondered if he could sense the irony of his words. Somehow, she convinced a smile to play on her lips. "I know that, Jeremy. I don't want to mess this up for us. I'll pretend to be someone else, and I won't tell anyone where I'm going or where I've come from. Don't worry about that. To be honest, I just want to go and buy a treat. Do you need anything?" Violet joked. "Because I could pick it up for you."

"Oh. So you want to go soon, then?" Jeremy asked innocently.

"Yes, I do," she said. "So much has changed and I just, I really want a moment to myself. But I won't be gone long. I'll be back before you even know I left."

Of course he would notice she had gone. Her absence would weigh on the house like a plague. The air would feel denser, more difficult to breathe, less colourful without her inhaling it. But he needed to come to terms with the way their situation had changed.

"Okay," he said. "I'll give you your car keys back. I trust you." He looked right at her, and Violet was surprised at how uncomfortable it made her. She shouldn't feel guilty about what she was about to do to him.

The date was June 2. Almost a year had passed since she had last seen her car keys. Jeremy reached into the drawer beside his bed. The very drawer Violet had been sleeping next to for the past few weeks. She didn't want to know what sort of things he kept in his bedside table, but cursed herself for not thinking to check there for the keys. She'd never really looked at all.

Would someone who truly wanted to leave, she wondered, who was genuinely attempting to plan an escape, forget to think about how to get their car back? Later, she told herself. Worry about that later.

Jeremy dropped the keys into her hand gently; more accurately, he lowered them. Violet spotted her house key.

How simple it would be to get in the car and drive to her mom's house, to unlock the door, walk in and announce she was home. She knew she couldn't though, not without Ben. Her mom would never let her leave to come back and get him. And she couldn't risk that.

"Thank you," Violet said, hoping he heard the sincerity behind her words. "This means a lot to me."

"You know where your car is, right?"

She shook her head. He had mentioned once that it was in the barn, but she'd never gone looking for it. Another stab of guilt.

"It's in the barn," he repeated simply. Not hidden, not buried or sunk. Just sitting inside a barn. "The big one, towards the back. Not the mouse house, the bigger one."

She knew where, and nodded her head to let him know. How had she never peeked in there before?

"Do you think it'll run after sitting for so long?" she asked. Almost a year is a long time for a car to sit abandoned, especially through a Canadian winter.

"It should be fine," he said. "I checked on it every now and again and there were never any problems."

"Okay," she said, incredulous that even Jeremy had thought to check on her car and she hadn't. "Where's the closest convenience store?"

Looking around, Jeremy found a paper and pencil and began to draw her a map, a grid surrounding the prison whose gates were about to open. Violet wished he would write instructions instead. Her mind never mapped out anything; her brain didn't reconstruct lines to remember where streets met and led. Directions were simpler, like a recipe to follow.

When he finished, he handed her the napkin he had tattooed. "It's just called Bob's Corner Store. There's not much in there, but I'm sure you'll find something."

"And how long will it take me to get there?"

"Maybe ten minutes?" he guessed. "Fifteen?"

No wonder no one had found them, fifteen minutes from the nearest vendor called Bob's Corner Store.

"Okay," she said, trying to sound accountable. "So if I drive right there and back, it should take me about half an hour. Give or take five minutes in the store, I'll be back within 45 minutes. Does that sound reasonable?"

She hated that she was asking him, as if was any of his business how long it would take her to drive her own car to the store. But Jeremy seemed to like it very much, as Violet had planned.

321

"That sounds very reasonable," he said. "Ben and I will be waiting for you when you get back."

Reaching deeper into the drawer, he pulled out her wallet.

"Just don't use your credit card, okay?" She nodded.

Violet fought the urge to jump to the next part of her plan. Oh, and by the way, maybe I could take Ben for a drive tomorrow. I think he'd really like that. But she would wait until she got back, within 45 minutes, as promised.

Instead, she held up the keys. "Let's see if I still know how to drive!" she joked.

Walking out to the barn, she opened the large door that concealed her car. There you are, she telepathically communicated when she finally saw it.

The engine ran just fine, and as natural as if she had been driving every day for the last ten months, Violet began her way down the driveway. Her stomach turned at the memory of the last time she had been in this car. Excitement should have washed over her entire body, but she was leaving Ben behind, and she would be right back where she started within the hour. Not much had changed, not yet.

Jeremy's map was markedly accurate. His lines looked as if he'd used a ruler, all drawn to scale. Wide-eyed, Violet crept along the road, remembering the feel of the brakes and taking in the world around her.

Bob's Corner Store soon loomed before her. Getting out of the car, Violet felt an urge to turn and run. It had been so long since she'd made small talk with a stranger and she wondered if it was something you could forget how to do. The

322

thought of talking to unknowns didn't excite her one bit. It scared her. What would she say? What if they recognized her and reported her to the police?

As she entered the store, Violet was relieved to see a teenaged cashier flipping through a magazine disinterestedly while snapping chewing gum. She thought it would feel like Christmas; out on her own, able to choose anything she wanted. Finally to use the change that had been sitting in her wallet for almost a year. She grabbed a chocolate bar and a bag of chips from the narrow aisles. They could have been anything. She found herself in front of the cash register, waiting for the bored girl to look up and notice her.

A few seconds passed. What was proper etiquette here, Violet wondered? She couldn't recall. Should she clear her throat? Or should she stand patiently, quietly waiting for the girl to look up? She decided to go with the latter. When the cashier finally did look up, it wasn't with apology. Violet got the sense that the girl had known she was there all along, but couldn't tear her eyes away from the latest celebrity gossip. That's another thing Violet hadn't missed about the real world – how shitty people can be. She found herself craving the rocking chair on Jeremy's front porch. She fought the instinct to run.

"Hi," Violet offered.

No response. The girl rung through the two purchases and put them in a bag.

"Thanks," Violet said on her way out of the door. She breathed a sigh of relief once back in the open air.

Violet checked the clock when sat back in the car. She'd been gone about twenty minutes. She probably had enough time to take a joy ride; to use Jeremy's map-instead-of-directions and take a different route home. But she didn't. She drove back the same way she came. When she pulled back up that drive, fighting the guilt that came with it, only thirty-five minutes had passed. She was early.

Nearing the house, Violet wondered if she needed to hide her car in the barn again. She chose not to, parking in a way that would make it easy to drive off very quickly. Leaving the car, she almost forgot her bag of goodies and grabbed them at the last second. She was out of practise for running errands. Violet saw Jeremy standing in his bedroom window. She wasn't sure if he knew she'd seen him; she didn't let her eyes linger for long. Instead, she locked the car door and walked up to the house, as if it was the most natural thing for her to go out into the world and come right back.

Jeremy was heading down the stairs to meet her as she walked in the door.

"Welcome back," he said with obvious relief.

"As promised," she replied. "And ten minutes early!" She was trying her hardest to make light of the situation. She wanted it to be no big deal that she had just been the farthest away from Jeremy that she'd been in months.

"Good job," Jeremy said. "Did you have any trouble finding the place?"

"Not at all, your map was great. I ended up buying some snacks. You hungry?"

Her words had their intended effect. Jeremy's face lit up like a sunrise. "Starving."

"Good," she said, and led them to the kitchen. "It felt nice to be on the road again. What's Ben up to?" she asked casually, lining up her segue.

"He's in his room, as usual," Jeremy replied. "I wonder if he wants a snack."

Violet swatted her hand in the way that means, Nah. "Don't worry about him," she said. "But I was thinking, though, it might be nice for Ben to get out a bit tomorrow too. I could take him for a nice scenic drive, I still have that map in my car." She fiddled with her corner store bag. "We wouldn't need to go far, just long enough for him to get some fresh air. He's always loved going on country drives."

She could see Jeremy turning the idea over in his mind. There wasn't a real reason why he could or should say no. They had an agreement.

Just to reassure him, Violet said it out loud. "I have every intention of coming right back," she said, "I just know he'd really like to go for a drive."

Jeremy couldn't resist. He had a weakness for Ben, the same weakness most people got when they saw his brown eyes. There was a depth to them, something not innocent but not guilty.

"That sounds alright," Jeremy said. "Do you want me to talk to him?"

"Oh, don't worry about that," Violet said. "I'd rather leave it as a surprise and explain it to him in the car."

Jeremy nodded in disheartened agreement.

Looking at the clock, Violet realized it was only noon. There was still so much more of the day, so much more time before they could get out for good. She didn't know how to face it, so she excused herself from their little world.

"I think I'm going to take a nap," she lied.

"Sounds nice," Jeremy said, "Enjoy it."

When Violet got upstairs, she stopped in Ben's bedroom. "Did you miss me?" she asked.

The puzzled look he gave indicated that not only had he not missed her, he hadn't noticed she was gone.

"I just drove to the corner store!" she said with the enthusiasm of a young girl who'd just received her licence. "And I convinced Jeremy to let me take you for a drive tomorrow."

"Cool!" Ben exclaimed. Violet wondered if he thought she meant it; that it was a drive and nothing else.

"Ben, we're going to drive home," she said seriously, waiting for their escape to register. He paused, looked down at his hands.

"Which home?" he asked.

"Home, home," she stressed. "Back home to mom. Where we're supposed to be. And you'll get to sleep in your own bed, play with your own friends, get back to the life you're supposed to have."

Ben surveyed the room. Violet prayed she wasn't following his train of thought: that he already had a room, and toys, and people (albeit invisible ones) to play with. Their mother, though. He had been deprived of a mother, and that had to be something he wanted to go home to.

"I'll bet mom will have some chocolate chip cookies waiting for us when we get home, Ben. She's probably missed us so much. She's going to be so happy to see us."

Her words weren't having the effect she'd been looking for. There should have been an eagerness there that she wasn't detecting. She shouldn't have to convince her little brother it was a good idea to leave their kidnapper.

"Violet," Ben said in a voice smaller than his body, "What if she didn't miss us?"

Violet's heart rocketed into her throat, blocking her ability to breathe or swallow. She wanted to hug him, hold him tightly and assure him that of course, of course their mother had missed them. No doubt she had been searching for them everyday, wondering where they were, if they were alright.

But there was a tiny seed sprouting in her stomach that took root and twisted her insides every now and again when she allowed her thoughts to stray back home. It had been a long time. Much can happen in a year. What if they came home to find that their mother had already adopted two new children to take their place? What if she had given up, taken down all of their family photos, thrown away everything that reminded her of them? It might not have been something she had done out of indifference; it could have come from love and mourning. But it would mean they had been erased nonetheless.

Would Ben be able to enter a classroom with kids his age? Would he be held back? What about his friends, would they think he had changed? Maybe they would fear that he was cursed or tainted in some way. Whispers would undoubtedly tickle the back of his neck.

And how about herself? Would she still have a job when she left here? If so, she'd likely fall back into the same old schedule, working long shifts and doubles. No doubt she'd have to work additional hours to catch up on the time she had missed. She hadn't spent a penny of her own money, minus the few dollars in snacks at the convenience store, in almost a year. At least she still had savings in her account to use until she started to bring in money again.

These were all things Violet worried about. Things that made Violet say to herself, One more night here, just one more night before we leave. She wanted to make sure they were prepared as fully as possible.

Instead of reassuring her poor little brother that their mother still loved them and wanted them home, she had allowed her emotions to map themselves across her face. It registered through her lips, her eyebrows, her eyes. Ben started to cry.

"She's waiting for us, Ben," Violet said, a lump of apprehension clogging her throat. "She's waiting for us, just like she has been all along. And the sooner we get home, the sooner she can prove that to you." She pointed at him. "So that means we have to get ready to leave. Okay?"

Ben nodded.

"You're going to have to try really, really hard to seem like everything is normal. It's okay to act a little excited, but remember that we're supposed to be only going for a drive. We're going to pack up the things we need to take with us, but Jeremy can't know we're packing. If he suspects something, he'll spook and lock us up again. So you're going to have to be selective, do you know what that means?"

Ben nodded unconvincingly, so Violet explained.

"You can only choose a couple of things to bring home with you. Don't worry about clothes or toys or anything. We'll be able to get you whatever you need as soon as we're home, and don't forget that you have a whole room full of things waiting for you."

Fingers crossed.

"Do I have to leave my Jeep?" Ben asked, already knowing the answer.

"Yes, Ben. You have to leave it behind."

He hung his head for a moment, but he'd been prepared for that. He would have to leave behind his mud suit, too. He'd have to leave behind the days of driving in the dirt. It seemed to him that there was a lot he would be leaving behind; a lot that wouldn't fit into a small bag he could carry on his back.

"You won't miss it though," Violet said. "You'll be too busy enjoying all the wonderful things that were stolen from us. Just wait."

She said the words and tried to convince herself of their truth.

"I'm going to my room now," Violet said. "Jeremy thinks I went to take a nap. So as far as he's concerned, I stopped in here to tell you that I'm taking you for a drive tomorrow. And it's okay to be excited. If you're looking forward to it, there's less of a chance he'll change his mind. He won't want to let you down. But nothing obvious." Kissing the top of his head, she felt the lump in her throat dwindle slightly.

Arriving at the doorway, she turned to look back, to give Ben an encouraging smile. But he was already off the bed and on his way out the door as well. He headed right downstairs.

He went straight to Jeremy, who was sitting at the kitchen table reading.

"Hey, Ben!" he said happily as the boy walked into the room.

Without a word, Ben threw his arms around his captor's neck, buried his little head into Jeremy's scrawny chest, and held on tight.

"What's that for?" Jeremy asked, surprised. Ben didn't shy away from Jeremy's touch, but it was rare for him to show affection.

"Thanks, Jer," Ben said simply. His words sounded sadder than he'd meant them to.

"Did Violet tell you that you're going for a ride tomorrow?"

Ben moved his head up and down against Jeremy's chest.

"Well, you're welcome," Jeremy said gently. He wrapped his arms around Ben and held on just as tightly.

Something was happening inside Jeremy, and he couldn't put a finger on what. It was just above his stomach, just below his heart. It was something that had previously been hollowed out; heavy but void. Slowly, it had begun to fill up, like there was some small perforation where goodness was leaking in drip by drip. It should have felt heavier, but it didn't. Instead, it felt ever lighter with each increasing drop.

On that day, with Ben's arms around his neck and the woman of his dreams upstairs, the hollow expanse within him felt ready to burst, oversaturated with something unknown but so good.

"You're welcome," Jeremy repeated.

He missed all the signs. He didn't expect a thing. Ben's shaking, the tear that snuck down his cheek, all went unnoticed. It was if they didn't exist at all.

That was the last day that Violet and Ben spent inside of the house that was not Jeremy's.

31

When Jeremy looked back on the last night they spent together, he recalled an ordinary night. A regular dinner, some pleasant conversation, a little bit of television after the clean up. Nothing strange. He didn't see the unsettled way that Violet kept stroking her neck, tapping her foot. Or Ben's big, sad eyes that avoided Jeremy.

Violet went to bed early. She said she had a headache. On so many nights, Jeremy replayed those last hours in his head. What could he have done differently? What should he have said? Could it have been as simple as locking them up in the basement for a day? Maybe they hadn't been quite ready to be rid of their bracelets, the cameras, those burdenless burdens.

When Violet escaped to her bedroom, she couldn't sleep. She didn't have a migraine but her head ached with the thoughts ricocheting through the partitions of her skull. They bounced around ruthlessly, slamming into each other, breaking off into smaller, sharper bits. There would be no sleep for her that night.

Ben went to bed soon after Violet. He was worried he would slip up, say something he wasn't supposed to and ruin it all. Watching television was simple enough; he looked at the screen and pretended to focus on the image in front of him. The only times he had to tune in were when Jeremy laughed or said something Ben should respond to.

Finally, he forced a yawn and headed up the stairs.

"You're tired already?" Jeremy asked, surprised.

Ben wondered if he'd given in too soon; if it was too early to go to bed.

"I'm just going to read for a bit," Ben lied.

"Oh, alright," Jeremy said. He wasn't hurt or suspicious, just curious. "Goodnight then, sleep tight. See you in the morning, kiddo."

Ben paused upon hearing the nickname. Jeremy had only called him that once before, when they'd been doing a puzzle together and Ben found the tricky piece they'd been searching for.

"Way to go, kiddo!" he'd said, and Ben had beamed with the pride and glory that he assumed went with the title.

Seven years, that's how old Ben was as he walked up those stairs for the last time. A year older than when he walked in, but he'd aged so much more than that. He was old enough to realize it was the last time he would hear Jeremy call him kiddo. This was it. He also realized it wasn't supposed to be something he'd miss. He should be relieved to be free of it.

But Ben would miss it. He would miss Jeremy, the outdoors, the unstructured. He was wise enough, now, to know he would have to swallow the feeling, chew it up and digest it, hide it away deep down so no one could see. It was a feeling he wasn't allowed to speak of out loud because no one would understand; it wouldn't make sense to them. He wasn't sure how Violet felt. Maybe he could share the sentiment with her. She might hate him for feeling that way, she might yell and scream like she had done at Jeremy all those times.

"Goodnight," Ben finally replied as he walked up the last of the steps.

"Goodnight, Violet," he said to the closed doorway next to his. He heard no response, but she was sitting inside, alert, awake and wondering how the next morning would unfold. If it would ever come.

Ben fell asleep that night. He thought he might lay there for hours, unable to drift off from excitement or worry. But sleep claimed him quickly, as if his subconscious tried to save him with its murky depths.

And as for Jeremy, he fell asleep easily, lightly, happily. Blissfully oblivious.

The next morning was cloudy. Of course it was. Violet lifted herself out of bed early. Her plan was to make a big breakfast for the three of them before leaving with Ben.

First, she would say some goodbyes. Walking out of her room, she saw both Ben and Jeremy's doors still shut, sealing them off in their sleepy caverns. She tiptoed down the hall, the stairs, out the back door.

As she looked up, Violet wondered if she had appreciated the trees enough. She wrapped her arms around the hearty trunk of an old maple. The bark scratched against her cheek, an ant roamed across her fingers.

She walked past the forget-me-nots, plucked one and stuck it in her hair. The Mouse House; her failed sign of sticks that she had envisioned would secure them safety and rescue. They had gotten one but not the other, and it hadn't come from carefully arranged kindling. It was Jeremy who had kept them safe.

Violet let her legs collapse onto the lawn. She sat with her knees tucked beneath her, ignoring the dew that seeped and expanded through her clothes, clamming her skin. She remembered.

About a month ago, she'd been outside doing some gardening. Picking some herbs for that night's meal. The sun had been out in full force, and Violet could sense the rays sinking into her skin. She could feel their weight. But purple clouds billowed in, rolling across the sun's path without warning. Big, fat drops began to fall, so substantial that they made a noise upon hitting her skin. Holding her arms up, hands out, she collected the drops in her palm. Her chin was raised, her eyes closed to shield them from the downpour. She had stuck her tongue out, like a little girl catching snowflakes. Violet lapped up the raindrops hungrily, swallowed them and swore she could taste what made them rain, not just water.

Looking back towards the house, Violet had seen Jeremy open the back door suddenly. He ran outside carrying something in his hands. As he neared her, Violet noticed he wasn't wearing any shoes and that he had a closed umbrella hanging by his side. A present, not a tool.

Violet lowered her hands and stood waiting for him to get to her. He was a little out of breath, more pink than normal.

"Here," he said and swallowed loudly as he opened the umbrella and held it out to her.

"Jeremy," she laughed, "What are you doing? Where are your shoes?"

He looked down then, as if he hadn't realized he was missing them. Maybe he wasn't. "Oh," he replied bashfully. "Well, it started to rain. I wanted to protect you."

Protect, like the rain would slice into her skin, dissolve her flesh beneath its soggy blanket. As if she would be forever scarred without the saving grace he had provided.

She could have teased him for that, told him she didn't need or desire any shelter from the falling drops. She hadn't, though. She had stuck her hand out, taken the umbrella and held it over her head. "Thank you, Jeremy," she said softly.

He smiled and nodded, turned and ran back to the house. In his bare feet. She had smiled and shaken her head at the ground. She did the same thing in the present as she sat on the lawn for the last time.

Standing back up, Violet told herself she wouldn't miss this place. Not Jeremy, not the home, not the wide-open space. She knew she was lying, but it made her feel better for the moment. She walked inside and into the kitchen.

Eggs, bacon, sausage, home fries. She knew the smell would rouse the boys before her voice did. Sure enough, as soon as the bacon lay bubbling in the pan, Jeremy's soft soles descended the stairs behind her; Ben's furious feet followed soon after. Both seemed so excited.

Jeremy set the table, Ben poured some orange juice, Violet turned on the radio. No one danced; no one sang. But they came close, together in the kitchen, preparing for a feast. Jeremy tapped his foot, Ben bobbed his head, Violet hummed.

The meal was delicious. None of them remembers what they talked about, but they did talk. There were no silent spaces, save for the few moments when all three chewed in unison. Once, this didn't stop Ben, and the momentum of his words spewed his eggs across the table.

"Gross," Violet said, allowing herself to laugh after Jeremy snorted. It was a nicer breakfast than most people had on most mornings, and it passed too quickly for all three.

Jeremy insisted on doing the dishes. Violet objected, but had hoped he would offer. She wondered why she took a mental picture of Jeremy's back at the sink. Was that something she should want to remember? Regardless, she took it in. The window facing the forest behind them; the green tea pot sitting on the window's ledge; the clear vase with dried sprigs of lavender she had put there.

The cottage country blue curtains that were parted in the middle and pinned back like a little girl's hair. The shiny silver of the sink, the steam rising from the hot water that Jeremy never seemed to notice was blanching his hands.

"Thanks, Jeremy," she said on her way out of the kitchen, and he turned back and smiled. His foot still tapped along to the beat of a song Violet had never heard.

There wasn't much more for her to do, nothing to pack besides the clothes on her back and her purse. She wanted to bring the sweater she'd gotten for Christmas, but it was too hot outside. It would be suspicious.

Ben peered out from his doorway when she got upstairs. His room was as messy as ever. A small pile of things sat in the middle of his floor – a toy car, a pen, a photo Jeremy had taken of him.

"Is this okay?" he asked, pointing to his collection.

"That's fine," she said gently. "They'll fit in my purse so he won't see. Are you all set?"

"Yup," he said quietly. They headed down the stairs to Jeremy's back, which still leaned over the sink. Violet wondered how she would convince her voice not to waver.

"Well, we're going to head out," she shouted to him over the sound of the water. Forever.

Jeremy turned his head towards them, his long torso still facing the water. "Wow, you're not wasting any time, are you?" But he was joking, he was only a little worried, he was smiling.

"Yeah," she strained. "Just too excited to wait I guess."

"Where do you think you'll go?"

"Oh, I'm bringing your map with me from yesterday, so just on some back roads. We'll probably be gone for about 45 minutes, give or take," she said, hoping she sounded convincing. She had been tempted to tell him an hour, two, as much time as possible before he would begin to wonder. But she didn't want to push her luck and was planning on driving as far away as she could, as fast as she could. Forty-five minutes would be enough.

"Excellent," he said biting her bait. "Well, drive safe, I hope you guys have a really nice time."

Part of him had been hoping she'd decide to stay home instead. Every time she didn't leave would be another time he wouldn't have to wait for her return. He tried not to let it show, and thrust his shoulders up and back. He believed in the boomerang. But he would wait with bated breath for the sound of their tires returning up the driveway, the deep rolling grit of the trampled gravel.

Violet and Ben shouted, "Goodbye!" as they opened the front door and stepped outside. Ben stood on the porch for a moment, not sure what to do.

"Is there anything else?" he asked. Violet assumed he meant anything they had forgotten, anything they hadn't packed and should have.

"No, there's nothing else," she said, thinking she was offering reassurance.

Ben stared at her with a scared look on his face. He had meant, What if this is the best we've got?

Violet walked toward the car with long strides. She didn't look back, forced herself not to, in fear of seeing Jeremy in the window. If he looked out as she tried to escape, she would screw it up, stumble, or worse, turn around and go right back inside. Could he have that power over her? Could he hold up some invisible chain and reel them back in? She felt no strings, no strain, nothing yanking her back. Just the weight of her own body.

She opened the car door; Ben did the same. They buckled up. Ben stared at his big sister, knowing she would tell him what happened next, and next, and next, until the whole thing was over.

"Okay," Violet said as she turned the key in the ignition. "This is it. Take one last look back if you want to, because this is the end of it." She had no idea which way to turn when the gravel road became a T.

Ben did look back. And, even though she told herself she wouldn't, Violet did, too. It had been their home. Homes aren't always the happiest of places, but they have people within them who love. There had been love in that home. Strange love, maybe forced love, maybe unhealthy love, but all love is like that sometimes.

There was Jeremy in the window. He must have finished the dishes. He stood there with his hands crossed in front of him. They were far enough away that Violet couldn't read the expression on his face. She couldn't see the valleys etched in his forehead or the white line of his lips pressed together or how huge his eyes looked.

Violet's breath caught in her throat. She rolled down her window and waved goodbye to him, trusting that they were far enough away that he couldn't read her face either.

"Wave bye, Ben," she said quickly, desperately. "He's there in the window, so wave goodbye."

Ben did, and Violet pressed on the gas pedal to take them down the driveway. When they got to the bottom, she turned left. Why not?

She drove and drove. There was no way of knowing where she was. Ben was no help and she didn't recognize the streets. She hadn't brought the map Jeremy had drawn. She should have; it would have helped. She could easily have gone into Bob's Corner Store to ask for directions into town. But instead, she had left them in her bedroom, sitting out on her set of drawers. It would be one of the first things Jeremy would see if he walked into her bedroom. She had left her door wide open.

Both hands stayed clamped to the wheel. The gravel felt loose beneath her tires and she feared it would send her reeling in one direction or another if she hit it too quickly. She crawled along slowly at 20 kilometres an hour.

"Vi?" Ben finally said, "Why are we going so slow?"

"I'm just making sure we don't skid out. It's like driving on ice," she exaggerated, because it wasn't really like that at all. A year away from the wheel was enough to make anyone cautious. No one could fault her for that.

After driving straight for a long time, Violet turned to Ben. "Alright," she said, "What way?"

"Right," Ben said instantly. He had thought about this, had been sitting there wondering when it would be a good time to tell her they should get off this road, the same road Jeremy lived on, the first road he would take if he were to come looking for them.

She turned right, looked to the horizon. Just natural landscape, aside from the road, as far as she could see. Looking at the clock, she saw that only five minutes had passed. They had some time before Jeremy would begin to miss them.

Time crawled slowly after that, country scenery all around them. Sprawling fields, tall trees, a couple of brave squirrels who darted freely onto the gravel, unexposed to the graveyard most roads become with frequent car use.

"Now what way?" Violet asked.

"Left," Ben said. Farther away, was what he really meant. He wasn't sure how he felt. There were things he didn't want to leave behind, and a part of him would feel okay if Violet decided to turn the car around and go back. But now that he was here, in the car, driving away for the first time, he realized that he wanted his mom. He did want his own bed, his own friends. He wanted to tell them the story about the man who had stolen them, and suddenly felt a pang for back-to-school clothes, new haircuts and pencil sharpeners.

He looked over at Violet. She was so quiet, and he could see how high her shoulders were raised.

"We're gonna be okay, Vi," he said, unsure if it would be comforting or annoying.

She didn't say anything, just turned to him with a big, fake smile and nodded her head. The nod had been their code, for all the times when it had been too much to muster up the words for emotions they had no vocabulary for. When sometimes the only thing to do had been to just nod. Violet wondered if, going back into the real world, nodding would be enough. Maybe people would pry more out of her, not allowing her to fall back on a simple bob of her head.

In the distance, a barn appeared.

"Look!" they both said at the same time, as if they had never seen civilization before.

"Alright," Violet said, "At least that's a sign of another person. Maybe we're getting closer."

They were. Continuing straight on that road would lead them to Blind River, the town they had been absent from for almost a year.

When they saw the first signs of residential sprawl, twenty minutes had passed. They didn't recognize the area but the gravel turned to pavement, the street signs turned from numbers to words and cars began to pass them on the road. The presence of other drivers made Violet nervous. She felt as though she could easily swerve into the wrong lane at any moment. Her depth perception had always been shoddy and she was particularly jittery that day. She probably wasn't fit to be driving, and part of her wanted very badly to pull over, to sit and wait awhile until the sky got darker and all the other cars headed home.

"Do you recognize any of this?" she asked Ben. He shook his head.

"Me neither," she admitted. "Let's pull over at the next gas station and we'll ask how to get home. Sound good?"

The nod.

A gas station soon appeared before them. Violet flicked on her blinker, something she hadn't been doing on the back roads, and turned in. Parking wasn't as hard as she had anticipated, and she successfully maneuvered between the two lines.

"Wanna stay in here?" she asked Ben. He did.

Getting out of the car, Violet walked towards the entrance of the store and saw a line of three phone booths on the outside wall.

Her home phone number sprung into her head; she could see the seven digits display themselves behind her eyelids. The unique code that would allow her to access home, no matter how far away.

I could call. The thought leapt into her head as suddenly and vibrantly as the numbers. She fumbled in her change purse for a quarter. Remembering the price increase on phone booths, she dug out another.

Approaching the nearest booth, she lifted the receiver and felt the weight of it in her hand. She pressed it firmly to her head, feeling the vacuum seal against her ear. She dropped her two quarters into the machine and cringed at the monotonous drone of the dial tone. It was such a haunting noise; she wondered who had chosen it. Couldn't it be a song? A soft melody, or at the very least a more friendly pitch?

She entered the numbers into the phone slowly and deliberately. She didn't want to press the wrong one and have to start all over. The gap between entering the numbers and the connection lasted a lifetime. Violet could hear the suspension, the seemingly endless hollow. But finally, a ring.

Then another ring, and one more.

What if she doesn't answer? Violet wasn't sure if she would leave a message. Before she had to decide, there was a small click, a pause and a "Hello?"

Violet recognized the voice instantly, and was secretly relieved that she did. Thank god she hadn't forgotten.

"Mom!" Violet said quickly and loudly, "Mom, it's me!"

Another pause. "Who is this?" Anger laced her words in a way that Violet didn't expect or understand.

"It's Violet! Mom, it's me!" She hadn't imagined she would have to announce her identity so many times. Shouldn't her mom just know?

"This is cruel," the voice said, dripping with menace. "Is this funny to you?"

"What? No, mom, it's really me, it's Violet! And I'm okay, and Ben's okay too, and we're coming home! We're coming home right now!"

Violet wanted to shout out the whole story, tell her every word, but it would have to wait until after they were able to share an embrace. They would have to hang on to each other for a moment so they knew for certain it was real. Before she could say anything else to convince her mother or herself that she was really on the way home, Holly interrupted her with a shout.

"Fuck you," she said loudly. "Whoever you are, fuck you. How dare you put me through this. How dare you." She hung up.

Violet stood with the phone in her hand for a long time. The sound of the disconnection, that staccato beat, was even more eerie than the dial tone itself.

There was only one reason her mother could have reacted that way. She must have thought they were dead. Violet wondered how she could have come to that conclusion. She had hardly scoured the earth, searched the area thoroughly and completely. Had she given up on them? Violet squeezed her eyes shut, swallowed, shook her head and put the phone back down. She would pretend she hadn't made that phone call, that her change purse was still two quarters heavier. Their mother was, at this very moment, sitting at home. Thinking about them. She must be so upset. Making that phone call had only delayed them, and Violet chastised herself for her weakness.

Pressing open the door into the store, the chime sounded to alert the cashier. Stop picking your nose, stop reading dirty magazines, the bell announced. The young boy behind the counter jerked his head towards her. Violet wondered for a moment if he would recognize her. Maybe posters of them had been plastered around town, on signposts, the evening news. Perhaps her face would be forever recognizable to the town folk who had been haunted by her image for weeks on end as the devastating search for the missing siblings continued. The Stolen Siblings, that surely would have been their headline.

But nothing flickered over the cashier's face besides boredom. Violet's hand self-consciously snapped up to her hair; she ran her fingers through it. She hadn't striven for conventional beauty in so long. It wasn't as though she had given up the façade, the strategic placing of her hands on her hips. Those thoughts had come back to her after she regained access to a mirror and a shower within Jeremy's house. But that had been different, that had been easy. Back in the real world, the insecurity and constant self-evaluation began to creep back in.

She arrived at the counter before she even knew what she wanted to say.

"Hi," she started, "I was just wondering if you could give me some directions back into town."

"What town?" he asked, a fair question.

"Oh, sorry. Blind River. There are so many side roads out here that I have no idea where I ended up."

"Sure thing," he said. Immediately, he got out a pen and napkin and began to draw a map. What was with men and intersecting lines? It was as if they needed to know how to conquer from all angles instead of just one, Violet thought, as if they wanted to avoid the use of language at all costs, conveying messages by data alone.

"It'll take you about five minutes if you follow this road right here," he said as he gestured to his offering. "You're not far."

"Wow," Violet said. "Really?" It felt as if they should have to drive for days.

"Really," he handed over the scrap.

"Thank you," she said sincerely, "I appreciate it." She turned and walked out of the store, given a final farewell by its chime. When the car was back in her line of vision, and Ben within it, she gave a thumbs up and the biggest smile she could muster. Ben gave her a small one in return.

Violet climbed back in the car and hoped Ben wouldn't ask her about the phone call. But he did, and she couldn't blame him; it had been so long since a phone call had been an option.

"Did you talk to mom?"

"No," she said quickly. She was about to continue when Ben asked another question.

"Did you talk to Jeremy?"

"Jeremy? What? No," she said, alarmed that he would think so. "No, I called home, but no one answered."

"Oh," he said, sounding too downtrodden for someone of his size.

"I have a feeling she's at home though," she soothed. "And we're going to be there sooner than you think. How long do you think it'll take us?"

"An hour?" Ben said, time being a concept that didn't mean much to him yet.

"Nope, the person inside told me we're only about five minutes from town. I'll bet we can make it home in less than fifteen minutes. Are you excited?"

"Yes," he said, but he wasn't. Violet could tell. She wasn't sure why, but her heart wasn't as light as she imagined it would be either. It was alarming how neutral she felt towards the idea of being able to go home. Being behind the wheel and steering in the direction that would take her there, she felt nothing.

Not nothing, that wasn't accurate. She couldn't describe it, and wished she could draw a map of it to explain.

They drove on and urbanization began to explode around them. Grocery stores, fitness centres, cars and homes. Violet knew where she was but the landmarks had changed. She passed a plaza that had been a park when she left.

The traffic lights scared Violet a bit; the sun had come out and she couldn't see the colours changing very well.

"Is that – is that green?" she asked Ben more than once. He nodded yes, without pausing to think of the need to be accurate.

Three honks raged at her from behind as she had fouled someone again, somehow. She couldn't take the time to wave or apologize in fear of being lambasted with another honk from someone else she was sure to offend in the process.

"Here we are," Violet breathed. Their neighbourhood. The streets were the same, children out playing on bikes. Be careful, little ones, she wanted to say to them, Don't get into a car with any strange men. She knew she was the minority, that it didn't happen often, that most likely those children were safe. But she couldn't shake the feeling that they were bound to be snatched up as they sat passively on their bikes, while their mothers painted their nails or talked on the phone to a friend. Flirted in the backyard with men. Bad things could happen when no one was watching, and even when they were.

Violet looked over at her little brother. Mouth open, eyes wide, he looked back and forth without saying a word.

"Are you ready?" she asked him. As if he had a choice, as if they had ever had a choice. But he nodded, little sport that he was, lying for her benefit.

"Good," she said, making the final left turn onto Norwood Crescent. A big, friendly circle of a street. In the wintertime, the snow plough piled all of the snow into the middle of the court, forming a great white mountain, or at least a great grey one, depending on how fresh and pure it was or wasn't. As a child, Violet had played on that hill for hours, digging tunnels through its core, riding her bicycle down its side. At the moment, the centre of the court was an empty, concrete void. Right beyond it was home.

"Home," Violet said out loud, as if reinforcing it to herself and to Ben. "We're home."

The house was a bungalow; a squat, long structure made of mostly brown things. Brown bricks, painted brown trim around the windows. A chimney somewhere on the back of the roof poked up. The front door was painted a deep forest green, the same colour as when they had left it, but with fewer chips and scratches. Sparse, bedraggled gardens patched the front lawn, and Violet's heart sank a little in her chest. Their mother had loved the garden and been so proud when it flourished. Perhaps she had been too heartbroken to grow something new, something beautiful out of the earth when the two things that meant the most to her were gone. Violet held this thought close to her and hoped.

It amazed Violet that the house didn't look more beautiful. Shouldn't it appear to be glistening, glowing like the North Star beckoning them home? It should be an oasis, Violet thought. But it wasn't. It was a small bungalow that their mother had a very hard time affording. The tiled walkway up to the front door was still cracked; Holly hadn't gotten much farther than the door's paint job. No vehicle sat in the driveway, but the closed garage had always sealed their mother's red car away. It was probably nestled safely within right now.

Violet pulled into the driveway and slowed to a stop. Neither of them jumped out of the car. When Violet unclasped her seatbelt, she heard Ben do the same. As her hand reached out to pull the handle on the door, Ben's little hand did too.

"This is it," she said, preparing them. Ben didn't say a word. They got out of the car and shut the door gently. Neither wanted to make much noise. After pressing the power lock button on the car, she grimaced. The beep was far too loud. Violet looked expectantly up to the windows of the house. She thought for certain she would see the ruffling of a curtain, the curious peek of a mother who had been waiting for that sound for months on end. But there was no motion, and Violet realized she was just going to have to walk up to the front door. She did, and Ben followed along beside her, one step behind.

Reaching the doorstep, Violet hesitated. The key to their house was in her hand. Every other time she'd stood on that porch, she had used it to let herself in. But something about that seemed wrong now. She would feel like they were intruding. After the phone call to her mother, Violet figured it would be wise to simply ring the doorbell and allow her to come to them.

"Do you want to ring it?" she asked Ben, pointing to the little button. He shook his head no. Violet wondered why he looked so little to her right now; as if he had shrunk somehow. Maybe he had, just a little.

Violet reached her left pointer finger up, and pressed the button much harder than she needed to. There was that noise, that ring they recognized. Ben and Violet locked eyes at the familiarity. It felt comforting, which was a welcome relief.

Straining her ears, Violet heard nothing at first. Then there it was, soft padding footsteps. Tentative steps in their direction.

"Here she comes," Violet whispered. The emotion she felt most clearly was terror, and she had no idea why. She grasped Ben's hand tightly. He didn't resist, and gripped right back.

The door opened. They could hear the click of the latch and gathered that it hadn't even been locked. They could have just walked right in without a key, anyone could have. Violet held her breath.

When she saw them, Holly screamed and dropped to her knees. It wasn't a choice. Her hand flew up to cover her mouth and she screamed again. Violet dropped down next to her and put her hand on Holly's thin shoulder.

"Mom, we're home, we're okay." She wanted to say a million words as fast as she could to assure her everything was alright. She waited for Holly to say anything at all.

"Oh my god," she said wetly, the sound muffled by her hand. "I don't believe it."

Ben was on his knees by then. "It's okay mom," he said, "I love you," as if that had been the doubt on her mind, the reason she cried.

"Ohhhhhhhh," Holly howled as if she was in pain. "My babies," she said. "You're home, you're okay."

"We're okay," Violet said again. She felt as if she should say it over and over again. Tears flowed down her cheeks. It was all over. If she turned around, Jeremy wouldn't be there. No bracelet or camera would hold her back. She wouldn't have to hide in the basement if anyone came to call.

She belonged to herself again, to nobody else. She would be able to leave Jeremy behind. She repeated the mantra in her head and wondered why she still didn't believe it.

AFTER

Some people make it despite the odds stacked against them. Some glue within them holds stronger. They can compartmentalize the things that make them hurt into chapters they can turn the pages of and leave behind. They're forever changed because of it, but everything changes you somehow.

Violet never moved on. She stayed in that chapter, that prison in her mind. She remained contained long after being released. What was it about her that allowed Jeremy to stay in her bones? Her eyes became glazed over, and you could never tell if she was with you or back there with him.

If she was in the past, you might catch her fingering her necklace, the one with the stars Jeremy had given her for Christmas. A small shackle around her neck. Her mouth might twitch. Not a smile, not a frown, just the faint shimmer of a response to something from long ago.

Once, we were stolen. But one of us never made it out.

1

That was twenty years ago. I still can't believe so much time has passed. It's not as if it feels like yesterday, but I often find myself wondering how something so immense could happen during only one year out of my 27. I feel as though my life could not be defined without it.

So much happened after Vi and I went home. Our rooms were just as we'd left them. Mom kept them as a constant reminder of all she had lost. She really did think she had lost us. Everyone told her we were gone, to give up and move on. She didn't do either of those things, but she did stop actively looking.

Not long after we got home, Vi asked Mom to sit down with us and tell her side of the story, all that happened while we were gone. Mom seemed reluctant, as if it would hurt us somehow, but Vi said we needed to know. I wasn't sure if we did or didn't, but I still wanted to hear it.

Mom told us she'd been expecting us home for dinner that night. When we didn't show, she hadn't been too worried. A little pissed off, actually. She called Vi's cell phone, which Jeremy never told us.

When we didn't come home that night at all, that's when she really started to worry. She called my daycare to see if I'd been picked up, and they told her I had and that Vi had been the one to do it. No one had seen the man in the car; no one had noticed at all.

Mom didn't sleep that night. She drove to Vi's work. She thought maybe Vi was ignoring her, or had taken an extra shift, and she wanted to see with her own eyes that Vi was or wasn't there. But she wasn't; she had left hours ago. That was when Mom had called the police. She wanted to know if there had been any accidents, any suspicious characters in the neighbourhood, any reason they could give her why her two children hadn't come home. No one could tell her anything, except that she shouldn't worry, that we would most likely show up in the morning.

The morning came, we did not, and I became an Amber Alert. That's still neat to me, in a twisted way. Our house turned into search party headquarters. Mom says she had no idea so many people knew who we were, let alone cared enough to join the hunt to find us.

Police officers interviewed Mom for hours on end about things like whether Vi had a bad boyfriend, if there had been any strange people lurking around before we vanished. Because that's just it, we did vanish. We didn't leave any trace; we hadn't realized we would need to. Mom says she felt awful because some of the officers seemed to think we had run away from her, that she might have been an unfit mother. The thought ate away at her, that maybe it could be true. When she told us this, we gave her big hugs and comforted her, told her we never would have stayed so long if we could've helped it. I remember thinking, even then, that it was a lie.

They checked border guard records to see if any people of our description had left the country. For a while, our faces were even on the evening news down south. Vi asked which picture Mom had given for the posters, which I thought was a dumb question. She'd picked one of the two of us together, Vi's arm around me at Christmas. Vi said it was a bad picture. Girls are so strange; as if that mattered. We were both smiling and my hair was in my eyes. Mom used to always brush it off my face, telling me not to hide my brown eyes. By the time we got home after being with Jeremy, my hair was so long you could barely see my face. Mom took me to get a haircut the very next day. It was one of her top priorities, which I always thought was strange.

She told us our faces had been all over the place, not on the milk cartons because they didn't do that anymore, but everywhere else. I think Mom spent a lot of money on things like magnets. She told us she didn't want people to just walk by a flyer, see our faces and keep going. She wanted us in their houses, on their fridges, to remind them every moment that we still hadn't been found. Mom didn't sleep a lot during that time. I don't think she ate a lot, either. Hugging her felt different, less soft and more angular. She was smaller in various ways.

The worst part, she told us, was that there were no leads. Well, there were the crazies who called the tip line to spout conspiracy theories, and the police did the best they could to check up on all of the false alarms, but it got frustrating. Apparently, there were almost one hundred phone calls. Some were psychics, claiming our bodies could be found in the bottom of a well somewhere in the forest. The police didn't tell her about calls like that. The only time she heard such things was the night she volunteered to man the phone line. She didn't offer to do it again.

Nothing new developed. It wasn't like they were putting together a puzzle piece by piece, each bit bringing them closer to us. The pieces were all missing. It began with interviews, so many interviews, finding out who knew what. Searching different places they thought we might have ended up. There was a memo sent out about Vi's car so people could watch the road for it. Of course, by the time they were looking, it was locked in Jeremy's garage.

After a week of searching, they knew we hadn't just run away. We weren't heartless, we would have left a note or called to let Mom know we were okay. But that made it worse because it meant we were somewhere we didn't want to be. The police even asked Mom to speak on the evening news, to send a message to anyone who might know something. She broke down in the middle of it, couldn't finish the words. She told us she stayed awake all night after that newscast, thinking she might have blown her one shot, that she had muttered and mumbled the instructions people needed to get us home to her.

The worst part was what came next. That was when they started dragging the lakes, scouring the fields. Mom said it terrified her, but it wasn't as if she would ask them not to look. As she told us this, Vi and I both cried. They were the words we needed to hear. Our mother had been looking for us. She hadn't thrown in the towel or forgotten us. We shouldn't have wanted to hear that she'd been destroyed by it, but we did. It was music to our burning ears. I remember how important I felt, and how anchored. It was nice to know that someone grieved your absence. I don't think either Vi or myself truly realized how much we doubted our ability to be missed.

We asked so many questions, greedy for the knowledge of what had happened while we'd been suspended in time and space. It strained her to answer; she would stop to break down, but I think she understood why we needed to know. She told us the only thing that kept her going was that at the end of each day, our bodies hadn't shown up. Our corpses weren't lying in the bottom of any lake they had drug so far. Whenever the phone rang, her body would tense with the fear that it would be the worst news. For the first month or two, she actually drew comfort in the absence of that phone call. She told us she was living in a world of in-betweens. I wasn't sure what she meant at the time, and I didn't ask. I think I know now.

All in all, we were gone for ten months. Mom told us she was in denial for a long time, and Vi asked in denial of what.

357

"Of your absence," she said, and even at seven I thought that was silly. The only certain part of any of it had been that we were absent. That we were in danger, that we were being held against our will, that we could be harmed or damaged or tortured – it was the rest she should've been in denial of.

After four months of searching, the police told her they couldn't keep looking much longer. Things had been winding down, volunteers lost stamina and resources ran low. Mom offered to put more money in, more man-hours, but it was no good. They cancelled the tip line. Mom didn't have the heart to answer those calls, and there was no one else to do it. The house emptied. The hallways were still lined with markered maps, but now no one added to them, no one clustered around, delegating tasks based on where those red dots were and weren't. The task to find us fell to her. Our names stopped being read on the evening news. The newspaper stopped reporting on us, the journalist who had been covering our story stopped calling. Mom said she felt a little offended. With all the details she had shared with that woman, Jessica Valdez, she felt they shared something special. Mom couldn't believe their relationship had been about publishing a story and nothing more.

Family members rallied around Mom; people brought casseroles and called to invite her to barbeques on the weekends. She always declined. She lived like a hermit, only going outside for work and racing home every evening to check her messages, her mail, to see if there was any word.

I know my mother. I know she loves us, and I don't doubt that a large part of her was missing when we were missing. But I also know her well enough to know how she copes. Our house wouldn't have been empty. She wouldn't have said no to all of the offers. She would have needed the attention, the frames to lean on. When I think of our house in our absence, I imagine it teeming with men, like an anthill. I can see suitors coming and going, bringing flowers and food, each one an offering for her bleeding heart. That wasn't something I figured out when I was seven, but soon after, when I started to ponder the logistics of her sitting at home abandoned. That's when I started to whiteout some of her version of the story and paint in my own. I know Vi did this instantly, right as Mom told us.

When Vi called from the pay phone, Mom hadn't known what to think. It had been so long since she'd heard our voices, and Vi wasn't herself that day so the voice was likely unfamiliar. Regardless, when we showed up on our own front stoop, Mom told us she thought for a split second that we might be ghosts come back to haunt her. She said she was scared to touch us in case her fingers went right through.

People always ask me what it was like to be kidnapped, and they're always disappointed with my answer. It wasn't all that dramatic, not for me anyways. I wasn't deprived. And I know, I know, people always say that the things that matter most aren't the tangible ones, but I was a little boy. I didn't have all of that stuff figured out just yet.

Jeremy was never mean to me. I mean, he did things that were awful. Keeping us in the basement at the beginning was really negligent. It was a long time ago now, but I can still smell the bucket in the corner where we had to go to the bathroom. Vi even threw up in there one time, and Jeremy didn't come in until the next morning to clean it out. It was awful and cramped, but that didn't last long. For the most part, we had the run of the house and the whole property.

When people ask me how I feel about Jeremy, I never know what to say. I should hate him. I know this is what they want to hear. Since we escaped, the world has been waiting for Vi and I to condemn him, but we haven't. I was too young to understand that what he had done was truly wrong, and Vi was in too deep. I didn't know that then.

2

I don't know how long it took Jeremy to realize we were never coming back.

Later that day, Jeremy drove to the police station and turned himself in. He walked in, told the woman at the counter that he had kidnapped Violet and Ben Wrigley for almost a year. After he said it, he took out the gun that was tucked into his pants, placed it on the counter, and put his hands behind his head. The woman had no idea what to do. She radioed someone in the back, and they came out with handcuffs. They arrested him right away.

When they told me Jeremy had a gun, I knew instantly that he would never have wielded it against anyone. He must have purchased it after we left; otherwise he would have used it to kidnap us instead of the fake one. I found out it was fake years later, but I'll get to that.

The gun he carried that day, a real one, carrying one bullet only, had been meant for Jeremy and Jeremy alone. He would have turned it on himself before

360

anyone else, and this knowledge tingled inside of me even back then. I still don't know the reason why he didn't just do it; blow his brains out and get it over with quickly. I'm glad he didn't, but I can't help but wonder what changed his mind and gave him the courage to hand himself over. His last parting gift to us.

He's still in prison, twenty years later. It's minimum-security, and I know firsthand that he's fairly comfortable there. It isn't so bad. Twenty years for what he did for one year. I don't know, is that a lot? Maybe I'm biased.

We weren't involved in the trial. We never had to stand up in court and say that yes, Jeremy had been the one to keep us. We never got to defend or condemn him, not really, not in any grand way. We were sat down in interviews and asked how we felt about Jeremy, what had happened while we were gone. They asked me over and over if he had hurt me in any way. I always said no. They would rephrase the question, saying the same thing in different words. They were looking for me to say yes. I think it pissed them off when I refused to submit. A couple of times, they worded the questions so bizarrely that I didn't even know what they were asking, but I was smart enough not to answer those ones. I asked them what they meant, every time. I didn't know what was going to happen to Jeremy, but I wanted them to know the truth about what happened when we lived with him.

The newspapers loved it. Our faces were all over the papers again. They took an updated photo of us with our arms around each other and plastered it on every front page. They called us the Stockholm Syndrome Siblings. I had no idea what it meant. I do now, and they had it all wrong.

People try to tell me that Jeremy brainwashed us, that he told us he wasn't the bad guy so many times that we started to believe it. I told them that not once did Jeremy ever tell me he wasn't a bad guy. He didn't ever say he was a good guy. He didn't talk about what sort of guy he was at all. That's when they would tell me that the best manipulators are people who can do so without you even knowing, and that this must have been the case for us. I always shook my head at that. It didn't make sense to me. Jeremy hadn't conducted some strange voodoo, he hadn't swung a pendulum in front of our faces and told us we were getting sleepy and that he wasn't the bad guy. But people didn't like to hear that. People are dying to convict, to sentence, to condemn. I think they truly believed that if Vi and I admitted we'd been brainwashed then the world would be a little safer again. It was the in-between that was the scary part.

It would be a lie to say I've fully moved past what happened to us. I don't think there's a day that goes by that I don't think about it for some reason or another. People recognize me less now. Sometimes they still look at me with huge eyes, like they were the ones to discover me, as if they could call 911 right at that moment and set everything straight. I always feel like telling them that no one found me, not really. We might still have been lost if we had waited to be found. We turned ourselves in. We were the ones who finally brought ourselves home.

It happens less and less, though, that I'm confronted with questions about our time there. In the aftermath, it's easy to gloss over how long ten months is. You hear some stories of people who were gone for years, and their response afterwards was that they weren't able to escape. They were brainwashed. What the brainwashed bit covers up is the fact that they enjoyed part of it, somehow. They must have. Not in some sick masochistic way, but in a genuine, humble, coping way. It's hard for me to think back to my time with Jeremy and not think about Christmas, or my birthday, or that Jeep. There are a lot of good memories that come from that place.

The funny thing about our memory is that it protects us. It's like the way you can't remember the feeling of physical pain. You remember the ache; you know it was there, but you can't summon the throb. Your brain has done too good a job blocking it out. For me, it's the same. I don't remember pain, I don't even remember feeling all that scared. I remember feeling fairly safe, secure and happy.

That last bit is the part I try not to admit to many people. They get all suspicious. It doesn't work with their view of the world and the way it turns. But I did feel happy there. I wasn't traumatized for life. When we left, I readjusted to living with my mom, continued to go to school and grew up to be a relatively normal human being. I have my quirks like everyone else, but I don't think of myself as scarred, not really.

Other people do though. To them, my scars are visible. It's as if the lines slash across my face, huge creases where normalcy used to be. Sometimes people still shy away from my hand when I reach out to shake theirs, as if my scars are so vibrant they fear it might be catching.

I suppose I'm getting ahead of myself, though. It's been twenty years, and there are some gaps to fill in.

The day Vi and I returned home, we had no idea that Jeremy had turned himself in. We also had no idea, and would find out soon after, that it hadn't even been Jeremy's house at all. It had been an employer's home that he'd been entrusted to care for. The owners were horrified when they discovered what he had been using their property for, and they sued him.

The media went after Jeremy tirelessly. There was a picture, and I'll always remember it, of Jeremy being taken away in handcuffs. He's looking directly at the camera and his brow is furrowed, his eyes squinting. He looks sinister, and the press labeled him as such. But I knew that look, and it wasn't menacing. He'd been blinded by the flash of the camera, for god's sake. It was obvious to anyone who looked at it with a blank slate.

Our mother clipped out newspaper articles written about us while we were gone, and about Jeremy when we came back. At first I'm sure she did it for her own sanity; later, because she thought she was doing us a favour, documenting the many ways she'd tried to find us. I didn't read them when I was young; I didn't understand them or care to. Now when I look over them, I just feel hollow.

Vi and I experienced the press differently. I was the little boy who never had a choice. I was trapped in the backseat, too young to struggle or break free. Depending on who you asked, the same was true of Vi. Poor young girl who didn't know any better.

To many, however, it was as if she was a monster too. I never understood it. They painted a lurid picture of her as a lovesick woman who had some secret anger because of being adopted (because of course, that was a part of the whole circus too), and who had been willing to put her little brother's life at risk due to her own stupidity. Or promiscuity, again depending on who you asked. They were relentless. Even interviews that Vi agreed to do were edited against her favour, swooping in on tiny moments where she showed any sort of compassion towards Jeremy. Because she did. We both did. Because we missed him.

I won't go so far as to say I saw him as some sort of father, because even I know that's absurd. But when you're little and you don't have an older man around and then you do, sometimes it's hard to differentiate. He didn't always do the right things, but sometimes he did. If you look at his stealing us as one huge, massive mistake and error in judgment, he kinda did alright on the rest. That's how I feel about it.

I went back to school that September but I was held behind a year. The friends I had known were a year above me. Kids teased me and called me stupid, and never acknowledged that it was only because I'd been out of school for a year. No one seemed to pipe up with that information, and even I ceased to when I saw the looks it got me. I decided I'd rather be stupid than a freak. Kids were cruel but sloppy; they would tease you for whatever information you laid down in front of them. So I became stupid. Maybe that's the way I suffered after returning home; I didn't try. I didn't listen. I would stare out the window for hours with my head in the curve of my palm, thinking about where else I would rather be. If anyone else in the class did this, they were instantly called upon and disciplined. But teachers let things slide with me, as if they were afraid to reprimand me lest I fall apart. They assumed Jeremy had weakened me, thinned my skin, so that at the wrong word or look I could entirely disintegrate, crumple right before their eyes.

Kids saw this. They notice these sorts of things. I wished teachers would've gotten me in trouble sometimes, just so I wouldn't piss off the rest of the students. School was hell for me, plain and simple, but school was hell for many.

I got older, a little bigger, my voice grew deeper. I started chasing girls and was met with a staggering failure rate. I think I scared them. The damaged boy, the one who could explode at any moment. Everyone expected me to become so full of teen angst that I started to believe I should. I did all the drugs, I stayed out late at all the parties, I drank. I can remember a few occasions where I came home to liquor bottles lined up across the kitchen table, my angry mother standing, arms crossed, behind them. Essentially, I went through what every teenager under the sun does. Except I was still a special case. People always looked at me with a slightly cocked head, as if trying to figure me out. As if they were guessing the exact moment of my demise. I always disappointed them, though. I never broke.

A different story is true for Vi. Constant criticisms from the press followed her like a storm cloud. It gave some people the confidence to sneer at her on the street. While I was met with pitying looks, she got cold shoulders and glares. One woman, as we were walking through the mall together, spat on Vi's shoe. She shouted, "Shame on you," before scampering off.

Shame on Violet was a common judgment and after a time, I can't help but feel that even our own mother started to believe it. Once, a few weeks into our return, Mom couldn't resist her curiosity any longer. She'd asked us both in advance, made something of an appointment, letting us know she was going to ask questions about the time we'd been away.

Vi and I met her at the kitchen table and we all sat down. We drank some lemonade, ate some strawberries, and then Mom started to ask the things that everyone did. We thought we were safe from the questions in our own home, but we weren't. Homes are never completely safe.

"Do you still think about... him sometimes?" She would never say his name, as if she was scared of the power of it. As if upon speaking Jeremy Ridgeroy three times in front of a mirror he would climb through it and come after her in the night.

Vi and I looked at each other. The answer to the question was easy. Of course we still thought about him. We both nodded yes.

"Did he ever tell you why he kept you there?" she asked. No one seemed to be able to figure that one out. We knew, but it wasn't something that could be easily explained. It had taken us months to get it. Sometimes I still don't fully understand. I left this one to Vi.

"He was lonely," Vi offered. "He wanted someone to spend time with and he thought the only way he could do it was by force."

Mom gulped. "And was he? Forceful?"

Vi looked at the ground. "Well no, not physically. He didn't push us around or hurt us. But there were a lot of things he told us to make us think it wasn't an option to leave."

"So he tortured you?" Mom said, letting out a sob with her last word. It wasn't clear whether it had been a question or a verdict.

"No, Mom," Vi said, touching her hand. "He didn't torture us. We didn't suffer, not really."

"Of course you suffered!" Mom jumped in. "You were trapped for a year, of course you suffered!" I suppose this was true. But suffering is part of the human condition. We would have suffered had we been in the comfort of our own home. I don't feel any more haunted than you do, probably. We're all burdened by something. But I didn't have these words then, I didn't know how to say it. Neither did Vi. The words never came out right, or maybe it's that people just weren't listening when they were.

"Well," Vi conceded for our mother's benefit, "I guess we did suffer. He held us in a basement at first, with just a pot to go to the bathroom in and some blankets." The words were designed to pierce our mother's heart, and they hit their target. She sobbed into her open hand.

"My poor babies," she said over and over. "My poor babies."

Vi did get her job back at that diner. I'm not even sure she wanted it, but an old co-worker came around soon after we got back and told her the job was waiting for her. Vi knew she had to get back to real life at some point, and the sooner the better. She said yes, dug out an old apron from the bottom of her drawer, and went back to serving.

I'm not exactly sure what it was like for her to go back there, but she would come home from long shifts with purple rings around her eyes. When she entered the front door, she would close it quickly and lean against it, as if trying to keep something out. She would take deep breaths, ease her way back into comfort. For the most part, she would smile.

Vi's smile is something I really miss. I haven't seen it in years, not really. When we first got back, she tried it on as often as she could. As often as she thought people would believe, I suppose. But there was always a weight behind it, a strain that you could see in the way the corners quivered. I think it got harder for her, because she tried it less and less. It stopped being convincing. It screamed of forgery. Eventually, she decided it was better not to try at all.

She worked at that diner for another eight years and never went away to school. She made enough money; she worked as hard as she ever had, just as many hours. Maybe her tips weren't as good, but they were still there.

I asked her one day, why she never went away. She didn't like the question.

"What, so it's a bad thing that I didn't go to university? Not everyone does, you know," she'd said without pausing to conceal her offence. She fingered her shooting star necklace, that noose around her neck.

"Not at all, I thought that's what you'd been saving for, you know, before, so I just wondered what changed."

"A lot changed, Ben," she said. "Everything."

But the thing was, it hadn't. Not everything. It was possible to pick up and carry on. I had done it, and most other people do too, at some point from something or another. You fall down and no matter from what height, if you survive, you get up, brush off the dirt, and go on. Right? I mean, isn't that the way it works? Tragedy is all around us, all the time. I never saw why ours was so special.

The whole time Vi worked at the diner, she lived at home. Her friends had mostly gone away to school. They had new friends, new cities, new boyfriends, whole new lives that Vi wasn't a part of. A couple of co-workers came calling, frequently at first and then less so as time passed. Their sympathy only lasted so long. Vi didn't seem to mind. She'd work all day, come home, go to bed, and do it all again. She'd spend hours on the front porch, sitting in the rocking chair, never getting anywhere. Her brow would be scrunched up. I always tried to follow her line of vision, to find what she was staring at so intensely. But it was nothing; her eyes remained glossy and unfocused.

Vi never moved out of the house. From what I've gathered, she was afraid to leave Mom alone again. She wouldn't have been alone – I was there all the time growing up. But Vi felt some strange attachment, as if trying to prove that she hadn't been hiding from her life; she hadn't hated her mother and wanted to get away. Perhaps she felt it was her penance for the guilt she had been prescribed.

By the time I survived high school, I discovered something big about myself. My endless chasings of females were all for naught. Nothing had come from them, and more than that, I didn't mind.

When I was in my final semester of Grade 12, already itching to get away from home and from this town, I was walking home in the rain. Big, fat drops too, and I didn't have an umbrella. A car pulled up alongside me, stopped and rolled down the window.

"Hey, you," the driver said. A man, not much older than me. I was instantly struck by his electric green eyes, his turquoise shirt showing more of his skin than I'd ever had the balls to, and his big, welcoming smile.

I should have turned and ran, given my track record with men and cars. But I was older now, I was wise and stronger. There was nothing he could do to me that I couldn't prevent, I thought.

"Want a ride?" he shouted to me after I'd taken in him and his bright red car.

"Sure," I gambled. I'd just heard some lightning and figured it would only get worse, plus my backpack was no doubt allowing sufficient water in to smudge all the papers within. I opened the passenger door and sat down.

"Thanks, man," I said.

"No problem," he said to me, looking over. "So, you go to school here?" he asked, gesturing in the direction of the high school.

I nodded. "Yeah, just finishing my last semester. Then I'm out of here."

"Yeah," he laughed, "That's exactly what I said two years ago when I graduated. Soon, though," he stipulated.

"I'm Ben, by the way," I said then because I didn't know what else to say and I hadn't done it yet.

"Arthur," he said in response, extending his right arm out to me without taking his eyes off the road. I shook it, and I remember being surprised by the strength behind it, the grip and accuracy of his hand in mine. Handshakes, if you think about it, are just holding hands in a brief, firm fashion. I remember not wanting to let go.

"So where do you think you want to go when you're done school?" he asked.

"I'm not sure yet," I told him. I was sick of the question, and I hated it when anyone else asked it, but I didn't mind it from him. "I've always sort of wanted to be an architect."

This was the sort of response most people hear and think, Pipe dream. Never going to happen. I didn't have any specifics, I didn't know for certain where I wanted to go. I'd applied to a couple of schools already just because they force you to do it so early, but they were stabs in the dark at best. Arthur took my word for it, though.

"Amazing," he said, and I knew he meant it. "That would be an incredible job. Me, I've always wanted to be a yoga instructor. I've been training for awhile now, and I'm almost certified. I thought I'd have to leave town, head south somewhere, but the craze is spreading. I think I could even open up a yoga studio here and people would sign up. We don't have one yet," he said.

I looked over at him. His chest was enormous. To this day, I maintain that if he were fitted for a bra, it would be larger than the average female's. Those muscles were from yoga, from stretching, from holding his body in gravity-defying postures. It had never been something I'd pictured a man doing, but I was struck with the grace of it.

"I've never tried yoga," I admitted, "but I've always wanted to." That was a lie, by the way. I admitted it to him later, too. I wasn't sure why I'd wanted to impress him, but I know now.

"You should come by for a lesson sometime," he said genuinely. "I could give you a free trial." He looked over at me then, flashed me those eyes and his smile, and I felt a stirring inside of myself that I had never gotten from the opposite sex. I could feel butterflies hatching and taking flight, the ones I'd heard young girls tittering about with hearts for pupils. I thought boys weren't a part of that, but it's not true. We can feel love with the same giddiness, the same rosy-cheeked sincerity. Maybe we don't all know how to access and harness it, or heaven forbid show it, but it lies within like an untapped mine, a wealth of emotion waiting for someone to come digging.

I said yes, that I'd love to come for a yoga class. Before then, I'd never acknowledged my desire for men. I'm sure there were flare-ups in my youth, times when I looked upon them and felt attracted, but never in a fashion I marked as sexual.

No, I'd never lusted after Jeremy. People always ask me that, usually after they've had a few drinks. I'm not damaged, I don't feel deprived or scarred in my adoration of males. I have a vast and insatiable desire to give love. I'm not tainted. I don't know why I feel the need to clarify this so defensively, but people need convincing. They assume humans are so easily ruined.

Arthur drove me home that day, and the road flew by under our tires much faster than I hoped. When we arrived, I wondered if there was a way I could touch him somehow. I debated shaking his hand again, but that's sort of a one-time occasion. A hug would be outrageous and I knew it. I had no idea how to read him. Aside from the fact that there was no ring on his left hand, I hadn't the slightest idea. His smile though, it was something I felt he didn't share with just anyone. And those eyes, could he really look that way at a stranger he never again wanted to see? Something unpolished and inexperienced bubbled up in me and told me to go for it.

"Thanks again for the ride, Arthur," I started.

"No problem, Ben. I'm glad I could help."

"Do you think I should get your number then, if I'm going to call you about a yoga class?" I said it far too quickly, but he did me a favour and pretended it had come out just right.

"Good idea," he said and reached over, across my leg, into the glove compartment. It felt like static shock, the brush of his sleeve on my jeans. He pulled out a napkin and pen and scrawled his number and name, drawing the A like an arrowhead with no bar crossing it. I liked that.

"Perfect," I said. "I'll call you, then." I knew I should probably throw in a dude or a bro, but didn't feel up to it.

"I hope you do," he said as he flashed those eyes at me again, which had to mean something. And it did. He told me later that he'd seen me out walking before and always wanted an excuse to talk to me. I think that's bullshit, to be honest. There's nothing so striking about me that would have alerted his interest from afar, without hearing a word come out of my mouth. But I liked when he fed me the story anyways. I prompt him sometimes, Tell me the story of how we met, just so I can hear him say it.

I did call Arthur, soon after he dropped me off. I waited three days. Maybe it was four. Playing hard to get seemed silly, but I didn't know the code. When I got out of his car that day, I stood stock-still and watched him drive away. I had no idea what to do; I felt frozen to the spot. What I wanted right then, in that moment, was Vi. She wouldn't be hard to find; she would be in one of three places. On our front porch, where I could see she was not, at work, or somewhere inside the house.

She was in the kitchen baking cookies. I walked in and slumped down on a chair. "Hi," I said in what was supposed to be a neutral tone.

"Hi," she said suspiciously. Rightly so, I suppose. I hadn't been the most communicative. I wasn't around the house much and looked for ways to avoid talking to her or Mom. It wasn't anything personal, just one of those things teens do.

"When did you know you liked boys?" I blurted.

"Oh," she said, surprised. "I don't know, I guess I always sort of knew. I used to chase the boys around the classroom in kindergarten trying to kiss them.

But I think it was about Grade 3 that I had my first real crush." She paused. "If you're hinting that I should go out and find myself a boyfriend, I'm not interested."

"No," I said quickly, not wanting to offend her before I got to the heart of it. "That's not what I meant. It's just that... I don't think I like girls."

She responded in a way that told me she didn't understand. "Well, some people are late bloomers," she said, trying to make me feel better. "Maybe you need to get out of high school first."

I started to get nervous. "That's not it. I've tried to feel that way about girls, I've gone on dates and brought flowers and kissed them goodnight. I've fooled around."

Vi wrinkled her nose. I'm sure it was uncomfortable for her, but I couldn't stop. I barged on.

"I think the problem is that it's not girls I'm interested in. I think I might like boys instead. Like you do."

She put down the wooden spoon in her hand and looked at me hard. It wasn't a mad look, or even judgmental. Just serious.

"What makes you think that?" she asked.

"I just got a ride home from a guy named Arthur," I said honestly, "He made my stomach feel something that I've never felt with a girl."

As if everything inside of me was spinning around very quickly, gaining momentum and throwing off my centre of gravity. As if it could start to spin so fast that I might explode and it would rise up and out of me like a cyclone.

"Wow," she said. "So how did you leave it, what did you say when you got out of the car?"

"I got his phone number," I said with a smile.

"Jesus, you don't waste time. Do you know if he was interested in men?"

"I don't know. I don't know anything really, except that he kept smiling at me and offered me a yoga lesson. I really want to see him again. Should I call?"

"Okay, we'll get to that in a bit," Vi said. "First of all, do you think there's a possibility this is just a man crush? I mean, your sexuality doesn't have to be decided based on the way your tummy felt when a random dude picked you up on the street."

She sounded more like the sister I used to know than she had for months. I knew I'd made the right decision talking to her.

"There's a possibility," I admitted. "I have nothing to go on besides this one moment. But there's something about it, about him, that makes me think it's not just a fluke."

Vi nodded her head once.

"You don't think that's weird?" I asked her. I braced my body as if she might strike me.

"Ben, are you kidding? Look what generation we're part of. There's nothing wrong or strange about loving someone the same gender as you. No one has the right to judge you for how you feel and who you love. Because you can't help who you love, Ben."

Her eyes were so big when she said this. I couldn't help but feel that she wasn't only talking about me. I wondered what I could say to help her, but I realized she hadn't admitted anything to me, not really. Those words were supposed to be comfort for me, and they were, I suppose.

I stood up and gave her a big hug. It was meant to be a thank you, an apology, an act to show my love. My arms went around her but she was slow to respond. When she was ready though, she leaned right in. The weight of her whole body pressed against my chest. Her legs went slack. She started to sob. I always say sob in reference to her crying, because that's what Vi does. They aren't silent, small tears that trickle down her cheeks. Her eyes flow with the force of her whole body behind them. It makes you physically ache to hear her cry. I wasn't sure where her tears were coming from, or who they were for, but I just held on to her tight. One thing I have learned is that if someone lets you hug them, you just keep hugging until they're ready to let go.

Vi and I stood that way for a long time. It was her who finally pulled back, smearing her eyes with the back of her hand, rubbing flour along her eyebrows.

I laughed, wiped it away and she let out a giggle – a timid one I knew wasn't genuine. They weren't tears of disappointment in my decision to pursue a man. That's not her style. Part of me thinks she cried because she lost the little brother she used to watch over; that I didn't need her in the way I used to anymore. Another part, a bigger one, knew that wasn't the reason.

Arthur answered his phone when I called him three or four days later. I told him I'd seen a new coffee shop in town and was wondering if he wanted to try it with me so he could tell me more about yoga. It's funny, the safety scripts we develop to conceal the ways we feel. They never really work. It was obvious that I simply wanted to see him. I've always wished I said that instead. I just want to see you.

But he said yes, and he sounded excited, and we met the next day and that's how it all began. We've been together ever since. That was ten years ago. A long time, isn't it? People don't really have a problem with it. A couple of raised eyebrows, some whispering behind our backs, but people will always find something to whisper about.

Mom was the hardest. Not because she wasn't accepting, but because she seemed to view it as a consequence of something, a punishment for some action. It never felt that way to me, and I tried to describe that to her. She told me it wasn't that she didn't support my decision, but that she didn't want everything in my life to be hard. Things aren't much harder for me than anyone else, they're just hard for different reasons.

I think that's how I survived it. The knowledge that the first person I walk by on the street, and the second, and the third, are all going through something. They have each been bent and broken and on the floor, and here we all are, still walking around and smiling at each other. For the most part, anyways.

3

The year after I met Arthur, Mom got really sick. There was a day, a really awful day, when I came home to find her lying on the floor, a pool of blood around her head. Vi was at work and I wasn't sure how long she'd been lying there. I shook her. I know I should have been gentler, but she wasn't responding and I needed a response. Her eyes fluttered, and when they finally focused she didn't recognize me.

"Frank?" she had said, confusing me for her latest flame. Flowers from Frank sat on the very table she had banged her head against as she fainted and fell to the floor. I asked why she might have fainted and she got very quiet.

I lifted her. It's a strange feeling when your own mother feels small in your arms. She didn't want to leave the house.

"I'm fine," she told me, "I don't think I drank enough water today. Just get me a glass please, and I'll be just fine."

Just fine. It was breast cancer. She had been growing cancerous cells in her body for months, and had ignored the signs. No mammograms were on her doctor's records; she ignored the aches and swells. For months. That sort of denial is something I will never understand.

When we got to the hospital, because that's where I dragged her, they told her she should have come months ago. The doctor got as close to scolding her, and me, as I think he was professionally permitted to. Maybe more so. By then, it was too late. The cancer had spread to her bones. As if it had knocked on the door, stayed for a visit, enjoyed the hospitality and made the decision to move in permanently and invite all its friends.

Mom only lived for two months after that. By the end, she was a shrivelled ball in a hospital bed. Her breasts had been removed, but from what the doctor told us they didn't much resemble breasts anymore.

Vi and I sat by the bed that wasn't her own through it all. A selfish part of me wondered when it was going to be over with. We knew she was dying and had to, every day, watch her writhing in pain or completely incoherent (really, which is better?). The awful voice inside my head that brings out the very worst in me just wouldn't shut up. I didn't want her to die. I wanted her to be healthy, to live, to have admitted to her illness months ago. But since none of those things could happen, I wanted her suffering to be over. Soon it was.

She didn't leave a will. There was no money set aside for a funeral, no plans for the way her body would be dealt with. Vi spent her savings on Mom's funeral. Our grandparent's protested and said they would help cover some of it, but Vi refused. Her logic was that they still had their own funerals to save for, their own expenses to be covered by their pensions. So Vi paid for it all. It's incredible how expensive those things are. You don't want to cut corners when burying someone you love.

Feeling a bit like the black sheep of the family, I offered to pay for some of it. I didn't have much money since I was paying tuition for architecture school. She pointed this out to me. I'll never forget what she said to convince me she should pay.

"Ben, you're going places," she said. "You have potential and a future. You're still young. But it's too late for me. I missed out. I'm almost thirty, I live at home, I work at a diner. I have a high school education and that's it." She sliced her hand through the air in front of her. "I don't have a partner. I don't have friends. What is there for me to spend my money on? It'll collect dust in the bank. I want to pay for this so I can feel good about something I have done in my life. Mom is going to have the most beautiful funeral anyone has ever seen, and that will be something I did for her. It's the last thing I can offer her. Please Ben," she pleaded. "Let me do this?"

It was a beautiful ceremony. I didn't cry. Vi did. The ratio of men to women was three to one. I chuckled to myself about this, about how even in death she could attract hordes of men. It wasn't really all that funny, and I didn't share my dark humour with anyone but Arthur who smacked me on the arm for thinking such a thing at my own mother's funeral.

After Mom died, Vi stayed in the house. When the legalities were all sorted out, the property went to her. I didn't mind. She seemed to think I would be upset about it and told me that I could live with her if I chose. But I was happy to leave. If I stayed, each day I would walk with the ghost of my mother. Every ounce of me wanted to tell Vi she should get out too; sell the place and take a trip, take a class, do something different. She was so alone, and I know why it happened but I don't think it was inevitable.

Vi is beautiful, and all her features individually are striking. They used to come together so well. Now, she looks like a slightly distorted picture of herself. The pieces don't fit the way they're supposed to. Her smile doesn't glow the way it once did. Her eyes don't sparkle. But she still wears that necklace every day.

I've never seen her neck without it since we left Jeremy. She's always touching it, rubbing it between her fingers, as if it's a rune that will give her the answers. I'm not even sure what her questions are.

Vi stayed in that house when I moved out to live with Arthur. Every time I saw her, even when weeks passed between visits, I had the feeling I was the last person she'd seen. And each time, she was a little further out of my reach. A little harder to talk to, to draw out. I should've tried harder to get her out of that house. She withered in there.

Arthur had begun training to become a yoga instructor when I moved in. I had never been so in love. Well, more accurately, I'd never been in love, but I liked the way it felt. I loved waking up to the warmth of someone beside me. The nicest feeling in the world is needing a hug and being able to turn around and get one, and a really good one, anytime you want.

Arthur has a tattoo covering his back of giant wings. One on each shoulder, stretching down to his lower back. Amongst it are the words, Love means never having to say you're sorry.

The first time I saw him without a shirt on, I asked him about it. He told me he'd gotten it a long time ago. I asked if he believed those words and he tilted his head a bit, as if he'd never thought about it. "I'm not sure," he finally responded. "I don't think I really want them to be true. They just sound beautiful."

I was glad he responded that way. I've learned a couple of things about love. One is that there is always some love buried inside you, dying to be given out. Even when you think you're exhausted of it, completely drained dry of it, there's a backup resource deep within you somewhere.

Another is that love is having to say you're sorry. Probably at least once a day. I don't think it ever hurts to apologize. Arthur tells me I say sorry too often. He says I'm The Boy Who Cried Sorry. But I mean it, or at least I usually do.

I suppose my love life isn't exactly what someone would have in mind when searching for the dirty details of how fucked up I became after Jeremy. I'm sorry. But Arthur is a huge part of my life, and I think he's the reason I'm still sane today. So he has to be included. My story cannot be told without him now, just as it couldn't be told without Jeremy.

After graduating from university, I was in massive debt. I worked hard, for years, to pay it off. As a dishwasher in Vi's diner for awhile, random repair jobs here and there, until I finally got my heels dug in deep enough to start applying for real jobs. I don't mean that the others were fake. But I viewed them as a path I was paving to become an architect, and I finally got there. I was hired by a firm in town and I started to bring in more money than I ever had in my life. It wasn't a lot, but it was more than minimum wage. It astounds me how many people are willing to pay their human counterparts so poorly.

You're probably curious about Jeremy. Whether I hate him. The answer is that I don't. I'm fairly sure I even love him in a way. Is that crazy? I don't know. I spent a significant amount of time with him, and he took care of me. People shake their heads when I say this. Their eyes are so pitying, like I've gotten it so wrong and someone needs to help me see straight. The thing is, I'd rather not be a victim. I don't want to be someone seen as trampled on. What's the use in that? It's over, I'm alright and I've moved on. No one else seems to be able to.

He was wrong to have taken us. With the things he suffered through in his life, how could he possibly have a rational view of what was wrong and right? I can see his logic. It's hard for most people, but I've gotten there. He believed all his life that love and family were all you truly needed to be happy, and he'd never had either, not fully. How was he to know it was wrong to create that for himself? To scavenge some scraps he could glue together and declare as happiness? Maybe I wish it wasn't us that he scavenged. But I'm not even sure about that, and it was us, so there's no use thinking about the way things might have been otherwise.

Now, I know more about Jeremy than I ever did. Countless reporters and admirers have assembled facts about his past and put them on display for the world. Jeremy never told me about his childhood. I think Vi knew some of it; they confided in each other quite a bit. I was too young to understand, or at least I think that's why he didn't share his past with me.

Jeremy has a bit of a following, the way people who have done wrong always seem to. Young psychology students visit him and ask to write their dissertation on him. He never says no, but he also never offers up information willingly. They have to squeeze the details out of him, ask questions in just the right way. There's honour in the way he does it. He's not looking for handouts. He doesn't try to say he's been unfairly accused. The day he showed up at the police station with his hands on his head marked the end of the denial of anything he'd done wrong.

I remember reading the first exposé about Jeremy, written by a young female reporter for the local paper. The writer was very careful not to condemn or condone; she merely laid out the facts in chronological order. By the time you got to the bit where he kidnapped two human beings, it almost seemed like an inevitability instead of a crime. I suppose I've said enough on the subject, though. I don't think he's guiltless. What he did was wrong, and I wish he'd figured that out sooner than he did. Maybe it took Vi and I leaving to give him perspective.

4

Since Jeremy's incarceration, I have visited him four times. That's not a lot over twenty years, but most people think it's four times too many. The first time, Vi and I had to go to the station to identify Jeremy as our captor. We both nodded our heads and then hung them. It was Jeremy who was contained then, and we the ones keeping him there. Just as he had caged us, we had locked him up like an animal. But for decades instead of months. Doesn't that make us the guilty ones? Probably not, I know, but I can't help but think about it sometimes. We stole his freedom, too.

The second time I went to visit him was when I first started high school. By that point, I'd gotten used to the long looks people gave on the street, and the questions they couldn't resist asking. Sometimes I pretended I didn't know what they were talking about. It blew people's minds that I could be so nonchalant about something they deemed so tragic.

I am not a tragedy.

When I went to see him the second time, I took this sentiment with me. I wanted Jeremy to see that he hadn't ruined me. I wasn't sure if I meant it to be for his benefit or detriment. Whether it was a Look Jeremy, I'm alright! I turned out okay! A proud child displaying a painting to be hung on the fridge. Or a Jeremy, you were not capable of ruining me.

I didn't say much. He was still in a cell then, with a bed, a television, a desk, carpet. That was one of the things I was most glad to hear, that he had a carpet beneath his feet. I'm not sure why. I didn't actually see his cell because he came out to a common room for the visit. He told me about it when I asked. He seemed surprised both to see me and that I was concerned about his living conditions.

"Ben," he said, looking me right in the eyes. I knew his vision would be blurry; it had to be with the tears I saw forming in each duct. "I am so, so very sorry."

He meant it, I know he did. It wasn't just the next step his psychologist had advised.

"I know," I replied. I wasn't ready to absolve him, not then. I didn't know if I ever could. I was still young and a little angry.

He looked haggard. Black circles raccooned his eyes. You couldn't tell they were green anymore, too sunken. His red hair flailed wildly around his head. This was nothing new; I'd seen his hair crazy before, but it took on a particularly striking quality against the staunch grey and white surrounding us. He was aging at an alarming rate. His movements were small and silent; he did whatever he could to ensure no one feared him. I wondered what sort of a hell this prison was for him. I wondered if they tore him apart.

"I just wanted to tell you I'm okay," I said. "I just started high school and my grades are alright and my life is good." I didn't want to harm or help him at that moment, I only wanted to get it off my chest.

"I'm glad," he said.

There wasn't anything else I wanted from that meeting, and I didn't have the strength to stay any longer. I nodded at him, got up and walked away.

Years passed before I thought about visiting again, although he was often in my thoughts. Every Christmas, I get a card from him. I don't know if it's legal, and part of me thinks it's one of his followers, his sympathizers and cheerleaders who sneak the cards out for him. Vi gets one, too. Two separate envelopes, two chances of getting caught. But they come every year. Even after I moved out, Vi set aside my card for me every holiday season.

The third time was after I'd met Arthur. I was falling in love, and that was something I had secretly feared I would be unable to do. I assumed I would have walls, shields I'd use to lock people out.

I realized soon after that those seeds of doubt were planted externally. Every article written about us sang our sorrows. Our mother hugged us for minutes on end after each publication, and the urge I felt to squirm out of her grip made me wonder if everyone was right. Maybe I was ruined in some way.

But along came Arthur, and I knew I could prove them wrong. When I came out, I wanted Jeremy to know. This time, I wasn't bitter. I simply wanted him to see the person I was becoming. I don't think he hindered the person I became. I was so young, with so much time left to self-correct. Maybe I wanted Jeremy to feel a little less guilt. I was sure he worried and wondered about us, and I hoped it might make his imprisoned life a little easier if I told him I was okay, if I showed him.

I didn't tell anyone I was going. Not even Arthur, although I ended up admitting it to him months later, which was met with a long hug and a big squeeze, as if I must really need it. I probably did.

Jeremy was just the same, but with streaks of grey through his hair. The same tired face that lit up as much as possible when he saw me.

"Ben," he said instantly, "I'm so happy to see you." I could tell he was scared to say anything more; he had no idea why I'd come back.

"Hi, Jeremy," I said, this time determined to stay longer. "How are things?" A silly question, but I figured it was a nicety I shouldn't cast aside.

"Oh, you know," he said. "Same old. The food isn't the greatest, but I have my own space. I do a lot of reading, a lot of writing. I go for runs and work out, too."

I could see the wiry gristle of his body beneath his shirt. There was a sinewy strength about him, like he was made of barbed wire.

"Do people bother you in here?" I asked.

"Nah, not too badly," he said, but I could tell he was lying.

I remember being struck with the panic of not knowing what to say. I remembered the purpose of my visit, and I updated him on my life, on Arthur. Jeremy didn't blink when I told him I was in a same-sex relationship. Didn't flinch or cringe. I always loved people a little more when they responded that way. My own mother flinched.

"Are you surprised?" I asked, wondering if I'd given off hints I hadn't been aware of.

"Surprised?" he repeated. "Not really. I mean, I didn't guess either way. Does he make you happy?" Jeremy added, but not as an afterthought.

"Yeah," I said honestly. More than anyone else ever has, I held back saying. I didn't know for sure it was true.

"Well, I'm happy to hear it then," Jeremy said. "I imagine you'll face some people out there who don't understand. But honestly? Fuck 'em. It's too bad that they're so miserable, but it has nothing to do with you."

The word fuck out of his mouth hadn't been violent or vulgar. Only heartfelt.

"Thanks," I said, and I meant it. No one's words had made me feel better about the situation than his.

I didn't stay long after that. It depressed us to talk about how close Jeremy might be to getting out. The parole boards had never been on his side. Even with spotless behaviour, they weren't convinced. Maybe it was the length of time we spent with him, maybe it's because there were two of us or because Vi was a female or because I was so young. The facts stacked against him in the worst ways.

When I got up to leave, I reached out my hand. I wasn't sure why I did it, or whether I was even allowed to touch him. The guards permitted it though, and so did Jeremy. He grabbed my hand with force. I could feel all five of his fingers pressing into my palm. It was strangely comforting. We stood there for a moment in an awkward embrace that neither of us wanted to break.

We finally let go. I think it was Jeremy who initiated the release.

"Say hi to Vi for me, will you?" he asked as I turned to walk away. "She looked very beautiful the last time she came to see me."

The instant he said it, his face clouded over.

"Vi visits you?" I asked. She'd never mentioned it to me. To be fair, I hadn't mentioned my visits either, in fear of them hurting her. I wondered if she had done the same. "How often?"

"Oh," Jeremy said. "I'm sorry. I didn't realize she hadn't told you." He looked so disappointed it made me want to cry. "She comes every few months. Maybe don't mention to her that I told you? I don't want to upset her."

I knew that he meant, I don't want her to stop visiting me, and I understood. If Vi had made the decision, so many times, to come and see Jeremy without letting me know, then she should be able to keep making that decision on her own. I wondered what they talked about, what she told him about her life. Jeremy might be disappointed in her story. Maybe he feels responsible. Maybe he should. Vi could have sucked it up and gone to university and blossomed and met new people and fallen in love, but she'd chosen to avoid doing each and every one of those things. She lived like the whole world was a fright.

I've seen her mentally preparing herself to go to the grocery store. I noticed her breathing a little too quickly, and asked her what was wrong.

"Nothing," she minimized. "It's just that there are a million choices to make at the grocery store. Knowing how to pick the best of everything is tricky. And at the cash registers, everyone is always in such a rush, and they look at you funny if you don't have your own bags or if you fumble with your change."

Everyday tasks seemed to upset Vi increasingly. More and more, she asked favours of me – little errands she needed me to run. I knew it wasn't because she was too busy. It was that she was too scared, and it seemed as though she was becoming more so all the time.

I wondered if Jeremy could sense her increased fear of life. Did he council her on it? Did they sit and giggle like they used to around the campfire? I remembered with a pang the jealousy I felt when the two of them sat out there, conspiring.

When I walked out of the prison that day, I took Jeremy with me more than I ever had before. He stayed in the back of my mind, in my bones. I didn't mention my visit to Vi, but it sat on the tip of my tongue and I wondered why it was so hard to just say it. Something told me I shouldn't. Vi was becoming more fragile by the day. I didn't want to push her, or have her think I was judging.

More years passed; we all grew older. Vi stopped working at the diner. She said she couldn't face people anymore. I didn't know what to do about it, and I wasn't sure how she'd survive without an income but she told me not to worry. I tried to see her as often as I could, but life gets busy and every visit became more excruciating than the last.

Today, I'm still living with Arthur. We're not married, but we've talked seriously about it. It would be a small ceremony, nothing flashy. Neither of us has a big family or many friends.

And today, for the first time since the last time, I went to visit Jeremy. I finally assembled all the questions I had for him, sorted out the things I felt he owed me an explanation for. The things I'd been too scared or unsure of to ask. But I had a list this time, and I felt entitled to some answers.

I was nervous. I told myself it would be my last visit. Once I asked all my questions, I'd never need to rely on him again.

I arrived, and this time Jeremy was waiting for me in a brown padded chair. He looked shrunken, like a human-shaped casing that someone had loosely stuffed with scraps. The circles around his eyes were darkened; bruises rimming his eyeballs like glasses. His sunken cheekbones made him appear emaciated. I could see his belly beneath the table though; he wasn't starving. Excess material had collected around his waist like a lifesaver, but nothing about him looked like it had been, or could be, saved.

"Hi," I said to him, sitting down in a nearby chair.

"Hello, Ben," he said. I was amazed that his voice sounded the same. It wasn't scratchier, more gruff or mean. It was the same as it had always been.

"How are you doing?" he asked to break the silence.

"I'm good," I told him. "I'm good. Still with Arthur. We're living together now and thinking about getting married." I paused to read his reaction, cocking my head. He showed no sign of discomfort or distaste, and I loved him in that moment.

"How are you?" I continued, not wanting to say too much, too soon.

"Oh, you know," he said. "I'm good."

I took a breath and decided my next question was valid. "Is it hard? To be cooped up in here?"

"Well, how long has it been now?" he asked. "Twenty years?"

"Almost exactly," I confirmed.

"That's close to half my life. I've been here so long that I don't remember what it's like to be out. So I don't miss it too much."

I wasn't sure why those words shot a pang through me, but they led me to say to him next, "You don't remember the time we lived with you?"

"Yes," he corrected. "Of course I remember. But it's been long enough that I don't miss the freedom of being out of here. I'm out of practise."

It was a lie and I knew it. It was written all over his face, all over his body. No one forgets what freedom tastes like, not when they've had it once. I'd be willing to bet he stored the feeling somewhere deep inside, an internal vial he could open and sniff from whenever he felt particularly powerless.

I didn't call him on his lie. I knew it was for my benefit, so that I didn't feel bad about the fact that he was here because of something he had done to Vi and me. Or maybe that was just my own twisted reasoning, I'm not sure.

"Is there any hope you might get out of here someday?"

He nodded and took a sip of the glass of water in front of him. "It's not hopeless. I go up against the parole board again next year, so there's a chance they could let me go." His eyes told me that there wasn't really.

"I don't know how you do it," I said. I couldn't help it. "I'm sorry, I know that's awful to say, but it's just... It's been so long, so much in my life has changed, so much in the world has changed. But for all of it, you've been stuck inside of here. Doesn't it ever make you angry?"

He smiled, a sad suggestion of amusement. "Sometimes. But I only have myself to blame. I committed a crime, and it wasn't just a crime that took a second. It went on for a long time, you know how long."

"I know," I said. "But when I look back on it now, I just think about it as the time I spent with you. I grew up a bit, I had a birthday, we celebrated Christmas... It was just a period of my life, no better or worse than any of the others."

It wasn't a lie to make him feel better, it was as honest as I could get about emotions that made me uncomfortable. But emotions will do that to you.

His eyes grew wider then. Not any less sad or aged, just wider. "I'm glad to hear that," he said simply.

"Jeremy," I said, because I was ready, "Why us? Why us and not somebody else? Why at all?"

He had planned for this, I could see by the subtle nod of his head. He had practised.

"My life has been mostly miserable," he started. "But then your sister came along. You spend your whole life ignored, and when someone finally pays attention it feels really good. I convinced myself I had found someone who understood me. She smiled at me, she laughed, and you know how pretty she is. I honestly fell in love with her in an instant. I wasn't even aware of it, but I loved her from the start."

He paused for a moment. "One time, I thought I had struck up the nerve to talk to her. I was thinking about asking her on a date. I waited in the diner parking lot but when she finally came out, she was crying. She looked so hopeless. I remember thinking that nothing in the world should make a girl cry like that." He shook his head. "I still don't know what she was crying about, but in that moment, I convinced myself that maybe things were hard for her, too. Maybe she needed someone to help her out, and maybe I could be the one to do it.

"And then it all happened so fast. I hate to say it, but I never planned for you at all, Ben. You were just picked up along the way. I wasn't sure what else to do so I just let it happen." He was trying to meet my eyes but kept looking at the floor.

"There's no excuse. Everyone gets lonely. But I was beyond lonely. I was empty. My life was nothing until you and Violet became part of it. Those months with the three of us in that house were the best in my life. I know it's awful to say and I have no right to think it, but I did feel like we were a family. Maybe you weren't there by choice, and I know now that it was monstrous for me to have kept you there. But it was the closest thing to a family I've ever had."

I think he had more to say, but he lost his nerve. I could tell by his eyes that he wasn't sure how I would react; if I would scream and rage or just get up and leave. I didn't do any of those things. I did something that surprised even myself.

"I understand," I said. "I get it. Having a family, a support network, is something that everyone deserves. I know that, because I didn't get one right off the bat. I got lucky, and I ended up with a mom who did her best and a sister who loved me. And I got you." I started to cry, I couldn't help it. I didn't even feel ashamed.

"You taught me how to hunt for bugs. You let me stay up late and learn when my bedtime should be. You sang me happy birthday. You put bandages on my skinned knees and didn't call me a sissy when I started to cry. You let me have a wild imagination and even let two invisible people come for dinner." We both laughed a little. "I've become the person I am today because of everything that happened to me in my past. And you are a part of that." I wanted to touch him but didn't.

"When I think back, I'm struck with the sensation that you are the closest thing to a father I've ever had. It doesn't make sense. I've struggled with it for years. I should hate you, everyone tells me I should. But I don't. Not even a little." Years of turmoil boiled down to the next moment.

"Jeremy... I forgive you. I forgive you for everything you did and everything you didn't let us do. It's okay. It's done with now. You've paid your dues, far beyond what I think you owed. You're clean, Jeremy. There's nothing left to fix."

I couldn't say anything more. My throat was too raw. It might have been against the rules and against what anyone else in the world thought I should do, but I got up and I hugged Jeremy. I held onto him for a long time, and I held on tight. He did the same. We stayed like this, Jeremy still sitting in his brown padded chair, me standing beside him, squatting down, hugging. It probably didn't look very dignified. I'm not sure I was allowed to touch him, but no one said anything and we remained that way until I finally pulled back. I instantly missed the press of his fingers on my back.

"Thank you so much, Ben," he said softly. "You've given me more than you can possibly know."

I hadn't planned on laying out my forgiveness like a gift. I hadn't been entirely sure I was ready to give it, but I was glad I did. I left then. My list of questions seemed irrelevant.

Life plays tricks on you. It deals you cards you never learned to play, in a game with rules you aren't sure of. You never know for certain when something will slide over and knock you down. But you keep playing. I know this much is true. You have to keep playing.

Vi took herself out of the game. I've been thinking about it a lot lately. She hides herself away in that house so much that it's as if she were still living with Jeremy. Not much has changed, besides the fact that she has less company now. I worry about her. I worry, because I'm the little brother. I'm the one who everyone thinks it should have affected more. Maybe so, but I've found a way to cope with those nicks in my armour. Vi's got chipped away entirely, and now she lives in fear. She allowed her anxiety to grow around her like a shoddy shield that won't protect her from anything.

On the way home from visiting Jeremy, I decided I should visit her as well. I don't do it often enough. Sometimes it's hard to be inside that house, to think of the memories we were robbed of having within it. To sense the missing presence of our mother as strongly as if there was an absent window or a broken door.

It didn't take me long to get there. I always feel the need to knock now. I still have a key; I haven't taken it off my keychain just in case, but it's not mine to walk into anymore. It's Vi's house, and she doesn't fill it fully; it's a whole lot of love short of a home.

The doorbell is broken. It has been for months. When I offered to mend it, she'd brushed me off and told me she would take care of it. Her stubbornness had increased over the years.

I knocked. No answer.

"Hey Vi," I called out, wondering if the door was thin enough for her to hear from wherever she was hiding within. I considered announcing who it was, then realized she could figure it out. No one came to visit these days. Vi didn't like strangers coming to call, and she wouldn't let people close enough to become something other than a stranger. She lost the ability to let down her guard and allow people to see who she was. Maybe she was too ashamed, too afraid of what she would confess, what would come out of her if they stayed long enough to listen.

I circled around the house to see if she was sitting on the back deck. I've stumbled upon her like this before and been startled by the blank, flat look she greeted me with as I rounded the corner. It was as if she didn't know who I was and didn't care to. She didn't look worried or concerned, just indifferent. Detached and remote; gone to a place I can't reach her.

Today, there was no one back there. But I heard something. A rustling, a whispering. It reminded me of something far back in my memory. A shiver crawled down my spine and I turned quickly. Nothing was behind me. Just trees and the world. I heard it again and couldn't shake the unsettled feeling that was draping itself around my shoulders like an unwanted cape.

There is a basement window that faces the backyard. It was right below my feet, just to the left of the back door. That's the cellar. It's where Mom used to keep all of her wine.

Something caught my eye in that window. Something shimmered. I looked down. There, staring back at me, were two pairs of eyes.

Once, we were stolen. But one of us never made it out.

EPILOGUE

Violet was institutionalized. I turned her in, and rescued the little boy and girl being held in her basement. They had been there for a month. Violet hadn't shown them the mercy Jeremy did; they were still pissing and shitting in a pot and crying for their mother every night. Their family welcomed them home with open arms, and the media frenzy began anew.

Jeremy was released from prison one year after I made my last visit and discovered Violet's secret. Having been locked up for over two decades, Jeremy had no place to go. There was no halfway house for him, he couldn't call his family, and he had no friends to speak of.

One day, Jeremy showed up on my doorstep. His shoulders were stooped and he looked at the ground sheepishly. He asked if he could stay the night. He had nowhere else to go.

I stepped back and let him in. He stayed with Arthur and I until he found a place of his own two weeks later. Now, the three of us have dinner together once a week and talk about everything but the past.

Jeremy and I visit Violet in the hospital. We bring her flowers. We talk about the weather and tell stories, and she sits across from us but she doesn't hear us.

Her bright eyes have turned dark grey and they stare at the wall. Her wasted body lies almost motionless as she drowns in the days, absently thumbing the shooting star that still graces her collarbone.

DEDICATIONS

For those who know me, thank you for your unending support. My sincerest gratitude goes to all who supported my Indiegogo campaign and gave this project some legs. That includes Rachael Raven, Greg Mullins, Emma Jackson, Stephen Jardeleza, Christopher Symons, Danielle Houstoun, Jeff Symons, Em Jardeleza, Kristin Sawyer, Bruce Raganold, Erika Barber, Shannon Bush, Scott Read, Katie Frost, Lisa Elder, Troy Hughes, Chris Jardeleza, Doug Michaelides, Courtney and Carol Wendt, Samantha Schmidt, Brogan Van, Tim Bryant, Ryan Stuckey, Terry Jardeleza, Elizabeth Howell, Rob Elder, Douglas Irwin, Chris Goulet, Rayanne Lees, Lisa Symons, Greg Kolz and Kassie Greeley. I couldn't have done it without all of you.

My brother Cameron Symons ensured the success of that campaign with support I couldn't have dreamed up. He was the first to read the quivering mess of a first draft that no one should ever have seen. Still, he told me he loved it. I'm lucky in life to have him as a brother. Thank you, Cam.

To Emma Jackson and Samantha Schmidt for being early readers and my own personal support team. Life would not be nearly as good without you two in it.

To my editor, Ellen Keeble, who taught me to show not tell and to cut out the quirky bits that no one but myself would find entertaining. This novel is a million times better because of you.

To my graphic designers, Emma Lovell and Jen Morgan at Charm Media, who created a book cover as haunting and beautiful as I'd imagined.

To my family that has always believed I am a writer. Thank you for giving me the confidence to make it happen.

To Stephen Jardeleza, the most patient and supportive partner I could ask for. You inspire me every day.

Thank you also to those I don't know. I have always relied on the kindness of strangers, trusting more than (some thought) I should. I've left things unattended, lost things, dropped things, and have usually come out on top. People call me lucky, and I am, but I also think it's because of the good in people that shines through when it counts.

Thank you for taking a chance on me, a perfect stranger trying to get her words out right. I am floored by the generosity that has allowed my first novel to see the light of day. Thank you for that. I'll never forget it.

ABOUT THE AUTHOR:

Courtney Symons lives in Ottawa, Ont. where she works as a journalist. Her work has been published in various print and online media including the Ottawa Business Journal, the West Carleton Review, Metro Ottawa and The Landowner.

She writes non-fiction all day and comes home to write fiction at night. This is her first novel. Follow her on Twitter @CourtneySymons or @OnceWeWreStolen and on Facebook at Once, We Were Stolen. Visit her website at www.courtneysymons.com (a work in progress) and learn more about her at www.about.me/courtneysymons.

17460810R00233

Made in the USA
Charleston, SC
12 February 2013